INSPECTOR FRENCH:
JAMES TARRANT, ADVENTURER

Freeman Wills Crofts (1879–1957), the son of an army doctor who died before he was born, was raised in Northern Ireland and became a civil engineer on the railways. His first book, *The Cask*, written in 1919 during a long illness, was published in the summer of 1920, immediately establishing him as a new master of detective fiction. Regularly outselling Agatha Christie, it was with his fifth book that Crofts introduced his iconic Scotland Yard detective, Inspector Joseph French, who would feature in no less than thirty books over the next three decades. He was a founder member of the Detection Club and was elected a Fellow of the Royal Society of Arts in 1939. Continually praised for his ingenious plotting and meticulous attention to detail—including the intricacies of railway timetables—Crofts was once dubbed 'The King of Detective Story Writers' and described by Raymond Chandler as 'the soundest builder of them all'.

Also in this series

By the same author

*with other Detection Club authors

FREEMAN WILLS CROFTS

Inspector French: James Tarrant, Adventurers

COLLINS
CRIME
CLUB

COLLINS CRIME CLUB
An imprint of HarperCollins*Publishers*
1 London Bridge Street
London SE1 9GF
www.harpercollins.co.uk

HarperCollins*Publishers*
1st Floor, Watermarque Building, Ringsend Road
Dublin 4, Ireland

This paperback edition 2022
1

First published in Great Britain by Hodder & Stoughton Ltd 1941

A catalogue record for this book is
available from the British Library

ISBN 978-0-00-855415-6

Set in Sabon Lt Std by Palimpsest Book Production Ltd, Falkirk, Stirlingshire

Printed and bound in the UK using 100% Renewable Energy
at CPI Group (UK) Ltd

This book is produced from independently certified FSC™ paper
to ensure responsible forest management.

Find out more about HarperCollins and the environment at
www.harpercollins.co.uk/green

Contents

AUTHOR'S NOTE

I wish to acknowledge with gratitude the help given me in connection with legal matters by Mr Michael O'Connell Stranders, LL.B. (Hons.), Barrister-at-Law, of Lincoln's Inn.

Also the kindness of Mr William Carr in advising me on questions of chemistry.

F.W.C.

1

James Tarrant Starts the Ball

James Pettigrew Tarrant paused in the business of wrapping up a bottle of medicine in its clean white paper sheath, and glanced wearily out of the dispensing-room window of Barr's, the Lydcott chemist's. He glanced at nothing in particular, because, indeed, there was nothing particular to glance at. The shop was at the meeting of two ways, and while the entrance was in the High Street and overlooked the entire pageant of Lydcott life, the dispensing-room gave on a side road of what seemed to the young man quite incomparable dullness.

Tarrant was bored, and felt he would be bored no matter in what direction he looked. He was more than bored: he was fed up. Fed up with his job, with old Humphrey Barr, the owner of the antiquated little shop, with the village of Lydcott and—with one exception—with everyone who lived in it. He had obtained the post with profound satisfaction, some months previously, believing that as the single assistant in a small business he would have a better position than as a mere member of the staff in a large branch. But the move had proved disappointing. The trade was as tiny as the village, and though he was left in charge for considerable periods, he never had anything to do which really interested him or made the slightest demands on his not inconsiderable abilities.

Sighing gently, he turned back to his work. With automatic accuracy he folded the paper, tipped the ends against the hot wax and sealed them down, scorning string after the manner of his kind. Then, having written a name on the paper and ticked off an item in the day-book, he put the bottle aside and took up another.

Though working deftly and with speed, Tarrant's thoughts remained centred on what had always been his main preoccupation: his own prospects. He was ambitious, and what was more to the point, he knew just what he wanted. It was not professional advancement, except in so far as this might be a means to an end: the life of even a successful retail chemist fell far short of his aspirations. Nor was it scientific fame that he coveted. His desires were simpler and more direct. Tarrant wanted money—money and the luxury and, above all, the power which money brings. For money, if he could get enough of it, he would willingly have bartered his soul.

But as assistant to old Barr in this prehistoric jumble of houses called Lydcott, he would earn no money, not at least in the sense in which he interpreted the phrase. He had applied for Barr's job, believing that he was adventuring himself on a flowing tide, and instead he found himself floating in circles in a backwater.

Money, he told himself for the nth time, was not to be had by the conscientious performance of one's daily duty. Bread and cheese could be earned in that way, with perhaps a spot of jam occasionally, but for real money, the cakes and the cocktails, something more was required. Brains were needed—brains to make other people pay you for value that they thought they got from you, but did not.

That this conclusion was sound Tarrant was convinced, but rack those brains—of which he felt he had his full share—as he would, he could see no way in which the feat could be accomplished.

James Pettigrew Tarrant had always had an eye to the main chance. Even as a child it had somehow happened that the larger portions of cake and the best seats on excursions fell to his share, and at school his proclivities were known and guarded against. His youth passed uneventfully, then, financial difficulties descending upon his parents, it was found necessary for him to earn his living. He was fond of chemistry and had been well grounded in science at his school, and being of smart appearance and with good manners, he had little difficulty in obtaining a job as junior salesman in a chemist's shop. There he worked hard, having been twice promoted in twelve years. So far all had gone reasonably well, but now, at the age of thirty, he had made his first mistake. He had taken this job in this ghastly dead end, and unless he did something drastic, here for the rest of his days he was likely to remain.

Money! How could he make money? That was his growing preoccupation, and that was what seemed more and more impossible with every day that passed.

Footsteps sounded outside—light, rather thrilling footsteps, somehow suggestive of small neat shoes with high heels. Tarrant looked out with more interest. Down this lane—it was its one alleviation—was the way to the Wilton Grange Convalescent Home, a large establishment a mile or more out into the country, and along it nurses would sometimes pass. Tarrant had no objection to looking at nurses in the abstract, but there was among them that dainty little piece with whom he had recently scraped acquaintance.

Nurse Weir: Merle Weir, so she had told him. Nice name, Merle. It was just three months since he had met her, and by now they were pretty good friends.

The Convalescent Home was Barr's mainstay: only for it Tarrant was sure the little shop could never have survived. Every day the Grange van called for medicines, but on that evening three months ago a prescription was wanted in a hurry, and Nurse Weir, who was in the village on other business, called and took it out. She was a pretty girl, and Tarrant had been correspondingly attentive. She had responded in a quiet, friendly way.

Now Tarrant was accustomed to this. Somehow he was attractive to women. He did not know why, for he was not unduly conceited, but the fact remained. Girls fell for him with gratifying, indeed sometimes with disconcerting, readiness. He didn't care about them himself—not much at all events. They were amusing, and he would always take readily enough anything which came to him, provided that could be done without fear of matrimonial entanglement. But Merle Weir was different. This time he felt it was love at first sight.

Fate had then stepped in and settled the matter. On the following Wednesday afternoon, his half day, he had taken the bus to Bramford, their nearest town, only to find Merle seated opposite him. For a moment he had not recognised her in mufti, then he had smiled, crossed the gangway and sat down beside her. She had not objected, indeed she had appeared mildly pleased. Tarrant made the most of his opportunities, with the result that by the time they had reached Bramford she had agreed to have tea with him at the Purple Lizard. They had returned together, and later she had accepted his invitation to go to the Bramford Cinema. on their next free afternoon. That visit had been followed by many others, and now, after three months, Tarrant was surprised to find that instead of being tired of the association, as had so often happened under similar circumstances in the past, each meeting made him keener for the next.

The sharp *kling* of the door-bell recalled him to the present, and as shuffling feet sounded without, he put down the bottle he was wrapping and stepped into the shop.

It was old Miss Bellamy, one of those confirmed hypochrondriacs who rejoice the heart of the small chemist. Better still, she was a patent medicine fiend—there are few more profitable lines. Tarrant hated the sight of her, but business was business, and he wished her good evening civilly enough.

She had been, it appeared, in poor health. This Tarrant had foreseen, as also that he would have to listen to a detailed description of her symptoms. He could have foretold the course of this, though not which was the offending one of her organs. He soon learned. It was her stomach, and about her stomach he presently knew as much as any man. Half a crown, he thought, she should be good for, as with a fine appearance of sympathy he listened to the maundering statement.

The recital continued as if it would never cease. He presently became aware that she was prolonging the interview, smiling at him with her toothless gums, and suddenly he knew the reason. She also felt his attraction. She was enjoying herself, mouthing at him and making inane conversation. It was a pathetic and rather horrible sight, but Tarrant did not appreciate that kind of pathos. Girls, he told himself, were one thing, but this old hag was quite another. Suddenly he felt he could stand no more.

'What you want,' he interrupted with force and finality, 'is a bottle of Braxamin. Ever tried it?'

Braxamin, it seemed, was also her preference. She had used it before under similar circumstances and it had done her good.

'Fine stuff,' he assured her as he deftly jerked a bottle from the serried ranks, papered it, handed it to her with an air, and dropped the resultant half-crown into its appointed place.

Braxamin! he thought as he returned a moment later to the dispensing room. Now that was how money was made! He had once analysed the stuff and found it was nearly pure magnesia: that and a small quantity of inert salts to make up a patentable formula. Cost perhaps tuppence a bottle, including the wrapper. And sold for half a crown. That was it! That was the way to success: to be making the stuff, not wasting time, as he was, peddling it over the counter.

Braxamin had suggested a dream which had occupied his mind for years. Could he not make a similar mixture? Could he not add to some simple, cheap and efficient remedy for some common complaint, a few inert ingredients to enable the mixture to be patented, and sell it at a similar profit? There was a fortune in it, if only he could light on the right stuff.

And he could! He had worked out his formula at the time. It also was simply magnesia. The same essential as in

Braxamin, but with a different selection of inert additions. His remedy would be just as effective. It would really give relief and it would be harmless, just as Braxamin was.

He had been desperately anxious to market his product, but he saw that he could as easily market part of the moon. The actual putting out of the mixture on a small scale he might have managed: he had saved a few pounds and he thought he could borrow a few more. But the success of such ventures depended on advertisement, and advertisement was costly. Thousands of pounds would be wanted, and thousands of pence was his limit.

His cogitations were presently interrupted by another shuffling footstep—that of old Barr coming to see that everything was right for closing the shop. He was a thin old man, stooped and with glasses and a straggly beard, timorous and unprogressive in character, but upright and kindly at heart.

'Who was in?' he asked as he entered the room.

'Miss Bellamy,' Tarrant answered. 'Bottle of Braxamin: half a crown.'

'A good seller. I wish everything went as well. Did you find those Aloin pills for Mr Brown?'

'Yes, they were in the corner cupboard after all.'

'I've ordered some more. What was the other thing I had to order?'

'Sponges, you said.'

'That's right: sponges. I suppose you've nearly done?'

'About finished now.' Tarrant looked at the little heap of white-coloured bottles and boxes ready for the boy to deliver, and the second smaller pile packed in corrugated cardboard beneath greyish paper and secured by string,

7

which was to go by post. This lot, together with some half dozen letters, the firm's output for the day, he would take to the post office on his way to his rooms.

Barr pottered out into the shop and Tarrant heard him opening the cash register. There was the chink of coins, and he knew these were being transferred to a canvas bag, to be taken up to the old man's bedroom for the night. Then the steps shuffled about the shop and in his mind's eye Tarrant could see a bottle of Braxamin being taken from stock, and put in precisely the same place in which its predecessor had stood. A click indicated the shutting of the door and more drawn-out sounds that the blinds were coming down. Trade for the day was over.

Tarrant, having done a little tidying, collected his post office stuff, bid his employer a somewhat brief good-night, and let himself out into the High Street. In spite of his poor opinion of it, Lydcott was not an unprepossessing little place. It was, in fact, a typical Surrey village, one long, irregular street of brick and tiled houses toned by age to a mellow brownish red and relieved here and there by the green of trees and creepers. An old stone church with a squat square tower stood back on a tiny hill, with a lych-gate on the road in front, and a humped-back bridge with white handrails drew attention to a narrow sluggish stream. All unchanged for centuries, yet the signs of progress were not wanting. In front of a garage there were three petrol pumps of vivid scarlet, and a 'Surrey Trust' noticeboard showed on the gable of the ancient inn.

The place, however, had no beauty for Tarrant. Having finished at the post office, he was now free for the evening. But free for what? The church choir practice, which seemed the chief excitement of a Friday evening, evoked in him no answering thrill. And in the bar of the Green Horse, the sole alternative attraction, there were only yokels with whom he had nothing in common. There was no cinema, no dancing, no tennis, nor boating, nor golf; no girls—except Merle, and she was engaged on Fridays.

He went to his rooms, which seemed more deadly than ever, sitting down resentfully to a somewhat unappetising supper. Money! he thought. The first thing it would do for him would be to get him out of Lydcott. Oh, if he could only try his patent medicine idea!

Then in the act of raising his fork to his mouth he stopped, and for some seconds remained motionless. Why, he could try it after all! The snag had been the advertisement. Well, there was a way out of that!

Slowly he lowered the morsel to his plate, while an excitement rose in his mind such as he had not felt for years.

Why need he advertise? The Braxamin people were already doing all the advertisement that was necessary. Could he not take advantage of their work?

Suppose he were to approach retail chemists and say: 'You sell Braxamin? A very good line. And you get sixpence a bottle commission? Quite. Here is a similar stuff that I make: equally harmless and equally effective. When you're asked for Braxamin just say you're out of it and that here's something else that you can recommend. I give a shilling commission and you'll make an extra sixpence on every bottle.'

By Jove! It was an idea! Tarrant sat metaphorically hugging himself as he gloated over it. Money! Yes, there was money in it all right. In the first flush of his enthusiasm he could see no limit to what it would bring in.

Could he do it? He felt sure of it. Obviously with a small plant, and working by hand instead of machinery, it would cost him more to put out his mixture than it cost the Braxamin people. Suppose it took fivepence or even sixpence a bottle, delivered, instead of the twopence or threepence that he had estimated they did it for. Then there would be sixpence for the patent medicine stamp, if he should patent his stuff. That, with the shilling commission, would leave sevenpence a bottle profit for him. Or say he gave ninepence commission, his profit would go up to tenpence. For him that would be wealth. Besides, he would not be a fool. For a time at least he would put all his profits back into the business, and so buy plant and reduce his costs.

But would the retailers do it? Ah, there was the snag! Some of them would and some of them wouldn't. It would largely depend, he thought, on how they were approached. There he felt he was all right. He had a profound belief in his own tact.

It would, perhaps, be better not to make that remark about Braxamin. The idea should be conveyed more subtly. He would simply call as traveller for the new remedy. He would talk to the proprietor and so judge the man. If it seemed wise he would merely canvas for an order and leave it at that. But if things looked propitious he could go on: 'It's been well taken up in Manchester—or Aberdeen or Penzance,' or some other equally distant town. 'There I heard a story of what one man did to get our commission. When his customers asked for Braxamin he told them—' and so on. This would not be a suggestion, but a joke, but with the right man it would do the trick.

No longer was Tarrant bored. No longer were his rooms drab and Lydcott a dull place. Life had suddenly become adventurous and thrilling. At last there was something to be thought of: something to be done: money to be made.

Money to be made!

He got out his old notes and read them with enthusiasm. Then he settled down to re-estimate his costs. This was the one department in which he really had learnt something since coming to Barr. As he revised his figures, he became more and more excited. The thing would be a certain winner!

But he could not carry it out single-handed. With a small car or van it would take his entire time to do the travelling, so that someone else would have to take charge of the manufacture. Where could he find a suitable partner?

Then came the greatest idea of all. Merle Weir! Would Merle join in the affair?

She would, he told himself, be eminently suitable. She was competent and efficient in everything she did. She had a nurse's training, which, if it was not exactly what was required, at least had familiarised her with medicines and their sale. She was straight: on that he would have banked his entire future, and, best of all, he believed from odd remarks that she had dropped, that she had a little money in the bank.

Was she too straight? Tarrant smiled confidently. Merle was a girl and she was fond of him. Merle would be pliable. If she suited him, he would see to it that her scruples were overcome.

He looked at his watch. Too late, he was afraid, to ring her up that night. Besides, better sleep on a thing like that. Though he had no doubt that he could get rid of her if she proved troublesome, there was no sense in having unnecessary unpleasantness. He would take his time about the whole affair and not risk spoiling what was perhaps the most critical step of his life.

Probably she would want him to marry her. Well, there

was no hurry about that. Probably also he might do worse, but here the wise attitude would be to wait and see.

All the same, next day he telephoned to Merle, asking her to meet him on Sunday afternoon, as he had a matter of importance to put before her. He smiled confidently as she replied that she would come.

2

Merle Weir Takes a Hand

The Wilton Grange Convalescent Home was a luxurious establishment set high up among the pines of the Surrey Green Sand Ridge. Its fees were as lofty as its position, and its proprietor, by receiving only those patients who were already improving in health, had gained it a reputation for efficacy. This does not mean that it was run on fraudulent lines. If its visitors paid highly, they got value for their money. Their clinical treatment was of the best, the visiting doctors were specialists in their respective lines, and from the boarding and social point of view everything was the last word in efficiency and high tone.

The nurses, too, were of a superior type. More than mere professional skill was required of them, though technical competence was naturally a *sine qua non*. But they had also to reach the proprietor's high standards in social deportment, personal appearance, beauty of voice, and, of course, morals, though this latter requirement was usually taken for granted. Against these demands they received exceptional pay and privileges, such as separate bedrooms, admirably furnished staff-rooms and liberal leave. In fact, a billet at Wilton Grange was looked upon not only as one of the plums of the profession, but as a certificate of all round personal excellence. It was natural, therefore, that Merle Weir was delighted when some three years before Tarrant came to Lydcott, she was appointed to a vacancy on the staff.

Her father had been a doctor with a good country practice. She was an only daughter, and on her mother's death several years earlier she had taken her place, acting as housekeeper and secretary to Dr Weir. Characteristically she threw herself with energy into the work. To enable her to deal more efficiently with his accounts and correspondence she taught herself book-keeping, shorthand and typing. She did not attempt dispensing, though she picked up a good deal about it, but she drove his Armstrong-Siddeley with skill, and could hold her own with any chauffeur in the matter of running repairs. Finally, in character she was one in a thousand, straight and kindly and decent and unselfish.

Then, to her intense grief, her father died, and she found herself alone in the world. He had left her a little money, though barely enough to live on. Now she was free to follow her own bent. She had always liked nursing and she divided her capital, setting aside half for the necessary training, and retaining the rest against the proverbial rainy day. She worked hard, obtained high qualifications, and in due time reaped the reward in the Wilton Grange position.

She liked the place and the work, and, more important still for her happiness, her fellow nurses. One of them in particular had become her special friend, though she was not normally given to special friendships. This had arisen through an act of kindness on Merle's part. The girl was Elsie Oates, a tall, blonde young woman of about the same

14

age as herself. One day Merle surprised her, sobbing bitterly. She had noticed that she had been depressed for some time, but this betokened real trouble. At first Elsie was reticent, but presently the genuine sympathy in Merle's manner brought out the story.

It appeared that Elsie's young man, a budding accountant in a Fenchurch Street firm, was seriously ill. It was not quite clear what was the matter with him, and Elsie thought the doctors were themselves puzzled. But they were agreed that his best chance lay in a sea voyage. And this was the difficulty. He could not afford it. The cost would have been some forty pounds more than he and Elsie could jointly raise.

It was then that Merle surprised her friend and, indeed, herself. 'I happen to have forty pounds in the bank that I'm not at present wanting,' she heard herself saying, 'and I'd like to lend it to you. You can pay it back when it's convenient.'

At this Elsie wept again, declaring she could not take the money. But Merle insisted and presently her friend's despair became tinged with hope. With the aid of Merle's contribution the fiancé's passage was booked, and all looked promising. Then a further blow fell. Just before the boat sailed the young man had a relapse. Instead of going aboard the s.s. *Antonio*, he was taken to hospital. In a week he was dead.

Elsie was inconsolable, but here again Merle's friendship helped her to carry on. Gradually the sharpness of her pain became dulled and things settled down as before. Under the circumstances the shipping company generously refunded the whole of the passage money, and Merle's forty pounds was repaid in full. But the episode left Elsie Merle's firm friend determined to do everything in her power to wipe off the moral debt which she felt she still owed.

Another year passed, a year of hard work and of happiness, and then a new factor came into Merle's life. She called one evening at Barr's for some medicine and met the new assistant. Since then nothing had been the same.

In appearance James Tarrant was her ideal. Tall and slender, though not slight, he gave an impression of physical fitness and resilient strength. His complexion was pale, but clear and healthy, and made a foil for his dark hair and eyes. His long face was strengthened almost to brutality by the squareness of his firm jaw, and his lips were thin and rather tightly compressed. Only his eyes made the critical hesitate: they were too shrewd for complete confidence. But when he smiled they lost their calculating look and his whole face softened.

He had been pleasant about the medicine: neither offhand nor familiar, but just friendly, Merle had been lost in admiration.

Then on the following Wednesday had come the meeting in the bus. She had seen him the moment he entered, but he had not noticed her until they had gone some little distance. Then he had acted delightfully, moving beside her with just the right amount of deference and friendly interest. He had talked easily and entertainingly and in such a musical voice! When on arrival at Bramford he had rather deprecatingly suggested tea, she felt as if she had known him for a long time and that it would be churlish to refuse.

She could not get him out of her thoughts, and when a few days later a charming note arrived, suggesting a visit to the films, her heart leaped. Would she go? She laughed as she put the question to herself. Would she not? But she was careful to reply neither too quickly nor too enthusiastically.

Her admiration grew with each subsequent meeting until at last she made the great discovery. She loved him, and, if he asked her, she would marry him. Since then her love had steadily increased, till at last she had one fear and one fear only—that he might not ask her.

She began then to find that love included pain as well as pleasure. There was the thrill of eager anticipation before they met, but there was also cold fear and disappointment when they parted with no apparent progress made. Merle grew absentminded and irritable and her work began to suffer.

Then one Saturday morning her outlook changed. Tarrant rang her up to ask if she would meet him on the following afternoon. This had already often happened, but now there was an eagerness in his voice which had been lacking before. Besides, he intimated that he had something of importance to put before her.

At last a proposal! She felt it could be nothing else. There was nothing else between them, nothing that they had ever talked about or envisaged. No, at long last it was, coming—the greatest day of her life. By the next morning she would be engaged, and before many months had passed she would be Mrs Tarrant.

Everyone noticed the change in her that day, the matron with relief, the nurses with winks and shrugs and grins. Merle didn't see them, nor would she have cared if she had. The glorious prospect filled her mind to the exclusion of all else.

They were to meet on Sunday afternoon at a bus stop near the Home, from which they would drive still further into these wonderful Surrey hills, climb up to one of the summits from which they could look down across the Weald to the blue line of the South Downs, and then walk back to lower levels for tea.

Though she arrived at the rendezvous before the time, he was waiting for her. He usually kept his appointments accurately on time, and when she saw him so early her heart leaped. It was, she told herself, a portent.

He met her quietly, as he always did, though she could feel that he was secretly excited. He began at once talking commonplaces, which was natural enough in the little crowd which was waiting for the bus. All the same, a faint chill began to damp her enthusiasm. There was something on his mind, yes, but what was it? His glance, when it fell on her, had less than its usual ardour, and indeed it fell on her but seldom.

Then the cold breath of doubt was gloriously dispelled. Strolling slightly aside from the others, he looked at her, and in his eyes was all the old warmth and admiration. 'He does love me!' she thought thankfully. And when he murmured in that voice which always slipped under her guard and left her weak and helpless before him, that he had something to ask her and that it must wait till they were alone, she was once again in the seventh heaven.

The drive passed like a dream, and presently they had left the bus and taken the winding path which led up through the trees to the top of the hill. They let the other climbers pass on and were at last alone. Then her whole being became riveted to his words.

'It's coming!' she thought with a joy that was almost pain. 'It's coming at last!' For he was talking about himself, his early life, his prospects. 'A job like mine's all right in a way,' he was saying. 'It gives a man a start and all that, but there's no money in it. And what I want and what you want is money.'

'James, dear,' she wanted to cry, 'I know what you're thinking—that you must have a comfortable home to offer me before we can be married. But you're wrong! All we want is each other, and you know it.'

But that didn't seem to be what was in his mind. 'All my life,' he went on coolly, 'I've been thinking of money. I want money, and so do you, not, of course, for its own sake, but for what it brings. But I've never seen how I could get it.'

Again that faint chill swept over her. Of course she wanted money; everybody did, though obviously money was not everything. But he seemed to think it was. He continued about his prospects till she could almost have screamed.

'I've wanted money, but I never could see how to get it,' he repeated, 'until Friday night. Then I got an idea. Tell me, have you ever thought about patent medicines?'

A cold, numb feeling seemed to grip her heart. Patent medicines! What was he thinking about? She glanced at him quickly. His face was lit up with an eager interest, but it wasn't in her. He wasn't even looking at her. It was something affecting himself, in which she was not concerned.

She simply couldn't answer. Her mouth was dry and she felt physically sick. She hadn't known that disappointment could be so bitter. He glanced at her casually.

'Hallo,' he said, but in an offhand way and with some impatience, 'what's the matter? Not feeling well?'

Her pride came to her aid. 'Just the hill for the moment,' she said as steadily as she could. 'I'll be all right directly.'

'Perhaps I've been rather rushing it,' he answered. 'I'm apt to forget about things when I'm keen on anything.

19

Well'—and the interest crept back into his manner—'I was asking you about patent medicines. Have you ever thought of the money that's to be made if you can strike a good one?'

'No,' she murmured, 'I never thought about it. Tell me.'

He was only too ready. 'Well,' he went on eagerly, 'take Braxamin. Here you have,' and he gave her the figures he had estimated: the large profit on each bottle, the hundreds of thousands of bottles which must be sold every year, the thousands of pounds of clear gain. Desperately she fought to take in what he was saying and to forget that other nightmare.

'That's the way to make money,' he continued, 'and that's what I propose to do—to put another stuff like Braxamin on the market.'

She did her best to be sympathetic as be elaborated his plan. His trouble was that it wanted two people. He would do the canvassing and the distributing, but someone else would be required to mix and bottle the stuff.

When Merle realised where all this was leading, she experienced another revulsion of feeling almost as difficult to control as the first. Why, he wanted her after all! And the question of marriage was not ruled out! It was only postponed. This suggestion of his might—certainly would—lead to it! Warmth flowed back into her heart.

At all costs she must agree. If she turned him down she would lose him. Of course she would be sorry to leave the Home and to give up nursing. But these were nothing in comparison to what she would gain. In any case, she needn't try to deceive herself. She could not resist what would bring them so close together.

So far she had thought only of their personal relations.

Now, as her mind became easier on that score, she began to consider the scheme itself. To her distress, the more she did so, the less she liked it. Why, it was scarcely honest. Not actually dishonest, of course. James would never propose anything of that kind. But still not exactly what she would like to do.

'But tell me, James, I don't understand: is it quite—straight?' she said timorously.

'Straight?' he repeated, and for the first time she saw an expression in his eyes which rather frightened her. But it instantly vanished. 'Straight? What are you thinking of? Of course it's straight. You're not suggesting the Braxamin people are crooks, are you? What I propose is just the same.'

Merle suddenly realised that the point was vital to her peace of mind and that at all costs it must be settled.

'But is it so straight?' she went on. 'They're charging people half a crown for what you tell me is worth about tuppence. I don't know that one could stand over that.'

'My dear girl, you've got it wrong,' he said, for the second time that afternoon smiling in that entrancing way which broke down all her defences. 'Tell me, what do you think the Braxamin people are out for?'

'Money,' she answered promptly. After all he had said there could be no question of this.

He made an impatient gesture. 'Ah, yes, of course. Every business without exception is run for money—even nursing. But I don't mean that. What are the Braxamin people out to do for their money?'

'Why, to sell their stuff. I don't think I understand.'

'No, you haven't got what I'm driving at. They're out to cure people, aren't they? People with indigestion and tummy aches and so on. Isn't that right?'

'I suppose it is.'

'Of course it is. Now tell me, how could they do that if they charged two or three pence for the remedy? Don't you know that people, particularly uneducated people, only value things that cost them something? Don't you see that in this case the half-crown is part of the cure?'

She thought over this. 'That hadn't occurred to me,' she admitted.

'But you see it now that I point it out? Half the benefit of medicine and drugs comes from faith. Don't you know that? And the more you can stimulate faith in the remedy, the more good it will do. To produce that faith it must *cost* the patient something. Don't you see it?'

She was not satisfied, and yet his argument seemed unanswerable. She shifted her ground. 'But what about our taking advantage of the Braxamin advertising? Do you think that's quite straight?'

'Perhaps not. But we won't really do that. I only put it in that way to make you understand. People are always coming in and asking for something for indigestion or flatulence or pains in the tummy, and you sell them what you think will do them good. My stuff will definitely do them good, so why not sell it? Braxamin has got no monopoly on the market.'

That sounded all right, too. Perhaps she was being hypercritical.

'It's a big decision,' she said presently; 'big for me, I mean. If I did what you suggest it would ruin my present prospects. Then if this thing failed I should be finished. I should never get so good a job again.'

He moved impatiently. 'It won't fail,' he declared dogmatically; then with a change of manner: 'Don't you see that

22

it can't fail? The demand hasn't to be built up through years of advertising; the demand is there. Our mixture will meet that demand, and meet it well. It only remains to ensure our stuff is sold rather than our rival's! That will be done automatically by our larger commission. It's absolutely fair to our rivals. If they want the trade, let them increase their commission.'

He had an answer for everything, and yet she was not satisfied. But now once again her love for him swelled up in her heart, pushing all these points of technical morality into the shade. She loved him, and she believed that, in spite of his preoccupation with his precious scheme, he loved her. Very well, if she turned him down, as she had seen before, she would lose him. To go into the thing with him would bring them together, and even if he did not immediately propose marriage, she would still be in touch with him.

But in spite of her love she had not entirely lost her common sense. She told him that she was honoured that he had offered her a partnership in his scheme, but that it represented so tremendous a change in her life that she could not decide on just an hour's notice. Could they meet on Wednesday afternoon, and she would then give him her answer?

Biased as she was in his favour, she could not but see that her caution had a salutary effect on his manner.

During the next three days, free from the glamour of his presence, she was able to consider the proposal more critically. Gradually her ideas became clarified. She felt she would *hate* to give up her nursing and her career as she had planned it out. She realised that she loathed the scheme, which in spite of Tarrant's specious pleas, she did not

23

consider honest. She doubted that the various chemists would prove so compliant as he supposed, in which case the whole thing would fail. Finally, she doubted that even if it did succeed, money earned in such a way would bring happiness.

But over and above all these considerations was the fact of her love. Again and again she repeated to herself, 'If I turn him down, I lose him.' Could she face that?

She weighed the pros and cons in her mind, but all the time, deep in her heart, she knew what she would do. Her happiness was bound up in him. If she lost him, nothing else mattered. And what influenced her even more was the belief that she could help him and give him something of the love and companionship which up to now she feared he had missed.

When they met on the Wednesday she intended to tell him immediately that she had decided to join with him. But it suddenly was borne in upon her that if she were to continue working with him it could only be through marriage: any other basis would mean eventual misery. Almost without volition she heard herself saying: 'James, this is so important that I must be absolutely straight with you. I don't think we could work together on our present basis. I must tell you quite honestly that I cannot afford to give up my present life unless it means a home to me.'

He looked at her keenly. 'You mean marriage?' he asked quietly.

'I'm afraid so.'

'Afraid!' He made an eloquent gesture. 'My dear Merle, isn't that the one thing I really want? Isn't that what all this has been leading up to? Only I felt that unless I had money to support a home, I daren't ask you. Merle dear, you fill me with utter joy.' He bent suddenly, took her in his arms and kissed her again and again.

'Then I agree,' she murmured, as she relaxed in his arms. Yet the faint chill still lingered in her mind.

3

James Tarrant Gets Busy

Tarrant both smiled and shivered when he looked back on that Wednesday afternoon. He smiled when he told himself that he had successfully taken his first hurdle: the obtaining of Merle's help in the venture. He shivered when he realised the cost. Though he was attracted by Merle, he did not intend to marry her. Of course he wasn't really committed. No one had heard their conversation and there was nothing in writing. If the necessity arose, he could say that she had mistaken his meaning.

He saw that while he mustn't allow the engagement to be announced, in private he would have to assume its existence. This he felt he could do safely. He could surely find phrases which would satisfy her and yet would be capable of an innocent interpretation.

There were, then, two lines of activity stretching out before him: one, to keep Merle sweet and helpful, the other, to get on with the scheme. The first could largely be done by compliments and a little love making, but the second meant real work.

He began next day when old Barr went out for his usual afternoon constitutional. Looking up the files, he made a list of firms who supplied the various materials and appliances he would need, and that night wrote asking for catalogues. He bought a map of England and considered desirable sites for his works, and he wrote to a celebrated builder of light cars and vans for prices and running costs.

'We've actually got under way,' he told Merle exultingly when next Sunday afternoon they met. 'I'm getting prices and then we'll see how far we can launch out. I haven't got much capital, you know: only a few pounds, but it'll probably be enough for a start.'

'I've got a little too,' Merle said hesitatingly.

This was just what he wanted, but he saw that he would be unwise to be too eager. 'Oh, no,' he answered protestingly, 'I couldn't take that. You're giving quite enough in your time. You mustn't risk your money.'

She seemed relieved, as he had intended. He was satisfied that if they were actually held up for cash, the circumstances would make an appeal which she would be unable to resist. In such a case he would gracefully allow his objections to be overborne.

'I'm getting out these costs,' he continued; 'bottles and cartons and bins and tables, a small car or truck, a shed with water laid on, and what's necessary for washing and filling and despatching.'

'Where did you think of starting?'

'Now that's characteristic of you, Merle,' he declared, with one of his intoxicating smiles. 'You put your finger right on the crucial point. I'd like a biggish town where we would, so to speak, get lost. There's no use in advertising what we're doing, you know. Then it ought to be near a

27

port, partly because coastwise transport is cheap, and partly because we might eventually sell in Ireland and abroad.'

'I don't think you need worry about selling abroad,' she returned. 'By the time we're strong enough to attempt that, we shall want new premises and can move to a port.'

He nodded, noting again the unerring way she went to essentials, though unpleasantly conscious of the circumspection on his part that this would mean.

'I'll make a fist of suitable towns,' he said, 'and then go round them and see about sheds. Now another thing. When are we going to leave our jobs and what reason shall we give?'

Her face fell and he could see that this for her was going to be a wrench. 'I thought,' he went on, 'of saying I'd got some friends in the States who had written that they had a job out there for me.'

Her face fell still further. 'But, James, that wouldn't be true. Why not tell the truth? I'm going to. I'm going to say that I've got a good job with a new medical firm, but that I don't yet know where I'm going to be sent.'

Tarrant cursed himself for his carelessness. Her little manias and phobias must be respected. There would be enough of sailing close to the wind in their venture without worrying her with gratuitous prevarication.

'You're right,' he declared, as if he had overlooked the point. 'We should certainly keep to the truth. Yes. I'll say something of the same kind. Now about the date. I'll look about for the shed, then we could start directly I find one. I've only to give a week's notice, and I suppose it's the same with you?'

'I think so. But, James, wouldn't it be better to be quite straight about the thing? What about announcing our engagement? You say you're leaving to take over a better job, you needn't say what, and I can say I'm following you to be married.'

Again Tarrant swore mentally. That was the worst of women. They couldn't do business without dragging in their wretched personal feelings. If Merle was going to question the uprightness of every future word and deed, she'd be more trouble than she was worth.

Her suggestion confirmed his intention to avoid marriage; to be tied up to a Recording Angel with an inflamed sense of honour would be just hell. With a flood of relief he reminded himself that nothing irrevocable had been done.

Yet he must get her help with the scheme. He knew no one else that he could ask.

'My dear girl,' he gave her another melting glance and smile, 'I only wish we could. But I told you I couldn't afford to marry at present, as all I have goes into this. And I'm not going to let my wife support me, even if she would. So I absolutely refuse to tie you down till we're sure we've backed a winner. Directly the money begins to come in, let's announce the engagement: then just as soon as we have enough, let's do the deed.'

'But the announcing of the engagement wouldn't involve immediate marriage.'

He took her arm and pressed it beneath his. A kiss he thought was indicated, but as they were walking down the main street of Bramford that could be postponed. 'My dear,' he said softly and his voice was very ardent, 'don't you think we might have our own little secret just between the two of us?'

He saw, as he had expected, that she couldn't resist him, and gently switched the conversation in a less dangerous direction.

Next day he told old Barr that an American relative had just arrived in the country, and wanted him to drive round and show him the sights for a week. He therefore would be obliged for leave. If Barr thought he was due holidays, he would take them now; if not, he would forfeit his wages.

Barr, knowing that his assistant had really worked hard since his arrival and being a kindly man at heart, did what Tarrant had shrewdly calculated he would do, and agreed to consider the week as holidays, that is, with full pay. Again pleased with his successful manoeuvring, Tarrant's belief in himself was still further confirmed.

Of the list which he had made of towns suitable for their headquarters, he had visited only one, Exeborough. His sister had lived there, and on her death, three years earlier, he had gone down to the funeral. He had got away from the house as soon as possible and had spent the time till his train in walking around, and he had taken a fancy to the place. It was in the south-west, and was connected with the sea by a river navigable by coasters. Down by this river there were small streets of working-class houses, and it would be strange if among them he couldn't find a suitable headquarters.

On the following Monday he left Lydcott early, and by midday was in Exeborough. That very afternoon he found a suitable property. The position was good; it lay across the river on low ground close both to the railway and the diminutive harbour. It consisted, so far as he could see by squinting over the surrounding wall, of a small yard with a shed along one side and at the other a tiny office. The place wanted paint, but otherwise seemed in good repair. A board along the front bore the legend: 'J. H. Matthews, Produce Dealer', but it was evident that the produce

30

dealings of J. H. Matthews had come to a bad end, as across the letters was pasted a bill with the words: 'To be Let or Sold. Apply Grimmett & Mason, Boulter's Close'.

Some heads at windows in the adjoining houses, and a rapidly increasing ring of children watching his essays in sleuthing warned him to avoid inaugurating a mystery. He crossed the road and knocked at a door. One of the heads removed itself from a window and presented itself for closer inspection.

'Good morning,' said Tarrant, with his pleasant smile. 'I'm looking for a shed to start a small business. Can you tell me what there is across there? Just the yard and shed and office, or are there more buildings?'

The woman, obviously interested, confirmed his supposition. He chatted pleasantly for a moment or two, then threw in the essential question: 'Been long vacant?'

This she couldn't immediately answer, but by dint of obtaining the opinions of curious neighbours, the point was settled. J. H. Matthews had departed over two years previously.

A further question told Tarrant that Boulter's Close was off the High Street on the town side of the river. Ten minutes later he was Shown into Mr Grimmett's private room, and in another three he had stated his business.

'Very convenient little premises and apparently just what you want,' said Mr Grimmett; 'and in good repair also. Perhaps you'd like to have a look at it?'

'No use unless I can afford it,' Tarrant returned. 'It's a new business and I haven't much capital. What do you want for it?'

'It's a good site,' Mr Grimmett pointed out. 'A good pitch, so to speak. There's a keen demand for sheds and yards in that area. Would you buy?'

'Couldn't afford it. If I took it I'd want a short lease with an option to carry on from year to year.'

Grimmett hesitated, while he turned over some papers. 'Hundred a year, or two guineas a week for shorter terms,' he said at last, shooting a little side glance at Tarrant. 'I may tell you,' he went on with an engaging air of putting his last card on the table, 'that it's worth far more than that, but between ourselves the owner's hard up and wants the money.'

Tarrant considered this. 'A hundred a year,' he repeated; 'that seems a lot. I suppose it's because of the keen demand you mentioned?'

Grimmett shot him another little glance. 'Why, yes,' he said, 'and quite natural too. After all, value depends on demand, doesn't it?'

'I agree,' Tarrant assured him. 'And it wouldn't be anything like that figure only for the demand?'

'Well, supply and demand are the same all the world over,' Grimmett asserted, though with somewhat less assurance.

Tarrant bent forward. 'Now, sir, I can see that you're trying to do your best for your client, which of course I thoroughly appreciate. I'd want you to do it for me under similar circumstances. But when this shed has been vacant for over two years you needn't talk to me about a keen demand. If I find it suitable, what about fifty a year and I to pay the rates?'

Grimmett smiled. 'I don't suppose you're seriously putting that forward,' he declared. 'But there's no use in our talking unless the place suits you. Come along down and see it. My car's outside.'

The 'premises' when Tarrant inspected them, seemed

ideal. The shed was larger than he had visualised, but if the affair prospered there would be considerable storage of stocks, so perhaps this was an advantage. Having pointed out all the faults he could think of, Tarrant began bargaining, and before he left Grimmett's office he had a signed agreement in his pocket to take over the premises for one year at a rent of seventy pounds, with an option to carry on at the same figure year by year for the next four years, possession being obtained on the paying of the first year's rent. Tarrant wrote a cheque as if the matter were the merest bagatelle, instead of the paying out of exactly a quarter of his capital.

He wrote the news to Merle, asking her to resign and come to Exeborough as soon as she could. Next day he arranged with a firm of builders whose yard he had noticed in an adjoining street, to carry out some small alterations at the new property. The name board was to be re-lettered, certain bins and benches were to be put in the shed, and a desk and set of drawers were to be fixed in the office. Water and electricity were already laid on, and he gave orders for a large sink to be put in, beside several additional lights. In an excess of zeal he bought a can of oil, and went round lubricating all the hinges, locks, and other moving mechanisms that he could find.

That night Tarrant went up to London, and next morning he began a series of calls on firms which manufactured the various articles and materials he required. He gave orders for the delivery of bottles and stoppers, scales and measures, a cheap hand mixing machine, the various chemicals in bulk, wrapping paper, corrugated paper, cartons, and other similar requirements. At a printers and lithographers he ordered business writing paper and bottle and parcel despatch labels, all of excellent quality and lettered according to his own design. A vertical file, folders, and a typewriter he picked up second-hand, together with other necessary office equipment. Then he went down to Lydcott, paid for his rooms and collected his clothes. Finally he wrote to Barr saying his American relative had offered him a job in Philadelphia, that he regretted, therefore, that he would be unable to return, and would Mr Barr please take his week's holiday in lieu of notice. It was characteristic of him that he never even thought about the inconvenience to which his action would put the old man.

Returning to Exeborough, he found his work cut out for him. His cheque having been cashed, he received the keys of the shed, and harried the contractor to such an extent that work on the alterations was begun that very day. The evening he spent in searching for a room, which eventually he found in a reasonably satisfactory boarding house.

After some three weeks of high endeavour, Tarrant was ready to start operations. All legal and municipal requirements had been complied with. The tradesmen, through ceaseless badgering, had finished and left. The various bins and racks and cupboards were full; bottles, wrapping paper, cartons, chemicals: all were in place. The hand mixing machine was installed, the letter paper and typewriter were in the office and there was plenty of water and plenty of light for everything that was to be done. As Tarrant surveyed it all, his heart swelled with pride and confidence. In the meantime, Merle, inclined to protest owing to having been unable to give her employer longer notice, had left the Home and was coming down the next afternoon, a Sunday. Tarrant hoped that she would get a room without delay, so that actual production should begin on the following morning.

He was careful to greet her as a lover should, and even his hardened conscience smote him as he saw how she reacted to it. 'I thought,' he said, 'we'd have tea first, then go and see the premises—it's really a yard and shed, but "premises" sounds better—and then you will want to get fixed up about rooms.'

During tea he noticed that her manner showed strain, though it was some time before he discovered the cause. She was frightened. After so drastically burning her boats, it was, of course, no wonder. Now, he realised, was his opportunity. If he could comfort her and recreate her sense of security, he would bind her more closely to him than ever. He was careful, therefore, to pretend that she herself was all he wanted, and that his scheme, while important and thrilling, was yet completely secondary.

All the same he could not hide his pride when he took her down to Arbutus Street and showed her their new headquarters.

'Oh,' she said, evidently agreeably surprised, 'that looks fine. It's much larger than I had expected. Funny,' she glanced at the new name board, 'that it should have been used before for manufacturing a patent medicine.'

'But it wasn't,' he answered smiling. 'The last tenant was a produce merchant.'

'Then what about the board?'

'The board? That's all right. It's our board.'

Merle stared at him helplessly as she read the legend:

KOLDKURE
John Tinsley. Manufacturer of Koldkure.
Cures colds, sore throats, etc.

He chuckled.

'Before you you see John Tinsley, joint proprietor with Miss Merle Weir of Koldkure.' He grew serious. 'No, old girl, you haven't got the point of that. We want to be saved from visits from emissaries of Braxamin. If we trade under the name of Koldkure we shall be saved.'

'But our stuff doesn't cure colds.'

'Merle, dear, you must trust me to think of things like that. I have stuff that will, with labels and all complete. We'll make up a few dozen bottles in case anyone sees our sign and wants to buy the stuff. But our real work will be the other.'

He could see that she was upset. 'Oh, James, is that really necessary? I don't like it. Why can't we be absolutely straight?'

'It *is* absolutely straight. A business can call itself by any name. If we had called ourselves the Sun and Planets Manufacturing Company, would you have objected?'

'Of course not. But that's different.'

'Why? We wouldn't manufacture either suns or planets. No, you can call your business by any name you like, and you can manufacture all sorts of things that are not mentioned in the title. It's a perfectly common and legitimate practice, and there's nothing crooked about it.'

'No, but—'

'We *do* manufacture Koldkure. It's entirely up to us to push it or not to push it as much as our other lines.'

She was silenced, though he doubted if she was convinced. As they explored the premises, he realised that she had been bitterly disappointed. He tried to cheer her up by pointing to the stacks of bottles, the various-sized dishes which, filled from different bins, made the required mixture, the mixing machine, a little chute he had himself made for filling, and the arrangements for packing. Gradually her enthusiasm revived, but when they reached the office and saw the paper and labels it again became damped. And yet their heading was good. First, in small, discreet capitals, came the word 'Koldkure', followed by an even more elaborate account of John Tinsley and his achievements than appeared on the board.

'Only our trade name,' Tarrant assured her. 'Merle dear, I see you don't like it, but I assure you it's perfectly in order. Such devices are normal business procedure, well understood and approved by all concerned.'

'Then I don't think I like business,' Merle said in a small, strangled voice.

'Personally I hate and loathe it,' Tarrant returned earnestly, 'but when we go into it we must adopt its methods.'

Merle was fortunate in finding a room, and by the time she had moved in her two suitcases it was after seven. As a mild form of celebration Tarrant decreed that they should dine together in one of the better restaurants of the city.

When at last they were seated over coffee, he carefully steered the conversation towards finance. 'We've done pretty well on the whole, I think,' he declared as he balanced a lump of sugar over her cup and paused for her nod to drop it in, 'though it's come to a darned sight more than I esti-mated. But I expect that always happens.'

'Have you much money left?' she asked, just as he had hoped she would.

'None,' he grimaced. 'That's just the trouble. Not a blessed bean. Fortunately we've got most of what we want.'

'What's still outstanding?'

Better still! She was reacting exactly as he had intended. 'Well,' he answered, with what he considered the necessary hesitation, 'there's just one important item, and that's the car. I've looked over, I suppose, some scores of second-hand cars, and I've found one that would do—a Mornington twelve. It's four years old, but it's been well looked after, and really looks like new. Of course it's an expensive make, but I simply must look prosperous. And it has a tremendous roomy back that would carry a lot of samples.'

She thought over this. 'What do they want for it?' she asked at last.

'Seventy, and dirt cheap at that. I had it out. The engine's in fine order, runs like a bird, and the tyres are good. It's a bargain right enough, but I just haven't the cash.'

'Very well,' she said, 'that'll be my contribution. I was thinking it over as I came down, and I want to put a hundred into the thing. That's seventy for the car, and there'll be thirty over for any other small, items that we want.'

He protested, as he had intended to do if this admirable result were achieved, then graciously retreated, again according to plan. He had, indeed, difficulty in hiding his exultation. He knew how to work this girl. He could get what he liked out of her. And as to her conscientious scruples, a few amorous looks and kisses would put them right.

Next morning they bought the car, and then, going back to Arbutus Street, began the great work. Having rinsed a hundred bottles, Merle measured out the necessary materials, while Tarrant turned the mixing mill. Between them they filled the bottles, fixed in the stoppers with the necessary firmness and stuck on the labels. Then Tarrant gave his staff a lesson in putting them up in the light grey paper he had chosen, so that the printed name would fall in the right place. Lastly they packed cartons: half-dozen, dozen, two-dozen and five-dozen sizes.

By the end of that first week they had accumulated a fair stock, while Merle had grown highly skilful in each process. On Sunday they packed the back of the car with samples, and on Monday morning Tarrant started out to seek their fortunes.

While he was away Merle was to hold the fort, send more samples by carrier for him to pick up, reply to inquiries, supply any orders which came in, and between times continue filling bottles. If they were extraordinarily lucky, and Merle found herself unable to cope with the work, she was to look out for a suitable girl to help her.

Tarrant's hopes were high as he turned the bonnet of the Mornington to the north.

4

Merle Weir Develops Technique

If James Tarrant had disliked the condition on which Merle had agreed to join in his scheme, Merle herself was almost unhappy as she watched the Mornington disappear on its quest. Turning back to the yard, she felt weighed down with what for her was a most unusual sense of loneliness and foreboding.

The truth was that she had misgivings as to whether she had done the right thing in joining in the enterprise. The Convalescent Home now looked profoundly attractive and its loss seemed overwhelming. The others had been nice to her at the end. They had been interested in her plans and she had felt so mean in not answering their questions, for she could not bring herself to take the easy way out and lie. But James had been adamant about that. Again and again he had declared that no one must know where she had gone or what she was going to do.

Elsie Oates, the nurse to whom she had lent the money, had been particularly demonstrative. She had seemed so hurt at Merle's lack of response that Merle had been driven to saying, 'It's a secret for the moment, Elsie; please don't ask me. You'll be the very first I'll tell, as soon as I'm free to do it.' But Merle had hated it.

Now that the die was cast, she saw what she had lost. And what had she gained? Well, she had gained James Tarrant, and that would infinitely outweigh everything else. That, she now realised, was what she had really wanted and hoped for all the time.

But the very fact that she reasoned in this way was a confession of that little devil of doubt which was there, poisoning her happiness. Had she gained him after all? He had been—at times—so absolutely and perfectly charming that she felt that the least doubt was disloyalty. But she could not but see that his endearments were non-committal, and that on every occasion when she had proposed making their engagement public and irrevocable, he had found some reason why it couldn't be done. Her gnawing fear she would not admit even to herself: that he didn't really love her as much as he said.

Her pleasure in the scheme had also largely evaporated. All this business about false names and the Koldkure subterfuge worried her. Once again, if their venture was as straight as James assured her, why should such precautions be necessary? It was true that he had answered her objections, and no doubt he was right, yet it gave the whole enterprise an air of deceit which was hateful.

Then she rallied herself. This depression was wrong and harmful. It was only that James had gone off and that she was alone. The affair was only beginning. Had he not promised to marry her as soon as there was enough money? Very well, she must get on with the job and worry no more.

For the. next two days she continued filling and packing

bottles, and by keeping busy overcame to a considerable extent her loneliness. Then on the Thursday morning a letter was in the box which thrilled her. It was addressed in Tarrant's hand to Messrs Koldkure, Arbutus Street, Exeborough, and her heart beat more rapidly as she opened it. It read:

My dear Merle,

I do hope you are all right, liking Exeborough, comfortable in your rooms, not overworking and not too lonely.

I am having a marvellous time: extraordinarily, unbelievably successful. Practically every shop I've been to has promised to try the stuff, and I'm hoping that you will be deluged with orders and be so overwhelmed that you'll have to get that girl we talked about.

I have made a slight alteration in our selling plans, which I'm afraid will mean a bit of repacking. Or rather, better keep what you've packed for stock, and pack new lots to meet the orders.

I have dropped our name from the label. Most of the firms I have visited would prefer to have their own name on the bottles, so I have been having a series of new labels printed, and these must be stuck on both bottles and wrappers. These I am sending to you direct, and as you will get more and more of them, you will want to fix up a special file for them. You will have to be *terribly* careful to send the stuff to the right firms.

The car is doing magnificently. It is going to make our fortunes—thanks to you!

All the best to you and hoping to be back soon,
Yours ever,
James Tarrant.

This was excellent news, and yet the letter left Merle with a heavy sense of disappointment. 'My dear Merle', 'Yours ever': these were very different to the expressions she had hoped for.

Of course he had thought of her first: had asked about her health and so on before going on to his news. Yet that awful little devil of doubt whispered that this was just a concession to duty and that the writer's real interest began in the second paragraph.

Yet, she told herself, he was correct to write as he had. They were not actually engaged, and until they were the kind of letter she wanted would be impossible.

The label idea she could make nothing of. However, it did not seem to matter whether the bottles bore the names of the manufacturers or the vendors, and if the shops wanted the latter, she supposed it was all right.

On Saturday a package came from a Bath printer: sixteen different sets of labels all bearing the words 'Indigestion Remedy', with names of the sixteen different firms below. As yet there were no orders, but she began to prepare bottles in the hope that these would follow.

That afternoon she took her first half-day off work, intending to spend it looking for other rooms. Those she was occupying she had taken in a hurry, and they were far from comfortable. In this connection a strange coincidence took place.

At the cheap restaurant at which she had been lunching she had seen each day a tall, pleasant-looking girl. She looked pale and anxious, and as she took an extremely light lunch, only a cup of coffee and a roll and butter, Merle supposed that her trouble was financial. They had not spoken, but her eyes had on more than one occasion met Merle's.

On this Saturday the place was fuller than usual and the only vacant seat which Merle could find was at the table already taken by this girl. Merle asked if she might join her.

'Oh, please,' said the girl with a smile. 'Do sit down.'

Merle made a casual remark about the crowd, and they dropped into a somewhat desultory conversation.

'I've noticed you coming for about a week,' the girl said presently. 'Have you just come to the town?'

'Yes, I'm working at the Koldkure place that's just been opened. It's a new job.'

'I saw them repainting the sign. Have you a big staff?'

'Two of us at present,' Merle smiled, 'but if we've any luck we shall require more hands.'

The girl's eyes flashed. She hesitated and then spoke as if from some overwhelming internal urge. 'Oh,' she implored, 'do forgive me for worrying you at this casual meeting. But it's so terribly important to me. If you should have a vacancy that I might be able to fill, would you look into my qualifications?'

It was the first time Merle had ever been in the position of an employer, and she felt slightly embarrassed. But she also felt that if she would have to engage help, this girl was the very type that she would like. 'We don't want anyone at present,' she replied, 'but if we do I should be glad to talk it over with you.'

The girl beamed. 'Oh, thank you,' she returned warmly. 'May I give you my name?'

She wrote on a small pad, tore off the leaf, and handed it over. Merle read: 'Edith Horne, 12, Bouverie Lane.'

'Right,' said Merle, putting the paper in her bag. 'Are you out of a job?'

'Unhappily,' Edith grimaced. 'I was shorthand typist and clerk at Finlay's Laundry, and when the Eziwash people opened their laundry with lots of capital and the latest machinery poor Mr Finlay was ruined. He hadn't the cash to reorganize his whole place, as would have been necessary. We all got the bird.'

'Hard lines,' Merle said sympathetically.

'It was rather a shock,' Edith admitted. 'There's only myself and my invalid mother, you know, and she keeps the house while I do the supporting. We've managed fairly well, as we let our best room, but unfortunately our tenant left us just as the time I lost my job, and we haven't been able to get anyone since. We're afraid we shall have to give up the house, which, I need hardly say, we'd rather avoid.'

The more they talked, the more Merle took to the girl. Though she gave these details, there was no suggestion in her manner of a hard-luck story. She was obviously just explaining what she evidently thought had been a breach of good manners.

'Whereabouts do you live?' Merle asked. 'As a matter of fact, I'm half thinking of moving from where I am. Perhaps your room would suit me. Could I see it?'

For a moment the girl did not speak, and Merle saw there were tears in her eyes.

'Oh,' she said, 'if you wouldn't mind coming with me after lunch, or at any time that suits you. Of course I'd only be too delighted.'

The house was small, a tiny parlour beside the hall, a fair-sized room over both, and two small bedrooms to the rear over the kitchen, but Merle took to it at once. It was spotlessly clean and the upper front room, which was the one to be let, Was quite well furnished. Better still, there were no houses immediately opposite and from the windows there was a charming view of the river and lower town beneath a background of rolling hills.

'You could either have your meals here or join Edith and myself below,' Mrs Horne explained as Merle turned back from the window. She was a kindly, motherly sort of woman, though obviously in poor health. 'I'm sure if necessary we could suit our times to yours.'

The place was infinitely better than where Merle was, and the terms being moderate, she engaged the room, saying she would move in immediately.

On Monday morning the first batch of orders arrived from James. They were from eight firms, and they varied from six bottles to two dozen. Merle worked hard, and by evening they were all filled and packed. Then she carried her parcels to the station and booked them off.

Next morning there were no orders, and she made the necessary clerical records. She carded the firms with their orders, posted up her ledger and typed immaculate accounts, which, however, she held over until she could discuss with James the best date to send them out.

On Tuesday there were two postal packages, one from James with a letter and a dozen more orders, the second from the Bath printers with a new series of labels. James began with similar perfunctory inquiries as to her welfare, continuing with enthusiasm about his trip. He was doing, he said, *far* better than he had anticipated. Nearly every manager he called on was interested, and a large percentage had agreed to place orders. He hoped and believed she would soon be overwhelmed, and he advised her to look out for a suitable girl to help her.

This time it took Merle two full days to complete the

orders, and on the next morning there was another letter from Tarrant with nineteen orders. He also required a large number more samples. There were in addition three letters from managers of chemists' shops, two making inquiries about prices, and the third giving a firm order.

With delight Merle realised that she would be unable to cope with the work herself, and she went back to Bouverie Lane and asked Edith Horne to help her for one week. Edith's joy made her feel ashamed, though very happy, and they went back then and there to the shed and started work. Edith proved efficient and skilful, as well as being an exceedingly pleasant companion, and Merle soon made her permanent.

As the days began to mount up into weeks, Merle realised that she had backed a winner. More and more orders came in while Tarrant worked slowly across the lower Midlands. Money also began to arrive, and Merle opened an account in the bank. But so far all that came in was required to meet the bills, and Merle had to draw on her own money for board and for Edith's wages.

Before a month had passed the two women found themselves swamped with work. And here it was that Merle once again congratulated herself on having met Edith. For Edith recommended one of her former fellow workers at the laundry, and when a small, fair, blue-eyed girl with a cheery smile turned up and showed what she could do, Merle felt she could not have made a better choice.

Tarrant was now at Manchester, his letters still enthusiastic as to his reception. Merle was growing terribly anxious to see him, and wrote urging him to park the car and run down by rail for a day or two, she said to discuss several matters which had arisen. For some time he procrastinated, but suddenly he changed his mind and wired that he was coming that night.

He appeared really delighted to see Merle, though once again she was disappointed by a certain perfunctory element in his greeting. In one way he had changed. He had become more a man of the world, was better dressed, and had an indefinable air of living well. When they went to dine, it was not to a small restaurant, as on the evening on which she had arrived in Exeborough, but one of the best hotels in the town. He ordered an expensive hock, and instead of the cigarette of former times he produced a cigar from an elaborate case.

'I cashed one or two of the cheques,' he explained when Merle remarked on the change.

'But, you know,' she answered, 'I'm short of money here. So far I've only had enough to keep up our stocks. I've had to pay for myself and part of the wages of the girls out of my own money.'

'Don't worry, my dear child,' he answered, and this time his manner really did suggest that her comfort and welfare were his one concern. 'You'll get ten times, a hundred times, back for every penny you spend now. These clothes and cigars and so on that I've adopted are simply business, same as the car. If I go in to see a manager, he sizes me up and in nine cases out of ten his order is the result of what he sees. If I look prosperous he argues that my stuff must be selling and that it's therefore probably a good line. If I look like a down-and-out, he thinks: "No one else appears to be buying his stuff, I'd better keep clear of it." See?'

Plausible, as ever. What he said was probably literally true, and yet it left that perplexing little element of doubt which so distressed her.

'But shouldn't those cheques go through the books?' she asked. 'Edith Horne knows about book-keeping, and everything is entered up in the most professional way.'

He shot her a keen glance. For a moment his expression changed, grew ugly almost, then he was smiling as before.

'You're dead right,' he agreed. 'I'll send you a note of them all.'

This was satisfactory, and realising that he did not want to talk about themselves, she continued about the venture. 'We want some machines,' she asserted. 'A bottle-washer and drier, a mixer and a filler would save money.'

'Do you know how much these would cost?' he inquired.

'Yes, I've had catalogues and I've got all the figures. A bottle-washer . . .' and she went into technical details.

He was obviously impressed, and agreed that this should be their first major purchase. Then encouraged by his approval, she went on:

'Another thing I'd like very much, and that is to give Edith a small interest in the business. She's so good and willing, and she's been such a tremendous help.'

She expected him to agree as a matter of course. But he seemed much upset by the idea.

'Good Lord, Merle!' he exclaimed. 'What are you thinking about? An interest in the business—and to a blank stranger! That's not the way to succeed.'

For the first time since they had met, she felt really annoyed with him.

'But Edith's very exceptional,' she declared, 'and she's not a blank stranger. I've got quite fond of her, and she really has been such a help.'

'Isn't she paid for it?'

'Not for what she's done. Her pay would cover routine

work. But she's done much more than that: more than I could have asked.'

'Evidently trying to worm her way into the thing,' he retorted, 'and it looks as if she was succeeding. Keep her in her place, or else your authority'll be gone.'

Merle was intensely irritated. 'You don't understand,' she protested. 'You've not seen her. She's not that sort at all.'

He smiled contemptuously. 'You're too soft, Merle. You'll never run a business if you let any Tom, Dick or Harriet soft sawder you like that. Give her her wages, and if she doesn't like it, let her go. You can't mix up business and charity.'

Merle could have wept. Were they going to quarrel? But she felt that her whole future depended on this issue. Either she must assert herself or she would be no more than a paid employee herself.

'But I don't understand this,' she said quietly. 'I thought I was a partner. Do you mean that I don't have any say in anything at all?'

He was evidently surprised. Once again he glanced at her keenly. For a moment he seemed undecided, then his face changed and he gave one of his warmest smiles.

'My dear girl, I had no idea you felt so strongly about it. Give this Edith or whatever her name is anything you like. I'll agree. All I want is that you should be happy.'

Once again she could have cried; this time with relief. This was the old James, kindly and loving and considerate. If he were always like this, what a joy life would be!

The next six months made a record of unbroken success. James continued his trip into the North, and his passage was marked by an ever-increasing flood of orders. What was most satisfactory of all, re-orders were continuous. The

Indigestion Remedy was an obvious success and the future looked highly promising.

At the Works—now dignified with a capital W—the staff had grown to seven, and the large shed had proved so inadequate that a second had been erected in the yard. Merle had not in the end given Edith an interest in the concern, but she had introduced a system of bonuses for all the girls, Edith's being considerably higher than the others. This made a very contented and helpful team.

At this time also Merle made an appointment which was to have a profound and unexpected influence on the future. There was now so much local transport that a Works vehicle had become a necessity. She therefore bought a twenty-hundredweight van and advertised for a driver. She had a large number of applicants and of these she selected one, a young man named Temple, also recommended by Edith Horne.

Peter Temple had been educated considerably above his former position. He had indeed been intended for business, and it was owing to family bereavement and the consequent need for ready money that he had taken a minor job at Finlay's Laundry. From this he had been promoted to rounds-man, but since the closing down had been out of work.

Merle took to him at once. His square face with its firm jaw and honest eyes suggested reliability, and his movements and answers competence and intelligence. He started a fortnight after their interview, and she soon saw that her choice had been vindicated.

During this period Merle had a great deal to make her happy. Profits were increasing and she enjoyed her work. She had moreover begun to study chemistry seriously and had started a series of experiments in the hope of so improving the Remedy that it would become better than Braxamin and thus win success on its merits. But she knew that she had entered upon this new life, not to make money or have a pleasant time, but in the hope that James Tarrant would marry her. And this unhappily seemed just as far away as ever.

At first he had told her that he could not afford it, but that when the money began to come in, the situation would be changed. Then when the money did begin to come in, he said they must put it back into the business. Now, when they had bought their machines and cash was accumulating in the bank, she felt the time had come. It hurt her pride terribly to refer to the matter again, but at last in desperation she did so.

'My pet,' Tarrant said, with one of the fascinating smiles which broke down all her defences, 'what's the good when we're living at different ends of England? Let's wait just a little. This ghastly travelling won't last for ever. I'm going to appoint two men, one for the north and one for the south. Then I'll be able to do what I've wanted for the last nine months: come and live here. We'll take a decent house in the suburbs and then we can be married.'

On that occasion he was so kindly and loving to her that for the time being she was swept off her feet into temporary heaven. But next morning he had left again without anything further being settled.

Sore in spirit, Merle carried on: and all the time the business prospered.

5

George Hampden is Perturbed

George Hampden, general manager of Braxamin, Ltd, glanced at his Chairman as he sat opposite him at the boardroom table, and from him to the faces of the other six directors present. The usual monthly meeting of the Board was in progress, an event for the general manager. So far Hampden was pleased with today's proceedings. Routine business had been transacted with gratifying smoothness and now the directors were considering the customary reports of their officers.

They were a mixed lot, the directors, and Hampden could not help speculating on the chance which had brought them together. Sir Claud Munroe was the typical Chairman of fiction. A big man with a big face, there was mastery and domination in every line of his features. Piercing eyes beneath heavy brows, a hawk nose, thin compressed lips and a chin like a block of granite envisaged the ruthless drive and pertinacity of his character. A good Chairman, Sir Claud was yet reasonably considerate to those who did not oppose him. Hampden liked him, but usually thought it wise to hold similar views on the subjects under discussion.

At the Chairman's right sat Joynson Cooke, about as complete a contrast to his leader as could be imagined. Cooke's face was weak and his expression shifty. His lounging attitude across the table was typical of the man, and compared unfavourably with the other's martial erectness. His eyes were those of a dreamer and his mouth was large and loose. His features suggested dissipation and he was supposed to be no better than he should be.

Joynson Cooke was Deputy Chairman, not because of his business ability, a trait of which no one had ever accused him, but because he was the originator of Braxamin. He had been much impressed on hearing a rumour that a popular, highly advertised and by no means inexpensive brand of pills could be put on the market for less than a penny a box. Here was something which appealed both to his cupidity and his gambler's instincts, and the idea of emulation seized upon his imagination. For months he sought a suitable complaint and remedy for exploitation. Then one day when seized with a sharp attack of indigestion he took a dose of magnesia, experiencing almost immediate relief. Eureka! Here were both, ready to hand. All he had to do was to sell magnesia under a different name in artistically labelled bottles and his fortune was made. Knowing nothing of chemistry, he went to Hampden, then manager of the local chemist's shop. Hampden was also impressed by the idea, and the two attempted to put out the new remedy themselves. They soon found, however, that this was impossible and that capital was needed to start the business. Cooke, looking round among his acquaintances for a backer, found him in the person of Sir Claud Munroe.

That astute gentleman recognised the possibilities of the scheme and backed it so strongly that he became the virtual owner and controller, allowing Cooke a few shares and a seat on the Board, rather as a concession than of right.

Beside Cooke sat Leslie Bird, a bright young land-owner of sporting proclivities, selected partly for his money and partly because he was unlikely to have convictions on any of the subjects which might come before the directors. Next to him was old Lord Furberton, whose name gave a *cachet* of respectability to the entire undertaking and who, being over eighty, very deaf, and well advanced in his second childhood, was also unlikely to give trouble. The fact that he was retiring in a few months rendered any opinion which, unexpectedly, he might express, of even less importance than it might otherwise have been.

Of the three at the opposite side of the table, John Roberts, on the Chairman's left, was a porcelain manufacturer, shrewd and capable, chosen for his knowledge of business and markets; Lewis Palmer and Hunt Grayson, both retired civil servants, were pleasant, kindly men, but neither was of strong enough character to affect to any considerable extent the march of events.

On the extra chair at the end of the table next to George Hampden sat Pateley, the firm's advertising manager. He had completed the routine portion of his report, and the directors were now considering his suggested slogans for a new publicity campaign which had been agreed on. These slogans were to greet travellers arriving on British shores, were to be exhibited at ports only, and were to have an appropriate nautical flavour. A similar series for rail travellers had been a great success, and it was hoped that the new venture would prove equally lucrative.

'Surely,' Grayson was saying, slightly apologetically as usual when addressing Sir Claud, 'those last two rather—er—contradict each other. "Braxamin Keeps the Ship at Sea", yes, very good; or "Braxamin Brings the Ship to Port", excellent: but not both together. You see my point?'

'I take it,' put in Palmer, also a little deprecatingly, 'that they mean that Braxamin will do anything. Either keep the ship at sea or bring it to port, or—er—'

'Scuttle it or blow it to blazes,' suggested Bird helpfully.

'As a matter of fact,' put in Cooke, 'I don't like either of 'em. Why not stick to "If You're at Sea, Take Braxamin"? That covers all we want, doesn't it?'

'But surely,' Grayson objected again, 'though that's an excellent slogan, it scarcely applies to people who are coming ashore, as would be those we have in mind?'

'Those going aboard would see it too,' Cooke pointed out.

'True,' admitted Grayson, 'and yet I fancy something with a more general application would be better. You follow what I mean?'

'I should stick to "In Emergency Braxamin is Better than the Boats",' said Roberts with decision. 'What do you think, Mr Chairman?'

'I agree that should be retained,' Sir Claud pronounced, and each hearer instantly realised that it was the one that he also preferred, 'but we mustn't confine ourselves to one or two. I should like at least half a dozen.'

'I agree, sir, said Pateley. He was looking pleased, as the Board had given his efforts more consideration than he had expected. 'But I had thought that only one should be put out at first, and others added, at, say, two monthly intervals. That's what we did with the railway series, and it would mean continued novelty.'

'A dashed good shot,' murmured Lord Furberton, apparently in connection with a story he had told some ten minutes earlier. 'Twenty-four and a half brace!' He seemed to be addressing no one in particular, and no one took any notice of him.

'We'll consider that,' Sir Claud approved. 'What do you suggest for the later ones?'

'I thought, sir, we might start with "Braxamin Brings the Ship to Port",' Patcley answered. 'In deference to Mr Grayson's opinion we might drop "Braxamin Keeps the Ship at Sea" altogether. Then after a couple of months we might add, "Are You Seaworthy? If Not, Take Braxamin", and then, "If You're at Sea, Take Braxamin".'

'Too like each other,' Roberts objected crisply. He glanced at the typewritten sheet before him on which the various suggestions were set out. 'What about Number Five?'

'"Braxamin Will Keep You from Drydocking",' read Pateley. 'Yes, sir, I think that would do admirably for our third.'

'Eh?' said Lord Furberton, suddenly waking up again. 'What does he say?'

'"Braxamin Will Keep You from Drydocking",' Leslie Bird shouted.

'From what?'

'Drydocking!'

Lord Furberton nodded. 'Oh, yes. Wish we'd had it in '94 in the old *Medusa*. Haha! In the Azores. Struck something submerged. Stove in her bows. We had to drydock at Port Delgada. Brings it all back.'

'It's a good slogan,' Bird shouted.

'A good what?'

'Slogan!' Bird roared.

'Be gad, yes! Brings it back as if it was yesterday. Bows stove in. I remember—'

'I think,' broke in Sir Claud's incisive voice, 'that we may accept "Braxamin Will Keep You from Drydocking" as one of the later in the series. Do you agree, gentlemen?'

The gentlemen agreed.

Hampden wondered why they were spending so much time on the matter. Usually Pately merely reported that he was about to start a campaign to the extent that their appropriation would permit, and that his slogans would be chosen from the list which had been placed before each of them. Usually they passed his proposals without giving them much apparent thought. But today they had questioned every single item. Hampden was pleased and in a mild way tried to keep the ball rolling, for the last item on the agenda was a troublesome one, and the more time they spent on slogans, the less would be left for it.

They went on to discuss Pateley's further efforts:

'Braxamin is Your Sheet Anchor: Hold to it', 'Braxamin Keeps the Engines Working Smoothly', 'The *Gigantic*'s Overhaul Costs £200,000: Yours a 2s. 6d. Bottle of Braxamin', 'Braxamin is the Beam that Pierces the Fog' and similar imaginative gems. But now their interest seemed to have waned, and Sir Claud presently drew the discussion to a close by an ultimatum, delivered in the guise of an appeal for their opinions, that Pateley might be left to carry on as he suggested. Needless to say, this produced unanimous agreement, the advertising manager with a bow left the conclave, and the meeting turned to the next item on the agenda.

They worked through some more business and in due course reached the last item.

'Number Fourteen;' the Chairman glanced at his paper; 'Falling off in Certain Sales.' He paused, looked round the little circle, and continued in grave tones. 'This item, gentlemen, represents possibly the most serious matter that we've had to discuss for several months, and I kept it to the last so as to get our routine work cleared away before we dealt with it. Perhaps I had better recapitulate the affair, particularly as you, Mr Roberts, were absent from our last meeting.'

'Thank you, Mr Chairman,' said Roberts.

Sir Claud again glanced slowly round the circle of faces.

As you know,' he resumed, 'since our business settled down after our early intensive efforts, our sales have shown a small but fairly regular increase, averaging about five per cent per annum or nearly half of one per cent per month. As you know also, during the last few months this satisfactory condition has ceased to obtain. In January last, instead of the customary increase of point five per cent, there was a drop of point four per cent. In February this drop increased, and in March our sales were one point three per cent down. Of course the same thing had happened before on various occasions and we naturally assumed that we were meeting a mere temporary setback which would quickly correct itself. But when Mr Hampden received the figures for April, which showed a falling off of no less than three point two per cent, he realised that something serious must be wrong, and he brought the matter specially before us. As the rest of you remember, he reported that he wished to make a more detailed analysis of the position than his existing clerical staff would allow, and he asked for some temporary expert assistance. He undertook to report the result of his investigation today. That correct, Mr Hampden?'

'Correct, sir.'

'We have all seen that the sales returns for last month show a still further decrease. Instead of being about five per cent. up to June last, as we should be normally, we are over four per cent down. This is most serious, and I think we'll hear what Mr Hampden has to say with interest. Now, Mr Hampden, if you please.'

This was the moment Hampden was rather dreading, for the report he had to make was by no means reassuring, and though he knew he personally was not to blame, he was by no means certain that he would escape criticism.

'Certainly, sir,' he answered. 'On considering the reports of our agents, with their frequent references to the continued popularity of Braxamin, I formed the opinion that this falling off was not general, but local. It was to settle this point that I asked you for additional clerical help. This enabled me to have graphs made of our sales to each individual shop, information which up to the present has not been considered value for the expense involved.

'The results have been well worth while. As I expected, the falling off was local. Eighty-six per cent of our accounts with the shops showed an increase. This averaged our usual half per cent per month, entirely normal and satisfactory. But in the remaining fourteen per cent there had been a serious drop. It varied in amount, but averaged forty per cent.'

'Good Lord!' Cooke ejaculated. 'Fine management that! How do you account for it?'

Hampden felt his pulses quickening with anger. He hated Cooke, and Cooke, he knew, hated him. If Cooke could make out that the drop was his fault, he would not be slow in doing so.

'I'm just coming to that, Mr Cooke,' he said smoothly, restraining his feelings. 'But first I should remind you that in a matter of this kind there must necessarily be a time lag. If our returns became affected four months ago, it indicates that the cause had begun to operate some months earlier still.'

'You mean while stocks in the shops were running out?' asked Grayson.

'Yes. Even with sales normal it might have been some time till an order was due.'

'Quite.'

'I thought you might like to see the places affected,' Hampden continued. 'I've got out some maps.' He passed round some white photographic prints of England, sprinkled over with little red and blue figures. 'These red figures beneath the names of the towns,' he explained, 'show the number of shops affected in that town. The blue figures I'll come to in a moment.'

They examined the maps, Hampden pausing to give them time. He was pleased with the maps himself, and he knew they would appeal to both Sir Claud and Roberts, the only two members of the Board who really mattered. He had put a lot of work into them, and had had fair copies of his results made in a surveyor's office.

Roberts presently looked up. 'A good map,' he said. 'It shows an interesting distribution. The leaven, whatever it is, is working more strongly in the south-west and tailing out to nothing in the north. Any cases in Scotland?'

'None, sir.'

'Very interesting distribution,' Roberts repeated. 'What do you make of it, Mr Hampden?'

'To me it suggests four points,' Hampden resumed, 'all,

unhappily, mere probabilities. First, I thought that all the cases were the result of one and the same agency. That seems to follow from the general circumstances.'

Sir Claud, listening carefully, nodded his appreciation of the point.

'Second, I imagined the activity started in the south-west and worked north. Mr Roberts noticed one of the indications which suggest this: that the red figures showing the affected shops are larger in the south-west, and grow smaller as they come north-east, dying out altogether about the mid-Lancashire Yorkshire line. The second indication is even more convincing. Look, please, at the blue figures after the red. These show the month in which the fall began, representing January as one, February as two and so on. From them it's obvious that it started in Cornwall, Devon or Somerset, worked across to Kent and Essex, then back to Birmingham, and so north.'

Again Hampden paused, while the directors made a show of examining the blue figures.

'That's convincing enough, I think,' Roberts said presently with a glance round.

'The third point which occurred to me,' Hampden continued when they looked up, 'is that the work, whatever it is, has been done by personal canvass, not by general advertisement or circular.'

Grayson interrupted. 'Perhaps Mr Hampden would make that a little clearer? I don't quite follow his reasoning.'

'Well,' returned Hampden, 'it surely follows from what we've just been talking about—the fact that we can follow the route which the traveller must have taken. If there had been a circular or general advertisement, this wouldn't have obtained. The falling off would have begun everywhere simultaneously and probably would have been more wide-spread.'

'I follow that now,' Grayson nodded. 'Very clear indeed, if I may say so.'

Hampden was breathing more freely. They were taking it better than he had expected.

'My fourth point,' he went on, 'has less to support it. In fact, I might call it a pure guess, but it might be useful to keep in mind during subsequent investigation. It is that if the canvassing began in Devon or Cornwall or Somerset, it's not unlikely that the headquarters of the persons responsible is in that area.'

'Doesn't follow,' said Cooke, and there was a sneer in his tone.

'I think it's a useful suggestion all the same,' declared Palmer, for which Hampden felt grateful.

Lord Furberton suddenly chuckled. 'Braxamin Keeps you from Drydocking,' he muttered. 'Ha ha ha! Very good! Brings back all that time at Ponta Delgada, just as if it was yesterday.'

'Got through, that has, at last,' Bird commented. 'He's waking up in his old age.'

'Eh?' asked Lord Furberton, putting his hand to his ear. 'It was the old *Medusa*, you know. D'I tell you?'

Bird waved his hand. 'You told me,' he shouted. 'Very interesting.'

The old man nodded. 'Stove in her bows. We had to dry dock.' He muttered something further, then again subsided into a kind of dream.

'One other interesting point struck me,' went on Hampden, as if there had been no interruption, 'and that is that in no centre are the whole of the shops affected that we supply.

63

For instance, in Avington'—he pointed on his map—'there are nine chemists' shops, and only three show reductions, the other six remaining normal.'

'Have you been able to trace any factors common to those which show reductions?' Roberts asked.

'Naturally, I've tried to do that,' Hampden answered, 'but not with great success. There is just one point which may or may not be significant. All the affected shops are privately owned. There is not a single instance of one of the chain stores showing a fall.'

'I think that's suggestive,' exclaimed Roberts, looking round the circle of faces.

'In what way, Mr Roberts?' asked Grayson. 'I don't follow that.'

'Well'—Roberts took a cigar-case from his pocket, half opened it, and put it back again—'the owner of a business is easier to get at than a manager working under a big company.'

'That's what I thought, sir,' Hampden continued.

'Very interesting, all this,' Cooke said in sarcastic tones, 'but I'm hanged if I can see that it's getting us anywhere. Can't you find out more about it than that?'

'Yes,' Hampden answered easily. 'I've only dealt so far with what we could all have deduced from the maps. Naturally, I didn't leave it at that. My next step was to write to each affected shop, pointing out the drop and asking if an explanation was available.'

'A letter's no good,' Cooke answered roughly. 'What you want is to go to see the people.'

Hampden controlled his temper. 'Certainly, Mr Cooke,' and his voice was silky, 'if you'd like that done, I'll do it. But to make the necessary hundreds of calls in the time, I shall require some extra representatives. I presume that'll be all right?'

'Of course not,' put in Roberts impatiently. 'Don't be an ass, Cooke.'

Cooke said nothing, but the glance he shot at Roberts was venomous.

'I had replies from practically all the shops and all said more or less the same thing: they did not think there was any special reason for the falling off. There had not been quite the same demand for Braxamin, but they were sure it was a mere temporary setback and that things would soon get normal again.'

'A put-off,' said Roberts.

Hampden nodded. 'I thought so. I had had Mr Cooke's idea of the personal call in my mind all the time, and now I thought I'd try it. I took a day's leave and went down to Bristol, where seventeen shops were affected. Bristol I chose because I'd never been there, and so wouldn't be known. At each shop I asked for a bottle of Braxamin, and I confess I was interested by the result. In ten shops they said something like this: "Yes, we've got Braxamin, and we've also got a remedy of our own which we recommend," and I was shown another bottle. I said: "Is this better than Braxamin?" They said: "We don't say that; they're both very good. Some people like one and some the other." I took the bottle in each case.

'In the remaining seven shops the procedure was slightly different. In these the assistant said, "Yes, we have Braxamin," and went away and began looking among the display bottles, then came back and said, "We stock it, but I'm afraid we're just out of it. We'll have it in tomorrow if you call, or if you'd prefer it, here's a remedy of our own that we recommend. It's not exactly the same as Braxamin, but it's very similar." When I had finished I had accumulated seventeen bottles of substitutes, all labelled "Indigestion Remedy", with the various names of the vendors below.'

'Very interesting, if I may say so,' put in Grayson. 'That seems to support your theory that all this activity has a single source?'

Hampden nodded. 'I thought so, Mr Grayson,' he agreed, 'and the matter was practically confirmed by my next step. I had all seventeen bottles analysed, and all contained the same ingredients: principally magnesia.'

'Now really, that's most interesting,' Grayson repeated. 'I think—er—you're to be congratulated, Mr Hampden, on your—er—detective abilities.' He gave a nervous laugh. 'What do you say, Palmer?'

'I agree,' Palmer admitted. 'I confess I should never have thought of those tests myself.'

It was nice of these two, Hampden thought, though he realised they were more anxious to oppose Cooke than to help him. However, even such praise was pleasant enough.

'Thank you, gentlemen,' he answered. 'These facts, I think, confirm the conclusion we came to from considering the map, namely, that some one agent is at work to sell his own stuff at the expense of ours.'

Bird sprawled back in his chair. 'You mean someone's trying out our own ramp?' he demanded.

'I don't know that I quite follow Mr Bird's reference to a ramp,' said Grayson protestingly.

'You don't?' Bird retorted.

'But how,' put in Palmer hurriedly, as if to pour oil on water which might become troubled, 'could X sell his own stuff at the expense of ours? He could scarcely put it out more cheaply, and yet, what with advertising and so on, we don't make such a vast amount out of it?'

'You ask what X would get out of the thing?' Hampden replied. 'It seemed to me he'd do very well out of it. First, he'd have our profit, not unduly large, but still not inconsiderable. Secondly—and this is where his scheme is really clever—he'd save our heaviest item of expenditure—advertising.'

'Quite,' said Roberts; 'if he made our profits, plus our advertising costs, he'd do pretty well.'

'That's not absolutely clear to me, I'm afraid,' put in Grayson. 'How can he sell his stuff without advertising it?'

'Hampden has just told us,' Roberts answered. 'The chemist sells it in preference to ours.'

'Ah, yes, I see that,' persisted Grayson. 'What I don't see is why he should do so.'

'I expect there's a reason for that. What do you say, Hampden?'

'Larger commission, I imagined,' Hampden replied, not too pleased at having some of his thunder stolen.

'That's it, depend upon it,' Roberts assented. 'He can afford it if he's saved his advertising costs. What do you think, Mr Chairman?'

Sir Claud, who usually reserved his remarks till the summing up or decision stage was reached, agreed that the theory was probably true. 'Have you any proposals to put before us, Mr Hampden,' he went on, 'as to what we should do about it?'

This was the point of which Hampden was afraid, and he thought he would be wiser to avoid it. 'Not today, sir,' he therefore replied. 'I suggest, if you are agreeable, that you postpone action till next Board. I haven't had time yet to make all the inquiries I should like, and I should hope by then to be in a position to put before you a considered recommendation.

The Chairman thought over this. 'That seems reasonable,' he said at last. 'Those in favour? . . . Against? . . . Carried unanimously. Thank you very much, then, gentlemen; that concludes our meeting.'

Hampden felt considerable relief as he collected his books and papers. They had certainly taken the matter better than he had expected, and both Sir Claud and Mr Roberts seemed to have approved his efforts. Sincerely he hoped that by that day's month his report would be more satisfactory.

6

George Hampden Practises Detection

Though the Board's reaction to his sales statement had been surprisingly satisfactory, George Hampden remained a good deal worried by the whole affair. Had he felt his position as general manager of the company more secure, he would not have thought so much about it. But the fact that Cooke, the Vice-Chairman, was his enemy and wanted to get rid of him, gave it an importance not its own. No better reason for replacing the manager could be found than that the business of the company was going down. Sir Claud, Hampden thought, would wish to be fair, but he was a hard man and his god was success. And none of the others, he was sure, would take a stand on the matter, should it come to a head.

Hampden's thoughts went back to the start of the enterprise and the gradual transformation of Cooke from an eager ally to an open enemy. At that time Hampden had been manager of the principal chemist's shop at Saxham St Edmunds, an East Midland town of about thirty thousand inhabitants. How well he remembered that summer's afternoon on which Cooke had come into the shop and asked, almost deprecatingly, if he could have a few words with him in private. It had been a sweltering day and Hampden had been impatiently watching the clock, anxious to get home to the cool of his little garden. Then Cooke had come in, and as their talk progressed, Hampden had forgotten about the heat, about closing time, about his supper and his garden. Was this, he had asked himself, the chance that he had longed for all his life—the chance of making real money? He had not, he remembered, been enthusiastic at first, and the discussion had gone on for nearly two hours before Cooke had suggested that they should join to carry out the scheme. Not till several more meetings had taken place had agreement to do so been reached.

It was a big decision for Hampden. His then position carried a reasonable salary, and unless an earthquake wiped the country out, it was secure. This venture might bring a fortune, but it might also mean complete disaster. And if it proved a failure, he needn't hope to regain his former state of comparative affluence.

When the two men saw that without the wherewithal for advertisement they could make no progress, Cooke approached Sir Claud Monroe. In the subsequent negotiations Hampden, unfortunately for himself, completely outshone Cooke, who knew nothing of the technicalities of business. The result was that Sir Claud deferred to Hampden and ignored Cooke, and from this grew that jealousy in Cooke's mind which was to poison the future of both men. Since then Cooke had made no secret of his desire to get rid of his former ally, but so far Hampden had given him no excuse to act.

The loss of his job would be a very serious matter for George Hampden. He was cursed with an extravagant wife, who always wanted just a little more than he was able to provide. His daughter Joan was also an anxiety: not personally, for she was a good girl and he was tremendously fond of her, but financially. Her school was expensive and she had large ideas as to what was necessary in the way of clothes and amusements. Thank heaven his son Edward was at last beginning to earn: he was a budding electrical engineer, but he still required an allowance to augment his salary. Hampden up to the present had been able to meet these calls, but to do so he had had to borrow, and now a sum of four hundred pounds would shortly be due for repayment. Where to obtain the money he did not know, and he was visualising having to move to a smaller house and drastically to cut down his expenditure. Experience told him the sort of reception his family would give to such a suggestion.

His thoughts returned to his immediate problem. At all costs he must stop this rot in the Braxamin sales. How should he set about it?

Obviously his first step must be to find its cause; in other words, the person or persons who were selling the new digestive remedy. From the replies to his circular it did not look as if he would get the information by asking for it. Was there any other way in which he could obtain it?

For three days he worried over the problem and then an idea occurred to him which he thought might succeed.

The next morning he took a holiday from the office. First he did what he could to alter his appearance. In a rough tweed sports coat and plus-fours, a green Homburg hat and a pair of plain glass horn-rimmed spectacles which he had once used in some amateur theatricals, he looked surprisingly different from the sprucely tailored manager of Braxamin Ltd. In this garb he went by an early train to Chelmston, a large town in the Eastern Counties, and one which he had never before visited. Here no less than seven chemists' shops were affected, and in each of these in turn he bought a sponge. It was a particular shape of sponge that he wanted, and he spent some time examining the samples shown him. This enabled him also to examine the staff, and for the first time in his life he was disappointed by their evident health, intelligence and contentment. It was not, indeed, till he had visited his sixth shop that he found the type of assistant he was seeking.

This was a young man of sallow and dyspeptic appearance. To Hampden's joy, he looked also as if he had a chronic grievance. It would be unfair to assume him a disloyal servant, and yet Hampden felt that had he himself been in charge of the shop he would have taken an early opportunity to get rid of him. But circumstances alter cases, and Hampden was not now on the side of the proprietor.

He duly bought his sixth sponge and left the shop. It was getting on towards lunch time and instead of looking for a restaurant, he began sauntering along the pavement, keeping a discreet eye on the door he had just left. It was not certain that the dyspeptic one would leave the premises for lunch, but if he did, it might save Hampden waiting till the evening.

Fortunately the street was one of the main thoroughfares of the town, so that Hampden could loiter without obvious intent. Not three doors away also was a large bookseller's, and at what shop window can one gaze so long without remark as one containing books? Between the bookseller's, a music warehouse, and a Corporation exhibit of electrical appliances, Hampden put in a good half-hour. But in spite of these distractions time began to drag, and it was a relief when at last the dyspeptic one appeared, turned off in the opposite direction, and moved slowly down the street.

Hampden followed. He had never seriously trailed anyone before, and he felt in a mild way some of the thrill of the chase. He soon found that it was easy to keep his quarry in view, but less so to avoid attracting the attention of others. Fortunately the man gave him no trouble. He walked, or rather shuffled, along without once looking behind him.

The chase led into a slightly poorer quarter of the town and ended in a restaurant, one of those large chain-store places which have few frills but reasonably good food at a minimum cost. Hampden followed the other in.

He was in time to see him taking his place at a table in a small alcove. Hampden had been hoping that a full house would force him to sit next to the salesmen, but it chanced that there was plenty of room. He therefore chose another gambit.

'Excuse me,' he said, stopping at the table, 'I rather wanted a word with you. May I sit here?'

The young man seemed surprised, but muttered that he would be pleased.

Hampden chatted lightly till they had both been served. 'I think you're in the pharmaceutical world?' he then essayed.

'That's right,' answered the young man, who after a brief period of reserve had considerably thawed. 'I saw you in Wagstaff's a while ago.'

'Yes. One of the staff, aren't you?'

'That's right,' repeated the dyspeptic one. 'What about it?'

'I'm in the pharmaceutical world myself,' Hampden declared, 'for my sins. Not much money in it, I find.'

This produced a more enthusiastic response, as Hampden had expected it would. He played for a time on that stop, then continued: 'For the first time in my life I've been on to a good thing, and now it looks as if I was going to lose it.'

The dyspeptic one's interest waned. 'How's that?' he said perfunctorily.

Hampden saw that he had strayed from the path. 'Yes,' he answered, 'and I think I could save it if I had a bit of information.'

Interest waxed again in the sallow face.

'And, of course,' Hampden continued, 'if I could save it, I'd be prepared to pay a bit. It might be worth the best part of a tenner to me.' He paused, then added carefully, 'I suppose that wouldn't interest you?'

This reacted more satisfactorily, but the dyspeptic one grew crafty. 'Can't say,' he replied laconically. 'It might.'

Hampden bent forward. 'I'm offering,' he declared crisply, 'ten pounds for a name and address. Care to deal?'

The other's eyes flashed and Hampden believed he had got him. But the young man only repeated, 'Can't say. I'd have to know more about it.'

'Of course,' Hampden agreed, and now he spoke with a cheery good fellowship. 'Well, I'll tell you. But it's confidential. That all right?'

'O.K. by me.'

'Fine. Well; here's my trouble. I've made up and am selling an indigestion remedy. It's something like Braxamin, same base and cost, but with different additions. It's good stuff, better than Braxamin, or at least I think so.' Hampden smiled.

'What do you call it?'

'Just "Indigestion Remedy". I don't put my own name on it, but the retailer's. They like it better.'

The young man, now keenly interested, nodded. 'And what *is* your name?' he asked sharply.

'Bolton,' said Hampden. 'Herbert Bolton. And yours?'

The dyspeptic one hesitated, then said with less gusto, 'Grimshaw; Arthur Grimshaw.'

'Well, Grimshaw, my stuff began to sell: I thought I had a good thing and all that, and then I'm hanged if the idea wasn't stolen.'

'Stolen?'

'Yes. Someone else is supplying it. My stuff. I've analysed it and it's the same. The shops are all right: I've nothing on them. It's someone else who's doing me down, making it and selling it to the shops. See?'

The young man nodded.

'Well, I can't find out who's selling it, and that's what I want.' Hampden paused and added, 'It would be worth ten pounds to me to know,' another pause, 'just name and address of suppliers.'

Grimshaw didn't reply and Hampden continued even more confidentially: 'Now your people are selling my stuff. But I'm not questioning their honesty. It's the man who's supplying them that I'm trying to get at. I want you to be clear that there would be no disloyalty to your people in your telling me.'

'I know the stuff you mean,' Grimshaw said after a still longer pause, 'but I don't know who sells it.'

Hampden shrugged. 'I dare say,' he returned easily, 'and I've no doubt it might give you some trouble to find out. That's why I'm offering ten pounds. I can't expect people to take trouble for me for nothing.'

'I don't like it,' Grimshaw objected. 'I'd have to search through the books. If I was found I might get the sack.'

'You'd have to be careful, of course.'

'It's a big risk. I don't like it at all.'

Hampden sat back as if disappointed. 'Oh, well,' he said, 'I'm sorry. But if you won't, you won't. I'll have to find someone else.'

This had the desired effect. After raising some more objections Grimshaw agreed to do what he could. Hampden immediately took a roll of notes from his pocket. 'Here's two pounds ten,' he said, 'as a first instalment. There'll be another two pounds ten when you give me the information, and five more when I check up that it's correct.'

'You're not risking much,' Grimshaw grumbled, though he took the money.

Four days later Hampden returned to Chelmston and once more lunched with his accomplice, this time by appointment. Once again he waited till they were served, and then put his question. Grimshaw was looking particularly unhappy and he shook his head despondently.

'I couldn't get it, Mr Bolton,' he declared in a whining tone. 'I did my very best, but I couldn't find it anywhere.'

Hampden overcame the temptation to reply cuttingly. 'Oh, well,' he said, 'one can't always succeed at one's first shot. What did you do?'

Grimshaw seemed relieved. 'I didn't tell you,' he answered with more assurance, 'that we've got special instructions about your stuff. The boss told us to sell it if we could. If we were asked for Braxamin we were to produce Braxamin, but we were also to show a bottle of your mixture and say that this was a stuff of our own that we could recommend. But we don't do that.'

'Then what do you do?'

'We generally say we're out of Braxamin and then produce yours. We say we'll have Braxamin in next day if they care to wait. But they never do. They always take your stuff. That's because the boss would rather have it sold.'

'Somebody paying a good commission on it, I expect,' Hampden said bitterly. 'Go ahead.'

'Well, there's no name on the label except ours, and nothing to show where it came from. So I took a risk, a big risk, Mr Bolton, and got into the office at lunch time and had a good look through our order book. Missed my lunch, I did. But I couldn't find it. There was no order for it in the book.'

'Well?'

'Of course there mightn't be. These travellers come in and they see the boss and no one else knows what they say to each other. The boss might give a dozen orders by word of mouth and he might forget to put them in the book.'

'That's not very helpful,' Hampden pointed out.

'I know, Mr Bolton, and I'm terribly sorry. After that two pound ten and all. But I've done my best. Missed my lunch and ran the chance of the sack. I couldn't have done more.'

Hampden was disappointed. It looked as if he had lost not only his two pounds ten, which was a trifle, but five precious days also, and these were important. However, something might still be got from this fool. He settled down to a pleasantly mannered but searching cross-examination.

In the end it was more by chance than good guidance that he came on the required clue.

'When did you run out of the stuff last?' he asked on the chance of stumbling on something.

'We never do run out. There's always more in before the last bottle's sold.'

77

'Then when did you last get some in?' Hampden continued patiently, and it was this which rather surprisingly worked the oracle.

'Quite lately. Let's see; about ten days ago.'

Here at last was something to work on. By means of suggestions about contingent details, Hampden contrived to fix the time as after lunch on the previous Tuesday week. It had happened that Grimshaw had been told off to unpack the consignment. Further questions brought out the facts that it consisted of a carton containing two dozen bottles, that it had been delivered by the railway van and that there was no sender's name on the label.

'Well,' said Hampden, who wanted to keep his fool keen, 'that's not so bad after all. I'll give you the other two pounds ten, and if this enables me to find what I want, you'll have the fiver as well.'

Hampden had brought a suitcase with changes of clothes, and after lunch he assumed a garb more in keeping with his next impersonation. Then he betook himself to the L.N.E.R. Goods Office.

'I'm from Messrs Wagstaffe's, the chemist's in the High Street,' he explained. 'I've called about a parcel you delivered on Tuesday week last, the eleventh. It was a box packed in brown paper about so big,' he demonstrated sizes, 'and we've had a mishap with it. We had a small fire in our office and it and the papers about it got burnt, and I'm hanged if anyone can remember where it came from. Can you give me the consignor's address?'

The clerk thought he could, and a few minutes' search justified his prognostication. The package had come from Messrs Koldkure, Exeborough.

Hampden's heart leaped. He knew something about

proprietary medicines and he was pretty sure there was nothing of this name on the market.

Instead of returning home that night, Hampden crossed the south of England to Exeborough. It was dark when he arrived, but he put up at an hotel, and next morning began a new investigation. A glance at a directory gave him the Koldkure address, and he presently located the shed. For the first time not very sure what line he was going to take up, he pushed open the door. The office was a tiny place, and the tall, good-looking girl who was typing at a large desk seemed to fill it completely.

'Good morning,' said Hampden, holding out his card. 'I should be glad to see the proprietor, if you please.'

Edith Horne looked at the card. 'Mr Tarrant's here today but he's out,' she answered, 'and Miss Weir has gone up town.'

'I'll wait for Mr Tarrant, if he won't be too long.'

Edith pulled out a chair. 'Then won't you sit down?' she invited. 'I'm sorry we haven't a waiting-room, but as you see, our premises are small.'

Hampden took the chair while Edith went on typing. A good reception for an enemy, he thought, though possibly this underling did not know the real business on which she was engaged. He could see some of the freshly typed letters, and on one, feeling that all was fair in love and war, he was able to read: 'With reference to your order for two dozen bottles of our Indigestion Remedy, we have pleasure in sending you herewith . . .' So that was that! He had come to the right place, and an order to view documents would prove it.

Presently there was a quick step and Tarrant swung into the office. He stopped on seeing Hampden and stood looking at him questioningly.

'This is Mr Hampden of Braxamin, Limited,' Edith explained, handing over the card. 'He has called to see you.'

'I called to see the proprietor,' Hampden amended.

'Well,' Tarrant returned, 'you've found him first shot. Come into my office and tell me what I can do for you.'

'I should have thought that my card would explain that,' Hampden suggested, when the door of Merle's sanctum had closed behind them. 'Does the name Braxamin awake no answering chord in your mind?'

Tarrant put on his best manner. He smiled amiably. 'It certainly does,' he admitted. 'Our only serious rival. If you people were out of the way we'd make a lot more money, and I expect you feel the same about us. Won't you sit down, Mr Hampden? I'm glad to meet you in this friendly way.'

'I'm afraid it's not likely to remain as friendly as all that,' Hampden pointed out bluntly, taking the indicated chair. 'You say that probably each of us looks on the other as a rival whose decease would mean a considerably increased profit?'

Tarrant shrugged lightly. 'A joke, I'm afraid; possibly ill-timed. But if you wish to be serious, it is perhaps none the less true.'

'I only object to your joke, Mr Tarrant, because it so completely misrepresents the situation. It suggests that we are in a similar position in this matter, whereas our positions are really entirely different.'

'Now that,' said Tarrant, 'is interesting to me, and I'd be glad to know how you make it out.'

Hampden nodded. 'I'll tell you. Six years ago we produced Braxamin. It is, as you know, a proprietary digestive medicine based on magnesia. I have no doubt that you know it's formula as well as I do. The remedy is a good and useful

80

one, and has helped thousands of sufferers without any resulting deleterious effects. We spent a fortune advertising it, and it is only now that we are beginning to get some return on our capital. We consider that because of our labour and outlay and the risk of failure which we ran, we are entitled to that return.'

'We're certainly not denying that,' said Tarrant.

'I'm sure you're not,' Hampden agreed. 'But our point is that *you're* not entitled to it.'

Tarrant laughed. 'My dear sir, this is fantastic. Our returns have nothing to do with yours. We also have put in trouble and money and taken a risk: probably a lot less than yours. But then our returns are probably correspondingly infinitesimal.'

Hampden made a gesture of disagreement. 'Better, I think, that we should put our cards quite openly on the table,' he suggested. 'Our point, and I think we could prove it in court if it became necessary—though don't let us talk about court—our point is that your indigestion remedy is really ours, and that—'

'I deny that *in toto*,' Tarrant was beginning indignantly, but Hampden waved him to silence.

'Please let me finish, then you have your say. We say that you've copied our remedy and that you're taking advantage of our outlay in advertising and then cutting us out by offering the retailers a higher commission than the standard: a secret commission, in fact.'

'I deny every word of it.' Tarrant's righteous wrath was very effective. 'But even if it were true, even if we had done everything you suggest, what's that to you? Everything that we've done has been strictly legal and you've nothing on us: nothing whatever.'

Hampden now took a more pacific line. 'I can well understand your being annoyed, Mr Tarrant,' he declared. 'If I were in your place I should be, too. But it's not what I say, but the facts that matter, and when you've thought over this more calmly, you'll see that if we were to bring an action against you, we'd not only get an injunction, but heavy damages.' Here he shot a speculative glance at Tarrant, as if wondering how far this statement would be swallowed. 'But,' again he waved him to silence, 'I didn't come here to talk about courts and actions. Myself, I'm always out to settle things amicably. Suppose now we adjourn until you have had a proper opportunity of considering the matter, and if you desire it, of taking legal advice. Suppose we then meet again and see if we can reach some satisfactory settlement?'

With intense interest tempered by slight misgiving, Hampden watched his listener's expression change from a fine registration of righteous indignation to the very essence of cunning. Tarrant had apparently taken his bait, and when he favoured Hampden with a quick but calculating look and said in an elaborately off-hand way, 'Well, that perhaps would be wise,' the guess was confirmed.

Hampden felt that an unnecessary word would now do harm. He therefore stood up.

'Good,' he said heartily, 'then when can we meet again? In a week's time?'

Tarrant shook his head. 'No point in waiting a week,' he declared. 'Are you staying overnight?'

'At the Station Hotel,' Hampden answered promptly, though he had intended to catch an afternoon train for Town.

'Then I'll call on you tomorrow at eleven.'

As Hampden went to the hotel to make his reservation, he smiled inwardly. He believed he was going to settle this troublesome business, and at the same time actually to save his company money.

7

George Hampden Scores a Hit

The clocks were striking eleven next morning as Tarrant was shown into the private sitting-room which Hampden had reserved.

'Good morning,' said Hampden, who believed in the oil of courtesy. 'You're punctual. Sit down and have a drink before we get to business.'

Tarrant appeared surprised by the friendliness of the greeting. He accepted pleasantly enough, though Hampden could see he was distrustful of what might be behind it. They chatted for a few moments and then Hampden remarked, 'Well, have you thought over what we discussed yesterday?'

Tarrant nodded. 'Yes, I've considered it carefully, and to be quite honest, I don't see that there's any need to make a change.'

'But we think there is,' Hampden smiled.

'I know, but look at it this way.' Tarrant's manner indicated how transparently he was putting his cards on the table. 'We're not really doing you any harm. We're getting a few pickings, I admit, enough to supply our very modest wants, but not enough to make any difference to you. I suggest that we both go ahead as we're doing and ignore each other. Armed neutrality, if you like.'

'I'm afraid,' Hampden answered, 'that we can't agree to that. I admit that you're not injuring us now to any appreciable extent, but you soon would begin to do so. We've graphed your activities, as far as we can get on to them, and the indications are unmistakable.

'But you can't stop us, Mr Hampden. Let me be quite frank. You virtually tell us what we are doing is a racket. Very well, you may be right; but if it is, you're doing the same. You can't get at us.'

'We can take you into court, as I said, and get not only an injunction, but damages.'

'No,' Tarrant spoke pleasantly and without heat, 'if you'll forgive me, that's just what you can't do. Even assuming, which we don't for one moment admit, that you've a good case in law against us, it would expose your own racket. Our counsel would see to that.'

'I deny that absolutely,' and Hampden's manner was equally suave. 'We have done nothing contrary to the law and you could therefore prove nothing against us. We could show that it was you who were guilty of sharp practice.'

Tarrant shook his head. 'We'll take the risk. I'm grateful to you for warning me and all that, but we've put our money and time into this thing and we couldn't see all that lost without making a fight for it. You'd do the same in my place, you know.'

Hampden grinned. 'I expect I should, Mr Tarrant, and I can't blame you. But perhaps we're foolish to talk about courts. Even if we won, I agree that that sort of publicity would be bad for Braxamin. So don't let us waste any more time fencing. Briefly, I have a proposition to put before you for an amicable settlement.'

'If that's so, you'll find me ready to meet you half-way. What is it?'

'This. Subject to confirmation by my Board, and that will be forthcoming, I ask you to discontinue making your indigestion remedy, to disband your workers, close down your works, and give up your entire business, lock, stock and barrel, signing an undertaking not to restart it. In return I offer you one thousand shares in Braxamin and a seat on our Board carrying a salary of five hundred a year.'

Tarrant thought this over and then a slow smile formed on his lips. 'That's ingenious, I admit, and would be fine for your company. But I hardly see where I come in. The five hundred a year wouldn't count, because I should work for that, and you'll forgive me if I say that I'd more than earn it. So that all I'd get would be the thousand shares. What are they worth, by the way?'

'They're standing at forty-five shillings at present, so that they would bring in £2,250. But of course you couldn't sell them while you remained a director. Holding them is a necessary qualification.'

'If I sold them I'd lose my £500 a year, you mean? Very valuable to me! What do they bring in?'

'We're paying fourteen per cent. on our ordinary shares,' Hampden answered. 'About £140 a year.'

'Very interesting. Our business is small, admittedly, but it's already worth many times that figure, and of course it's growing. No, no, Mr Hampden, you'll have to do better than that.'

'You haven't considered everything. Your time would be

your own, except for part of the first Monday of each month. You could therefore take on other work.'

'That's one way of looking at it. Mine is that I now have an interesting job that fills my whole time: a lucrative hobby, you might say. If I accepted your terms I'd be at a loose end.'

'As I say, you could take other work. Or if you cared to represent Braxamin on the road, no doubt that could be arranged. I assure you, Mr Tarrant, few firms in our position would make half so liberal an offer.'

'That may be, but I'm concerned only with yours. And there's no security of tenure in your proposal. What's to prevent your waiting until I have destroyed my business and then giving me the sack? I don't think you can really be serious.'

'I was never more serious in my life,' Hampden said earnestly; 'At the same time I appreciate your point. We'd meet you there. Give you a guarantee for a number of years as might be arranged, provided you dealt fairly with us.'

Tarrant shook his head. 'I appreciate what you're offering and I'm grateful to you,' he declared, 'but naturally I must consider myself. Your offer's nothing like good enough. I should want at least £1,200 a year, and you're offering £640.'

'£640 and the option of another job with us, or of taking on anything else you liked.'

'Ah, no doubt. But I prefer the job that I have.'

'May I suggest that you think it over?'

Tarrant shook his head decisively. 'No, sir, it would be no good. I'm afraid I couldn't seriously consider such an offer. Very good of you, but there's no use in wasting your time.'

Hampden wondered whether the moment had not arrived to indicate what lay beneath the velvet glove. He believed Tarrant was a bluffer. He believed indeed that he was bluffing now.

'Very well, Mr Tarrant,' he said, 'you spoke frankly just now: let me be equally so. I admit I was bluffing when I said we would take you into court. You're quite right there, it wouldn't suit us. But that doesn't leave us helpless. If we can't come to terms—and we would be glad to modify our suggestions to meet your wishes—there will be nothing for it but to fight. And if we fight we shall win.'

'Just how do you propose to do it?'

'In the obvious way. We shall simply increase our selling commission to fifty per cent above yours, no matter what you pay and no matter what it costs us. You might struggle along for a few months, but you'd be out of business by the end of a year, and you know it.'

Tarrant appeared neither surprised nor upset at this, though he looked more cunning than ever. Hampden once again felt a slight wave of misgiving lest the man should have some trump card still up his sleeve.

'There's something in that,' Tarrant admitted, 'though not, I'm afraid, as much as you seem to think. What you suggest would cost you much more than you've any idea of. All the same, if you'd offer reasonable terms, I don't say I wouldn't accept them.'

'What would you consider reasonable terms?'

'£1,200 a year for myself to begin with.'

Hampden smiled. 'I'm afraid we couldn't consider that. But let's hear it all. What else do you want?'

'Provision for my partner, Miss Weir. What do you propose about her?'

Hampden considered. 'We might be able to find Miss Weir an executive position in our works,' he said presently, 'though I couldn't promise that till I looked into it.'

Tarrant shook his head. 'That would be a comedown for her after being practically boss. Then there are our stocks. We have a lot of our stuff made up and bottled, and bins full of magnesia and the other ingredients for making more. How would you deal with that?'

'We'd let you sell on your old terms what's made up ready for sale and take your stocks and bottles off your hands at cost price. We could put in a chartered accountant to fix up the figures.'

'That might do,' Tarrant returned, 'though I'm sure your offer for Miss Weir wouldn't be good enough.'

Hampden thought it was time to put down his foot. 'I'm sorry,' he declared, 'but I can offer no more, either to you or to her. You are, Mr Tarrant—forgive me, I don't want to be offensive—but in plain speech you're swindling us, and because of the difficulty of our own position, I've made you an extremely generous offer. It's for you to take it or leave it. If you take it we become friends and allies, I'm sure to our mutual advantage. If you don't, we fight. Will you please decide?'

'That's an ultimatum?'

'Yes, I'm afraid it is.'

Tarrant sat silent, evidently thinking deeply. His face had lost its hearty hail-fellow-well-met expression and now looked mean and crafty. He shot little speculative glances at Hampden, as if wondering how far he could be trusted or bribed. Hampden did not break the silence, which grew oppressive. At last Tarrant made a sudden gesture, as if throwing everything to the winds.

'I accept, Mr Hampden!' he exclaimed. 'I know when I'm beaten.'

A wave of satisfaction swept through Hampden's mind. He was going to have to work with this man, and if he could not have him for a friend, he could at least avoid increasing his enmity.

'You're not beaten,' he said, with a short laugh. 'Very far from it. But no one in your position could stand up against our resources. I congratulate you, Mr Tarrant, and am glad we are going to work together for the future.'

After a drink to their association, they put the heads of their settlement on paper, from which the solicitors would make a firm agreement. As they worked, Hampden grew more and more concerned about the other's attitude. Tarrant did not seem in the slightest degree upset by what had occurred, and once again little qualms of doubt began to worry Hampden. He did not think he had made a mistake, yet his defeated rival's manner was disquietingly suggestive of victory.

Now another idea which had lain dormant in Hampden's mind during the negotiations came forcing its irresistible way to the top. That debt of his! That four hundred pounds which he must soon find, or face hell in his home! He had just brought off a fine *coup*. Could he add to it a second, easing his own position as he had that of the Braxamin Company?

He had felt that its success would depend on Tarrant's personality, and now he was sure that had he been given a choice, Tarrant was the very man that he would have selected. But what he proposed was a serious matter: nothing less than to have underhand dealings with a swindler. Yet he thought he would be safe. In as far as he placed himself in Tarrant's power, Tarrant would be equally in his. He turned to the man, his expression graver.

'Now, Mr Tarrant,' he began confidentially, 'I have something else to say to you. You are a man of the world and I am another. As such I suppose neither of us is accustomed to refuse any little gift the gods may offer us?'

Tarrant stared, and an expression of extreme wariness appeared in his eyes.

'Meaning just what, Mr Hampden?' he answered pleasantly.

'I'll tell you. I have an idea there's something for both of us in this affair. Now I don't know whether a few hundred would mean anything to you, but I confess I could do with the money. Question is, would you be interested?'

Tarrant remained wary and non-committal. 'I might,' he admitted. 'Depends on what I'd have to do for it.'

'Nothing that would give you either trouble or anxiety. A mere technicality, I can assure you.'

'It's the first time I've heard of getting a few hundred by a mere technicality,' Tarrant declared. 'What's the great idea, Mr Hampden?'

Hampden drew closer and lowered his voice.

'Suppose,' he said confidentially, 'I were able to induce my people to pay you an additional thousand in cash for your business, what commission would you offer me?'

Tarrant stared, then his features broke into a slow smile. 'Oh,' he returned, 'so I've been a sap, have I, and sold for a thousand less than my business was worth? That's not my usual line.'

'I believe you.' Hampden said with feeling. 'But there it is: if I do what I suggest, what would you pay?'

'Ten per cent, I think, is usual under such circumstances.'

'You like your joke, I see. Now look here, Mr Tarrant, we needn't waste time over this. Here's my proposition. I'll get you an additional thousand in cash, provided you hand over five hundred of it to me. That's clear, I hope. Now what about it? Is it on or off?'

For some moments Tarrant thought intently, then he made an emphatic gesture. 'On!' he declared. 'I congratulate you on the idea. But will your people stand for it?'

'I think so. Our agreement would naturally be contingent on that.'

'And what,' asked Tarrant, 'is to prevent my keeping the whole thousand, if your people are so generous as to pay it?'

Hampden's answering smile was not so happy. 'I can trust you, as you can trust me. I should naturally want a promise from you to pay me five hundred in settlement of some hypothetical loan, just as you would want the thousand included in our notes for the agreement.'

'That's only business,' Tarrant agreed. 'Very well, let's initial an amended note of the agreement, and then I'll give you my I.O.U. for the five hundred.'

They did so and then Hampden became once more the efficient manager of the Braxamin Company. 'Good,' he said, rising to show that the interview was over. 'I'll put the essentials of this before our Board at their next meeting, though it'll only be a matter of form. Then I'll send you the draft agreement. And in the meantime you'll order no more stocks.'

'Right.' Tarrant answered, getting up. 'I'll keep my part of the bargain.'

'I'm sure you will, Mr Tarrant. Let's have another drink before you go.'

Hampden was glad when the interview was over. It had been a strain and he had wanted the whiskies and sodas. In spite of those little qualms of doubt, he was well pleased with the result. He really had done extraordinarily well. With regard to official business he had found the source of the trouble, no slight achievement in itself, and he felt that his dealing with it amounted almost to a stroke of genius. Even Cooke would be bound to compliment him.

But better even that his success in his official business was the solution he had found for his personal difficulties. What an untold and overwhelming relief that five hundred pounds would be! Now he could carry on without shipwreck in his home. Admittedly the cost had been high. It was the first time in his life that he had departed from the straight road in business, and of course he was now to some extent in Tarrant's power. However one couldn't have such benefits without paying for them.

Before any part of the official business could be gone on with, he must get his Chairman's approval, and he now rang up Sir Claud and arranged an interview for the next day. That afternoon he returned to London.

Sir Claud heard him through without comment, and then a slow smile spread over his rugged face. 'You propose to give him Furberton's place, I suppose?' he said at last. 'Good; very good indeed. But I'm surprised he accepted.'

Hampden remembered his qualms of doubt, and for him, became unusually expansive. 'To tell you the truth it surprised me. He looked perfectly satisfied too, indeed almost pleased. I don't deny that it made me wonder had I slipped up somewhere.'

Sir Claud pondered. 'I don't think so,' and the words immensely relieved Hampden. 'We've only the two interests to consider: his and our own. This agreement'—he tapped the notes—'fixes him all right. If he breaks it, we'll break him. Why, with this agreement, we could take him into court and properly salt him: it's an admission of fraud on his part. Nothing wrong with it.'

'I'm glad to hear you say so, sir.'

'What about the girl? Can you really fix up something for her?'

'Not unless we create a special job. But he didn't seem to worry about her. I imagined it was a nominal partnership and that they're probably living together.'

'I'm surprised at you, Hampden.'

This delighted Hampden more than all that had gone before, because when Sir Claud joked it meant that he was very pleased indeed.

'Now,' went on the magnate, 'with regard to ourselves, we're going to save money. What do we pay Furberton?'

'A thousand for acting as director and the interest on five thousand shares. These shares are ours; Furberton only holds them nominally. He accepted those terms, but I couldn't have settled with Tarrant without handing his shares over absolutely.'

'That's all right. Now let's see: we pay Furberton £1,000 plus £700 of interest: £1,700 a year. That right?'

'Quite correct.'

'And we're giving this Tarrant £500 plus £140, that is, £640 a year, plus the equivalent of £3,250 in the first year.'

Hampden nodded.

The Chairman did sums on his blotting-pad. 'That is, in about three years we shall have paid off the lump sum and then—let's see: £640 from £1,700—we'll save over £1,000 a year.'

'That's what I made it.'

'Good: very good indeed. You've saved a thousand a year *and* got rid of the competition. I congratulate you, Hampden. You've done really well.'

'Thank you very much, sir. I'm very pleased that you think so.'

'I take it you'll delay Tarrant's joining the Board until Furberton has left, so as to avoid paying double fees?'

'I intend to do so.'

'Right. Then as a matter of policy I think you should see Roberts and Cooke before you fix up. The others don't matter.'

Hampden's relief was overwhelming. No question about the £1,000 had been raised, and now that the item had got past Sir Claud, it was to the last degree unlikely that it would arouse comment elsewhere.

Being anxious to get the major affair settled and off his mind, Hampden decided to take the remainder of the day in interviewing the two directors. Roberts was easy to reach. His porcelain factory was in North London, not twenty minutes' drive from the Braxamin headquarters, and in less than an hour Hampden had his full approval.

To see Cooke, on the other hand, would take most of the afternoon. Since the last Board he had met with an accident and was confined to bed at his home in Little Bitton. Hampden rang him up and after lunch set off alone in his car.

He was pleased to be making the journey, because it took him into old haunts. Little Bitton was some five miles beyond Saxham St Edmunds, itself thirty miles from Town, where he had lived when managing the chemist's shop. That had been a pleasant period in his life. The work had been congenial, there had been golf and boating, and he had made many friends. As he passed through Tottenham he decided that he would get away as quickly as possible from Cooke and drop in on one or two of his old cronies on the way back.

Once clear of London he drove fast, and reaching Saxham St Edmunds forked right for Little Bitton. This was a more pleasant country than that through which he had already passed; moreover he knew every inch of it. A little outcrop of hills in the generally flat land gave it a distinctive character and there was a lot of fine old timber and a number of small rivers and streams, most of them, as Hampden knew from happy experience, well stocked with fish. Little Bitton was a charming village, picturesque and unspoilt, and was surrounded by the 'places' of the fortunate.

In one of the smaller of these 'places' lived Cooke with his two unmarried sisters. Old Mr Cooke had been in the hardware trade, and having amassed a fortune in South Lancashire, had come south to end his days in more rural surroundings. He had bought 'Greenbank', a pleasant cottage with grounds sloping down to the River Webble. But he had not long survived his retirement. In less than a year after settling down he died, leaving the place and half his money to Joynson. At this time Joynson was some two and twenty and was still studying for the diplomatic, but on coming into his £20,000 he felt he was set up for life and need no longer work. He got into a racing set and developed a passion for the turf, particularly that side of it which 'features' the bookmaker and the pool. In a short time he found the interest of his legacy insufficient for his needs and began nibbling at the capital. This melted in a way which shocked even himself, and in desperation he began to look for some way of making good the deficiency. It was then, eight years after his father's death, that the proprietary medicine idea occurred to him, which had led to the floating of the Braxamin Company.

During the six years which followed, his financial position grew more and more precarious. His director's fees and the dividends on the shares he had received as the originator of the idea, brought him in some £1,500 a year, but of his original capital little was left. Hampden had heard that he was paying devoted court to the local heiress, a Miss Jean Woolcombe, though whether these facts represented cause and effect, Hampden didn't know. The Misses Cooke, who had inherited the remainder of their father's money, were both older than Joynson. Though they continued to live at 'Greenbank', they had developed their own interests and had little in common with their brother.

Hampden found Cooke querulous from pain and boredom, but for the same reason glad to see him. 'Fed up with this ruddy bed,' he grumbled, 'and the doctor says I'll have another fortnight of it. Ruddy waste of time.'

'Sorry to hear that, Mr Cooke; though you've done me a good turn by giving me a drive down here.'

'You're not as sorry as I am; not by a long chalk. Well, what's the trouble? It wasn't to inquire for my health you've come, I'll be bound.'

'Well, since you must know, it was not,' answered Hampden, trying not to be irritated by the other's manner. 'A spot of business to talk over. I want authority to act about that fall in our returns. I've seen the old man and Roberts and they're quite satisfied, so if you agree I can carry on without waiting for next Board.'

'What do you want?'

'I'll tell you. I've found . . .' and Hampden went on to describe his proposed settlement with Tarrant.

Cooke at once objected. He did not see why a man who had been trying to cheat them out of their just profits should be rewarded with shares and a seat on the Board. 'Far better to fight,' he declared, jerking himself irritably about. 'If he's been working against us up to now, how do we know that he won't continue to do so as a director?'

'He was never working against us,' Hampden pointed out. 'He was working for himself and he didn't care two hoots about us. All he wants is money and he's found out how to get it from us. If we have to pay, in any case we may as well have the benefit of his advice, for he's certainly able.'

Cooke grumbled again. He was damned if he was going to be cheated by any ruddy swindler. Let them fight him and put him out of business. What did it matter if it did cost something? It would be cheaper to be rid of the swine and be done with it. And so on for fifteen minutes on end.

Hampden let him talk, and when he seemed about to run down he asked quietly: 'Then you'll carry the Board with you, I take it? You'll talk round Sir Claud and Roberts?'

This had a damping effect. Cooke flung himself across the bed. 'How the hell can I do anything tied down here?' he retorted. 'Have the ruddy thing your own ruddy way, and don't bother me about it any more.'

Having achieved his victory, Hampden turned the conversation to horse racing, and presently Cooke had thawed and was discussing eagerly the chances of Mellon King and

Buttercup for the Nossex Stakes. When, half an hour later, Hampden left, Cooke was in a more friendly frame of mind than he had been for years.

That night the firm's offer in writing went to Tarrant and two days later the agreement was back in Hampden's hands, duly signed. Lord Furberton was leaving the Board after two more meetings, so Tarrant was given three months to wind up his business and shift his allegiance to his former adversary.

As the time passed slowly on, Hampden grew more and more satisfied that he had done the right thing. Tarrant was playing the game. Within a fortnight the firm of chartered accountants had been appointed, and in due course their agent reported the closing down of the business.

That same week Tarrant came up to Town and took rooms in Jermyn Street. Hampden called and had a drink with him, partly as a gesture of politeness, partly to inform him as to the Board meeting on the following Monday, and partly to make discreet inquiries about a point which had been giving him some anxiety—the fate of Miss Weir, about whom nothing more had been said either in the agreement or out of it.

Tarrant he found disposed to be agreeable.

'Miss Weir?' he answered, 'Oh! she's all right. Been lucky, she has. Got a good job. Curious how it worked out. She was a nurse, you know; a good nurse too, tiptop qualifications and all that. One of her patients was a wealthy South African. He was interested in a hospital out there and they wanted a matron, and he wrote offering her the job. She had turned it down, but only just posted the letter. So she cabled accepting and cancelling the letter and she's sailing next week. Lucky, wasn't it?'

'Very.' Hampden answered promptly, glad to have possible claims from this source wiped off the board. 'And you don't want a job with us yourself?' he went on. 'We're doing a new drive in Ireland, and you can take charge of our representatives in that country if you like. Five hundred, expenses and a bonus.'

'Thanks,' Tarrant answered, 'we did talk of that, didn't we? By the way, are you ready for some more whisky. Say when . . . Soda? . . . I'm obliged for your offer, but I'm not going to accept. As a matter of fact,' he grew more confidential, 'I'm joining with another man in a small venture. It's a hobby really, but if we've any luck we should do quite well out of it. It's rather confidential, but I'm sure it's safe with you.'

'Of course, but don't speak of it unless you want to.'

'No, it's all right. It's a medicine bottle with the lines marking the doses radiating from the neck, instead of being stepped down the back. That's to say, you pour till the surface comes down on to the line, instead of having to upend the bottle to see where you are.'

'That sounds interesting. You're not going to make the bottles, are you?'

'That's the idea. My friend's taking over a small glass works, and doing the financing. I'm to do the selling—if I can.'

'If you can't, nobody else could,' Hampden laughed, as he took his leave. 'Then we'll see you at eleven next Monday?' About the £1,000 they had shared, neither man said a word.

Tarrant turned up at the Board and made an excellent impression. He was deferential to Sir Claud, and friendly to the others. He quickly grasped the business at issue, and his remarks, though few, were helpful and to the point. Once again Hampden felt he had done well and he left the boardroom more easy in his mind about his own position than he had been for a good many months.

8

Peter Temple Achieves an Ambition

Peter Temple had been delighted by his appointment as van driver and general handyman at the Koldkure Works. In the first place, it marked the end of a period of unemployment which had lasted since the laundry closed down, and in the second, this new job was more varied and gave him greater scope than his last. He was glad moreover to be again with Edith Horne and his other old workmates, and last, but not least, he had taken a great fancy to Merle and felt she would be an ideal employer.

There was only one fly in the ointment: Tarrant. Tarrant he disliked at sight. Tarrant had come into the yard one day—the first time he had seen him—and had called roughly to him as if to a dog: 'Here you! What are you supposed to be doing? You're not paid for loafing. Get my cases in from the car.'

Peter had indeed been standing about, but he was waiting for a package to start for the station. There was nothing, of course, in the greeting to upset him: that was the way countless bosses spoke to their men. But after Merle's kindly manner and pleasant way of giving instructions, it grated. Fortunately, Tarrant seldom appeared, but when he did so the happy atmosphere of the Works dissolved and frowns and bad temper were the order of the day.

'He's a blight,' Edith Horne once said. 'I wish he'd stay away. It means trouble all round when he appears.'

'Thank goodness we don't see much of him,' Peter agreed.

'Funny how much the way you're asked to do a thing matters,' Edith went on. 'It's more important than the thing itself. Now there's Miss Weir, and anything she asks you to do is only a pleasure. But let Tarrant ask you to do anything and your back's up at once.'

'Oh, well, what would you expect? There aren't many like Our Merle.'

'You're right,' said Edith, he thought a little dryly.

Certainly having Miss Weir for a boss did make a difference. Peter began to look forward to seeing her when he got his daily instructions. She was so kindly, and never unduly asserted her authority. It was as Edith Horne had said: when Merle asked one to do something—she never gave an order—the doing of it became a pleasure. And it was worth taking trouble to get her smile and word of approval.

Sometimes Peter thought she was looking worn and unhappy, and the thought moved him strangely. If anyone ought to be happy, it should be a person like her, whose chief object seemed to be to give pleasure to others. If anyone in the works had been making trouble for her, he felt he would have had something to say about it. But as far as he could see, no one had. She got better service than any other employer he had ever heard of.

One day an incident took place which left him amazed

and horrified, revealing as it did a strength of feeling in himself which he did not know he possessed.

He had been delivering packages at the station, and owing to some delays, returned to the yard after closing time. He let himself in with his key and put the van away, then instead of immediately going home, he stayed on for a few minutes preparing some stuff for the morning. While thus engaged he overheard voices.

'I don't like it,' Merle was saying and her voice was troubled. 'Why can't we be straight, James? That's the one thing that I hate about the whole business: all this crookedness and subterfuge.'

'For goodness sake, Merle, don't be so tiresome.' It was Tarrant's voice and there was a rasp in it. 'If I've told you once, I've told you a dozen times, there's nothing crooked about the thing.'

'But I think it *is* crooked.'

'Well, you think wrong. It's just business. Pleasant for me to come back and hear all this whining. I wish to heaven you'd pull yourself together and be like other people.'

For a moment Peter couldn't think what was happening to him. The blood was pounding in his temples and his throat was congested. He started forward and his hands clenched as he fought his desire to seize Tarrant by the throat and squeeze and squeeze and squeeze till the man's face grew black and his eyes started from their sockets and that foul voice was choked for ever. Tarrant! *Anyone* to speak in that tone to Merle! No one should live to do it twice!

What he might have done if the voices had continued, he didn't know, but Tarrant went on in a more apologetic tone, as if sorry for his outburst.

'Well, let it alone for the present at all events. Come, let's have some dinner.'

There was a murmur from Merle and the slamming of a door. They had gone out.

For a good fifteen minutes Peter stood in the garage, fighting for sanity. He was horrified by the strength of his feelings. He had been as near to murder as to fill him with dread. If things had not been as they were, if he had not been separated from Tarrant by the office wall, he dared not picture what might have happened. He might now be a *murderer*, a fugitive with a price on his life. Hideous!

But it was not till later that he realised the truth. While completing his forward notes Edith Horne began to talk of Tarrant. 'He's a nasty piece of work, if you ask me,' she declared. 'I don't know what Miss Weir sees in him.'

Peter stared, while a curious constricted feeling grew in his throat. 'You don't mean—' he stammered hoarsely.

'Of course I mean it,' retorted Edith. 'She's just dotty about him. Between ourselves, they're engaged: she let it out once when we were talking. Though what business of yours it is, I don't know.'

Then Peter understood. Yes, it was true. He loved Merle! More than his life. He would do anything for her. He would even kill Tarrant for her and hang, if it would please her and remove a trouble from her path.

But if she *loved* Tarrant! No, never, it couldn't be! And yet Peter realised that Tarrant might be attractive enough if he chose. He was big and good-looking—Temple was undersized and no beauty himself—and no doubt he could mend his manners if he thought it worth his while.

Now a cold hatred took possession of Peter's mind. If Tarrant were worthy of Merle, he would, he told himself,

105

have nothing to say. But that such a low swine should attempt to lift his eyes to a woman like Merle was an insult. Fed by his jealousy, Peter's hatred grew till he was scarcely sane. Fortunately Tarrant was away from Exeborough, and by the time he returned Peter had had time to cool.

Now that he knew what had happened to him, Peter was careful to control himself in Merle's presence, and he was satisfied that she never guessed his feelings. Though she was always kind, he felt instinctively that she would never tolerate any approaches on his part, and he therefore never made any. His love, however, gave him an insight he mightn't otherwise have had, and he realised that she was far from happy. But here again he did not dare to speak to her on the subject, though he would have given all he possessed to help her.

Then one day something serious evidently happened, for she became more upset than he had ever seen her. It was during one of Tarrant's visits—all trouble seemed to come through Tarrant—and it took place in the morning, for early in the morning she had been completely normal and when Peter saw her just before lunch she looked pale and frightened. Tarrant, whom he saw once during the afternoon, also looked upset, though with him it seemed excitement rather than fear.

Things, however, settled down and work went on normally. Though Merle still seemed worried, she said nothing to indicate that trouble was brewing. At the same time rumours began to circulate. Edith Horne told how on that morning the manager of Braxamin had called. The staff knew that Braxamin was their big rival and deduced that war between them had been declared. But only one actual fact was noticed: a fact which gave rise to deep misgivings—that the stocks of their raw materials **were** running down and were not being replenished.

Some six weeks later the blow fell. A notice was posted by Merle with the stupefying intelligence that the firm was being dissolved and the works were closing down. Notice was given to everyone, but instead of the week which was due, this would not take effect for another month.

Peter Temple was heartbroken, not so much for the loss of his job, but for the fact that he would be separated from Merle. What, he wondered, were her prospects? Was she going to marry Tarrant? Or would she, like the rest of them, be simply turned adrift?

He worried so much over this question that at last he took his courage in both hands and asked her.

'It's cheek on my part, I know, miss,' he pleaded, 'but I don't mean it as cheek. You've been very good to me and I'd like to know that you were properly fixed up.'

She usually called the girls by their Christian names and had dropped into the same habit with Temple.

'Nice of you, Peter,' she smiled. 'I appreciate that greatly. I've got work, though not such pleasant work as here. I'm a trained nurse, you know, and I'm going back to nursing.'

Then she was *not* going to marry Tarrant! Peter's spirits rose with a bound.

'I suppose, miss, you wouldn't let me have your address?' he begged, 'just in case I heard of anything in this neighbourhood that you might like? Your name has become known and you'd get anything that was going.'

'Nice of you,' she repeated. 'I'll certainly give it to you, and I'll be glad to hear how you get on yourself.'

It took all Temple's resolution to reply normally. He longed to pour out all his love for her and to assure her that he cared nothing for himself if only she were happy. But he did just control himself.

Preparations for the closing down now went on apace. All the finished Remedy was sold, the stocks of materials were removed to the Braxamin works, the premises were sublet and most of the staff were taken over by the newcomer. Goodbyes were said, and for the time being at least, Merle passed out of Peter's life.

Peter was not one of those taken over with the premises and for some weeks he remained unemployed. Then he got a temporary position as assistant postman in a rural area near Exeborough. He covered a good many miles every day and learnt a new technique, and was the better for both. He believed he was giving satisfaction, and began to hope for permanency with the Post Office.

It was then that Merle's letter came. It was headed Lincaster, a large town in the eastern Midlands, and read:

Dear Peter,

If you have a job this probably will not interest you, but if not, there is a vacancy here which I think you could have if you were able for the work. I admit I am doubtful about that; not anything against you, but simply that it is outside the sort of work you did at Koldkure.

If you would like further details, I'm afraid it means an interview. I would meet you half-way, i.e., in London. I am going up on Saturday, 23rd inst., and will arrive at King's Cross at 12.35. Perhaps you could meet me there? If you are still at Exeborough you could get back the same evening.

I need not say that I shall entirely understand if you decide not to come.

Yours sincerely,

Merle Weir.

Once again Peter's difficulty was to keep out of his acceptance the exuberant delight, the love and the longing that filled his mind. He had saved very little, but he immediately sank a large proportion of his capital in a new hat, shoes and a suit, this latter a vast extravagance. He retained indeed little more than enough for his fare and to give Merle a decent lunch and perhaps a mild excursion, if she would accept either.

His frame of mind was shown by the fact that when his postmaster refused him leave on that particular Saturday, owing to the head postman being off duty, he unhesitatingly threw up the job rather than ask Merle if another day would suit her as well.

With his heart beating high and arrayed in his new apparel, Peter reached King's Cross at the earliest moment that the journey from Exeborough would allow; an hour before Merle's train was due. The minutes dragged like lead, but at long last the train drew in. Peter's heart fluttered more than ever as he watched the crowd pouring from it. There she was! The station brightened as if the sun had come out beneath the roof. Acutely conscious of his new clothes, Temple hurried forward.

Heavens, but she looked adorable: more charming and lovely even than he had seen her in his dreams I. But tired surely and worn and anxious? If that unspeakable swine Tarrant had been unpleasant to her, he would—

'Hullo, Peter! Nice to see you again.'

109

The voice, cool and musical and friendly, brought Peter to his senses. He forgot his hat and his clothes and Tarrant, and greeted her as he should.

'This is good of you, Miss Weir, first about the job, and then letting me come up and meet you,' he went on. 'I don't think anything in my life ever pleased me so much.'

'You haven't got the job yet,' she smiled, 'and you may not get it at all. But you probably don't want it. You seem very prosperous.'

'I want it terribly,' he assured her. 'I've just lost my present one.'

'Oh,' she said sympathetically, 'how was that?'

He didn't want to tell her, but she quickly found out.

'Oh,' she cried, 'how shameful of you? Really wicked! I'm surprised at you, Peter. Why didn't you write and fix another day?'

'Oh, it's nothing; don't think of it,' he returned easily. 'I wanted to see you and hear your news. But look here, we can't talk on the platform for the rest of the day. I wondered—if you could spare the time—if you would—come and have some lunch.'

There, it was out! He held his breath. Then there came a wave of relief. She was not offended. Instead she replied as if his astounding feat had been perfectly normal. 'I'd love that. Where shall we go?'

The meal was practically finished before she referred to the subject of her letter. 'We've started a new firm,' she explained. 'James and I, but he is now unable to give much personal attention to it. What we want is someone to oversee the works, so that I could attend to the books. And the question is, could you do it?'

The mere suggestion made Temple's heart leap. It was *her*

job, and not only that, but an almost infinitely better offer than he had expected. He gulped once or twice, then found his voice.

'I can't thank you enough, Miss Weir,' he said earnestly. 'I could do it if only you'll give me the chance.'

She gave a tiny gurgle of laughter. 'You've a good opinion of yourself,' she declared. 'Why, you haven't even asked what we're going to make!'

'Only let me try,' he begged. 'If I'm a washout, you can get rid of me.'

'I'm to run the thing without James's help, and I confess I'd like to have someone I knew and that I was sure I could get on with. We prefer the evils we know, and so on. What's the quotation?'

For a moment Peter couldn't speak. To work as a partner, if an inferior one, with Merle; to see her every day; to talk to her; to be able to help her and make things easy for her: why, it would be heaven!

He wondered later if his feelings had shown in his face, for suddenly she looked at him doubtfully and her manner became a little uneasy. 'Remember,' she said in an altered tone, 'that this would be purely a business matter between us. I'm sure you wouldn't do anything to give me trouble.'

'Of course not, Miss Weir,' he said, and at the moment he meant it.

Her face cleared. 'Good,' she said. 'Well, on that understanding, and as we're to work together, you'd better call me Merle. The alternative is for me to call you Mr Temple, which would be ridiculous.'

Remembering his last remark, Peter controlled himself and made a joke in replying. Then he went on: 'This is wonderful news, Merle. Won't you tell me more about it?'

Her expression again grew grave, and for a moment he thought he had put his foot in it. Then he saw that she was not thinking of him.

'To be quite candid, I'm rather worried about it,' she said slowly. Then, as if coming to a decision, she went on: 'I suppose, if we're going to work together, I'd better tell you the whole thing. You know why we closed down Koldkure?'

'Not exactly. Of course there were rumours. It began the day the Braxamin manager called, so we supposed that that had something to do with it.'

Merle nodded. 'Well, he came and saw James. He was very polite, so James said, but he indicated that we were swindling the Braxamin firm, and, that we'd have to stop. He threatened us with legal proceedings and all kinds of horrors, and then said perhaps James would like a little time to think it over. All this James told me when he had gone.'

Peter was indignant. 'But that wasn't true,' he declared. 'The Koldkure firm was perfectly honest.'

'I hope so,' she answered with, he thought, some lack of conviction. 'However, James agreed to see the man next day, and he did so. When he came back he was a good deal upset; and as you probably know, it takes a good deal to upset James. He said that he had told Mr Hampden, that was the manager's name, that we were acting perfectly legally and that if he took us into court he could prove nothing against us.'

'Well, that's correct, isn't it?'

'Apparently they both agreed that it was, for Mr Hampden admitted that he had been bluffing. Then he went on to deliver his real ultimatum. If we closed down, the Braxamin firm would let us sell off all our finished product and take

112

our stocks off our hands, as well as paying us a lump sum to carry on till we got other jobs. James, I may tell you, got a hundred pounds and I got fifty. Not too unreasonable, I suppose.'

'I think it was damnable,' Peter said thickly.

'If we didn't accept those terms, the Braxamin people would fight us. They would offer double our commission, whatever that might be, and put us out of business. James was terribly depressed: I've never seen him so upset. You know, the Remedy was his idea, and he just hated giving it up.'

'I should have let them fight,' Peter declared pugnaciously.

Merle smiled a little sadly. 'You would have been right, as a matter of fact, but we couldn't know that then. Remember, we only sold the Remedy because we offered a higher commission than Braxamin. If they had doubled ours, we shouldn't have sold another bottle.'

'It seems ghastly to have given up without a. struggle.'

'*Ghastly!* That's what I felt, and it hurt me to see James's distress. However, he said that he wasn't finished yet. Though the Remedy had proved a washout, he had other ideas. Perhaps with luck we might get going on something else. He said I would remain his business partner, and that if he did start again I would be in on it.'

'Then this is one of the other ideas?'

Merle smiled a little unhappily, but went on in her own way. 'We closed down, as you know. Fortunately, most of the girls were taken over with the works, but you and Elsie and Mabel and I were out of work. I had my fifty pounds; they paid that on the nail, but you other three had nothing. I was sorry about it, but I couldn't do anything, and, of course, you three had only recently come to us.'

113

'That was all right, Merle. We had no grievance whatever.'

'That was what James said. Well, I went up to Town and got a post in a nursing home, a small place, badly run and all that. I didn't like it, but I couldn't get anything better. And you, you tell me, became a postman.'

'Yes, and not a bad job either. But go on with the tale.'

'Then I had a letter from James, asking me to meet him. He was full of a wonderful story he had unearthed. He said that some four years earlier, when Braxamin had only been on the market a couple of years, a small firm had done just what we had done—put a rival remedy on the market. Braxamin had threatened first to go to law, then, when their bluff was called, agreed it was bluff, and said they would fight by increased commissions. All so far exactly the same as in our case.

'But this firm, James had found out, had not been so weak as we were. They told Braxamin to go ahead and fight all they wanted to, and what do you think? Braxamin climbed down and made a settlement.'

'I should have fought,' Peter put, in with a grin.

'Luck—not guidance! Braxamin offered this man a large block of their shares and a seat on their board in return for his business. He accepted and they immediately closed it down.'

'Pity Mr Tarrant was in such a hurry.'

'Ah, but he had a scheme to put that right. That was why he wrote to me. He now wanted to be treated in the same way as that earlier manufacturer, but he said we were too late: that our bargaining power was gone because we had closed down. Then he made this suggestion:

'"Why not," he said, "start again?" The same remedy, the same plant, the same sales methods? Then as soon as we had got going we would have a lever to compel the Braxamin people to treat us properly.'

For a moment Peter did not reply. He could see nothing wrong with the scheme, and yet he did not like it. Before he could speak Merle went on:

'I see you don't think much of the idea. I didn't either. I thought it—well, I may as well say it—I thought it—not quite straight. But James was so full of it and so sure it was absolutely correct, that, though I did object, he persuaded me to go into it. So that's the job. It's not permanent because the Braxamin people will close it down, but when we leave we will do so with good compensation. He insisted on having everything put in my name, so that in the settling up I should not be left out. Well, after all that, are you still willing to join in?'

Peter laughed. Merle did not realise how idiotic a question that was! How could she know that he would do *anything* or go *anywhere* to be with her?

'Well, what do you think?' he answered, as coolly as he could. 'Do you suppose I could resist the chance of being works manager? Don't you know it's my life's ideal?'

'Then that's all right,' she smiled. 'Next question: when can you start?'

When Peter left to catch the last train to Exeborough it had been arranged that he should go to Lincaster in ten days' time, as by then they would have taken delivery of their new premises. As the train sped on through the night, he could scarcely remain seated in his carriage, so full was his heart of delirious joy. But though he didn't see it, already a cloud was coming up over the horizon.

9

James Tarrant Goes Social

As James Tarrant slipped on the coat of his new dress-suit he glanced with a self-satisfied smirk at the white bow he had just succeeded in tying. He had tied it well, as he did everything well, though he had only had two or three minutes' instruction from the shopman. His success in what so many found difficult was, of course, only a trifle, but, he told himself, it was symptomatic: an omen of success in this new social world into which he was now for the first time about to penetrate.

He had, he felt, reason for self-satisfaction. His advance had been—he smiled as he thought of the *cliché*—meteoric. Ever since that moment when he had decided to trust in himself and his luck, and giving up his lowly though safe job, to stake his all on the Indigestion Remedy, he had had an unbroken record of success. The Remedy had done well, better than he could have hoped. When he closed it down it was bringing him in a clear profit of over six hundred pounds a year, and he reckoned that in another twelve months the figure would have been doubled.

His complacency reached its climax as he thought of the Braxamin *coup*. Here again he was going to come out on top. Hampden, no doubt, was a smart man, but James Pettigrew Tarrant had been one too many for him. Hampden had handed over his shares and money and directorship in exchange for the Koldkure business, but he, Tarrant, had not handed over the business! He had kept both.

It had really been a brilliant idea! To accept the shares and the directorship, and only to pretend to close down the Remedy: for this new business he had started was, of course, the Koldkure works under another name. A difficult manoeuvre, most people would have found it. But not James Pettigrew Tarrant! He had done it and done it cleverly. With the Braxamin people there had been no trouble at all. Humdrum old Hampden could never have imagined such audacity. It had been necessary only to close down the Exeborough shed, and let Merle and the other workers separate and take fresh jobs. Hampden's spies and chartered accountants had reported everything O.K. and—there it was!

But at every point he had been up against Merle's morbid conscience. The silly fool thought the scheme was not straight. And this was where his cleverness had come in. He had put her off at the time with a tale of a hundred and fifty pounds compensation between them both. How he had regretted that fifty pounds he had had to pay her! But there was no other way; it was necessary to support his story. Then he had only to pretend that the shares and directorship had been given to an earlier rival, and that they would be offered to them if they strengthened their position by starting another business.

Merle had been really extraordinarily difficult. He wished to goodness he could get rid of her. She was nothing but a nuisance with her scruples and her sentimentality. But he couldn't do without her.

Only she knew enough to run the business, and this time it would be too dangerous to appear in it himself. He had therefore taken care that she should make every move. All the papers were in her name, ostensibly to insure her participation in the profits. He would let her run the thing as long as it seemed safe—he would learn on the Braxamin board what Hampden was doing—and if danger threatened, he could easily find some excuse for closing down.

Another darned nuisance was that in the end, to get her agreement, he had had to renew his promise to marry her. Not that he intended to do anything so silly. It was obvious that he must marry money: that was the whole point of his learning to make a good bow on his white tie. But there would probably be an unpleasant scene with Merle later on. Well, never mind: he needn't worry about his fences till he came to them.

When a few weeks previously he had reached this decision to marry money, he had gone about the business in the same careful calculating way in which he did everything else. Where were rich marriageable girls to be found? Why, in society. Therefore he must get into society. Which of his new acquaintances could best help him there? He skilfully pumped them about themselves and each other, and came to the conclusion that only Sir Claud and Cooke moved in the charmed circle. To cultivate Sir Claud would be beyond him, but Cooke was a different proposition. Cooke's heart could be reached through the medium of either whisky or horses. Tarrant could already put away a good deal of drink without showing it, but of racing he was completely ignorant. This, however, is a subject about which anyone with a little cash can learn, and Tarrant took an intensive course. Then his opportunity came. He overheard Cooke say that he was going to the Eastshire meeting. He went himself, accidentally met Cooke and was much surprised to find that he was also a devotee. Over drinks a life-long friendship was cemented.

In his cups Cooke had given him a general invitation to 'look him up' should he ever be in the neighbourhood, and by a strange coincidence it happened that the very next week Tarrant drove through Little Bitton. Naturally he paid his call. That was ten days ago, and tonight's white tie was the result. Tarrant was to make the fourth of a *partie carrée* to dine at Rimini's and to go on to the show of the moment.

The evening need not be described, as it was like any other evening of the same type. All the same, it marked a turning point in Tarrant's life, for there he met Miss Jean Woolcombe and decided to marry her.

He did not make this decision all at once, because it was only gradually that he learnt the essential fact upon which it depended. On that evening he recognised the young woman and her friend, Miss Maudsley, only as representatives of the class he was cultivating. Luckily he felt in great form and kept the party amused, being careful only not to outshine Cooke and so turn him into an enemy. When they said good-night he felt he had done well and would be received on equal terms by both ladies when next they met.

It was then that through books of reference and skilful inquiries he learnt that Jean Woolcombe was the only daughter of the late General Sir Swinton Woolcombe, K.C.B., C.B.E., D.S.O., a man of great wealth and position in the county. What was more, his charming place at Little Bitton and practically all his money had gone to Jean! Miss

Maudsley was, it appeared, a companion friend, and the two ladies lived nominally alone, though usually the house was full of guests.

Another factor in the situation which Tarrant quickly learnt was that his idea had already occurred to Cooke. He felt, however, that it would be a mistake to allow Cooke's desires or priority of claim to affect his own choice. If Cooke were in his way, well, like George Stevenson's cow, so much the worse for Cooke.

A week after the theatre, on a day on which he knew Cooke would be at a race meeting, Tarrant with some difficulty borrowed Leslie Bird's new sports car and drove down to Little Bitton to call on Jean. She greeted him, he considered, on weighing the point later, quite satisfactorily: in a rather off-hand manner perhaps, but then she *was* off-hand. She was a big woman with a high colour and plain features, and though her clothes were obviously expensive, she somehow never looked tidy. Her voice was loud and she walked with a mannish swing. She was pleasant in a slapdash way and seemed kindly, though kindliness was a virtue about which Tarrant was never enthusiastic.

Jean Woolcombe was, in fact, an unattractive woman. The thought delighted Tarrant. It doubtless accounted for the fact that, in spite of her money, she was still Jean Woolcombe. Splendid: it reduced the competition! For himself he didn't care what she was like. If once he married her and so solved his exchequer problems, he could take his pleasure wherever he chose.

He was careful to stay only a short time, and though Jean asked him to wait for tea he excused himself with obvious regret, giving a cast-iron pretext. She must not suspect he was trying to climb.

Now a difficulty presented itself. How was he to meet her again? Their ways lay apart. He could not constantly be passing through Little Bitton and taking the opportunity to call, nor could he very well ask her up to Town. Certainly in his present position he could not hope to compete with Cooke, who lived within half a mile of her house.

He gave this problem careful thought, and at last decided that in order to succeed in his plan he must move to Little Bitton. He would have to take a house, of course, but he had noticed for sale close to Cooke's place a charming cottage which would exactly suit a well-to-do bachelor. It stood in a couple of acres of ground on the slopes of the River Webble, a stretch of the left bank being actually included. The purchase of this would show reasonable wealth without ostentation, and once living there he would meet Jean on all sorts of occasions. As for his motive, he could say that he disliked Town and wanted to move to some part of the country where there was fishing. He knew nothing about fishing, but, like tying a white bow, the art could be learnt.

To this scheme there was but one snag: where could he get the money? Profits from the first Remedy were dwindling rapidly, and those from the second had scarcely begun to come in. With his Braxamin receipts he had now less than £1,000 a year. This enabled him to live as he was doing, but left nothing over. Of course there were the Braxamin shares, worth about £2,250. He could not sell these and retain his directorship, but he might pledge them with the bank. If the house also were handed over to the bank, that might advance him enough for the purchase.

He did not know if this was possible, but he thought he might at least see over the house, which he had noticed was still occupied. He therefore told Cooke of his idea and asked for his views.

'By Jove, Tarrant, so you're thinking of The Gables, are you? Well, you could do a lot worse. It's a nice cottage and you get the fishing rights on a couple of hundred yards of the Webble.'

'Not enough to be any good, I should have thought.'

'Oh well, a lot of people would give their eyes for it.'

'What's the place going for, do you know?'

'Haven't an idea. Better call with Margetson Jones, the agents. They're a Saxham St Edmunds firm and you'll find them all right.'

Later that week Tarrant visited the agents, and armed with an order to view, went to The Gables. The owner was a Mrs Wentworth, a mild-mannered old lady with an invalid daughter. Her husband had just died and she and her daughter wished to reside in Italy.

Tarrant was delighted with the place. There was a good hall and two other sitting-rooms, one a delightful lounge with a glass wall opening on to a loggia. There were three bedrooms and a maid's room, all fitted with running water. There was central heating as well as open fireplaces, and mains electricity. The house stood on the side of a rather steep valley, looking out across the river at the slope ascending from the opposite bank. The grounds were a huge garden, but running to shrubs and trees rather than flowers. The price was £5,000.

As owner of such a charming home, Tarrant felt that his hopes of marrying Jean Woolcombe would be raised to an entirely new level. Before he had completed his inspection, he had decided that he must have it.

But how to set about getting it? More chance with this

gentle old lady than with the agents, who were doubtless competent business men. Putting on therefore his best manner, he began the assault.

'What an absolutely charming place it is,' he remarked as he rejoined her on the loggia. 'I don't know when I have seen one I have liked so much.'

'Then perhaps you would like to take it off my hands?'

'Nothing I should like better: it's absolutely my ideal. I should offer to buy it today only for one rather serious objection.'

He was delighted to notice her face drop. 'And what is that, if I may ask?'

Tarrant laughed ruefully. 'Money,' he said, speaking as if the affair was some kind of mild joke. 'I'm afraid I couldn't rise to your price.'

'Oh,' she answered, 'what a pity. I should like to reduce it to meet your wishes, but I'm afraid I couldn't. We want the money to live on, you see.'

'I shouldn't dream,' he declared in horror, 'of suggesting such a thing. I know something about houses and I can assure you it's worth every penny you're charging. No, it's simply my misfortune, but it can't be helped.' He rose to go.

She seemed unwilling to close the interview. 'My misfortune also,' she said in a troubled voice. 'We are both anxious to leave and we can't do so till the house is disposed of.'

Tarrant's air of respectful sympathy was admirable. 'You're not as sorry about it as I am,' he assured her. 'I felt when I came down the drive that this was the place I had been so long looking for, but unfortunately even if you were disposed to meet me to some extent, I couldn't go to anywhere near your figure.'

'Well,' she said, 'I'm sorry too,' and she held out her hand in a friendly way.

'Of course,' Tarrant said, pausing after he had shaken hands, 'there *is* one way in which both our wishes might be met, though I don't know if it would appeal to you. It would at least let you go to Italy with adequate money and it would let me have the house.'

She smiled. 'That sounds magical. What's your proposal?'

'Simply, Mrs Wentworth, that you should continue your attempts to sell, but that until you do so you should let your house to me, just as it stands, furniture and all.'

'But if you were once here, you wouldn't be willing to leave, say, in a couple of months, if I sold.'

'Not if I furnished it: no. But if I had your furniture, it wouldn't matter. Perhaps I should say that I'm not married, but my aunt keeps house for me, and she's a very particular old lady and would be most careful of everything.'

'This is a completely new idea to me,' the old lady said a little helplessly. 'You see, I'd quite made up my mind not to let, but only to sell. I wanted to be rid of all the trouble of the place.'

Tarrant nodded. 'I can well understand that and I only put forward my idea in case it might interest you. Oh well, there's no harm done, and may I say that I hope your efforts to sell will soon be successful.' He bowed and began to move off.

'That's very kind of you,' she returned, 'but please don't be in such a hurry. I should like to consult my daughter.'

'I'm at your service,' Tarrant declared. 'If you'd like to do that at once, I can wait, but would you not be wiser to think over it for a day or two, and if you wish to consider it further you could drop me a card and I'd run down again. I have rooms in Jermyn Street.'

This seemed to impress her, as he hoped it would. 'If you don't mind sitting down for a moment, I'll have a word with my daughter.'

He could not help smiling as she left the room. *By George!* He was going to pull this off, as he pulled off everything that he really tried for! And if he pulled this off, he certainly would not fail with the larger affair which lay behind it. Married to Jean Woolcombe with an adequate settlement— he'd see to that—what could he not do?

For the next fifteen minutes he abandoned himself to rosy dreams, and then Mrs Wentworth returned and to some extent at least confirmed them.

'My daughter likes the idea,' she said. 'She wants to get away as soon as possible, thinking the Italian sun would help her. I propose, if you can spare the time, to ring up Mr Margetson and ask him to come down, when we could perhaps talk it over.'

'Well,' said Tarrant, this time truly enough, 'I don't want to do anything which might seem to be hurrying you, but if you really wish it, I can't pretend not to be delighted.'

Mr Margetson proved to be a large bucolic-looking man with a hearty manner countered by a cold shrewd eye which made Tarrant feel that his one for the interview would be the literal truth.

They had a preliminary talk in which the proposal was stated, and then Tarrant diplomatically withdrew to the garden while the others continued their discussion. That the plan would go through he now felt sure. Only on one point was he still doubtful: how long a lease he could manage to secure, for he had no intention of leaving at the end of two months, whether Mrs Wentworth sold or whether she didn't.

In the end agreement was reached. The place was let to Tarrant from the beginning of the following month, some three weeks later, at an annual rent of £500, the term to be for one year, renewable from year to year by the consent of both parties. An inventory of the furniture and so on was to be made and on that day week the parties were to meet at Margetson's office in Saxham St Edmunds to read, and if approved, to sign the completed documents.

'And about a reference?' said Margetson politely as they rose to leave.

'Reference?' Tarrant returned, 'I'll do better. I'll give you a cheque for the first year's rent.'

'That will be quite satisfactory,' returned Margetson.

A week later the lease was signed. With the consent of the Braxamin directors Tarrant had borrowed £1,000 from his bank on the security of his shares, and this sum added to his ordinary income would, he reckoned, keep him going for a year in The Gables. By the end of the year, he also reckoned, he would either be engaged to Jean Woolcombe, or know that his plan had failed.

He did not wish to show eagerness, so waited a month before moving in. He had, after interviewing many applicants, selected an elderly lady named Lestrange for his companion-housekeeper. She was to undertake the entire management of the tiny estate.

The monthly meetings of the Braxamin board now gave Tarrant a lively interest. As the sale of the Remedy from the Koldkure establishment began to fall off, Hampden had shown increasing satisfaction. His charts and graphs proved that the competition had been overcome and that the Braxamin receipts were once more expanding.

But now that the new business at Lincaster was expanding,

Tarrant waited for Hampden's reaction with genuine anxiety. After all, though he thought he was safe, he knew he was taking a risk. Hampden had found the Koldkure works, and if he became suspicious he might find those at Lincaster. And Merle of course would give everything away with both hands. Merle indeed was a complete fool in some ways. She had actually re-engaged their previous vanman: a man who knew all about the Koldkure works! She had even been going to engage another Exeborough man as a travelling representative, but fortunately Tarrant had learnt about that in time to stop it.

With regard to his own connection with Lincaster, he believed that in spite of anything Merle might say, his denials would be accepted, coupled as they were with the fact he had not appeared in the matter and that every document was in her name alone. But this was by no means certain, and his game was to prevent suspicion arising. After all, he had only to hold on for a year, by the end of which, as he had already decided, he would either have married Jean or have given up the attempt. Once sure of Jean, he would close Lincaster down.

The first month on which the Braxamin sales once more diminished provoked but little remark, and the same on the second. But by the end of the third, the trend had become too strongly marked to be dismissed as merely accidental. Hampden was obviously worried as he pointed out the deterioration. A long discussion ensued, but no step was taken except that Hampden was asked to make another set of maps and graphs and to report more fully at the next meeting.

This time the figures were even worse, and the graphs showed that the same kind of thing was happening as on the previous occasion. Hampden's anxiety became positively painful as Cooke attacked him for faulty management.

After an indeterminate discussion Roberts turned to Tarrant. 'What do you say about it, Mr Tarrant?' he asked with a crooked smile. 'We look upon you as a sort of authority on this sort of thing.'

Tarrant, who had so far kept silence, now used the answer he had so carefully prepared. 'I don't like even to speak about it,' he said with a convincing air of contrition, 'because I feel that the whole thing is my fault. There's no use of course in saying I'm sorry, though I am, desperately.'

'What do you mean?' Roberts answered, while the others looked up with interest. 'How is it your fault?'

Tarrant now simulated mild surprise. 'Well, I don't know, of course, but it seemed to me clear what's happening. I showed the managers of a good many shops that I could double the standard commission on my Remedy and yet make a profit. I can only suppose they have learnt the lesson.'

They looked at him. 'You mean,' Roberts said after a pause, 'that these managers are making the stuff.'

Tarrant shrugged. 'Any chemist who knew his job could analyse my mixture and find out its composition. If I could make it up and transport it to his shop, and presumably make a profit on it, how much greater the profit if he made it up himself? My profit, transport and overhead would be added to his double commission.'

At this they were silent, then Roberts suggested grimly, 'Alternatively, someone may have copied you and set up a works.'

'I thought that less likely, though of course it's possible,' Tarrant admitted.

'Why less likely?'

'Because it would be easier to get at a works. The individual could say that what he sold had been obtained from me.'

'That's true enough.'

All of them considered the matter serious. There was a good deal more talk on the subject, though again no definite conclusion was reached. Tarrant, however, held himself in readiness to close down the Lincaster works at short notice, should this appear advisable. It would be a pity as the business was beginning to pay quite well, but until the affair of Jean Woolcombe was settled, he could not be too careful.

He had now settled down at The Gables. Miss Lestrange had proved a pleasant old lady and an admirable housekeeper, and had engaged an efficient maid. Tarrant had himself selected a chauffeur-gardener named Hughes, and had in consequence bought a second-hand Lancia for him to drive. He had also found establishments in Town where they taught fly-fishing and golf and he was making good progress in both pursuits, as well as, with another coach, improving his tennis. Finally, and most important of all, he had been invited to cocktails at St Aidan's, Jean Woolcombe's house, and given an offhand invitation to come in for tennis when he felt like it. He had felt like it on several occasions and was delighted to find himself received as an acquisition into the Woolcombe circle.

Now he worked as hard at social accomplishments as formerly he had studied chemistry. So far he had passed muster by being quiet and retiring, but he felt that to gain his ends he must assert himself, and for that he wanted more knowledge and the assurance which it brings. Every day he increased in both.

10

Hilda Maudsley Watches the Game

Jean Woolcombe was what is usually called a good sort; well intentioned, straight, kindly and generous. Yet she was weak, a sentimental fool upon whose feelings any smooth-tongued rogue could successfully play.

So at least thought her companion, Hilda Maudsley, as she attended one morning in her employer's sanctum to discuss the day's programme. For Hilda was a good deal more than a companion; She was Jean's secretary, house-keeper, agent, business manager, deputy hostess, occasional chauffeur and general factotum. She ran the house, even to the length of appointing and dismissing the servants. She dealt with Jean's correspondence, issuing invitations, refusing subscriptions other than those socially desirable, advising on knotty points raised by correspondents, and interviewing business callers. Hilda had admirable manners—when she chose—and she always did choose where Jean and her friends were concerned. In fact she made herself indispensable to Jean, who had come to depend on her far more even than she realised. In return Hilda lived like an Indian ranee and pocketed a substantial salary, most of which found its way into her satisfactorily swelling bank account.

'And then the afternoon?' she was now saying, having reminded Jean that a General Mitford and his wife were coming to lunch.

'Tennis in the afternoon,' Jean declared. 'I forgot to tell you, but I met Mr Cooke and Mr Tarrant and asked them to come. I thought we needn't ask anyone else: just a quiet set between the four of us.'

Hilda raised a mental eyelid. This Mr Tarrant! They had first met him in Town when Joynson Cooke had invited them to dinner and a show. But Cooke had not particularly wanted to make Tarrant known to them. What he had wanted was to monopolise the heiress himself, and he had done so with constancy. Tarrant was a mere make-weight, and as such his place was with the companion. But Tarrant had proved unexpectedly entertaining, indeed embarrassingly so to Cooke, and Jean had presently found an occasion for a change of partners. On saying good-night she had asked both men to call, and Tarrant had done so a week later. Then had come his renting of The Gables, after which the acquaintanceship had ripened fast. Now the parties to which Tarrant was asked were getting smaller, which Hilda considered significant.

She had been a good deal attracted to Tarrant herself on that night of the dinner. He had plenty of self-assurance without being aggressive, listened carefully to what was said to him, spoke little but to the point, and gave the impression that his companion of the moment was of all others the person whose company he most enjoyed.

But subsequent meetings caused her to change her opinion. She soon realised that a colossal selfishness was Tarrant's ruling passion, and that if he played up to Jean, it was only for what he hoped to get from her.

Perhaps it was Hilda's own character which gave her this understanding of Tarrant's. For Hilda also was an adventuress. While outwardly murmuring how nice the tennis *partie carrée* would be, her mind had really dipped back into the past and was recalling her own entry into this magic circle of wealth and luxury.

Hilda Maudsley had not always lived in luxury. In her early youth her surroundings had been happy enough, but at the age of fourteen both her parents had been killed in a motor accident, leaving her with some shares which brought in £30 a year and what personal treasures she could save from the wreck. Among these she had unrighteously secreted a pair of tiny chased duelling pistols of her father's: really the creditors' property. But she had for them a sentimental attachment, and she longed for some tangible memento of her former estate. She had gone to live with an aunt under conditions which she found very different from those of her home. It was not that her aunt was unkind, but she was poor and had found it a struggle to make ends meet before opening her house to her niece. Hilda had not only to do without a great deal that she had previously taken as a matter of course, but she had to run errands for her aunt and help in the house. Also she had to work very much harder at her new Council school than at the select establishment at which she had up to then boarded. Hilda loathed the life and everyone connected with it.

She endured it for several years, deliberately preparing for the great day on which she could strike out for herself. She was efficient, and left school with a good education, including a smattering of physical and domestic science, as well as the shorthand-typewriting and book-keeping of the commercial classes. She found a post as typist in a florist's, and shared a room with one of the sales girls. In this companionship she was unfortunate. The girl at intervals made a great deal more money than the florist ever paid her, and Hilda presently found out how it was done and began to copy her. But Hilda was ambitious, and laid her plans for a very different future than that to which her companion seemed to be heading. Hilda was discreet, and she saved money. Then on her twenty-fifth birthday she went to Monte Carlo. She had provided herself with simple but admirably cut clothes, and had enough money for a fortnight's stay in one of the best hotels. During this time she told herself that if she couldn't find some rich old man who would set her up permanently, she would throw up the sponge and put her pistols to a use of which up till now she had never thought.

Then it was that she met Jean Woolcombe.

It was in a lift in the hotel, and as always to wealthy looking strangers, she was smilingly polite. Jean took to her, and they later had some conversation, in the course of which it came out that Jean and three other women had formed a party, intending to travel by the easiest stages and most luxurious services, through Italy, Greece and the Near East. They had come as far as Monte Carlo, and here they were likely to stay, for Miss Brownlow, their courier, who had arranged everything and who alone knew where they were going or how, had met with an accident and could lead them no further.

This was Hilda's chance and she leaped at it. Though she had been willing to pay the price for its advantages, she had loathed the idea. of the elderly protector. If she could net Miss Brownlow's job, she would have the money without the man. With a charmingly deprecating air she asked Jean for an interview.

She was, it seemed, a qualified secretary, for so she described her typing. She had moreover an intimate knowledge of travelling and hotels (she had herself worked out the route to Monte Carlo and gone minutely into the tariffs of the leading hotels), and though regrettably she was poor at languages, she was from every other point of view an admirable courier. She was looking for a new post: would Miss Woolcombe give her a trial until Miss Brownlow was able to resume?

To Jean, who had been in despair about the hitch in her plans, the proposal seemed providential. Charmed by the stranger's admirable manners and elegant appearance, and urged to engage her by her friends, who were tired of Monte Carlo and wanted to move on, she forbore to take up the references to non-existent personages which Hilda had so glibly given her, and came to terms.

Hilda spent the afternoon in a desperate effort to cope with the masses of tickets, coupons, exchange regulations and official documents which the tour had amassed, and for the first time a flickering of dread that she had undertaken something beyond her capabilities began to oppress her. But as always, she proved equal to the emergency. Going to a large English travelling agency, she offered one of the clerks a fat fee if he would devote his evening to giving her a child's first guide to travel. This he did, and she spent the remainder of the night studying the documents he had left. To be bright and fresh next morning was a strain, but she managed it, and when the limousine appeared at the door, spotless and softly purring, at the precise hour arranged overnight and they left the hotel to the bows of the smiling staff, Jean felt she had obtained a treasure.

Hilda now played her cards with care and skill. She bought guide books and worked up the tour so as to know what should be looked at, and those little anecdotes which supply the salt to sightseeing. She effaced herself as much as possible, while being there on all occasions when she was wanted. Finally she tactfully waited upon Jean, forestalling her wants so unostentatiously as never to cause her embarrassment. Jean grew more and more delighted with her find.

At the end of the tour things for Hilda fell out better, not than she could have hoped, but than she could have expected. Jean asked her to come and stay at St Aidan's. Now came Hilda's most difficult problem: how to make that invitation permanent. Characteristically she gave the matter careful thought, making no move till she had worked out a satisfactory programme, and then setting herself to carry it out with deliberate efficiency.

Her first step was to ask if she might not help Jean when she saw her busy on small household duties. Jean was delighted. Hilda pursued her policy, finding, as she expected, that more and more duties were delegated to her. At last she thought herself in a strong enough position for her next step. One morning she announced sadly that she would shortly have to leave. When Jean remonstrated, she persisted: 'It *is* good of you, but I really must. You know I must get work, and as long as I stay here, I shall never do it.'

She had hoped that Jean would make the required rejoinder, but very disappointingly Jean failed to do so, and she had herself to insinuate her idea. It happened that a number of visitors were coming to the house, and deprecatingly she suggested that she might stay during this period and take over the running of the house, so as to enable Jean to spend all her time with her guests. Once again Jean was delighted and once again the experiment was a success. Then came the most critical action in Hilda's entire campaign. Once again she brought up the question of her leaving.

'Oh, stay a little longer,' Jean cried impetuously.

'Ah,' Hilda returned sadly, 'I'm afraid that's just what I can't do. You see, I can't go on like this. I must have an income. I'm not rich, you know, like someone I could name!'

This treatment by suggestion presently bore the desired fruit. Why should Hilda not stay on and run the house for Jean? The salary was nothing: that would be paid as a matter of course.

Hilda was overwhelmed by this new and unexpected idea. She didn't really think she could. She wasn't satisfied that her friend really wanted anyone, and she feared she was creating the position for her. If so, it was sweet of Jean, but of course she couldn't possibly agree. The objection sounded high minded and rather touching, though she was careful not to overdo it.

Jean reacted admirably and Hilda then began to manoeuvre for the highest salary obtainable. If Jean did mean that, she would like to do something that was *really* helpful for her money. Could she not look after the servants, the most troublesome part of Jean's work? One thing followed another. Eventually Hilda found herself practically mistress of the house, and the salary, of imposing proportions, was duly settled.

To do Hilda justice, she earned it. The household ran as

smoothly as had the tour to the Near East. As has been said, she was not only a shield between Jean and domestic trouble, but she helped to make life easy for her in countless minor ways.

They played their set in the afternoon. To big bouncing untidy Jean games were almost a religion, though Hilda's more feline temperament despised them. She, however, considered it part of her business to play, and like everything else, she did it well. The set was hotly contested, but Hilda saw to it that Jean and Tarrant won.

The time devoted to amusement, the large houses and the evidence of wealth on all sides in this charming area of Little Bitton, made Hilda bitterly jealous. These people had security, and security was what she wanted. The more of the frills of life she could add to that, the better, but security was her real goal.

This desire now turned her thoughts to what she hoped would be the last and greatest step of her upward progress: the marrying of money. In her present position she was continually meeting wealthy men. So far none of these had been possible husbands, but her chance would come. In the meantime her life was pleasant and she was saving money.

Then Tarrant appeared upon her horizon. At first she wondered was this the monied scion of nobility whom she would presently allow to lead her to the altar? But gradually she began to see through Tarrant, perhaps because his tricks were so similar to her own. Better for Jean to amuse herself with him: in the case of such an obvious adventurer nothing serious would come of it. It would at least fill her mind and enable her to take Hilda as a matter of course. Hilda therefore welcomed Tarrant and was pleasant to him, but with discretion.

From Tarrant her mind swayed towards Cooke. Cooke she disliked intensely, with his ungracious manners, his self-centred outlook, and his obsession with the turf. But he lived in a charming house on the bank of the Webble, and though tiny compared to many of his neighbours, the grounds with a comparatively small expenditure could be made delightful. It was true that Cooke came to St Aidan's with the obvious hope of marrying Jean, but to Hilda that was a minor difficulty. She felt she could deal with it easily, were it only worth her while. Of this two points aroused her doubts. The first was that obviously required renovations in the Cooke establishment had not been carried out, which might represent a lack of money. The second was that Cooke's two sisters also lived at Greenbank, and she wondered how far they had claims of ownership. They were both older than their brother, and on the few occasions when she and Jean had been at the house, they had assumed the direction of affairs.

They were an interesting, if not an attractive pair, the Cooke sisters. Miss Elmina, the elder, was tall and spiky with a large nose and a slight stoop, and was given to ritualistic observances in the village church. Miss Charlotte's preferences ran towards dachshunds, and out of her kennels at the back of the house she was reported to make a very good thing. Hilda disliked both at sight. Cooke she felt she could manage easily, but if these two overbearing women couldn't be got rid of, the game wouldn't be worth the candle.

On the whole she felt that Cooke and his doubtful assets and his omnipresent relatives were better left alone. It would be wiser to encourage him to join in the race for Jean, still further directing her attention away from herself and the grip she was obtaining on the household.

Beside Tarrant and Cooke many had entered for the Jean Woolcombe stakes. Jean was nice to them all, but so far Hilda would not have given a great deal for the chances of any of them. They seemed mildly to amuse Jean and gave her an interest in life, but Hilda imagined she saw why most of them were there, and except perhaps in the case of Tarrant, she appeared to remain completely heart-whole. But Tarrant was the newcomer, and it was in accordance with precedent that he should have a temporary advantage.

Unhappily none of these fortune hunters would be of any use to Hilda. And the monied men who came to St Aidan's were mostly elderly and brought their wives. Altogether the prospects for her next step were not so bright as she could have wished, and she began to consider whether a season in Town was not indicated. She decided to suggest the idea to Jean.

11

Peter Temple Faces Panic

The months which brought James Tarrant a growing anxiety in connection with the new Works were for Peter Temple a period of increasing satisfaction in the same. Tarrant feared for discovery and the consequent loss of all his hopes. Peter rejoiced because his management had proved a success and pleased Merle.

They had had a strenuous and to Peter a wholly delightful time in setting the business going. Under Tarrant's secret direction Merle had found a suitable shed and fixed up a five-year lease. He had given her the necessary money in cash and she had banked it in her own name, paying it out by her own cheques. Tarrant had also designed the name boards and paper headings: 'Patt's Powders for the Pate. J. A. Patterson. Manufacturer of Headache Powders, etc.,' but Merle and Peter had ordered the plant and materials and engaged the staff.

During these months Peter never once saw Tarrant, though very occasionally Merle met him in Town. On these occasions she invariably returned in low spirits and Peter's hatred of Tarrant as invariably flared up again.

Peter was now satisfied from his own observation that Merle loved Tarrant, and he had been careful never to say or do anything which might reveal his own feelings. But he found that this repression meant an ever-growing struggle, in which the fear of defeat was always present.

As one result of his attitude, they had become much better friends. She now took him into her confidence, not only in everything connected with the Works, but also in many small personal interests. Among these was her chemical research, which she believed was at last going to yield that improvement to the Remedy which she had so long sought. Unsatisfactory as the position remained, to Peter this intimacy seemed wonderful.

Then it was that the first of two incidents occurred, each of which was profoundly to affect both their lives.

One day when going on business to Town, Peter idly began to read a paper which some earlier traveller had left in the compartment. It was the *Saxham St Edmunds Weekly Gazette*, and under the heading of 'Little Bitton' his eyes caught a familiar face. It was a small inset photograph and the adjoining paragraph read:

We understand that for reasons of health Mrs and Miss Wentworth of. The Gables are going to reside in Italy. The house has been let to Mr J. P. Tarrant, of London. Mr Tarrant, who is interested in the chemical industry, is also a fisherman, a golfer and an expert tennis player.

Peter could scarcely believe his eyes. Tarrant then had come into funds. He had understood from Merle that the man had nothing, that all his savings had been put into

141

the Koldkure Works, and that all the resultant profits had been used to start their present venture. Tarrant must therefore have lied to Merle. Peter's hate for him once again seethed up hot and furious. Tarrant was paying Merle—and Peter himself—comparatively tiny salaries, on the grounds that the business could afford no more, while he himself was renting expensive country houses and amusing himself with fishing and golf! Bitterly Peter determined that imperative demands for increases for them both must at once be sent in.

The paragraph had angered him, but he was not prepared for the effect it had on Merle, when that evening he showed it to her. She grew deadly pale and for a time seemed unable to speak. Then after a few rather tremulous remarks she decisively changed the subject.

It was not till a week later that she told him she had written to Tarrant. He had replied by telephone that he had hired the house as a surprise for her, and that it had used up all his money, but when he was able to accumulate a little more they could be married.

Peter received the information with mixed feelings. That she could tell him such a thing showed what excellent friends they had become. On the other hand, he was depressed by the suggestion of losing her, though not so much as if he had believed in Tarrant's intention. He scarcely admitted it to himself, but Peter's hope was that Tarrant would let Merle down—and what a magnificent thing for Merle!—and that he himself might marry her, as he put it, on the rebound.

At the same time he saw that a joint demand for increases was out of the question. If Tarrant was really saving up to marry Merle, she wouldn't, and he couldn't, make it.

A few days later Merle surprised him by saying: 'I'm feeling a little tired and run down and I'm going to take an occasional holiday. Tomorrow I shall not be in. You might look after things for me, and Rose Jordan will keep you straight on the clerical side.'

'Why not take a proper holiday?' he answered. 'Rose and I could carry on.'

'I know you could,' she smiled, 'but I don't really need that. Just a day now and then.'

Rose Jordan was the new Edith Horne, an efficient girl, though neither so helpful nor so pleasant as her Koldkure predecessor. However, there was little to be done on that particular day and things went as well as if Merle had been present.

The same thing happened on other occasions. Merle did not say where she went, but after each absence she seemed more depressed and unhappy. Peter grew greatly concerned about her, but he dared not try to force her confidence. Then one day she told him of her own accord where she had been.

'I suppose it was very bad of me, Peter, but I just couldn't help it. I felt I must see that house. I went to Little Bitton and had a look at it.'

'I can well understand,' he assured her. 'Did you see Tarrant?'

She appeared slightly embarrassed. 'Well, no,' she answered. 'I didn't actually go to the house, you understand. I just wanted to see what it was like. It's on a river and at the other side of the river there's a road, and I walked along the road and—had a look.'

Once again fury against Tarrant boiled up in Peter's mind. He did not dare to glance at Merle, for he felt she was not far from tears. That she would confide in him on such a subject gave him a shock. It showed him how desperately lonely she must be. The urge to take her in his arms and smother her with kisses was almost insupportable. But he resisted it.

'That's interesting,' he said with creditable detachment. 'I wish I had been there to have a look with you. What's the place like?'

'Charming,' she said. 'A delightful old house, covered with creepers. Of course, it was some distance away and I couldn't see all the details.'

'It must be delightful.'

Merle was evidently relieved at having told him and was now speaking more normally. 'An extraordinary coincidence happened,' she went on. 'As I was walking along the road opposite The Gables I met an old friend whom I hadn't seen since before I went to Exeborough: Elsie Oates.'

'Who is Elsie Oates?'

'Oh, you wouldn't know, of course. She was a nurse at the same place where I nursed, Wilton Grange Convalescent Home. I told you about it.'

'I remember.'

'She was rather a pal of mine, too, but I hadn't heard of her since I left. It seems they live there, she and her mother, along that very road. Extraordinary, isn't it?'

'Small world and all that.'

'They came in for a microscopic legacy, she told me, and that allowed her to leave the Home and nurse her mother, who's an invalid.'

'Pity, I should say. She might have had a career, but now her life will be spoilt.'

He was delighted to hear a faint gurgle of laughter. 'I

don't know that "career" is quite the word for a nurse in a convalescent home,' Merle observed. 'At all events she's pleased with the change. She insisted on my going home with her and having tea. Tiny cottage they live in, but all so nice and comfy.'

'But then,' said Peter, and suddenly he would have stopped if it hadn't been too late, 'she must have known Tarrant? I mean, if they were living in the same village?'

'She didn't know him personally,' and the change in Merle's tone made Peter's heart ache; 'but she knew who he was. She was full of the whole thing. She had met Miss Lestrange, his housekeeper, who, she says, is very nice. He's believed to have come into a legacy.'

Merle took one or two other holidays, and though she did not say where she had gone, Peter imagined it was back to Little Bitton. His blood boiled when he thought of the situation. Tarrant he believed to be a thorough paced scoundrel and he thought no fate could be too bad for him for his treatment of Merle. Peter could see how Merle's longings and her pride were urging in opposite directions. She could not resist going to see the house, but her pride would not allow her to approach Tarrant. Peter went to see it, too, though he did not tell Merle. The visit made him more than ever determined that some day, somehow, Tarrant should be made to pay.

Months passed and then occurred the second incident which was so profoundly to alter both their lives.

It happened that after supper one Friday evening—it was the 17th of March and neither of them were likely ever to forget the date—Peter went round to see Merle at her rooms. Owing to some business in a neighbouring town he could not be at the Works next morning and he had remembered certain matters which he wanted her to see to in his absence. He went in with a cheery word, but on seeing her stopped dead and stood staring blankly.

'For goodness sake, Merle! What's wrong?' he stammered at length. She was ghastly, with an expression of utter despair on her face.

She made no answer, simply shaking her head. Then his eye fell on a paper and very gently he picked it up. She watched him as if dazed.

It was the current number of the *Saxham St Edmunds Weekly Gazette*. He had seen the paper in her room more than once since the day he had found the copy in the train, and could imagine why she was taking it. Now it was turned to the Personal and Society column and the first paragraph read:

The engagement is announced between J. Pettigrew Tarrant, of The Gables, Little Bitton, and Jean, only daughter of the late General Sir Swinton Woolcombe, K.C.B., C.B.E., D.S.O., of St Aidan's, also in Little Bitton.

Peter's heart leaped. Here was news and no mistake! What a vista it opened up! Merle could no longer consider herself engaged to Tarrant and in her loneliness she might turn to him. Peter was not selfish in this. He honestly believed that she would have been miserable with Tarrant and that he himself could make her happy.

'Merle dear,' he murmured, 'I'm sorry.'

She stared vacantly, then began to laugh unpleasantly. 'Sorry!' she repeated. 'Is that all you can say?'

'No,' he answered earnestly. 'I'm sorry for anything that

distresses you, as you know very well. But I'm not sorry you're not going to marry Tarrant: let me say it, there's no use in pretending. My dear, he wouldn't have made you happy. He only thinks of himself.'

Merle roused herself. 'Happy!' she cried, and her voice rose and got shrill as she talked. 'Happy! It's been just hell since I met him. Just hell all the time. He took everything. He took my love. He took my job. He took my money, my conscience, my honour: everything! And he promised to marry me! He never meant it: not from the first. He lied to me from the very beginning.' She sprang to her feet and began pacing up and down. 'Oh,' she cried wildly, 'how I *hate* him! I wish he was dead. I hope he may suffer and suffer!'

She frightened Peter. She seemed as if possessed, so different from the steady, well-balanced Merle he had always known. He realised that it was that very steadiness, those feelings always so carefully repressed, which had caused the present outburst. There had been no safety valve, and the pressure had risen too high. He got up and put an arm round her in a brotherly way.

'My clear,' he said in a steady voice, 'you mustn't give way like this. Pull yourself together, and you'll be better in a moment.'

'Everything he said was false,' she shouted in a complete frenzy. 'He was just a living lie! I wish he was dead! I could kill him myself! I will kill him!' She struggled for a moment in his arms, then suddenly burst into a wild fit of crying.

He held her without speaking or trying to check her tears. It was pure hysteria of course, though none the less serious for that. Presently she began to quiet down. He remained with his arms round her, and at last the sobbing died away and she turned to him.

'Oh, Peter, what a comfort you are. I've been mad, I think. Don't mind what I said. I didn't mean it.'

'Of course you didn't,' he answered stolidly, though again his heart leaped. 'You're just a bit upset, and very natural, too. You could do with a drink. Got any spirits in the place?'

'No: I don't want any. Oh, I'm so ashamed of myself,' she went on, 'I don't know what came over me. It never happened before. Peter, you must forget all this. I wasn't normal, but I'm all right now.'

'It was nothing,' he assured her. 'We all get little turns like that. A mere momentary—what shall we say?—aberration. And now a tactful change of subject. I forgot to ask you to do a little job for me in the morning, as I'm going over to Fowler's.'

That night for Peter Temple the world was a brighter and more glorious place than it had been since the day on which Merle made him works manager, 'Oh, Peter, what a comfort you are!' What could he have hoped for more than that? She would get over this Tarrant business after a time, and then—then would come his turn!

Next day Peter duly paid his call at Fowler's. He did not get back till after the Works had closed, then after lunch he went again to Merle's rooms. She would, he was sure, be lonely and depressed and she might be persuaded to come for a walk or a bus drive out into the country. What joy that would be for him!

Merle's landlady, Mrs Benson, opened the door. 'Miss Weir has gone out,' she told him. 'Came back at the usual time and went out about half an hour ago.'

'Oh!' Peter felt dashed. The afternoon which had been bright and sunny suddenly grew grey. 'She didn't say where she was going, I suppose?'

'No, not a word.' Mrs Benson looked at him searchingly. 'To tell you the truth, Mr Temple, I'm not too happy about her. I don't think she's well.'

'Good Lord, Mrs Benson! What's the matter?'

'She didn't eat any breakfast or lunch to speak of and she was quite short when I asked her was the egg not fresh. Quite short! And that's not like Miss Weir. Then she seemed all upset in her manner.'

She was a good sort, Mrs Benson, kindly and fond of Merle, but a terrible talker. Peter crushed down his own anxiety. Her mouth must be stopped.

'She's a bit worried about a small fire we had at the Works,' he lied. 'Lost some papers that she valued. Nothing serious really, but hard lines on her.'

It was not a very good effort and Peter was not proud of it, but on the spur of the moment he could do no better. Mrs Benson looked at him, he thought, a trifle sceptically. 'Oh, well,' she said, 'I'm glad if it wasn't serious.' Peter cursed himself as he turned away. Why had he not stayed at the Works that morning? His business with Fowler's people was not urgent, and could have been postponed. He thought for a moment, then his anxiety got the better of him and he walked down a smaller street and rang at another door.

It was opened by a big middle-aged woman with a clever dependable face. This was Joyce Caldwell, the Works' forewoman.

'Sorry to worry you, Joyce,' Peter greeted her, 'but I'm looking for Miss Weir and she's gone out. I wondered if she said where she was going?'

He didn't for a moment expect that she had, but he was anxious and wanted to be sure that nothing abnormal had taken place at the Works. He thought Joyce looked at him strangely.

'She didn't say, Mr Temple.' She spoke slowly as if choosing her words and he felt sure that there was more to follow. His fears mounted.

'What is it?' he asked, though smiling as if it was a joke. 'I can see you're not telling me everything.'

Joyce was obviously unwilling to speak, but at length she told him. Merle, it appeared, had been very strange in her manner all the morning. She was preoccupied and evidently had something serious on her mind. When Joyce had reported a mistake in one of the letters, she found Merle had not been listening, and she had had to repeat her story all over again. Even then Merle had not appeared to grasp the matter and had told Joyce to see Peter about it later, though it had nothing to do with Peter. This was utterly unlike Merle. Then about eleven she had gone out. She had given Joyce the impression that she had wanted to do so all the morning and that she had suddenly found herself unable to resist her urge any longer. When Peter suggested that this was rather fanciful, Joyce admitted that it might be so, but that it was the way it had struck her. Merle had returned some half an hour later and she seemed then very much excited and upset. Another girl had been waiting with a question about her work, but Merle had refused to listen to her, telling her to wait till Monday. She had remained in her room with the door shut until the Works had closed.

'She looked very badly,' Joyce ended up, 'like I never saw her before. Not ill, you know, but sort of—I don't know how to describe it—sort of desperate. I was a bit frightened. She looked as if—as if she might do herself harm, if you know what I mean.'

150

Peter's anxiety was now very real. He could not banish from his mind the look he had seen in her eyes, when she had cried: 'I hate him! I could kill him myself! I will kill him!' At that moment, given the opportunity, she would undoubtedly have done what she said. It was true that she had quietened down later, but she had probably been brooding for the entire night over her injury. Even with Merle, it was impossible to say to what dreadful conclusion an abnormally heated brain might not have driven her. Again Peter bitterly regretted that he had not cancelled his engagement, so as to be available in case of need.

But being wise after the event was merely futile. Suppose Merle had gone to Little Bitton to see Tarrant? If so, was there a fear of her doing anything rash? Still more important, could he help her? It was at least worth trying.

How did you get to Little Bitton? He turned into a newsagent's and bought a time-table. It was not so very far; about forty miles in a westerly direction. Rail, he quickly saw, was no good. But a bus left at half-past every hour for Saxham St Edmunds, from which after ten minutes' wait another bus went on to Ralston, this latter passing through Little Bitton. Merle had left her rooms about a quarter-past two, and it was about ten minutes' walk to the bus station. It looked as if she had gone for the two-thirty bus. Peter's face grew graver. Oh, how he hoped she was all right! At all events it was now clear what he must do. He must catch the next bus. Perhaps he could find her and see that no harm was done.

He had time, sitting in the bus, gazing with unseeing eyes at the whirling trees and hedges, to indulge his fears to the utmost. Had she really gone to see Tarrant? Normally, of course, she would not do anything seriously wrong. But

151

last night she had really seemed off her head. She had threatened murder, and worse still, she had looked it. Of course Tarrant had asked for it. Peter felt that he could kill him himself.

He wondered what he should do when he reached Little Bitton. Off at once to The Gables, he supposed, and ask there for Merle. Or would it be better to take that road she had described at the other side of the river, and enlist that nurse's help? What was her name? Oh, yes, Elsie Oates. But this would give Merle away to Elsie. Well, that couldn't be helped. Elsie knew the district and might be an immense help.

The bus stop in Saxham St Edmunds was in front of a municipal park and under the trees at the back of the footpath were seats, all well occupied on this fine day. Peter began pacing up and down in front of the seats. Suddenly he heard his name called.

It was Rose Jordan, the Works' clerk, who had obtained leave that day to help with her sister's children, and who was now taking them for a walk.

'Hullo, Rose,' said Peter, trying desperately to appear normal. 'Sorry to hear you've been having trouble. Your sister, is it?'

'Yes, Mr Temple. Taken ill last night suddenly. My other sister'll be here on Monday, but there was no one to help today but me.'

He smiled with a great effort. 'That's all right. You'll hardly believe it, but we managed to get on.'

'What's all the Works coming to Saxham for?' went on Rose, speaking jokingly, but eyeing him closely. 'Here am I, and I saw Miss Weir not an hour ago getting into the Ralston bus. And now you're here.'

Then he was right! Merle had gone to see Tarrant! He controlled himself with a supreme effort.

'Well,' he joked, 'I suppose you know why *you're* here.' Then, proud of his presence of mind, he went on: 'As for Miss Weir and myself, we were asked to tea in Ralston, but I was delayed and so I'm following her.'

'She looked worried, did Miss Weir. I hope there was nothing wrong.'

'She probably thought she was going to be late,' Peter improvised. 'Did you speak to her?'

'No, she didn't see me.'

That was not so bad. Peter made another joking remark, then feeling he could stand no more, began his pacing again. When a couple of minutes later the Ralston bus drew in, he stepped on board.

In his mind was a growing feeling of foreboding. What would he find at Little Bitton? Pray God, Merle had not lost her head. As for Tarrant; if he had been making Merle suffer, then—

Peter set his teeth to choke back his almost insane fury. His impatience became an agony as he sat waiting for the bus to start.

12

Joseph French Receives a Call

At just eleven o'clock on the following morning Chief Inspector Joseph French emerged from his kitchen door into the tiny strip of garden at the rear of his house. He was dressed in a disreputable pair of grey flannel trousers and an old brown paint-spotted coat, and his pipe hung lazily from the corner of his mouth, as it would never hang if he were really at work. He crossed to a small shed, took out a spade, and then stood directing a predatory eye upon his microscopic plot of grass.

Though it might be thought that a spot of gardening on a fine Sunday morning was an innocent amusement enough for a typical British householder, there was something furtive in French's manner. He looked as if he was doing what he knew he ought not, and taking a risk about it too. For a moment he hesitated, then seeming to screw up his courage afresh, he boldly plunged the spade edgewise into the grass, the first step towards cutting a sod.

The truth was that he was now about to settle an age-long controversy with his wife. He wanted the path to their little

154

summerhouse in the corner of the garden to wind across the grass, round two small trees, instead of going, as it did, in a mathematically straight line down the centre. His Em was for the *status quo*, not because she did not like curves, but because the work would 'upset' the garden. She had, however, now gone to church, and French, having more than a clear hour at his disposal, had determined to take the bull by the horns and present her with a *fait accompli* on her return.

He had surreptitiously marked the line of the new path on the previous evening, and now he began lifting the sods, cutting them thick, so that they would bring the old path, after the gravel had been removed for re-use, up to the proper level. He did not expect to have finished before Mrs French returned, but he hoped to have done so much that it would be easier to complete the work than to restore it.

Unhappily his efforts were not destined to be successful. He had scarcely cut a dozen sods when his telephone bell shrilled. Placidly he said 'Damn,' and went in to get the message.

It was from the Yard, as he had feared. It appeared that Major Carling, the Chief Constable of Greenshire, had applied for help in a case of suspected murder which had just been discovered, and the A.C. would like French to go down. The Major was at the police station at Little Bitton, a village some five miles north-east of Saxham St Edmunds, and would wait there for French.

'Right,' said French. 'Call Carter and I'll be along directly.'

He stared ruefully at his embryo path, wondering if he might take the time to replace the sods already cut. Then duty triumphing over desire, he had instead a quick wash and change, packed a suitcase, left a note for his Em and set off to the Yard.

He was too old a hand to give more than a passing thought to the tragedy in which he was so soon to become involved, but he did wonder about Little Bitton. The location of his work made a difference. In picturesque surroundings and with a comfortable hotel to retire to, a country job might become pleasantly like a holiday. He had been lucky in having some such, but they were few and far between.

Sergeant Carter was waiting for him at the Yard. 'I've got your murder bag in the car, sir,' he greeted him. 'Shall I put that suitcase in with it?'

French handed it over while he went to see Major Carling's message.

'No details,' he was told. 'Just that they're on to a murder and they haven't the staff to deal with it. Better get on. The C.C.'s waiting for you.'

'Unless they give me an airplane, he'll have to wait,' French snorted, and went down again to the car.

He enjoyed the drive north. The country he loved at all times, but on this fine mid-March day it was vibrant with the fresh life of spring rising all around. The air was thin and clear and invigorating and the sun bright, if not actually hot. He appreciated the change the more, because for several months he had been but little away from headquarters. In fact, since that case of the burning of Forde Manor, which had taken him a good many times to Paris, he had only once had an outside job. It was a strange thought that what was giving him this healthy pleasure should be in itself foul and evil. He supposed that he and those like him were a sort of moral scavengers, trying to get rid of crime or at least to clear away its effects.

They drove along the main northern thoroughfare to

156

Saxham St Edmunds, then branched right for Little Bitton. French was delighted when he saw the beauty of the district and the charm of the little village. More like Devonshire or the better parts of Surrey, he thought, than the flatter country of the Eastern Midlands.

A sergeant met them at the tiny police station.

'The C.C. said that as it's nearly one, it would be better to begin with lunch,' he explained. 'He's gone back to Saxham, and I'm to show you the hotel. He's fixed the conference for two o'clock.'

'Right, sergeant,' French answered pleasantly. 'Lunch will suit us down to the ground. Where is the hotel?'

It was a small place but surprisingly comfortable. 'It's the fishing folk,' the sergeant explained as he helped them in with their suitcases. 'There's not much fishing about this part of the country except just here, and anglers come, and they want everything just so. You'll be comfortable all right. Then two o'clock, sir?' Again he saluted and withdrew.

The fulfilment of his prophecy began with an admirable lunch, and an hour later the two Yard men returned to the police station. A Lancia outside the door showed that Major Carling had already returned. He proved to be a middle-aged man, with a bald head, a clipped moustache and a military bearing. His manner was pleasant and his expression kindly, and French at once took to him.

With him was a big heavy-faced man, Superintendent Hawkins of Saxham St Edmunds, the headquarters town for the area. Their friend the sergeant was now formally presented as Sergeant Osborne, head of the local force, with Constable Coleman representing the force itself.

'Sit down, Chief Inspector, and you, sergeant,' Major Carling looked at Carter. 'Can we all fit in? What about you, super? If there are no more chairs, can't Coleman get a couple of boxes?'

They found seats presently and all looked expectantly at the Chief Constable.

'We asked your people to send us help, Chief Inspector,' he began, 'because we have just discovered what looks like a murder, and our C.I.D. inspector who looks after this area is ill and we can't spare anyone to replace him. You have your own sergeant to help you, but I wish to begin by saying that all our resources are naturally at your disposal.'

'Thank you, sir,' said French dutifully.

'You'll find Mr Hawkins very helpful if you want anything, and of course Osborne and Coleman will work under your direction.'

Rather unnecessary, all this, French thought: it surely might be taken for granted. But he only repeated his acknowledgment.

'Now,' continued Carling, 'I'll give you an outline of what has happened, and then you can ask any questions that occur to you.' He made the orator's pause, glanced at some notes, then went on:

'About 8.30 last night, Saturday, Osborne was rung up by a Miss Lestrange, housekeeper to a Mr Tarrant who lives close to the village, to say that she had just found Mr Tarrant's body in the river which flows past their grounds and that she feared he was drowned. She seemed very much upset and wanted help at once. Osborne sent Coleman for Dr Hands and hurried down to Tarrant's house, The Gables. There he found Miss Lestrange almost in a state of collapse, but she was able to tell him that the body was in a pool just below a certain footbridge. "I couldn't lift him out of the water," she added; "do go down quickly." Osborne reassured her and hurried down to the river. Be sure to correct me, Osborne, if I go wrong.'

'Quite correct, sir.'

'The Gables is a pleasant little cottage on the side of the Webble Valley, 'and its grounds slope down to the water's edge. Across the river is uncultivated ground, with boulders and rough grass and a few trees and bushes. It forms a really charming little valley and the river is a typical trout stream with deepish pools separated by stony reaches. Rather unexpected for this part of England, but I believe it's a volcanic outcrop of rock which gives us our broken country.'

'It reminded me of Devon,' French said as the other paused.

'Yes, it's very similar. You'll see it for yourself, of course, but you must know the setting to appreciate the story. It seems that ownership of the cottage includes the fishing rights along the river adjoining, and Tarrant had put up a plank footbridge opposite his place so that he could also fish from the opposite bank, which is open to the public. Osborne crossed this and found the body as Miss Lestrange had said, in a pool immediately below it. He dragged the body ashore and started artificial respiration, though he believed it would be no use. Dr Hands then came on the scene and took it over. Between them they kept it up for an hour, but the man was dead. They then brought the body back to the house and Osborne began to get statements.

'Miss Lestrange had somewhat recovered. She said that the deceased had taken the house about nine months earlier and had engaged her as housekeeper. There was one maid, Kate, and a gardener-chauffeur, who at that time had gone home.

'Mr Tarrant had been in London for a couple of days

159

and had returned that morning in time for lunch. He said he was going fishing after lunch and gave orders for his tea-basket to be ready. He was very fond of tea and when going fishing invariably took a thermos and a few sandwiches. He left about half-past two, saying he would be back for dinner at half-past seven.

'On such occasions he was usually in by seven, but this time he didn't turn up. They held back dinner, but when eight o'clock came and there was still no sign of him, Miss Lestrange decided to go and look for him. Then it was that she saw his body in the pool. Rather pluckily she tried to drag it out, but she couldn't do so, and she ran back to the house and telephoned here.'

Major Carling once more paused and glanced at his papers. Telling his story rather well, French thought. He could see it all happening. It was true, as he remembered with secret amusement, that he had frequently received a definite and vivid mental image of a locality from someone's description, and when he had afterwards seen the place, it had proved quite incorrect. However, the tale was all very clear and circumstantial.

'Though at this time Osborne has no suspicion that the death was other than accidental, he was puzzled as to what exactly had taken place. It looked as if the deceased had slipped off the bridge while crossing, but he was wearing waders, and he might have been fishing at that point. Osborne glanced round to see if he could find a rod or basket, but nothing of the kind was in view. He realised of course that a fisherman scrambling about over the stones in the river bed might easily have fallen. But the pool in which the body was found was not deep: four or five feet, you thought, Osborne?'

160

'I guessed that last night, sir,' the sergeant answered, 'but this morning I measured it. It was four feet six deep.'

'Quite. Well, the pool was not, only not deep, but it was easy to get out of. Osborne therefore supposed that the deceased must have hurt himself when he fell. But he had noticed no injury on the body. You therefore asked the doctor to make an examination?'

'Well, sir,' the sergeant moved uneasily, 'I didn't just like to do that. But I mentioned to him that I didn't see why the man was drowned.'

'Ah, quite so. And what did he say?'

'He gave me a queer look, sir. "I don't either," he said, "and therefore I'm going to suggest a P.M. He might have had a heart attack, but I naturally couldn't tell that from a mere inspection."'

'So that was how the question of a post-mortem arose? I see. Well, it was carried out last night by Dr Hands and the police doctor from Saxham. I have the report here. You can study it at your leisure, Chief Inspector, but in layman's language it simply says that death was directly due to drowning, that the deceased was in a perfectly healthy condition, that there were no traces of violence, *and*—and—this was really rather unexpected—that the body contained a large dose of aconitine, large enough to have caused death.'

'Very unusual indeed, sir,' French commented, feeling that appreciation was desired.

'Well, to go back to Osborne. He had a walk along the opposite bank of the river, and there he found the tea-basket. Tea had been taken and the basket repacked. He marked the spot and brought the basket back to the house.

'When he heard of the aconitine, he saw that the basket might be important. He therefore went early this morning

161

to The Gables and got the basket put under lock and key, as well as everything that remained of the deceased's lunch. I think you did very well, Osborne.'

'Thank you very much, sir.'

'Osborne of course had reported to Superintendent Hawkins, and Mr Hawkins told me. We both came over here early this morning and had a conference. The first thing obviously was to arrange for the analysis of the food Osborne had collected, and the examination of the teacup and flask, in the hope that there were sufficient dregs for testing purposes. Then we discussed the possibilities.

'First, there was accident. On the face of it, accident was unlikely. Few people are normally in possession of aconitine, and even if there had been some in the house, it was difficult to see how it could have accidentally got into the deceased's food. We had to keep an open mind, of course, but provisionally we dismissed accident.'

The C.C. paused and French dutifully made his comment. 'Only a very remarkable coincidence could account for it, I should think, sir.'

'So we thought. Then there was suicide. This seemed no less improbable. Here was a man in good circumstances, possessed of a delightful house and place, and engaged to an heiress. He was in excellent health and in a perfectly normal condition at lunch and had gone to amuse himself fishing. It seemed beyond belief that he could have had intended to kill himself. Again we had to keep an open mind, but again we provisionally dismissed suicide.

'That left murder. Here the probabilities were more obvious. The very facts which tended against suicide pointed towards murder. The deceased's prosperity and his engagement might have fed some rival's jealousy. We knew nothing

162

about the man and had no idea what cause for hatred he might have given. It was evident that murder couldn't be ruled out and that the affair must therefore be fully investigated.'

This pause French met with a half bow, half nod.

'The question then arose: who was to investigate? As I said, the inspector who does such work in this area is ill and all our people are busy with a wave of burglary cases: I therefore rang up the Yard and asked for help and I think, Mr Hawkins, we're fortunate in having the Chief Inspector here.'

The super smiled heavily. 'He won't bless us, sir, doing him out of his Sunday.'

'No: too bad, Chief Inspector. However, that's life. Now what would you like to do? The inquest opens at five o'clock this afternoon, but there will be an adjournment after evidence of identification and so on has been taken. You could attend that or go and see the body or the place or whatever you like. Osborne will be at your disposal if you want him.'

French considered. 'I'd like to see the place first and then the body. I think I'll give the inquest a miss.'

'Right. Then Osborne can go with you, but he'll have to come back shortly to prepare for the inquest.'

'If he shows me where it happened, he can go.'

'Right. Then the best of good luck to you.'

Ten minutes later French turned his car into the drive of The Gables, and with Carter and Osborne walked across the lawn towards the river. It was certainly a charming place. The house, small but dignified, nestled among fine trees on a sort of little plateau projecting from the side of the valley. From there the sward and flower beds sloped down to the water's edge. The other side of the valley was picturesque in a different way with its coarse grass, outcroppings of rock, gorse and shrubby trees. Some little distance beyond, on what seemed the edge of the valley, French could see vehicles passing along a road.

At the bottom of the garden was a primitive footbridge, a single plank with a rope handrail. The river was, however, just a large stream, not more than twenty feet wide, and anything up to three or four deep. About ten feet below the bridge was the fatal pool. French stood looking round while Osborne pointed out just where the body had been lying.

'Very good,' said French. 'Now show us where you found the tea-basket and you can get away.'

Osborne led them a couple of hundred yards down stream.

'That's the place, sir,' he pointed. 'He must have sat on that rock while he was having his tea.'

'Very good,' French repeated. 'Don't let's tramp it more than we can help.'

Osborne pointed across the river to a house which marched with Tarrant's.

'That place is empty,' he explained, 'and the deceased had taken the fishing rights as well as his own. That gave him over half a mile of the stream. He was very fond of fishing, I understand, but not particularly good at it.'

'Is it good fishing?' French asked.

'I believe so, sir. I'm not a fisherman myself. Then if that's all, I'll be off.' He saluted and disappeared.

French stood looking round him.

'Now, Carter,' he said presently, 'go down stream and see if you can find any fishing things: rod, creel, or anything of the kind.'

Carter moved down the bank while French stood looking about the little knoll. He scarcely expected to find anything useful, but there was always the chance. Matches, tobacco ash, footprints, scraps of paper: in all such many a clue had lain. But none such were to be seen. Not even could he find traces of tea leaves or milky spots on the ground which might furnish material for analysis.

Carter, it presently appeared, had had more luck. A little farther along the bank he had found a rod and a basket containing two small trout. There were flies on the hooks and the rod was evidently ready for a cast.

'I walked on beyond where the rod was lying,' went on Carter, 'and I found some footprints. I think you ought to see them, sir, though of course I can't say that they're anything to do with this.'

'I'm sure you can't, Carter. All right, come along.'

As they went down stream the valley narrowed and the road, drawing gradually in, crossed it by a bridge which French imagined would lead direct into Little Bitton village. The rod was lying just in sight of this bridge.

About fifty yards beyond the rod a colony of rabbits had thrown out a number of patches of yellow sand, and these were covered with prints. French stood trying to read their story. At first they seemed just a confused medley made by many passers-by, but gradually he came to the conclusion that only two men had been present and that these had been standing facing each other, though stepping about while they talked. None of the prints was very clear, but French selected the four sharpest—one right and left of each man—and with material from his 'murder bag' took casts. Whether or not they had anything to do with the affair, it was wise to make records.

Before leaving, the two men had a general look round, not only along the bank itself, but also over the whole uncultivated slope. The road, they found, was narrow and bore but little traffic. It was separated from the bank by a straggling hedge in which were a number of unfenced gaps. In two of these they found footprints.

The gaps were close together, both nearly opposite the knoll on which the tea-basket had been found, and each bore two sets of prints, one going and one returning. Here unfortunately the sand was soft and running and the prints were completely blurred: French could not even say whether they were men's or women's. All he could tell was that one person seemed to have passed in each direction through each gap.

French then returned to the pool in which the body had been found. After some consideration it seemed to him that Tarrant must have fallen off the bridge. A slip from it into the stream would almost certainly lead to the pool, and though Tarrant was wearing waders, the fact that the rod was some hundreds of yards away showed that he was not fishing. But why he should slip off the bridge, or why, having done so, he should not have climbed out of the pool, was not so clear. French felt that before he could get much farther he must see the doctor, and returning to the car, he drove back to the village.

Dr Hands was tall, thin and stooped; efficient-looking, but with a rather pedantic manner. 'I heard you had come, Chief Inspector,' he greeted French gravely. 'Won't you sit down and tell me what I can do for you?'

'It's about the poison principally, doctor,' French returned. 'I'd be grateful for anything you can tell me about it.'

Dr Hands leant back in his desk chair and put his

finger-tips together. 'The poison was aconitine,' he answered, 'and the deceased had taken a comparatively large close. I cannot of course say how much, as our test was purely preliminary and the organs have gone for a more detailed analysis. I am, however, safe in saying that it was enough to have proved fatal if the man had not been drowned.'

'I follow you. Now about that drowning. It's not at all clear what took place. Would you please tell me the effect of the poison?'

'It's a rapid poison as well as deadly,' Hands answered, a faint suggestion of the lecturing professor in his manner. 'The first effect is a tingling in the mouth, which rapidly becomes numb and then painful. This may occur within a minute or two of taking the poison. Pains in the stomach usually follow, with increasing numbness in the limbs, which eventually may lose their power altogether. The—eh?' he asked as French interrupted him.

'That explains the fall off the bridge,' French declared with sudden enlightenment. 'He took the poison, felt ill, and started to return to the house, By the time he reached the bridge his legs had grown weak and he. slipped into the stream. How does that theory appeal to you, doctor?'

'I think it's quite likely,' Hands agreed, 'and it also explains why he was drowned. Owing to the loss of power in his limbs he was unable to scramble out of the pool.'

French was pleased. This was progress.

'Quite so, sir. Now you say the symptoms would appear in a very short time. Do you think the deceased could have been poisoned at lunch, having regard to the fact that after it he got his rod and tea-basket, walked some hundreds of yards, and fished for at least a little time? He had apparently caught two trout.'

'I should think,' Dr Hands returned, 'that most unlikely. Had the poison been taken at lunch, I don't think he would have gone out to fish at all. He would have felt too ill.'

'Then it's more likely that he took at it teatime?'

'That of course I couldn't say. But assuming he did take tea and that he took nothing else, I should then agree with you.'

'Quite,' said French, repressing a smile. 'One other point. How can aconitine be obtained?'

'It could be bought at any chemist's, though the poison book would have to be signed. Or it could be extracted from a number of plants, *aconitum napellus*, for example. This plant is not a native of this country, but is grown here for its showy flowers.'

'What sort of taste has it?'

'Very little. Scarcely any in fact.'

'Then it could be disguised in tea?'

'Oh yes.'

French stood up. 'Thank you, doctor,' he said. 'That's all I want at present. Later I may have to come back with more questions.'

'I shall be pleased to help.'

French made only one other call on that Sunday evening, for it was getting late. After hearing about the opening of the inquest, he went to the mortuary with Osborne and examined the remains, as a precautionary measure taking prints from the fingers. Then he looked over the clothes and the objects taken from the pockets. In neither case was there anything which interested him, until he came to the shoes. From these he saw at once that Tarrant had been one of the two men who had met on the river bank just beyond where the rod was lying. Here at last was something positive, and an obvious 'line' would be to find the other man. The meeting had clearly taken place shortly before Tarrant's death and the unknown might well have offered him a drink from a poisoned flask. Even if he had done nothing so dramatic, he might have helpful news.

French wondered could he deduce anything from the number of prints visible. Apparently the men had been there for some considerable time. Or was it that the continual movement meant emotional tension? Could they, for instance, have been quarrelling? He felt that the marks gave some support to this view, but obviously nothing in the nature of proof.

However, that could wait till next morning. Satisfied with his progress, he returned to the hotel for a belated supper.

13

Joseph French Clears the Ground

As early on Monday morning as he well could, French called at The Gables and asked to see Miss Lestrange.

She was a little old lady with old-fashioned clothes and a placid manner. Competent, in a quiet methodical way, French thought, though not gifted with much initiative. She had recovered from the shock of finding the body and replied to his questions calmly, giving preliminary thought to each answer. She was in fact a good witness.

But she had little to tell which French did not already know. She described her engagement by Tarrant, her moving into The Gables and with Kate preparing it for him, his arrival, their normal life and his engagement to Miss Woolcombe. This, she said, had taken place on the previous Wednesday, though she had not known of it till later. Then she told about Tarrant's going to London on the next day, Thursday, she believed with Miss Woolcombe, and his return about midday on Saturday. He had said on Thursday before leaving, that he was going to fish on Saturday afternoon, and this he confirmed on arrival. He had had lunch and gone out in his customary way, and it was only when an hour had passed after his usual time of returning that she had gone to look for him.

'He took a tea-basket with him, I understand?' French asked.

'Yes, he was fond of tea and always did so. Just a thermos, you know, and something simple to eat.'

'Who prepared the tea on this occasion?'

'I did. I help Kate a good deal with the cooking because she has all the other work of the house.'

'Now, Miss Lestrange, I have to tell you something that may shock you and which you must keep strictly to yourself. Mr Tarrant had taken a dose of poison, aconitine, which would have killed him if he hadn't been drowned.'

She was obviously distressed, though she remained calm. 'How amazing!' she said presently. 'Is it known where he got it?'

'No,' said French, 'that's just it. We're trying to trace everything he ate or drank, and, of course, the tea comes under suspicion with the rest. Now, tell me, is there any chance that aconitine could have got into the tea or the sandwiches or whatever he had?'

An expression of horror passed across her face. 'Oh, no,' she declared. 'What a dreadful thing to suggest!'

'Accidents happen, you know,' French said dryly. 'Just tell me what you did in detail.'

'There's nothing to tell. I boiled the water, made the tea, strained it and put it in the flask, put in a, bottle of milk, and made some egg sandwiches. I also put in a piece of fruit cake. That was all.'

'I want to be sure the aconitine couldn't have got into any of these things.'

'You can be sure. With regard to the sandwiches and cake, I had the same for my own tea later, and the milk came out of the same jug.'

'So that only the tea remains suspect?'

'It couldn't have been the tea. I used the same kettle and tea from the same caddy.'

'That certainly seems conclusive. Now when was the flask washed? I mean, could the aconitine have already been in it?'

'No, because I heated the flask with hot water before putting in the tea. If there had been anything there, it would have been washed out. Besides, the idea's absurd. There couldn't have been any poison in it.'

'What did you do with the basket when you had finished with it.'

'I gave it into Mr Tarrant's own hands. He was in the hall ready to go, and he took it with him.'

'Is there as a matter of fact any aconitine in the house?'

'None. Of that I am perfectly sure.'

French turned to the next item on his list. Tarrant, Miss Lestrange said, had lived a quiet life, though he was absent a good deal from home. Where he went to she did not know. He entertained, though not a great deal. He had Mr Cooke in fairly often and once or twice a Mr Hampden, she imagined from London. Mr Hampden had always come on a Saturday and they had spent the afternoon fishing. Mr Cooke lived close by, but didn't fish, though she thought he had been out with Tarrant while he did so. Then Miss Woolcombe and her friend Miss Maudsley had been to lunch and one or two other people, mostly neighbours. French heard a good deal of local gossip, but nothing that seemed to him helpful.

'Now tell me,' he went on, 'who besides yourself knew that Mr Tarrant was going to fish on Saturday afternoon?'

'As I said, he told me on Thursday before he left, and Kate may have overheard him. Then two people rang up asking when they could see Mr Tarrant, one on Friday afternoon and one on Saturday morning, and I mentioned to each that he would be home on Saturday afternoon, but would be fishing.'

'Oh,' said French, 'who were they?'

'I don't know, neither gave their name. On Friday it was a man's voice and it was familiar though I couldn't place it. On Saturday morning it was a woman; a quite strange voice to me.'

'You didn't ask who they were?'

'I asked in both cases. The man seemed very much annoyed about something and rang off in the middle of my question. The girl said it was of no consequence and that she would ring up later.'

'And did she?'

'No.'

'Did you tell Mr Tarrant?'

'Yes, but he didn't seem to think it mattered.'

These calls, French thought, might be important. But the local police could more easily trace them. He therefore rang up Superintendent Hawkins and asked that this should be done.

'I want now to have a look at Mr Tarrant's papers,' he said, returning to Miss Lestrange. 'Could you show me his sitting-room?'

The library was a charming apartment, well stocked with the books of Tarrant's predecessor. In one corner was a large roll-top desk. It was locked, but French had brought with him the keys found on the body, one of which fitted.

'Have a general look round, Carter,' he directed, 'while I go through the papers.'

From the desk alone French could have deduced Tarrant's efficiency. It was tidy, the current papers being divided into 'For attention' and 'Pending' heaps, and dead matter being carefully filed.

A rapid examination led to a number of discoveries. The first and most surprising was that the deceased was a poor man. His current balance was small, and as far as French could learn, he had nothing on deposit receipt. More startling still was the fact that he had practically no capital, his one valuable asset, some 1,000 Braxamin shares, having been deposited with the bank to cover an overdraft of £1,000. French was completely puzzled. Surely, he thought, a man of so little substance would never have leased so expensive a property?

In the light of these facts, his next discovery was even more astonishing. The man had no job. He was a director of Braxamin and this brought him in £500 a year, but he appeared to have no other income. What could he be living on?

Then a more careful examination showed French that he was in receipt of other sums. For the lessee of The Gables these were not large, amounting to some £700 or £800 a year. But where they came from there was no indication. Another significant fact was that there were no records of Tarrant's early life, or indeed of anything that had happened to him prior to his renting The Gables. If this meant that there was something in his past which he now wished to forget, it might be a useful line to follow up.

174

Having completed his search, French turned to Carter, who had been prowling restlessly about the room. 'Got anything?' he asked.

'Nothing, sir,' Carter replied comprehensively.

'Then let's get on.'

They drove to Tarrant's bank and saw the manager. Here French confirmed his discoveries as to the man's finances. Tarrant had opened an account before moving to Little Bitton, and then had asked for an overdraft of £1,000, handing over 1,000 Braxamin shares as security. As these were worth over twice that amount, there had been no difficulty about obliging him. With regard to the odd sums, amounting to some £700 or £800 a year, which Tarrant had received, the manager said these had always been paid in in notes of small denomination, and there was therefore no record of their source. All this seemed to strengthen the suggestion that there was something in Tarrant's pre-Little Bitton life which he was anxious to keep secret.

When French returned to the police station he found that a reply had come in about the telephone calls. It had been possible to trace both, as they were trunk-calls and so had been recorded. That on Friday afternoon was from the Braxamin firm in London, and the later one on Saturday morning was from a box in the head post office at Lincaster. In this case the identity of the caller was not known.

French rang up the Superintendent at Lincaster and asked if he could trace this caller, then he sat down to consider his own next step.

The two most urgent matters seemed to be, first, to find out who had rung up Tarrant from the Braxamin firm, and second, to learn some details about the deceased's earlier life. French thought that both these matters could be best dealt with by a call on the Braxamin manager.

In five minutes he and Carter were on their way, and an hour later were shown into Hampden's office. The manager listened gravely as French told him what had occurred.

'That's a very disquieting statement,' said Hampden. 'I know that you people from the Yard are not called in unless there's a strong suspicion of foul play.'

'Hardly that, Mr Hampden, hardly that. Say rather, we're called in when there seems to be a reasonable doubt of what happened.'

'Under the circumstances, I fancy, a somewhat subtle distinction. However, we needn't waste time over that. What do you wish me to do for you?'

'Just to answer one or two questions, sir. First, I know nothing about Mr Tarrant. Can you tell me who he was and anything of his history?'

Hampden shook his head. 'I'm afraid very little. I didn't know him well personally and he never mentioned his family or early life.'

'You fished with him sometimes? Or was that another Mr Hampden?'

'No, it was I. It's true that I did fish with him and that I met him here on our Board days, but we never became really intimate.'

'How long have you known him?'

'About eighteen months. I met him in connection with the negotiations for his joining our Board, which he did just a little over a year ago.'

'I follow. How did you come to select him as a director?'

Hampden looked embarrassed. For a moment he did not reply, then with a slight shrug he leant back in his chair. 'I see,' he said, 'that I shall have to tell you. I'm sorry to say anything to discredit a dead man but this is not the time to prevaricate. In a word Mr Tarrant started an opposition medicine and we bought him out.'

'Tell me please,' said French, who felt there must be more than this in it.

Hampden thereupon gave him a fair account of what had happened, with the single exception of the division of the £1,000, neither accusing Tarrant of sharp practice, nor whitewashing his character, but from the facts letting French draw his own conclusions.

'Thank you,' said French when he had finished. 'All that may prove helpful. What became of his staff in Exeborough?'

'They were paid off and got other jobs, or most of them did. Our chartered accountants put in a man to see that the terms of our agreement were carried out, and if the matter interested you, you could see them: Messrs Carruthers & Lightfoot, of Arundel Street, Strand.'

French noted the name. 'Now just one other question. About five o'clock last Friday afternoon Mr Tarrant was rung up by someone from these offices. Can you tell me who it was?'

Hampden looked taken aback. 'How did you know that, Chief Inspector?' he asked uncertainly.

French smiled. 'Well, I now may ask you who it was, since you have shown that you know all about it.'

Hampden also smiled, but in a rather sickly way. 'You're very quick,' he returned uneasily. 'I am glad I am not a criminal trying to pull the wool over your eyes. Yes, I know who it was.'

French observed these signs of perturbation with interest. It might be due to a guilty conscience or merely to fear of giving someone else away. 'Good,' he said heartily, 'that will save me trouble. Who was it please?'

Hampden seemed to resign himself to the inevitable. 'It was Mr Cooke, another of our directors,' he said. 'He spoke from this room, that is how I know. He lives close to Mr Tarrant and I understand they saw a good deal of each other.'

'What was the purpose of the call?'

'He wanted to ring up Tarrant,' Hampden said doubtfully. Then, with a gesture as if coming to an unpleasant decision, he went on: 'I suppose I'd better tell you the truth, Chief Inspector. He had just seen in the paper the news of Mr Tarrant's engagement. He was ringing up, presumably to congratulate him.'

This seemed to French extraordinarily unlikely. Miss Lestrange had said that the caller had seemed annoyed, even ringing off in the middle of one of her questions. A man congratulating his friend on his engagement is not usually annoyed about it and his acquaintance does not try to keep the matter dark. He thought for a moment. 'What was the paper Mr Cooke had?' he asked.

'The *Saxham St Edmunds Weekly Gazette*,' Hampden answered. 'It is his local paper and it had been forwarded by post as Mr Cooke had been staying in town. He happened to glance over it while I was signing my letters and then saw the notice.'

An idea. suddenly occurred to French. Miss Lestrange in speaking of Tarrant's delight in the engagement, had mentioned that Miss Woolcombe was an extraordinarily rich young woman: the local heiress, in fact. Now he wondered whether Cooke might not have had similar aspirations. If so, it would account for the annoyance and excitement in his manner. French decided to bluff.

'The news must have hit Mr Cooke hard, I'm afraid. He was upset, I expect?'

Hampden replied more promptly. 'You think he wanted to marry her himself, do you? Well, you may be right. I personally thought it not unlikely.'

'If so, it was scarcely to congratulate the deceased that he rang up?'

Hampden shrugged. 'I don't know what he wanted with him. He only asked when he could see him.'

The last part at least of this statement was true. Now if possible to dispel Hampden's fears.

'Well, Mr Hampden,' French said, 'that is very clear, but I don't think it really affects my inquiry. What I really wanted to know was whether Mr Cooke made an appointment with the deceased, and from what you tell me he evidently did not. One more question and I have finished. You said you had fished with the deceased: did he bring his tea-basket on those occasions?'

'Always: he brought it along to where he happened to be fishing at the moment and had tea there: a simple tea, just a thermos and a few sandwiches.'

French rose. 'That is all at present and thank you for your help.'

He had noticed on the wall a framed photograph of a group and in moving he edged close to it. As he had hoped, it included Hampden. 'Is Mr Cooke in this group?' he asked.

Hampden pointed out the directors and French noted the photographer's name. When he left the office he called at the studio, ordering enlargements of each separate figure.

'From there he went on to Messrs Carruthers & Lightfoot, Arundel Street. There he learnt little fresh, except that

Hampden's account of the Koldkure affair was strictly accurate.

As French drove back to Little Bitton he felt he was getting on. First, it was evident that Tarrant had been something of an adventurer. That whole business of the Koldkure medicine was, at least, a moral fraud, and the Braxamin people had bought him out because their business was also a racket and they could not afford to take him into court. It looked as if the £700 or £800 a year which Tarrant had paid into his bank had been profits still coming in from Koldkure. But as that was closed down, these profits would soon come to an end, and then Tarrant would have to look elsewhere for supplies. Evidently he had done so and found them in the person of Miss Jean Woolcombe.

French ruminated over the engagement, and then a further possibility occurred to him. What if the renting of 'The Gables' had been a move to bring it about? Tarrant was a pauper, according to Miss Woolcombe's standards, and as there was no chance of her marrying a pauper, an appearance in the role of a well-to-do landed proprietor seemed desirable. This would account for his depositing the Braxamin shares with the bank as security for the overdraft with which he rented the house.

This view, added to French's previous ideas that Cooke might also have wanted to marry the heiress, produced a quite promising theory of the crime. French saw that his next steps must be: first, to settle definitely if Cooke had really been paying court to Miss Woolcombe, and second, if so, to interview Cooke.

In pursuit of these objectives, after dinner at the Bitton Arms he slipped into the private bar, which, luckily, was empty, and ordering a pint of bitter, engaged the barmaid in conversation. Miss Duke was a round-faced girl with blue eyes and light, fluffy hair, who seemed thrilled by the identity of her customer. French found that the way to her heart was to talk from the inside about the tragedy, and with a highly confidential air he told her all the things which she could learn next morning from her daily paper.

'You know,' he then essayed, 'I thought Mr Cooke was going to be the lucky man. The news of the engagement was a big surprise.'

That a complete stranger should so quickly have formed such an opinion did not seem to her at all remarkable. She heartily agreed.

'That's what we all thought,' she replied, evidently delighted to be exchanging confidences with a celebrity. 'It was generally reported that they were both in the running, but Mr Cooke was the favourite.'

'A nasty knock for him,' French said sympathetically. 'Do you think he'll take it hard?'

Miss Duke thought he would take it very hard, and French, having obtained the information he desired, steered the conversation into more innocuous channels.

It was still only nine o'clock and French thought the time as good as any other for his next visit. With Carter he walked round to 'Greenbank', where Cooke lived with his sisters. Cooke saw him at once.

'I am sorry to call so late, Mr Cooke,' French began, 'but you will understand that in a case like this the sooner we can get our information, the more valuable it is.'

'I can understand that all right,' Cooke admitted, 'but what I can't understand is how I can help you in the matter.'

French was interested in the man's bearing. He was unquestionably nervous and looked as if he were bracing himself for an unpleasant interview. These were signs with which French was well acquainted, and they very often, though not always, indicated a forward step in his investigations.

He began with some quite innocuous inquiries: how long had Mr Cooke known the deceased? What sort of man was the deceased? Had Mr Cooke seen much of him since he rented the Gables?

Under this treatment Cooke's apprehension melted: in fact his manner became slightly contemptuous. Then after French had asked a particularly innocuous question, he added in the same tone: 'What was the message you wished to give the deceased when you rang him up from the Braxamin offices on Friday afternoon?'

This was evidently unexpected. Cooke sat still for some moments, while his expression changed from nonchalance to concern and then to actual fear.

'Why,' he said at last, 'how did you know I rang him up?'

'Information received,' French returned. 'The police have ways of learning of such matters.'

'But I didn't get him: he wasn't at home.'

'I know he wasn't at home. I know also that your call was in reference to your discovery of his engagement to Miss Woolcombe. That must have come as rather a shock to you.'

'What,' he stammered uncertainly, 'do you mean?'

'You rang up to know when you could see the deceased, and were told that he would be fishing on Saturday. Did you see him then?'

Cooke hesitated.

'I see you did,' said French quickly. 'When was that?'

'I didn't say so,' Cooked answered uncertainly.

'Of course not, but your manner has. Come now, Mr Cooke, this is a murder case, and any kind of prevarication may prove serious. Tell me about your interview with him on Saturday afternoon.'

Again the expression of fear showed in Cooke's eyes.

'I am not trying to hide anything, Chief Inspector, because I have nothing to hide. I did see Tarrant that afternoon, and why shouldn't I?'

'No reason whatever,' French said pleasantly. 'All I want is the facts. Just tell me about it.'

It appeared that about three o'clock on that Saturday afternoon Cooke saw from his sitting-room window, which looked up the river, Tarrant fishing on the opposite bank. He crossed the river by the road bridge and went down the bank till he met Tarrant. When Tarrant saw him approaching he pulled in his rod, laid it on the bank and came to meet him. They chatted for a few minutes and then Cooke returned home while Tarrant resumed his fishing.

'Just whereabouts on the bank did you stand?'

When Cooke described the place French saw that it was where Carter had found the impressions.

'I saw your footprints,' he said. 'I should be obliged if you would lend me the shoes you wore so that I might check them up. Unknown prints are a worry, as you can understand, but once they're accounted for they're off one's mind.'

Without a word Cooke left the room, returning in a moment with a pair of shoes.

This was all right so far as it went, but French had not yet got all he wanted.

'What was the conversation about?' he asked.

'Why, about Tarrant's engagement, of course. I thought you knew that.'

183

Once again French decided to bluff. 'I knew that. And strictly between ourselves there are a couple of other things I know also. One is that the deceased was an adventurer, who wanted to marry Miss Woolcombe for her money. The other is that you wanted to do the same.'

Cooke paled, but attempted to bluster. 'I'd like to know what right you have to make statements of that kind,' he demanded. 'That's a pure guess on your part, and you know it.'

'Then, still strictly between ourselves, I'll guess again. Tarrant was murdered that afternoon, and you are believed to be the last person to have seen him alive. Now I'm making no accusation, but I put it to you that if you're innocent, your best plan is to be open with me. A moment,' French held up his hand as the other would have spoken. 'Before you say anything, I must warn you that you needn't reply unless you like, and that the sergeant here will take down what you say, which may be used in evidence.'

There was no mistaking Cooke's reaction. His bluster had gone and naked fear had taken its place. He was now only too anxious to oblige French.

'Well, Chief Inspector,' he said, evidently fighting hard for composure, 'as you know so much, I see I must tell you everything. It's not very creditable, perhaps, but it's the truth.'

'That's all I want, Mr Cooke, and if you're innocent the truth won't harm you.'

'Very well. It's true that Tarrant was an adventurer. You know perhaps about his Koldkure ramp?'

'Yes, I've heard about that.'

'I don't know how you've managed it in the time. However, that's not my business. Tarrant was hard up and wanted Miss Woolcombe's money. It's quite true that I and a dozen others did too.'

'Quite. Then when you saw in the *Saxham Weekly Gazette* that he had pulled it off, you were naturally upset. You rang him up, but couldn't get through to him then. But you did meet him on Saturday afternoon. Now, remembering my caution, what took place at that meeting?'

'I don't care a damn for your caution. I see that you're right and that I must tell you the truth, and I'm going to. I saw him and taxed him with all you've said. I said if he didn't clear out I'd see that Miss Woolcombe knew his whole history.'

'And what happened?'

'He smiled and admitted the whole thing. Then he went on to agree that I could wreck the engagement, but he said if I did, I couldn't take his place. He could play the same game and see that the lady learnt my motives. Well, he was right there. Under such circumstances she wouldn't have accepted me.'

'And how did you break the deadlock?'

Cooke seemed ashamed to go on, then made the effort. 'He made me an offer.'

'An offer?'

'Yes, he said we'd go into it together; he'd marry Miss Woolcombe and divide the spoils with me. He would pass on one-third of all he got.'

'And you agreed?'

'What else could I do? It was that or nothing. I could hardly be expected to give up such a chance.'

It was not a pretty scheme, though quite in accordance with what might be expected from the author of the Koldkure racket. If it were true, it would tend to clear

Cooke from suspicion. If Cooke had really agreed to such a plan, it would be in his interest that Tarrant should live to contract the marriage. In fact, the motives would be reversed. It was much more likely that Tarrant would wish to murder Cooke, than Cooke Tarrant.

After learning that Cooke had spent the hour after the interview over his betting records and had then called on a friend in the village, French returned to the hotel. At all events, there was here a good deal to think about, and he was not dissatisfied with his progress.

14

Joseph French Meets the Principals

Before going to bed that night French retired to a corner of the tiny lounge to consider his programme for the following day. This process he had always found a great time saver, and he never grudged the labour involved. In the present instance it resulted in an early call on Sergeant Osborne.

'I want your help with some local inquiries,' he began. 'I think you could do them better than I, as you know the place. But I fancy they will require more than your staff. How about it?'

'That's all right, sir,' Osborne answered. 'Superintendent Hawkins told me I could draw on him for any help that might be wanted.'

'Fine,' said French. 'There are five points so far. The first is to search The Gables for aconitine. That's a job a stranger could do.'

'Right, sir.' The sergeant made a note.

'Then I want a call made on all chemists in the district, including Saxham. I'm afraid this is rather a last hope, for a local purchaser would naturally go further afield. On the other hand, the stuff's not easy to get without a doctor's prescription, which might cramp a stranger's style.'

'Worth trying, at all events,' and a second note went down.

'Next I'd like inquiries made as to whether anyone was seen near the river on Saturday afternoon—either Tarrant or anyone else. Also if any local people passed along the river or the road above it and the approximate hour.'

'The same man could do both of these, I think.'

'I agree, sergeant. One thing more: I'm afraid also not very hopeful. I've had it in my mind that the aconitine might have been in a flask: that some fellow might have offered Tarrant a drink, you understand. If so, it's just possible that he might have wanted to get rid of the flask immediately and have thrown it into the river. You might make a search.'

'I'll attend to it at once, sir.'

'Thank you. That's the lot. Do you happen to know it Miss Woolcombe is at home?'

'I believe so, sir. I heard she came back and was terribly upset when she learnt of Mr Tarrant's death.'

'Waste of a lot of good sentiment. It's wonderful how often nice women fall for rotters. You might ring up and say I'm going round and should be grateful if she could see me.'

The reply being favourable, French went round. He found St Aidan's slightly overwhelming. Wealth tastefully displayed was its keynote, from the massive gates and pillars of the drive to the needlepoint chair in which he presently sat to await the coming of the owner. Wealth exuded from the velvet lawns, from the huge cedars which stood like giant sentinels about the house, from the profusion of exotic shrubs, as well as from the pictures and art treasures of the interior. It was not difficult to see why Tarrant should have adventured everything on the chance of becoming the master of such an establishment.

'Miss Woolcombe will see you, sir,' the butler answered French's inquiry, somehow contriving to suggest a veiled disapproval of the decision.

Jean Woolcombe, when some five minutes later she impetuously appeared, proved to be a large bouncing, rather untidy young woman with plain features and light wispish hair, but with really beautiful eyes. Honesty and steadfastness looked from their clear depths, and French felt instantly that from this witness at least he would get nothing but the truth.

He had no difficulty in inducing her to talk; in fact his questions were like the opening of sluice gates to a flood of conversation. She spoke of herself and her engagement without reticence, as if she had been bottling it all up and found a relief in putting it into words.

'We were to have been married in a month,' she declared, and French felt that she was not far from tears, 'and now . . .' She paused, but went on again before he could speak:

'I have had many proposals—for my money. But *he* never thought of that. I saw that he loved me: it was evident in his every word and look. But he wouldn't speak about marriage, and I could see the reason: it was my money. Of course, I couldn't let that stand between me and my happiness. So I had almost to tell him that I was fond of him, and then he explained that he wasn't a rich man, and that that had kept him silent. I said: "But you are able to keep up The Gables," and he made so little of it. "The Gables," he said. "Oh, yes, but The Gables is very small beer compared with this." Disinterested, I mean. You know. I tell you, Chief Inspector, it is the one thing anyone in my position longs for—*disinterestedness*. If you knew how one doubts even one's best friend! But there, I mustn't talk so much. What can I do for you?'

A few leading remarks, steering her conversation into the required channels, soon gave French all that he wanted to know. She told him about the dinner given by Cooke in Town at which she had first met Tarrant and at which she had asked Tarrant to call if he were in her neighbourhood, how he had done so during the following week, about her surprise when a couple of months later she had heard that he had rented The Gables, how she had asked him to tennis, and how they had gradually grown more intimate until, largely as a result of her own prompting, he had proposed.

Though French always tried to keep his sympathies separate from his business, he could not but feel intensely sorry for the rather flamboyant young woman. Apart from the craving for sympathy shown by this laying bare of her feelings to a complete stranger and a police officer at that, her disillusionment when she learnt the real character of Tarrant would be terribly bitter. This disillusionment, moreover, would be inevitable. Only if he failed to find the murderer could it remain secret, and to contemplate such a contingency was beyond French's powers.

His feeling for her rose to actual indignation as he remembered the infamous arrangement between Cooke and the deceased to share the spoils of the marriage. He felt he should tell her the truth; that she was well rid of her fiancé. Then he saw that not only was this not his business, but that there was no chance of her believing him and that the knowledge would have to come by the natural process of events.

'Now, Miss Woolcombe, when did you last see the deceased?'

This produced another flood. 'On the Saturday, the very day of his death! At twelve o'clock that very day!'

It appeared that Miss Woolcombe had had an invitation to spend that weekend with some people at Huntingdon, a long-standing engagement which she had felt she couldn't very well break. Tarrant had actually proposed on the previous Wednesday. She had not wished to announce the engagement immediately, and at her suggestion they had gone to town on the Thursday, so that they could be together without attracting attention. Miss Maudsley, her companion, had accompanied her: she was most helpful as well as very tactful. On the Saturday both Miss Maudsley and Tarrant had seen her off by the twelve-noon train from King's Cross. Miss Maudsley usually went with her on these visits, but on this occasion she had expressed a wish to spend the weekend at Bournemouth, where some friends of her own were staying.

French next interviewed Hilda Maudsley. She confirmed all that he had heard from Miss Woolcombe. Tarrant had driven them to King's Cross, and he and she had seen the train off. Tarrant had then excused himself on the ground that he was leaving at once for Little Bitton. He had asked her if he could put her down anywhere, but they were going in opposite directions. As a matter of fact, she went to a cinema, continuing to Bournemouth by the six-thirty train. She must admit that her story to Miss Woolcombe was a tactful little stratagem. She felt she was not particularly wanted at Huntingdon. Miss Woolcombe was so kind that she would never have said so, but Miss Maudsley could see from the eagerness with which she approved the excuse that she was quite pleased. This was not, of course, her only motive. She was glad of the chance of a couple of days to herself. Though she did go to Bournemouth and enjoyed it, her friends there were non-existent, and she stayed at the Ridley.

This, French could see, was a different type of woman from her employer. Small, dark and pretty, she was obviously highly intelligent. She made her statement clearly and with that minimum of words which is at once so admirable and so rare. A perfect witness, French thought, as he thanked her and took his leave.

'Hard luck on Miss Woolcombe, Carter,' he said as they left the house. 'I'm afraid she's in for more trouble.'

'Rough on her for the time being, sir,' Carter responded with insight. 'But it'll cure her when she learns what an escape she's had.'

French wondered. People's reactions to one another seldom worked out in this reasonable way. He also wondered about Tarrant. What was there in the man to have aroused such devotion in this nice woman? For he felt that Jean Woolcombe was really good and straight and kindly. Now that he came. to think of it, he had noticed something of the same kind in the two women at The Gables. So different in age and outlook, Miss Lestrange perhaps sixty and having evidently moved in good society all her life, and Kate, the maid, a raw country girl of perhaps a third of that age; both showed something more of personal feeling than could be accounted for by even such a tragic loss of their employer and incidentally of their posts. Some men were irresistible to women, and perhaps Tarrant was one of them.

192

If so, it opened up another theory of the crime: that it had been an affair, not of the head, but of the heart. The murder had followed so hard upon the engagement that it was difficult to believe they were not connected. Poison was a woman's weapon. Had the news of Tarrant's engagement turned some other woman's love to hate? Or, as he had already wondered in the case of Cooke, was the murderer a man cheated by Tarrant of the hope of the Woolcombe thousands?

Once again French took himself to task. This was not the time for theories. Resolutely he banished these intriguing possibilities from his mind and turned firmly to the next item on his list.

This read '*Johnson, Analyst*', and after ringing up Mr Johnson he turned the bonnet of the car towards Saxham.

Johnson proved to be an energetic man with greying hair and a precise manner. French was apologetic, realising that he was asking for results which the analyst probably had not had time to reach. But Johnson was pleasant enough.

'I've not completed the quantitative analysis,' he explained, 'but I may be able to answer your inquiries qualitatively. What do you want to know?'

'I want, as you can imagine,' French answered, 'to fix the time at which the deceased took the aconitine. And first, did you find any traces in the tea?'

Johnson shook his head. 'Unfortunately there wasn't enough tea left to test. The basket had been repacked and the flask and cup had been emptied. The test of the sandwiches and cake showed that there was aconitine in neither.'

'I thought as much,' French replied. 'I think I need scarcely ask you if you found traces in the lunch?'

'None in the food I was given, but, as you know, some of the dishes were finished and so couldn't be tested.'

'The medical evidence suggests that the deceased must have taken the poison later than lunch-time. My other question is: can you tell me what the deceased had after lunch? I have, for instance, wondered if someone gave him a drink from a flask?'

'I think I can help you there, Chief Inspector. There were no traces in the stomach of alcohol.'

It seemed then to French that the poison must have been in the tea, and he much regretted the fact that this could not be established. However, the inquiry was only beginning and he could not expect too much all at once.

He had decided that an early call must be paid to Sir Claud Monroe, Chairman of the Braxamin Company. He had been a good deal interested in Hampden's manner on the previous day. Hampden had seemed embarrassed through the entire interview and French had received a definite impression that he was keeping something back. French had thought it wiser not to probe too deeply at that early stage of the affair, but he felt that if Hampden were hiding anything, an approach to the Chairman might give him the hint he required.

On leaving the analyst he therefore rang up Sir Claud and made an appointment for an hour later.

The Chairman lived at Wolseley, a village about half-way between Saxham and London. It seemed a pleasant little place, and here again the house and grounds showed evidence of wealth, though on nothing like so lavish a scale as St Aidan's.

Sir Claud was seated at the desk in his library, where French and Carter were shown on arrival.

'Good afternoon,' he greeted them curtly though not unpleasantly. 'Sit down and tell me what I can do for you.'

French explained. He was engaged on the case of Mr Tarrant's death, and while he understood that Sir Claud could give him no information about the actual tragedy, he would be glad to learn anything possible about the deceased and Sir Claud's relations with him.

Sir Claud looked at him curiously. 'Do you know the circumstances in which Tarrant entered our firm?' he asked.

'I know about the Koldkure establishment at Exeborough,' French answered. 'I saw Mr Hampden and he told me of that. But I should like your own account of the matter in the hope of getting a fresh sidelight on it.'

Sir Claud briefly stated the facts, just as Hampden had done.

'That's very interesting, sir,' French remarked. 'Do you happen to know anything of the deceased's private life? Where he came from, or who his friends were?'

'Nothing; I didn't care for him and I never discussed anything with him but business.'

'Or about his finances? I may tell you that he was paying into the bank between seven and eight hundred a year from some unknown source.'

The Chairman raised his eyebrows. 'Unknown?' he repeated. 'Surely the source of sums of that amount could not remain hidden?'

'They were always paid in notes of small value. It obviously suggested a secret source.'

Sir Claud considered this. 'That interests me a good deal,' he said presently. 'I'm not suggesting that there's any connection, but a rather strange thing has recently been happening. When the Koldkure Works were shut down, the falling off

I mentioned in our sales continued for three or four months, then began to recover.' He looked at French.

'You mean as the retailers' stocks of the Koldkure remedy were sold off?'

'Exactly. Our sales began to approach normal in a fairly steady curve. By producing that curve we were able to forecast that they should have reached normal by last August. But here it is, Chief Inspector,' he sat up and demonstrated with his finger, 'that curve never did reach normal.'

'You mean?'

'I mean that it turned and began to go down again.'

French looked his question.

'Hampden was very much distressed, and I admit it was, and is, disconcerting. Tarrant at once said it was his fault.'

'His fault?' French echoed.

'Yes; he said: "I'm afraid I've given a good idea away broad-cast. I've shown a lot of chemists how to make a larger commission on their indigestion remedy sales. It would be strange if some of them didn't take the hint."'

'And did you, sir, believe that that was happening?'

Sir Claud shrugged. 'You know as much about it as I do, Chief Inspector.'

French paused in thought. 'What has happened to the curve,' he asked presently, 'since that discussion took place?'

'It has continued to fall. Hampden handled the Koldkure business admirably, but he hasn't done so well this time and it's worrying him. He's rather hard up and he's afraid his job's threatened.'

This seemed to French a strange statement for the Chairman of a large business to make about his most highly paid officer. Something of his thought must have shown in his face, for Sir Claud added: 'Extravagant wife. Been a drag on him ever since he married. I'm sorry for it, as he's a nice fellow.'

'Will he lose his job, Sir Claud, if the fall continues? But that's not my pigeon and perhaps I shouldn't have asked?'

Sir Claud shrugged again. 'I can't, of course, say what the Board might do in hypothetical circumstances, but it's obvious that we must have a manager who can stop the rot.'

Sir Claud now seemed to reach the end of his helpfulness. His manner indicated with no uncertainty that he thought the interview had lasted long enough.

French made tentative movements of departure. 'Just one more question, if you please. Mr Hampden did not tell me of this new development. Can you suggest the reason?'

Sir Claud's manner grew frosty. 'I don't know that I care to continue discussing Mr Hampden,' he said shortly, 'but I think you might answer your own question. The fall is a confession of his own failure, and I don't suppose he wants to talk about it more than he can help.'

This certainly was an explanation, though French was not satisfied as to its sufficiency.

'I'm sorry, sir, but there is just one other point. Can you tell me what the relations are between Mr Hampden and Mr Cooke?'

'As a matter of fact they don't pull. Cooke's jealous of Hampden and is always trying to get him out of the concern. Now is that all?'

French stood up. 'That's all at last. Thank you very much: I'm grateful for your help. It may be that our interests will prove the same and that I also may have to work on this puzzling fall in your profits.'

French indeed was interested in two aspects of the matter.

First, in the problem itself, the continued drop in profits after the cause of the drop had been eliminated, and second, in the fact that Sir Claud had connected it in his mind with the mysterious seven or eight hundred a year which Tarrant had paid into his bank. This surely could only mean that the Chairman suspected that Tarrant was once more at the root of the trouble. French saw that the matter was one which he must investigate. This whole episode of the fraud against the Braxamin Company might well have borne the seeds of the murder and might therefore concern him directly.

Sir Claud had also given a hint which might explain Hampden's reluctance to speak of Cooke's telephone call. When French tackled Cooke about it, as he obviously would, Cooke would know that only Hampden could have given him away. Hampden no doubt wished to avoid thus increasing his animosity.

French glanced at his watch. It was getting on to four o'clock. Here he was, half-way to Town, and if he went on at once he could see Hampden before he left his office. He borrowed Sir Claud's telephone, rang up Hampden, and set off. An hour later he and Carter were shown into the manager's room.

'Sorry to trouble you again so soon, Mr Hampden,' he began pleasantly, 'but I've just been having a word with Sir Claud Monroe and he happened to mention that your profits, which had dropped as a result of the late Mr Tarrant's activities, had not yet become normal. I wondered if you could give me any more information about that?'

Hampden was clearly anything but pleased by the question. For a moment he did not reply, then he said with an obvious assumption of ease: 'I don't know that I can. What exactly do you want to know?'

'Anything you can tell me,' French returned accommodatingly.

Hampden could not—or at least did not—tell him very much. With an air of great candour he produced the master graph, upon which the entire sales movement had been shown, and said that that was how the matter stood.

'May I ask what steps you have taken to investigate the matter?' French went on.

'You may, and if you do I shall have no objection to telling you,' Hampden returned. 'But I understood your inquiry related to the death of Mr Tarrant, rather than to the conduct of the Braxamin business?'

French looked him straight in the eye. 'Are they not connected, Mr Hampden?' he said sternly.

Hampden was taken aback. His eyes dropped and he moved uneasily in his chair.

'I don't know why you should say that, Chief Inspector. Have you any reason to assume such a thing?'

'Have you?' French retorted.

'I? No, none whatever.' He was pulling himself together and now began to register indignation.

'Did the idea never occur to you, sir?' French persisted.

Hampden cleared his throat. 'Oh, yes, it occurred to me. It would occur to anyone under the circumstances. But I've yet to learn that I should report fancies to the police instead of facts?'

French thought the confidential approach was indicated and smiled. 'I appreciate your attitude, Mr Hampden,' he said more pleasantly, 'which is, of course, perfectly correct. But this is a murder case and you, as a good citizen, if from no other point of view, are interested in my success. The question is, can you help me?'

An expression of relief showed on Hampden's face. 'Since you put it like that,' he declared, 'I may say that I should be glad to help you if I could. But I can't. I simply don't know.'

Whether he was or was not speaking the truth French could not be sure, but he realised that at the moment he would get no further. He therefore thanked Hampden and took his leave.

Being in Town, French called at the Yard. There was nothing there requiring his attention, but he seized the opportunity to instruct a subordinate to investigate the statements of Miss Woolcombe and Miss Maudsley as to their respective visits to Huntingdon and Bournemouth on the day of the crime. This was not that he suspected either lady, but as an ordinary piece of routine. It may perhaps be mentioned here that, so far as the statements could be checked, both proved completely accurate.

Leaving the Yard, French thought he would go home for a meal and drive back to Little Bitton in the evening. Then another question filled his mind: how to explain to his Em without serious loss of face, the strange condition of the lawn with its best portions denuded of sods. He found this a more difficult problem than the fate of George Tarrant.

15

Joseph French Visits Exeborough

That night French let Carter—who also had delightedly seized the chance of going home—drive back to Little Bitton, while he himself sat back in silence thinking over his case, reviewing his progress to date and considering his future action.

He began with the continued fall of the Braxamin profits, not because this seemed more important than any other point, but because his mind at the moment was full of it. And first as to its cause.

It was certainly possible that numbers of retail chemists had copied Tarrant's trick and were making up his preparation for themselves. Admittedly this would be extremely difficult to establish. The retailer had only to say that any given bottle sold had been obtained from the Koldkure works. He would have invoices to prove that he had obtained bottles from there, and there would be nothing to show that these had already been sold and replaced from his own manufacture. All this was possible. But there was one objection to the theory, and the more French thought over it, the more serious it seemed. The proceeding was dishonest. Retail chemists were probably no more and no less honest than any other class of men, but French didn't believe any considerable number of them would be guilty of the trick, particularly as the profit was so small. It was not even as if it was something shady which could happen in the ordinary course of business and be allowed to slide. This would be a deliberate action, involving the purchase and mixing of the ingredients, the printing of the special labels, and the wrapping of the bottles to look as if they had come from a factory. It certainly didn't seem to French that the average retail chemist would stand for it.

Yet this was the solution which Tarrant had suggested.

French wondered if this were Tarrant's real opinion. Tarrant was reputed to be a good business man, and he should therefore be a judge in a matter of the kind. It seemed doubtful that he could believe it. But if not, why had he put it forward?

Did not the man's action support a very different explanation: that he himself had repeated his fraud under another name? This would also have been quite feasible, and in accordance with his character, as well as accounting for his secret income of seven or eight hundred a year.

Of course this theory did not account for Hampden's manner. But Hampden's manner could be explained innocently enough. Sir Claud's suggestions would cover it, or it might have been due to fear of being mixed up in a murder case. All the same, French wondered if Hampden knew more about the affair than he pretended. Could he indeed have taken a leaf out of Tarrant's book and be himself putting out the Remedy?

There was a good deal to support the idea. Hampden

was in need of money, so there was no difficulty about motive. Hampden had visited Exeborough and gone into the Koldkure affair and therefore had the necessary knowledge. But had he the time? Yes, given a good manager, weekend meetings would be sufficient.

On the other hand, this idea failed to account for Tarrant's secret income. Was it not then more probable that the two men had gone into partnership? Such a theory would certainly meet the known facts. Yet French did not think it satisfactory. For one thing, neither would be likely to trust the other to such an extent. Then it would be too dangerous for Hampden. The least breath of suspicion and he was lost, for no such scheme could bear a rigorous investigation. And discovery would mean ruin. Even if he avoided prison, Hampden would never again get a responsible job.

Then still another idea occurred to French. What if Tarrant had been working the swindle and Hampden had discovered it? What if Hampden had even been blackmailing Tarrant?

For a moment this seemed to French likely enough, then once again he grew doubtful. It did not explain the murder or point to the murderer. Even if Tarrant or Hampden, or both, were selling a Remedy, that would be no motive for murder, while if Hampden were blackmailing Tarrant, that would supply a motive for keeping him alive.

But steady! Suppose the converse were true? Suppose Hampden were making the preparation and that Tarrant had discovered it and were blackmailing him? That brought in the murder. In such a case there would be motive, good and strong! It also supplied an explanation both of Hampden's manner and of Tarrant's money.

French grew quite excited as he considered this, his first really satisfactory theory of the crime. It was true that the objection of Hampden's risk still remained, but the man's circumstances might have been desperate and the risk therefore unavoidable. At all events, Hampden was now definitely a suspect.

Then French saw that this theory, good as it was, left out yet another important factor: the engagement. The engagement had been announced in the paper on the Friday—it was a Saturday paper, but for some obscure reason it was published a day earlier—and the murder had taken place on the Saturday afternoon following. Was this cause and effect, or was it pure coincidence? Cooke's story had been plausible, but was it true? Had Tarrant supplanted some other man? Was there some discarded woman friend—or several—whose thoughts had turned to murder on hearing the news . . . ?

French sighed as he realised how nebulous his ideas still remained. But he could do nothing more at the moment. Here was Little Bitton, and it was close on midnight.

On calling at the police station next morning, he found that some information had come in. A careful search had been made of The Gables and no trace of aconitine had been discovered. Nor had anyone recently bought it in the local chemist's or at Saxham. The valley and river had been searched for the length of a mile and no flask or other likely receptacle had been found. All this was negative, but the last of French's questions had produced something positive.

A Mrs Bordon, a local resident, had been walking towards Little Bitton along the Webble Road, which ran on the edge of the valley opposite The Gables, about a quarter past four on Saturday afternoon. She had seen a woman coming towards her from the direction of the village, but before they met the stranger turned off the road into the valley. When Mrs Bordon passed the gap through which the other had disappeared, she looked after her and saw her walking down towards the river. The gap was one of those in which footprints had been found.

'Mrs Bordon lives not three minutes from here,' Sergeant Osborne concluded, 'so I can bring her over if you'd like to see her.'

'I'll go there myself,' said French.

But Mrs Bordon, when he saw her, had little to add to the sergeant's report. The woman had been about thirty yards from her when she had turned aside and she had not observed her very closely. She seemed young and of middle height and build. She was dressed in a darkish hat and coat and skirt, brown, Mrs Bordon thought, though she could not be sure. In spite of her poor description, she believed she would recognise her if she saw her again. One point of the story interested French. The woman had been in a hurry. Not only that, but something in her walk had conveyed the impression of anxiety. She had seemed to be hastening to the river on some urgent and disturbing quest.

French railed at his witness's lack of observation when he returned to the station. 'How can we get her on that description?' he grumbled. 'What have you done about it?'

'Mrs Bordon said she was a stranger, sir, and she's probably right there, for she's a busybody: knows everybody and everybody's business. So I thought perhaps the woman had come into the village by car or bus or train.'

'Good,' French approved.

'From the bus stop to where Mrs Bordon met her is about ten minutes' walk. A bus arrives from Saxham at five minutes past the hour, so if Mrs Bordon's right as to the time she

205

saw her, she might have come by that. No other bus and no train get in anywhere near that time.'

'Very good. Can you get any further?'

'I have a man on it. He's seeing the conductors as they pass.'

'That's fine. What about inquiries along the road between the two points? I've got help before from invalids. They look out of the windows and notice who goes by. Nothing else to do, poor souls.'

'I'll see to it, sir, though I don't know of any invalids living along there. But someone may have been at a window.'

French found this information of considerable interest. A woman had rung up The Gables on that Saturday morning and he wondered whether this could be the same. In any case it was essential that she should be traced.

However, Osborne was doing all that could be done in the matter, leaving French himself free for other work. What, he wondered, was the most urgent item?

From the analysis he had made on the previous evening three main lines of inquiry had emerged: first, who besides Tarrant had wished to marry Jean Woolcombe? second, who besides Jean Woolcombe had been in love with Tarrant? and, third, had Tarrant been involved in whatever activities had caused the drop in the Braxamin profits?

'I say, Osborne,' he called, 'I want some more information. Have you a good-looking young constable with an eye for a skirt?'

Osborne grinned. 'I may be able to find one, sir. What do you want him for?'

'Let him go and make up to the maids at St Aidan's; you know, take 'em to the movies and all that. I want to know what other men were friendly with Miss Woolcombe. It'll have been discussed in the servants' hall, and if he's tactful he'll get it without giving anything away.'

Osborne nodded. 'I can arrange that, sir. I'll send him to ask about the deceased's last visit, and that'll break the ice.'

A good man, Osborne, French thought, as having called to Carter to bring round the car, he drove once again to The Gables and asked to see Miss Lestrange.

'I'm anxious,' he told her, 'to trace the woman who rang up Mr Tarrant on the morning of the tragedy, and in the absence of direct information, I can only do this by getting a list of his feminine acquaintances and trying each in turn. I'd be grateful for your help. Can you give me any names?'

Miss Lestrange shook her head. 'I'm afraid not,' she answered. 'I can't recall a single case of his entertaining. a lady here, except of course Miss Woolcombe and her friend, Miss Maudsley.'

'Then I must ask you to let me look again at his papers.'

In spite of his meticulous care, in this he had no luck. An exhaustive search failed to reveal a single name. He therefore decided to start work on his third line of inquiry: Tarrant's possible connection with the fall in the Braxamin profits.

If this had not been due to the action of individual retail chemists, what he had to look for was a factory or business resembling the Koldkure establishment. The first step must therefore be to learn just what the Koldkure place had been like.

'Exeborough tonight,' he told Carter. 'It's too far to drive. Look up the trains.'

'Koldkure, sir?' asked the sergeant, as he moved off to borrow a Bradshaw.

'Carter, you'll be a detective one of these days,' French

told him. 'As soon as you've done that, get the Exeborough super on the phone.'

'I'm coming down to see you this evening, sir,' French went on when his call was through. 'Murder of a man named Tarrant, who ran a patent medicine business called Koldkure in Exeborough a year or two ago. I'd be grateful for any information about the place you can give me.'

When late that evening French reached Exeborough, he found that his request had not been overlooked.

'The Super was sorry he had an engagement and couldn't meet you tonight, sir,' the station sergeant explained, 'but the place was on my beat before I got this step and perhaps I can tell you what you want to know.'

'Fine,' French returned. 'Then tell me anything you can.'

'It was in Arbutus Street, sir; that's down by the river, a working-class neighbourhood. It was a small place, just a yard and a couple of sheds. I can show it to you in the morning if you wish.'

'How long was it open?' French asked, the sergeant coming to a stop.

'About a year. It started about two and a half years ago and closed down about eighteen months ago.'

'Do you know where any of the people who worked there are to be found?'

'I heard that some of them had been taken over by Forster, that's the man who took the yard. He's a small printer.'

'I'll see him in the morning. Obliged to you, sergeant, but I'll not trouble you to come down. You might tell the Super that I'll hope to have the pleasure of seeing him before I go back.'

Forster proved to be a small anxious-looking man with a glass eye and a stammer. 'Yes,' he said, in answer to

French's question, 'I t-t-took over from those K-Koldkure people. I had no t-t-trouble with them. They seemed all right.'

'You took over some of their staff, did you not?'

'Five g-g-girls. Have th-three of them still, if you'd like to see them.'

Thus it came about that French met Edith Horne and obtained her views on Tarrant's works and their personnel. Edith was at first uncommunicative, but under the influence of French's manner she presently thawed.

'Have you ever,' French began, handing her a photograph of Tarrant, 'seen that man?' and when she had identified the portrait, he went on: 'I'm sorry to tell you that Mr Tarrant has been murdered, so you will understand the reason for my questions.'

She was obviously thrilled, but gave no indications of regret. If anything, there was satisfaction in her manner.

'You didn't like him?' French asked.

'Hated him,' she returned with decision.

'Why was that? Did you see much of him?'

'No, thank goodness. He was usually away. He did the travelling, you understand. Miss Weir managed the works.'

So French learnt Merle's name. Then he learnt a good deal more about Merle, some of which interested him extremely. He learnt that Merle was a saint on earth, and that there was nothing that Edith or any other member of the staff would not have done for her. He learnt also of the existence of Peter Temple and of their reputed loves, Temple's for Merle and Merle's for Tarrant, and finally that Tarrant's treatment of Merle had not been all that it should.

'Was Miss Weir engaged to Mr Tarrant?' he asked.

Edith nodded. 'She thought so, or at least she told me so.

But you couldn't count on Mr Tarrant. He would promise anything and then wriggle out of it.'

French smiled. 'No love lost on your side I can see, Miss Horne,' he declared. 'Well, from all I've heard, a good many people agree with you. Then you say Miss Weir was a partner as well as manager?'

'We imagined so, but of course we didn't know. She didn't talk much about herself, except one evening at supper when my mother was lying down and we were alone: I told you she lodged with us, didn't I? Then she seemed tired and sort of dispirited, and gave me to understand that she wished she had never come into the business at all. Not in so many words, you know, but that was what she meant.'

'What is her present address?'

'I don't know. She didn't give it to me and I have no idea where she is.'

French was surprised, and the suspicion which had flashed into his mind when he learnt Merle's relation to the dead man, became intensified. Why had she not left her address with this girl, who apparently had been more than a mere employee? It was obvious that he must find Merle, and at once.

'Where did she live before she came to Exeborough?'

'That I don't know either. She never said.'

'She wasn't telling much about herself. Do you know if she was in any kind of job, or was trained for anything? She must have had some training or she could never have managed the works.'

'She was a nurse, she did tell me that. When the place closed down and she was leaving, and I asked her what she was going to do, and she said, "Go back to nursing, I suppose. I can get a job at that easily enough."'

'I see,' said French. 'About what age was Miss Weir?'

'Thirty, I should think.'

During this interview French asked some questions about Peter Temple. But Edith Horne was not interested in Peter Temple. 'Good sort of chap,' she described him; 'straight and all that, and a good worker. Well-educated for a vanman, too. Intended for something better, I always thought. He was with some of the rest of us at Findlay's laundry before the Koldkure business started. He got a job as postman when the works closed down, but I don't know if he's in it still.'

'Tell me, did you ever hear of a Mr Hampden in connection with the business?'

Edith smiled. 'The manager of Braxamin? Why, he was the cause of the whole thing; at least, that was generally supposed. It was after his call here that the works closed down,' and she told him all that she knew on the subject.

French felt that his journey had not been wasted. Here in the person of Merle Weir was at least one of the women who had figured in Tarrant's life. An interview with her was obviously the next item on his programme.

But how could he trace her? Application to the various training schools would seem to be the first step. As he knew her approximate age, he could give reasonably close limits for her time of training. He rang up the Yard and asked that the inquiry be made.

This seemed all he could learn about the Koldkure works, but now, as often before, his characteristic thoroughness stepped in and suggested otherwise. While he was in Exeborough should not he interview all the remaining Koldkure employees he could find? Rather reluctantly he decided to do so.

The girls he found easily, as Edith knew where they were working, but from none of them did he learn anything fresh. Then he went on to the postmaster to ask about Temple.

'I happen to have heard of him, the official answered, 'because he left his district under unusual circumstances. It appears . . .' and he went on to tell of Peter's request for leave, and because it could not be granted till two days later, of his taking his own date and throwing up the job.

'Something pretty urgent there,' French smiled. 'Where did he go?'

This no one knew. French was not particularly interested in Peter, and yet he felt he ought to trace him also. Merle Weir had disappeared and Peter Temple had disappeared, and if Edith Horne was correct that Peter was in love with Merle, might they not have gone off somewhere together?

Having paid his respects to the Super, French went up that night to Town, calling next morning at the Yard. There he found that some information about Merle Weir had come in. She had been trained at Bart's and had then spent some time working as a private nurse. From this she had gone to the Wilton Grange Convalescent Home near Lydcott in Surrey. The Wilton Grange people had not been approached, but French could do this if he so desired.

French did so desire; in fact, instead of ringing up, he went down to Lydcott and called at the Home. There he learnt about Merle's period of service, ending in her sudden resignation to take up some unspecified and mysterious job. As the date of her leaving corresponded with the setting up of the Koldkure works, French had no difficulty in deciding the nature of that job.

But the matron did not know this. 'We thought indeed,'

she went on, 'that she was going to be married. I don't suppose there was any reason for thinking so, except that she had been seen a number of times with the chemist's assistant in Lydcott. I was sorry to lose Miss Weir. She was a really nice girl and an excellent nurse.'

'You don't happen to know the name of the chemist's assistant?' French asked, an idea flashing into his mind.

The matron didn't think she had ever heard it. French, returning to Lydcott, called at the single chemist's shop the village contained. Old Barr appeared.

'You had an assistant here, Mr Barr, about three years ago,' French began. 'Will you tell me his name?'

'I had three at that time,' answered the old man. 'First I had Fox, had had him for years, a good man. Then he left, got a better job somewhere, and Tarrant came. He didn't stay—'

'Tarrant!' said French with satisfaction. 'That's the man I mean. Can you tell me anything about him?'

'Got into the hands of the police, has he? I'm not surprised. He played me a dirty trick,' and Barr told of his having granted Tarrant leave with pay which had not been fully earned, and Tarrant's leaving him in the lurch at the end of the paid period. 'What's he been up to?'

'He's just been murdered,' French returned.

Barr was taken aback. 'Murdered, has he?' he repeated. 'That's bad! Though I've no doubt he asked for it.'

'I expect he did,' French agreed. 'Can you tell me anything more about him?'

Beyond the address of the firm from which Tarrant had come, Barr had nothing to say, though he handsomely admitted that the man was highly efficient, and in his work had given every satisfaction.

All this, French thought, was progress, and was therefore satisfactory. But none of it indicated the present position of Merle Weir. Upon this, he decided, he must concentrate until he found her.

16

Joseph French Beats the Organisation

In his search for Merle Weir, French considered that the time had come to enlist the help of his organisation. On reaching the Yard therefore he drafted her description, synthesised from the recollections of various witnesses, and sent it for insertion in the 'Wanted' column of next day's *Police Gazette*. Unhappily, he had been unable to obtain a photograph to accompany his paragraph, but unless she had changed her name, which was unlikely, the available information should be sufficient. Within a few hours every constable in the land would be looking out for her.

Hampden had shown him his graphs of the Koldkure activities, and French had noticed that at Aylton, a small town some twelve miles north of London, these had been particularly virulent. He now went with Carter to Aylton, borrowed a directory, and made a list of the chemists' shops. Then, followed by the sergeant, he went into these in turn, asking in each for a bottle of Braxamin.

In the first four he was served without comment, but in the fifth he had a return for his trouble. Here the assistant said, 'Yes, sir,' went away, and presently came back with a bottle in his hand.

'I'm sorry,' he explained, 'that we're out of Braxamin at the moment. We'll have it in tomorrow, if you can call again. But here's a preparation of our own which is quite good. Perhaps you'd care to try it?'

French took the bottle. It was labelled *Indigestion Remedy* with below it the name of the shop. 'Thanks,' he said, manfully repressing his satisfaction, 'that'll do as well. How much?'

'Same price, sir. Half-a-crown.'

French paid the money and took the neatly papered bottle. 'I'll be glad of a word with your proprietor,' he went on. 'Say Mr French would like to see him, though I don't suppose he knows my name.'

'Mr Jobson's in the office.' The assistant motioned with his head. 'Just go in.'

Jobson was a thick-set man with a heavy jaw and an aggressive expression. He looked his callers over inquiringly, but without speaking.

'Mr Jobson?' French said briskly.

'That's right. What can I do for you gentlemen?'

'We're police officers,' French declared. 'Here's my card. And this is my assistant, Sergeant Carter.'

'Sit down,' Jobson invited, scrutinising the card. 'Well, what's the trouble?'

'I came into your shop just now,' French went on, 'and asked for a bottle of Braxamin. Your assistant explained that you were out of it for the moment and sold me this instead,' and French unwrapped the bottle and laid it on the desk before him.

Jobson glanced at it. 'What of it?' he asked shortly.

216

'First, what not of it?' said French. 'We're not interested in you or your assistant or your sale of this preparation. We're not asking any questions about that.'

'Then what are you interested in?'

'The firm who sold you the stuff.'

Jobson looked uneasy. 'Koldkure?' he returned. 'What have they been doing?'

'No,' said French, deciding to bluff; 'that's just the point. I know all about Koldkure. It's the name of their successors that I want.'

'That stuff was bought from Koldkure,' Jobson asserted, but with considerably less assurance.

French felt sure he was lying, and decided on a further bluff. He leant forward and spoke more impressively. 'Now, Mr Jobson, I'd better be straight with you. This is a murder case: the murder of a man called James Tarrant at Little Bitton. You may have heard of it. We think we may be able to get some useful information from the firm which is putting this stuff out. If so, and if you try to mislead us in the matter, it may become a very serious thing for you.'

'Threatening, are you?'

'No; simply telling you where you stand. I presume you are aware that any attempt to withhold information from the police in a murder case may involve a charge of being an accessory after the fact?'

Jobson seemed taken aback. 'I've done nothing wrong,' he declared harshly. 'I don't see why you should attack me about it.'

'I can assure you,' French told him, 'that if you give me a correct answer to this one question, you'll hear no more of the matter. I know all about this Indigestion Remedy racket, but as I said, I'm not interested in it. All I want is to get the murderer; and you can help me.'

For a moment Jobson remained silent, then he picked up a pad, wrote on it and handed the sheet to French. It read: 'Patterson, Grantham Lane, Lincaster.'

French repressed a desire to cheer. Lincaster! It was from Lincaster that the unknown woman had rung up Tarrant on the morning of his death. Here at last was progress! He smiled at Jobson.

'Thank you, Mr Jobson, that's all I want. Assuming this address is correct, which I don't for one moment doubt, you'll not hear from me again. Good morning.' They went out, leaving Jobson with a mixture of resentment, bewilderment and fear stamped on his heavy features.

'Now, Carter, how do we get to Lincaster?' said French cheerily as they turned down the street.

'It's only about thirty miles from Little Bitton,' Carter returned. 'How'd it be if we went there and collected the car? We'll probably want it if we've to run about Lincaster.'

French considered. It was Saturday afternoon and the works would be closed.

'A better idea,' he said. 'We'll go by an early train on Monday. Arrange for Osborne to send the car to meet us.'

When about ten on Monday morning the two men left the train at Lincaster, they found the car waiting for them, and they drove to Grantham Lane.

It was a small working class street similar in appearance to Arbutus Street, Exeborough, and the firm's headquarters, when presently they found them, were not unlike those in which the Koldkure preparation had been produced. The resemblance persisted even in the sign. The legend 'Patt's Powders for the Pate. J. Λ. Patterson. Manufacturer of

Headache Powders, etc.' suggested the same authorship as 'Koldkure. John Tinsley. Manufacturer of Koldkure. Cures Colds, Sore Throats, etc.', from the underlying mentality to the final 'etc.'

'A bull's eye!' said French as he absorbed these particulars. 'That's Tarrant all right.'

He pushed open a door labelled 'Office' with the intention of asking for the manager. Then a better idea occurred to him. 'Is Miss Weir in?' he asked the sharp-featured girl who came forward. He could have hugged her when she replied: 'She's out at the moment, but she'll be back directly, if you care to wait.'

'We'll wait, thank you,' said French, subsiding into the chair she pushed forward.

It was seldom, he thought, that he had had so easy and so rapid an inquiry. It might have taken him weeks to find this woman and now in a few hours he had run her to earth. Good work! It was the sort of progress it was a pleasure to report.

He glanced about the office. It was tiny, match-boarded, and furnished in the cheapest way. There was a table with a typewriter on which the sharp-featured girl was pounding, a steel filing cabinet, another table bearing miscellaneous papers, a gas stove, a small cupboard and the three chairs at present in use. From the window was a vista of a yard with a small van being loaded by hand from an open door.

For ten, fifteen, twenty minutes they waited, and then another young woman entered. French admired her instantly. Not only good-looking but good, he felt sure, and not only good but capable. But she was pale and seemed tired and sad.

The sharp-featured girl glanced up. 'These gentlemen have been waiting to see you, Miss Weir,' she explained.

'Oh yes?' said Merle, looking questioningly at French. 'Will you come into my room?'

They passed into an even smaller and more cheaply furnished office. It contained little more than a table and two chairs, and Carter had to bring his chair with him so that all might be seated. French carefully closed the door, at which Merle raised her eyebrows.

'Our business is confidential,' he explained.

'What is it then?' Her manner was not short, only very tired.

'Here is my card,' said French, watching her as she read it.

It produced on Merle the effect it had had on so many before her. Slowly her face paled while an expression of alarm sharpened her features.

'Yes? What is it?' she repeated in a lower tone.

'Don't you know?' French asked quietly, still keeping his eyes fixed on her.

She shook her head. 'I'm afraid not. Please tell me what you want, as I'm anxious to get on with some work.'

'I'll keep you no longer than I can help, and I'm sorry to worry you.' French said this in spite of himself as he looked at her drawn face: it was not the gambit he had intended. 'It's about the late Mr Tarrant.'

French, watching her keenly, noticed a familiar phenomenon. Fear darkened her eyes, and he could see that she was bracing herself as if to meet a pressing danger.

'Oh yes,' she said again. 'What about him?'

'Everything that you can tell me, please. You know, of course, that there's a suspicion of foul play in the matter?'

'Yes, it was in the local paper.' She spoke with evident difficulty.

'You can see then why we want to learn all we can about the deceased,' he went on. 'When did you last see Mr Tarrant?'

'Last Sunday three weeks,' she replied after thought. 'We met in town, as we did at intervals.'

This was a fundamental question and French wondered if the answer were true. He doubted it, for Merle's manner was far from straightforward. Here, he thought, is a normally honourable woman, and she's lying and doesn't take kindly to it. However, he pretended to accept the statement without question.

'Was that meeting,' he continued, 'on business or pleasure?'

'Business principally. He was the owner of these works, you understand, and we met to discuss what was being done.'

'Then you were not joint owners, as I was informed was the case at Exeborough?'

She seemed surprised at the extent of his knowledge. 'I don't know how you learnt all that,' she returned, 'but you're quite correct. I put some money into Koldkure and therefore was technically part owner, though Mr Tarrant really was in control. But this business is different. It was his alone, and he paid me a salary as manager.'

'I understand,' said French. 'Now, Miss Weir, how did you first meet Mr Tarrant?'

She told him without hesitation, and the further the tale went, the more Tarrant's duplicity stood out in all its naked ugliness. He had cheated and deceived this girl, as he seemed to have cheated and deceived everyone with whom he had come in contact. And as French's questions became more

221

searching, he saw that she had hated and fought against the man's twisted methods, even though she had not realised how crooked these were. He saw that all through she had been driven on by her love, which had overpowered every other motive and desire.

'Tell me,' said French, with some relief passing on to another point, 'did you ring up Mr Tarrant on last Saturday morning?'

Again she seemed surprised at his knowledge. 'Yes and no,' she answered. 'I rang up his house wishing to speak to him, but he wasn't there and I therefore didn't do so.'

'And did you get into communication with him later?'

'No.'

'Now I'm afraid I'll have to ask what you wanted to speak to him about.'

For the first time she hesitated. 'Must I really answer that question?' she asked. 'It was so entirely personal and—remote from—anything connected with his—death.'

'You're not legally bound to answer any of my questions.' French returned, 'but you would be well advised to do so, as otherwise you may arouse unnecessary suspicions.'

She thought this over, looking more tired and worried than every 'Then if I needn't, I won't,' she said at last. 'I can assure you that it had nothing to do with—your inquiry.'

French decided to waive the point for the moment. 'Were you engaged to this man, Miss Weir?' he asked quietly.

She shook her head, apparently on the verge of tears and unable to speak. Then she qualified the negation. 'He had promised to marry me—many times, but no date had ever been settled, and I knew—he didn't mean it.'

French felt acutely sorry for her, though he could not but recognise how damaging was the admission. But the question was a proper one and he had given her an adequate caution.

'I'm sorry,' he said, 'just one more unpleasant question. Do you know of any other woman in Mr Tarrant's life; other than Miss Woolcombe, I mean?'

Again she shook her head. 'No,' she murmured faintly.

'Now something less personal,' he went on more happily. 'Did you ever meet a man called Hampden?'

She seemed relieved at the change of subject. 'Do you mean Mr Hampden of the Braxamin firm? No, I've heard of him, but I never met him,'

'What have you heard about him?'

'Well, I don't know that I can tell you very much. He called at the Koldkure works and saw Mr Tarrant, who happened to be there. I was out at the time. Then he and Mr Tarrant had a meeting next day at his hotel. It was a result of that meeting that the works closed down.'

'Last question. As a matter of form I shall want a list of your staff and their addresses. Can you let me have that now?'

'Certainly.'

More progress! French felt he had learnt a good deal from the interview, though not all he would have liked. He could not quite make up his mind about Merle. His instincts told him that she was a normally innocent and upright woman, but that on this occasion she was lying. Whether or not she was guilty of the murder was another matter: he felt he would require strong evidence before he could believe it. He had not asked her to account for her time on the Saturday afternoon, but he had not forgotten the question. It might be a useful line during a second interview, should such become necessary.

When French looked at the list which Merle presently handed him, the first name he saw was that of Peter Temple.

'That's familiar,' he said. 'Was Peter Temple employed at the Koldkure works?'

'Yes,' she answered, explaining how he came to be in Lincaster.

French next saw Peter and heard an abridged history of his life and the details of his present appointment. Peter answered the questions with readiness but with skill, leading French to suppose that his obvious admiration for Merle was due to appreciation of a kindly boss, rather than to the fact that he loved her to desperation. But when French went on to question Rose Jordan, the sharp-featured typist, he learnt some facts which interested him a good deal more. Rose he summed up as competent and intelligent, but as a busybody and a talker, and rather spiteful at that. French believed she envied Merle, probably for her prettier face and kindlier manner—at all events she seemed to derive a malicious pleasure from speaking slightingly of her.

All the same there was not much about Merle with which she could find fault. Grudgingly she admitted that she was a good employer and kindly to the girls under her. All she could urge against her was that she was often unpleasant to Mr Temple, and this she did with a malevolence which argued a strong personal interest.

'He's ready to worship the ground she walks on,' Rose went on bitterly. 'One would think she might show some consideration for all he does for her, but no, she takes it all as a matter of course.'

'Perhaps he wants to marry her and she won't agree?' French suggested mildly.

Rose rather sulkily said she knew nothing about this and that anyhow it wasn't her business.

'That's true of course,' French said easily, 'but one can't help noticing what's before one's eyes, can one? Now tell me, did you see much of Mr Tarrant?'

The girl stared. 'Mr Tarrant?' she repeated. 'Who's he?'

French was interested. Tarrant then had kept his connection with the place a real secret. Or had he been there under an alias? He took out his sheaf of photographs. 'He's among these,' he told her. 'Seen any of them before?'

She turned them over with a revealing eagerness. This girl's interest was in men, and if so, it accounted for her feelings towards Merle. French saw he must discount her statements accordingly.

But there was no need to discount her next remark; in fact French took it very seriously indeed.

'Is that the one you mean?' she said, holding out a card. 'I've seen him.'

So Tarrant had used another name! French took the photograph and then caught his breath. It was not Tarrant's face which looked up at him, but Hampden's.

'Oh,' he answered, 'you've seen this man, have you? Tell me about him.'

'He came in, let's see, it must have been about a month ago. I was alone in the office. He said, "I was passing and saw your sign. I'd like to try your headache powders. I'm a martyr to headaches and I can't get anything that does any good."'

'And you gave him some?'

'Well, naturally.'

'Did he make any other remarks? '

'Yes. He said, "Don't you make an indigestion remedy as

225

well? I'd like to try some of that too. I believe my headaches come from indigestion!" So I gave him another bottle.'

'Quite. Was that the only time you saw him?'

'The only time.'

'Now one other question: have you had any correspondence with a man named Hampden lately?'

'Hampden?' She shook her head. 'No, I never came across the name.'

So Hampden was mixed up in it after all! Apparently not as a partner, though indeed if Tarrant had kept his connection with the place so secret that the confidential clerk had never either seen or heard of him, why not Hampden also? Yet the visit did not look proprietorial. Much more it suggested the investigator. Was it not more likely that as Hampden had traced the first Braxamin rival to its source in the Koldkure establishment, so he had traced the second to Lincaster?

But if so, why had he not said so? French's entire information on the matter had come from Sir Claud Monroe. Here was something to be looked into.

He put a few further questions, but without learning anything more of interest, then asked that Joyce Caldwell, the forewoman, should be sent to the office. She proved to be a large woman on the wrong side of forty, slow speaking and placid, but he thought quietly efficient.

She was enthusiastic about Merle and liked Peter, but had never seen or heard of either Tarrant or Hampden. Obviously she hadn't the slightest idea—nor had Rose Jordan—that there was anything questionable about the honesty of her industry. But from her French learnt something which gave him a good deal of thought.

They were speaking about Merle, when Joyce remarked that she had seemed very depressed lately.

'Since when have you noticed that?' he asked, supposing that the cause was the news of Tarrant's death.

'Since last Saturday morning,' she replied unexpectedly.

'Saturday *morning*?' he replied with a sudden quickening of interest. 'What happened? Tell me about it.'

Then came out Merle's movements on that fatal day; her preoccupation, her excited manner, her going out about eleven and returning some half hour later, her shutting herself up in her office and refusing to deal with further business that day, and finally her going off to Saxham St Edmunds in the afternoon.

'Oh,' said French. 'How do you know that?'

Joyce Caldwell hesitated. 'Rose Jordan told me. Rose was on leave last Saturday; her sister was ill and she went over to Saxham to look after the children till they could get other help. She saw her at Saxham.'

'Yes?'

'And then an hour later she saw Mr Temple. She hadn't spoken to Miss Weir, but she did to Mr Temple. He said they were both going to tea in Ralston, but that he had been delayed.'

French called Rose in again. She confirmed the story in every detail.

He was intensely interested. The Ralston bus passed through Little Bitton. It looked as if both Merle and Peter had been there: Merle shortly before the hour at which Tarrant was murdered. Was there any connection between these two events? French remembered the woman Mrs Bordon had seen on Webble Road. Could this by any possibility have been Merle? If so, it should be a pointer to the end of his case.

During lunch he made a poor companion for Carter. His

227

thoughts remained full of what he had just learnt. At last, light was beginning to dawn. That morning his views on the tragedy had been nebulous; now, if they weren't crystalline, they were at least suggestive and promising. He had imagined that Hampden might somehow be mixed up in this medicine swindle, and he was. He had imagined that there might be some woman whom Tarrant had treated badly, and there was. Moreover, there was a man who was in love with the woman who loved Tarrant, and who might have turned to murder to rid himself of his rival. Lastly, there was the man he had already known—Cooke—who had wanted to marry Miss Woolcombe, and who had been supplanted by Tarrant.

Here were four persons, any one of whom might be guilty. And there might be others in a similar situation to Cooke's.

Admirable as his progress had been, French felt there was an immense lot of work still to be done. And his next item was obvious: to interrogate Merle Weir and Peter Temple as to their movements on the previous Saturday.

Before returning to the works he rang up the Yard to report his whereabouts and was told that an answer had come in to his 'Wanted' notice. Merle Weir was employed in Patterson's works, Grantham Lane, Lincaster, but the officer giving the message expected from French's address that he had discovered this already.

'Once again I've beaten the organisation,' French told himself as he and Carter walked back to Grantham Lane.

17

Joseph French Narrows the Issue

Merle had returned from lunch when the two men reached the works. French could see that his request for a further interview alarmed her.

'This is a confidential matter,' he began, looking pointedly at the match-boarded walls. 'I suggest that you send your typist on a message.'

With obvious unwillingness Merle put her head out of the door. 'I'm sorry, Rose, that we want this office: mine's too small. Will you move into Mr Temple's for a few minutes?'

'That's better,' said French. Then, looking squarely at Merle, he went on more gravely: 'Now, Miss Weir, I have to ask you some questions which may be important to us both. But first I must warn you that you are not bound to answer them unless you like, and also that anything you say will be taken down and may be used in evidence should this matter go into Court.'

The expression of fear in Merle's eyes grew more pronounced, though she spoke with continued assurance. 'I can't understand that,' she declared. 'What's the good of asking questions if I needn't answer them?'

'I can explain it,' French answered a little grimly. 'No one is bound to say anything which might incriminate him. If I ask you anything which you think might incriminate you, you will be well advised not to answer.'

'Incriminate me?' she repeated falteringly. 'Why, are you going to accuse me of anything?'

'I sincerely hope not,' French returned, and he meant it. He could not but feel sympathy for this nice young woman. 'I am giving you the caution, as I am bound to do, before asking you any questions.'

'Is it the business?' she asked. 'I admit I wasn't altogether satisfied about it, but Mr Tarrant assured me it was all right.'

'It's not the business. What I want to know is where you went and what you did on the afternoon of last Saturday week?'

She stared, while her face grew dead white. 'Oh,' she cried, 'you can't suspect—that I—?'

'Better not say anything about that,' French interrupted. 'If you feel you can answer my question, do so.'

'Of course I can answer it,' she replied more sharply. 'I went for a walk, a long country tramp. I—I felt it would do me good.'

'I must have some further details, I'm afraid. Where did you walk?'

'At Dunsfield. It was a place I had passed through and admired, and I had wanted to explore it for a long time.'

'Where exactly is Dunsfield?'

'The first village from Saxham St Edmunds in the direction of Ralston.'

'I remember. Well, we'll get your exact route presently. But another point first. You say you felt the walk would do you good. Just why? Weren't you well?'

Merle hesitated, and then made a gesture as if throwing caution to the winds. 'I suppose I had better tell you,' she said in a low voice, and now French thought that she meant to speak the absolute truth.

'I read in the local paper of Mr Tarrant's engagement, and I felt rather miserable. I shouldn't have, of course, because I had really known before this that I should never marry him. He did not love me and I could not have made him happy. So I was wrong to have taken it so much to heart. But I'm afraid I did. I thought the long tramp through this interesting scenery might help me.'

It was reasonable, yet French was not satisfied. He began to probe for details. She had not been able that morning to concentrate on business. She had caught the two-thirty bus for Saxham, had changed there and waited ten minutes for the Ralston bus. At Dunsfield she had taken a four-mile round, then, as she was back too early for the return bus, she had walked on the two miles into Saxham. She had bought some raisins and chocolate in a little shop in Dunsfield during this second visit. No, she hadn't met anyone she knew during the whole excursion, until on leaving Saxham on the return journey she had found Temple in the bus. He had followed her to Dunsfield, but had missed her.

'Now tell me, Miss Weir, had you ever been to Little Bitton?'

The question took Merle aback. She sat staring helplessly before her.

'Yes,' she answered at last.

'With the deceased?'

231

'No, alone.'

'For what purpose?'

'Just out of curiosity. To see the place.'

'Did you know The Gables?'

'I've seen it from a distance. I've never been near it.'

'Did you know where the deceased fished?'

'No; though, of course, I could guess.'

French paused, turned over his notes, and then began again. 'Now, you rang up The Gables on Saturday morning and were told he would be fishing there that afternoon. The suggestion is that you went to Little Bitton to see him. Remembering my caution, have you any comment to make on that?'

She was now ghastly. 'I did think of going to see him,' she admitted. 'I had some crazy idea that if I could speak to him again he would change his mind and give up Miss Woolcombe. But in the bus I saw that was absurd. I saw it would be useless and only painful for us both. I didn't go,'

Once again French was puzzled. 'You should have told me all that at first,' he said more mildly. 'Holding back essential facts naturally makes me suspicious.'

Her statement seemed consistent and yet French was profoundly dissatisfied with the interview. What he had been told might be the truth, but if so, he was convinced that he had not heard everything. However, he could do nothing more about it at the moment, and he turned to the next item on his programme: a similar interrogation of Peter Temple.

Peter's manner he found as suggestive as Merle's. Here also was doubt and an anxiety amounting to fear. French imagined that the two had agreed on the tale they would put up. His opinion was strengthened by Peter's statement. It was clear and reasonable, yet he made it with an absence of that ring of truth which counts for so much.

He began by admitting that Merle was, or had been, fond of Tarrant and that on the Friday evening, when she had seen the news of his engagement in the local paper, it had caused her great pain. He was away from the works on Saturday morning, and when he called at her rooms after lunch it was to learn that she had gone out. He imagined that she had gone for a long tramp, as she had more than once mentioned that nothing quieted her nerves like walking. He guessed that she had chosen Dunsfield, as they had discussed a walk there on various occasions, and he knew she intended to take it at the first opportunity. This opinion was confirmed by the hour at which she had left her rooms. It would have just enabled her to catch a bus for Saxham, the first stage of the journey. He thought she would be better for having a companion, so started in pursuit. Through a strange coincidence, when changing buses in Saxham, he met Rose Jordan, the office typist, who that day was on leave. By a still stranger coincidence she had seen Merle taking the Ralston bus an hour earlier. He therefore knew that he was on the right track. He got down at Dunsfield and walked over the route he imagined Merle would follow, but without overtaking her. Eventually he had given up the search and was returning home when he met her in the bus from Saxham.

French felt that without corroboration he could not accept this statement either. Was there not a more likely explanation of these mysterious journeys?

Suppose Merle, feeling herself deceived, jilted and injured by Tarrant, had gone down to see him, perhaps to ask him to fulfil a promise to marry her? Suppose she had made preparations to take her revenge on him should he refuse to do so? A passionate woman, wronged by the man she had loved, might well go to great lengths.

This seemed possible enough, but it was not without its difficulties. There was no evidence that Merle had been to Little Bitton on the afternoon in question, nor that she knew about Tarrant's tea-basket. Nor that she had the aconitine. It was true she was in charge of a chemical business and had been a nurse, but the business did not use aconitine, and she was no longer practising nursing. There was also French's conviction, which, of course, was not evidence, that a woman of Merle's personality would never commit a premeditated murder, whatever she might do under sudden emotional stress. But if ever there were a premeditated murder, this was one.

It was therefore clear that he must not only test the statements of these two, but also investigate the movements of other possibles, of which the first two were Hampden and Cooke.

Before leaving the works French called Peter and Merle in together. 'You must recognise,' he said, 'that a certain suspicion naturally attaches to every acquaintance of Mr Tarrant's who was near Little Bitton on Saturday afternoon week. I'm not suggesting that I doubt your statements, but obviously I must test them. To do so I should like your photographs in the clothes you wore on that Saturday. Any objection to Sergeant Carter taking them?'

With evident unwillingness Merle agreed, and Peter followed suit. In French's 'murder bag' was a camera. Neither he nor Carter were experts, but both could take a reasonably good picture, and soon the job was done. Half an hour later the two men were *en route* for Little Bitton.

'I don't know whether I'm getting sentimental in my old age, Carter,' French observed, 'but I should be sorry to have to bring those two in on such a charge.'

'I feel the same,' Carter answered. 'But lord, sir, you know better than I how misleading appearances can be. Particularly with women prisoners. I've seen them in Court looking like plaster saints with the dock for the niche.'

French knew that this was horse sense. It was the facts, not his feelings, which mattered, and he must not forget it.

After learning next morning from Sergeant Osborne that no further local discoveries had been made, they drove to the Saxham police station and French asked for an interview with Superintendent Hawkins. He told him what he had learnt and then went on:

'There are a couple of small jobs that you could have done for me, if you would. To develop my photographs and fix them up with a few others for selection purposes. That's one.'

'Right. And then?'

'To send copies to Osborne, so that he could find out if either Weir or Temple were at Little Bitton.'

'I'll do it. Anything else?'

'To cover the routes they ostensibly took: bus conductors, the shop where Miss Weir said she bought chocolate, and so on. I want to see Hampden as to why he kept dark Tarrant's connection with the second ramp, otherwise I would do it myself.'

'That's all right, Mr French. I'll see to it.'

'Thank you. Then I'll go and see Hampden.'

The Braxamin manager frowned when he recognised his visitor. 'Well, Chief Inspector,' he said, 'is it the Tarrant affair again? I had hoped we had finished with it on your last call.'

French avoided the obvious reply. Instead he said politely: 'I'm sorry to trouble you again, but one or two matters have arisen since I was here last.'

'I'm at your service, of course,' Hampden answered shortly, 'but I hope you'll be quick, as I have an appointment directly.'

'A couple of questions will give me all I want,' French returned. 'The first is this: Why did you not tell me that the late Mr Tarrant was behind the Lincaster Remedy?'

This was evidently both unexpected and disagreeable. French could see that Hampden was thinking deeply.

'I don't think I understand you, Chief Inspector,' he said at last. 'Are you suggesting that I deliberately held back some material information?'

'I asked you the direct question and you said you didn't know.'

Hampden's manner grew more assured. 'I'm afraid you've get the affair wrong,' he returned. 'I can't now tell you anything about Tarrant's activities, for the same reason that I couldn't do so on your first call: that I don't know anything about them.'

'What exactly do you know about the Lincaster Works?'

Hampden made a gesture of irritation. 'I hope this is really material to the Tarrant case, as my time should be otherwise occupied,' he said with an unpleasant intonation. 'What I know about the place is: firstly, that the rival remedy is being sent out from it: a lot of work went into finding that out; secondly, that it's being run by a man and woman called respectively Temple and Weir; and thirdly, that these people had been employed in the Koldkure Works in Exeborough.'

'That all, sir?'

'That's all. As I have already told you, it occurred to me that Tarrant might be behind those others, but I discovered nothing to back up the idea.'

'Then, when you knew all that, why did you not act?'

'I wasn't ready. These people were swindling Braxamin, but I wasn't satisfied that I could take them into Court and get satisfaction. In fact, to be quite candid, I wasn't sure of my next step.'

French felt dissatisfied with this statement, though he realised that it might all be true. He therefore answered more pleasantly: 'Thank you, Mr Hampden, that answers the first of my questions. The second is much easier. As a matter of form, I have to ask everyone who was connected in any way with the deceased gentleman to account for his time between 2 p.m. and 5 p.m. on the afternoon of Saturday week. Will you please tell me that, so that your name may be crossed off my list?'

Hampden stared. 'Look here, Chief Inspector,' he said brusquely, 'let us understand each other. Are you accusing me of murdering Tarrant?'

French made an easy gesture. 'Of course not, sir. We have our routine and we have to carry it out. This question is invariably asked in murder cases, and shouldn't be offensive.'

'I find it offensive, particularly after what has just passed between us.'

'I'm sorry, sir, but I'm afraid I must press it.'

'I needn't answer it.'

'Of course not,' answered French, 'if you don't object to my asking myself why you have refused.'

For some moments Hampden sat without replying, tapping his fingers impatiently on his desk and whistling through his teeth. Then he shrugged. 'All right, have it your own way. You want to know what I did between 2 p.m. and 5 p.m.?'

'If you please. I should add that your statement will be taken down and you will be asked to sign it, so that no misunderstanding can arise as to what you said.'

'I thought the phrase was "and will be used in evidence against you"?' Hampden put in bitterly.

'Only if the police officer has made up his mind to charge the witness with an offence. I have already made it clear that I have no such idea in your case.'

'Oh, very well. Let's see. Saturday is our early closing day, and I left with the others at half-past twelve. I went home. I live in Primrose Road, close to Primrose Hill, about ten minutes' walk from here. I lunched and then I went for my usual Saturday afternoon walk. I do that as a matter of health. I returned home somewhere about six. Is that all you want?'

'That's all, sir, if you'll just give me the itinerary of your walk.'

'And if I met anyone I knew, I suppose? Well, I didn't, as it happens.'

'Then the itinerary?'

Hampden sighed with ostentatious irritation. 'I lunched at one, as I always do, and went out—I can't tell you exactly at what time, but it was about half-past two. That near enough?'

'Quite, thank you.'

'I walked to Chalk Farm Station, took the tube to Golders Green, and went up on Hampstead Heath. There I spent the afternoon walking about and sitting at various places. I had tea at a little shop at the far side of the Heath and then walked home.'

'Where was your tea-shop, sir?'

'It was in Highgate Road, where the Heath comes right up to the road. I don't remember the name if I noticed it.'

'About what time did you have tea?'

'Ah, there you have me, I'm afraid. Some time about five, I think.' He paused for a moment, then continued: 'But if it's a matter of real moment you can find out for yourself. I walk fairly slowly on these solitary excursions, say, about three miles an hour. I spent perhaps twenty minutes over tea, and then walked directly home. So if you like to walk back at that pace, you can find out.'

This was exactly what French proposed to do. After getting details of the route—via Mansfield Road, Parkhill Road and Haverstock Hill—he set off, Carter following with the car.

It took just forty minutes, so if Hampden's recollections were correct, he must have reached the tea-shop about five, as he had said. French wondered if he could confirm this. There were two tea-shops close together, and he inquired in the first without result. In the second, however, he had better luck.

There, after a good deal of questioning, he found the waitress who had attended Hampden. She remembered him because he was faddish about his tea. He had, she said, ordered toast and butter and she had brought him buttered toast, and he had made a fuss about it and sent it away and asked for fresh dry toast with separate butter. Bit of nonsense, it was, as if they weren't really the same thing after all. But people were like that, and you just had to put up with it. However, he wasn't so bad as some, for he left a good tip.

There was no doubt that the man had been Hampden,

for the waitress unhesitatingly picked out his photograph from French's collection. But she could not say at what time he had arrived or left.

This was satisfactory so far as it went. Hampden's statement as to the close of his afternoon was true. Could anything be learnt as to the earlier part?

French drove with Carter to Golders Green Station, but there he had no luck. No one knew Hampden or remembered ever having seen him. This of course was not surprising. It was unlikely that a chance traveller should be recalled.

They went then to Chalk Farm and here encountered the converse difficulty. The entire staff knew Hampden, who was, they said, a regular traveller. But they saw him so often that no one could remember whether he had been there at 2.30 p.m. on the Saturday in question. At last, after much suggestion, a ticket collector recalled that Hampden *had* gone for a Golders Green train at forty minutes past two. He had stopped to ask this man about his son, who had just left his employment at a tobacconist's with whom Hampden dealt. When they had discussed the boy's future for a moment the collector had said: 'Your train's about due, sir,' and then Hampden had returned: 'Oh, I'm going the other way this time: Golders Green for a stroll on the Heath.' The down train was two minutes later than the up, so Hampden had had plenty of time to catch it.

Here also was confirmation of the manager's statement. Fairly complete confirmation too, French thought, for no more could be expected. Indeed it was so complete that French wondered whether the discussion about the collector's son and the buttered toast were not intentional: designed to fix Hampden's presence at the hours of two and five. Then he thought not. Hampden could not have known that the collector would have made that remark about the train, and after all many people dislike the greasiness of buttered toast.

Could Hampden then have visited Little Bitton and murdered Tarrant? It depended on whether or not a car were available. If a car had been waiting for him at some nearby station and further, if he had been able to dispose of it near the tea shop, he could have done the journey easily enough. He had two and a quarter hours, and the actual running would have taken little more than two hours, leaving perhaps ten minutes for the crime. French noted that the matter must be gone into exhaustively.

He rang up the Yard, asking that the necessary inquiries should be made. Was Hampden's car out that afternoon, and if so, who had taken it and where had it gone? Particularly, had a car been hired from any of the garages in the Camden, Hampstead or Highgate areas, or anywhere easily accessible from these?

One inquiry still remained which, while it would provide no actual confirmation of Hampden's statement, would reflect generally on its credibility. He drove to Primrose Road, and leaving Carter at the end of the street, walked on alone to No. 15 and asked for Hampden. As it was still within business hours, he was not greatly surprised to be told that he was not at home.

'It's about cricket, the Kenilworth Club,' he went on to the maid. Then as an apparent afterthought he added: 'I hope this is the Mr Hampden I'm looking for. I wonder if you can tell me? He's a great cricketer, is he not?'

The girl shook her head. 'I'm afraid you've come to the wrong house,' she declared. 'This Mr Hampden doesn't play.'

French registered sudden enlightenment. 'Oh, then I've got them mixed. I knew there were two Mr Hampdens and one was a cricketer and one a great hiker. This one, I suppose, is the hiker?'

A faint smile hovered on the girl's lips. 'He's not what I would call a hiker. He goes out for walks on Saturday afternoons, but I never heard of him going any distance.'

'Ah,' French concluded, 'then I have got the wrong address. Sorry.'

So that part of the story at least was true. Hampden did take Saturday afternoon walks, apparently like that across the Heath. No confirmation of the man's statement, as French had foreseen, yet it tended to support it.

Once again it did not look as if Hampden was his man. Slightly despondent, French drove back to Little Bitton, determined next morning to reconsider the case against Cooke.

18

Joseph French Reaches a Decision

When that night French re-read everything relating to Cooke in the file, he came to the conclusion that he had dismissed the man too quickly from his calculations. A strong case enough could, he now saw, be made against him, stronger indeed than against Merle Weir, Temple or Hampden. With reviving interest he began to collect the relevant details.

First he recalled Cooke's statements, both admitted and implied. The man was hard up and had been paying court to Jean Woolcombe because he wanted her money. Like Tarrant, he was sure that, once married, he could wheedle what he wanted out of Jean. He had not put this so brutally, but there was no question as to its truth. On the Friday afternoon he had learnt from the *Saxham St Edmunds Weekly Gazette* that Tarrant had out-manoeuvred him and was in a fair way to net the cash. He had rung up Tarrant from Hampden's office, only to learn that his supplanter was from home, but would be back on the Saturday afternoon. On that afternoon he had seen Tarrant fishing from his own grounds and had met him on the river bank. There he had told him that if he didn't clear out, he would anonymously suggest to Miss Woolcombe that she investigate the Koldkure affair. On this Tarrant had coolly suggested a division of the spoils, to which Cooke had agreed!

A sordid and unpleasant story, French had concluded, but was it true? He had thought so when he had heard it, but now he was far from sure. Even if it were, Cooke's motive for the murder remained strong. According to the proposal, Cooke would get only one-third of all that Tarrant could screw out of his wife. Why should Cooke put up with a third when there was a chance of his getting the whole?

The division-of-the-spoils tale might well be an invention on Cooke's part, designed for the very purpose it had up to now achieved: to suggest to inquisitive policemen that Cooke's interest was to keep Tarrant alive. Had he, French, fallen for an amateur's trick? He was glad he had kept his conclusions to himself.

Whether he had been wise or foolish, it was clear that Cooke's story must be more carefully investigated. What lines should that investigation take?

Ordinary routine had corroborated one item of the story. It was true that the two men had had a discussion on the river bank. The prints Carter had found were those of Cooke and Tarrant respectively, and their number and position indicated an emotional interview.

Suppose that after the interview Cooke had gone back along the bank, ostensibly to return to his home? Suppose when he reached Webble Road he had turned right instead of left, walking along the edge of the valley till he had passed where Tarrant was fishing? Suppose he had then gone down again towards the river, found Tarrant's tea-basket and put the aconitine into the tea?

244

It was difficult to see how this theory could be tested. Cooke had stated that after leaving Tarrant he had worked at home for an hour before going to see a friend in the village, and during that time no one, he believed, had seen him. Of course, were he guilty, he might have been observed on his way to or from the actual insertion of the poison, but unhappily the local police had already unsuccessfully searched for persons who were in the locality at the critical time. However it might be possible to learn something, and next morning French began with a visit to the police station.

'I've got some news for you, sir,' Sergeant Osborne greeted him. 'A report has just come in from Saxham. Miss Merle Weir bought some raisins and chocolate at Mrs Kent's shop in Dunsfield on the Saturday afternoon of the murder. Mrs Kent is not exactly sure of the time, but thinks it was after five.'

'That's good,' French. answered. 'How did the shopkeeper happen to remember?'

'Picked out Miss Weir's photograph and said she noticed her particularly because she was a nice-spoken young lady but seemed unhappy.'

'Any trace of Miss Weir having been here?'

'Yes, sir. That's the particular thing. It was she that Mrs Bordon saw.'

For a moment French thought that he had reached the end of his case. Did this not mean Merle's guilt? Then he saw that it might not do so, and that in any case a great deal more information must be obtained before he could be sure.

Having called on Mrs Bordon and satisfied himself as to her statement, he returned to Osborne.

245

'I want to trace her journey by bus,' he explained. 'Can you do that here, or shall I run into Saxham?'

'Saxham would be better, sir. The depot's there. If you think it's worth it, I'll try again here along the road and so on.'

'I wish you would,' said French. 'Then I'll do the buses.'

At the transport headquarters French saw the manager, explained what he wanted, and asked could he interview the conductors of the buses in question.

The manager looked up his rosters. Four men were involved, three of whom would shortly be available, while the fourth was at his home.

The first three could give no helpful information, and French went on to the address of their colleague.

Thomas Cullen was a small wizened-looking man with sharp eyes and an independent manner. French was pleased with his appearance, thinking that he would prove a better witness. And so he did. He said promptly that he had been the conductor on the three-fifty run from Saxham to Ralston on the day in question, and on the five-fifteen return run from Ralston to Saxham.

'You're the man I want,' French returned heartily. 'Here are some photographs. Did any of those people travel on either of those buses?'

The man cocked a humorous eye at French. 'Ten days ago,' he remarked. 'You wouldn't 'ave me remember everyone who travelled ten days ago? 'Ave a 'eart now, would you?'

'See what you can do,' French urged him.

The man turned over the cards, paused, considered one appraisingly, laid it aside, and went on with the others. Then he repeated the operation with a second card. Finally he handed his selections to French. With satisfaction French saw that they were Merle and Temple.

'Those two travelled on that day,' Cullen said with decision; 'the lady on the three-fifty from Saxham and the man on the five-fifteen from Ralston.'

This was satisfactory evidence. French already knew that Merle had travelled by the three-fifty and Peter Temple had admitted returning by the other bus from Dunsfield to Saxham. This showed that Cullen was a highly reliable witness.

'Good,' he said encouragingly; 'that's going to be helpful. How do you happen to remember them so well?'

'Because they looked so unhappy. I noticed the lady first, she seemed in bad trouble. I was sorry for 'er, for she was nice-looking too. Then when the man got in I said to myself, "'Ere's another of them," I said. "'E was looking worse; as if 'e'd seen a ghost. '*Orror*, if you take me; 'orror and despair; somethink terrible.'

'Right,' French approved. 'That explains how you remembered their faces. But how did you remember which journeys they made?'

Cullen did not reply so readily, and when he did speak it was with a slightly shamefaced air. 'To tell you the truth, sir, I don't 'ave much to think about on these runs, and I'm fond of inventing stories about the passengers. And when I saw those two, both sort of miserable and going to the same place, I made up a tale about them 'aving 'ad a lover's quarrel, so to speak. It ain't no 'arm and it passes the time.'

French wondered if he had heard aright. Merle had gone to Little Bitton, but Temple had got on at Dunsfield. 'Both going to the same place?' he repeated sharply. 'What do you mean?'

Cullen stared. 'Why, 'er going from Saxham to Little Bitton and 'im from Little Bitton to Saxham.'

Then not only Merle had lied! Temple also had been at Little Bitton, and he also had denied it. But their story was consistent; therefore they had jointly invented it. A conspiracy to defeat justice!

What terrible tale of tragedy did these movements and these falsehoods indicate? Had Merle interviewed Tarrant, and furious or despairing at his attitude, had she put the poison in the tea? Or had Temple discovered how Tarrant had received Merle, and driven to distraction by his love, had himself used the aconitine? Or had they met and conspired together to commit the murder?

French was loath to believe any of these alternatives, yet it was evident that these two must know something of the crime. Only such a knowledge could explain their conduct. Regretfully he saw that there was a case for arrest against both of them, though in the last resort this would not be his responsibility.

He spent some hours that afternoon considering the whole case afresh. It seemed to him that he would not be justified in keeping back what he had learnt from his temporary superiors, for whom indeed he was working and to whom he was responsible. He therefore rang up Superintendent Hawkins and a conference was arranged for the following morning.

This was held at headquarters at Saxham, and there were present Major Carling in the chair, Superintendent Hawkins, French, Carter, a shorthand typist and, by the Chief Constable's special invitation, Sergeant Osborne.

'Well, gentlemen,' Carling began when greetings and a little sublimated chaff had been exchanged, 'we're met to hear a statement from Chief Inspector French on the Tarrant case and to consider with him what action, if any, should be taken. We'll be glad to hear all that you can tell us, Chief Inspector, but I should like to know before you start whether you propose to recommend an arrest, or whether this is merely a report progress conference?'

'I regret, sir,' French answered, 'that I've not got a very satisfactory case to put before you. As for an arrest, that will be for you and Mr Hawkins to decide when you have heard the evidence.'

Major Carling nodded. 'Very well. Then please go ahead.'

'I might begin, sir, by telling you what I did and the facts I learned in my investigation, and then go on to the rather unsatisfactory conclusions I have reached. My first step after leaving you on Sunday week was to visit the scene of the tragedy. There I found . . .' and he briefly recounted his activities from that preliminary walk on the bank of the Webble, right down to his latest discovery through the evidence of bus conductor Cullen.

They heard him with close attention. 'That's very interesting,' Carling said when he had finished. 'You certainly have done some work in the time. And your conclusions?'

'Perhaps I'd better give you my line of thought consecutively,' French answered; 'that is, apart from the actual facts which I've just stated. From the medical evidence I assumed that the aconitine had been put into deceased's flask of tea, that after drinking it he felt ill and tried to reach his home, but that owing to the increasing paralysis he fell into the river and was drowned.

'I also had reached that conclusion. You agree, Super?'

'Yes, sir, I think there is no doubt about it.'

'The question then of course was: who could have

administered the aconitine? Here I sub-divide the question into: one, who had the necessary motive? Two, who had the opportunity? And three, which of the above could have got the aconitine?

'As you have no doubt realised, my investigations gave me four suspects: Hampden, Cooke, Merle Weir and Temple. I may perhaps state the case against each of these as I see it.

'Hampden first. I have to admit, sir, that I'm greatly puzzled about Hampden. I've been unable to prove anything directly against him, but his manner throughout has been extremely suspicious. I know of course that that's not evidence, but it's very unsatisfactory, and I think his case should be discussed.'

'By all means, Chief Inspector. Let's hear everything.'

'Hampden's position for some time has been rather critical. Owing to an extravagant home life he was hard up. Cooke, as the originator of Braxamin, was jealous of his greater influence in the business and was trying to oust him from it. Then in these strained circumstances there came the fall of the Braxamin receipts, increasing his anxieties. He found that the deceased had been underselling his firm and bought him out. The returns improved, but presently began to fall again. Hampden investigated further and found that the same ramp was being repeated, and by the same staff. Whether or not he knew that the deceased was behind it, I've not been able to find out, but there is at least a strong presumption that he did. He also knew that if the business were not stopped, it would eventually ruin him.'

'You can't prove his knowledge?'

'No, sir, but I might if I had a search warrant. If it's true, there would have been a motive all right.'

'Motive for murder? I don't quite see that, Chief Inspector. If he submitted his proofs to his Board, no doubt proceedings against the deceased would have been taken.'

'No doubt, sir. They could either have done that or they could have fought him commercially by increasing their vendors' commission till they put him out of business. But either of the courses would have involved them in heavy loss, because Tarrant was a man of straw from whom they could have recovered no damages. Hampden doubtless believed, and probably correctly, that it would have cost him his job.'

'No doubt you're right, but even so I don't see how murder would have helped.'

'Murder would have brought the Lincaster business to an end without any trouble or cost to the Braxamin Company.'

'But why? If the deceased was out of it, wouldn't those others, Weir and Temple, have carried it on?'

'I don't think so. Though I'm going to put the case for murder against them presently, I think they're honest. I feel sure, now that the deceased is out of it, that they'll close down. Weir, I'm satisfied, wouldn't stand for carrying on, and Temple would do whatever she tells him.'

Major Carling twisted in his chair. 'It's not very convincing, you know.' He smiled to take any sting out of the words. 'What do you say, Super?'

'I agree with you, sir,' Hawkins answered heavily. 'There might be a motive in what Mr French says, but it seems to me there's no proof of it.'

'I don't wish to argue that Hampden is guilty,' French pointed out, 'only that there might be a motive. There would be personal feeling in it too. Owing to the deceased's

251

Koldkure activities, Hampden had recommended his company to pay out a considerable sum of money: for nothing whatever. That would rankle. Now through the deceased they were threatened with a much greater loss: again under Hampden's handling of the situation. If Hampden was satisfied that he could murder the deceased without fear of suspicion, and so not only get rid of the present drain and prospective loss, but re-establish his own position, I think he might have done it.'

The Chief Constable considered this. 'So far as you're only trying to establish motive,' he said presently, 'I'll accept your suggestion provisionally. Given opportunity and something to connect Hampden with the affair, we can reconsider the motive.'

French nodded and went on to his second point.

'Now, with regard to Hampden's opportunity. He had the knowledge that the deceased would be fishing that afternoon, for Cooke rang up The Gables in his presence and was told so. He had fished with the deceased on previous occasions and therefore was aware of his tea-basket proclivities. Further, he was a qualified chemist and could have extracted the aconitine from the monkshood plant, of which there was a quantity in the public gardens not far from his home. He would also have known what was a fatal dose. So much for knowledge.'

'We may pass that, I think. Yes?'

'Then with regard to his whereabouts. He put up a statement which was almost, but not quite, an alibi.' French told of the walk over Hampstead Heath, then went on, 'He definitely left Chalk Farm Station at about two-forty, and reached the tea-shop about five, that is nearly two-and-a-half hours. Now, if he had had the use of a car, he could

252

undoubtedly have run down to Little Bitton, put the poison in the tea, and got back again in the time.'

'Opportunity established,' Carling agreed. 'But you want something more, don't you? Something definitely connecting him with the crime?'

'And that's just what I haven't got,' French admitted. 'I was unable to find any car that he might have used. His own was in his garage and I couldn't trace his having either borrowed or hired one. Further, I have no proof that he went to Little Bitton or actually did extract the aconitine.'

Carling shook his head. 'While I fully appreciate what you have done, Chief Inspector, I'm afraid something more would be necessary to justify an arrest. What do you think yourself?'

'I'm quite aware that it would, sir,' French admitted, 'but I thought it right to let you know all my conclusions. I confess I'd like a search warrant to go through his papers and particularly his finances.'

'We can consider that when you've finished your statement. You mentioned three others?'

'Yes. Cooke is the next. Cooke also had motive and opportunity . . .' and French put up the case he had so recently revised. 'But here again,' he went on, 'I have no proof. He has a motive for doing it, he had all the necessary knowledge and he was within easy reach of the place at the critical time, but once again my information just stops short. I can't prove he did it.'

They discussed Cooke for a little time, finally deciding to retain him also as a suspect. Then French came to the real reason for which he had asked for the conference, the cases of Merle Weir and Peter Temple.

'I'll deal with these two at the same time,' he explained,

'because they are closely associated in their private lives. And first a word about each. Merle Weir comes into the story as a nurse in the Wilton Grange Convalescent Home near Lydcott in Surrey,' and he sketched her career, following it with that of Temple. 'We see then,' he continued, 'that the situation prior to the murder was as follows:

'Weir and Temple were running this semi-fraudulent business for the deceased, he paying their salaries, but no bonus on results. Weir had obviously gone into the business, not to make money, but for the deceased's sake, as she was then deeply in love with him. He had treated her badly, taking her money and character in return for a promise of marriage, which he had renewed from time to time and as regularly broken.

'On the Friday before the tragedy she sees in the paper the news of his engagement to an heiress, and as a result she has an attack of hysteria. On the Saturday morning she acts in a distraught manner. About eleven that morning she rings up the deceased. She is told that he is from home, but will be back for lunch that day, and that he is going to fish in the afternoon. That afternoon she travels to Little Bitton and is seen walking on the river bank in the direction of the tea-basket. Here again I can't prove that she put the poison in—*but* she lies to me about the visit: first, she makes no mention of it, and then she says she was elsewhere at the time.'

The Chief Constable looked up with interest. 'That's more promising, Chief Inspector.'

'Temple is in love with Weir,' French continued, 'and natural jealousy would tend to make him hate the deceased. He knows or suspects how badly the deceased has treated Weir, and that is an additional cause for hatred. He also goes to Little Bitton that afternoon and he also denies absolutely having been there.'

'Did they go together?' asked Major Carling.

'No, sir. Weir travelled from Lincaster by the previous bus one hour earlier.'

'And had they the necessary knowledge?'

'Both were studying chemistry and had chemical reference books. Weir in fact was continuously experimenting. It's practically certain that either could have extracted the aconitine from the monkshood. I have not yet found the monkshood to which they had access, but it's a common enough plant and I don't think this is a difficulty.'

'It's that spiky plant which goes to a pyramid of bluish-purple flowers, isn't it?' asked the superintendent. 'I have some in my garden.'

'That's it, Mr Hawkins. It's also called Blue Rocket, I suppose, from the colour and shape. Then Weir and Temple knew of the engagement and of the fishing, but whether they were aware of the tea-basket I cannot yet say.'

They continued discussing the matter in all its bearings, and then Major Carling summed up.

'It seems to me,' he said slowly, 'and if any of you people disagree with me, please say so, that you have proved motive against all four of these suspects, though Hampden's is slight. You have also proved opportunity. In the cases of. Hampden and Cooke you have failed to prove direct connection with the crime. It seems to me therefore that in neither of these cases have we evidence to justify an arrest.'

'I agree with you, sir,' Hawkins said heavily. 'I doubt if we'd even get warrants.'

'Then we come to the cases of Weir and Temple. Here you have proved not only motive and opportunity, but you have to a certain extent connected both with the murder. Both went from Lincaster to Little Bitton that afternoon and Weir was actually on the river bank close to the tea-basket. Moreover, both denied having been there. I think you have a case for an arrest there. Now, superintendent, what do you say?'

'I'd certainly be for an arrest, sir. If they were there innocently, why didn't they say so?'

'Exactly. What do you say, French?'

French hesitated. 'I confess, sir, I'm not at all satisfied about the case, and that's really why I asked for this conference. I felt that I had got so much against these two, that I shouldn't be justified in keeping it to myself any longer.'

'There I'm entirely with you. Then what is your difficulty? Don't you think the evidence sufficient?'

'It's not that. If they're guilty, the investigation after arrest would build up the case. My difficulty is less tangible. It's their personality. I simply can't see those two guilty of so premeditated a murder.'

Carling frowned. He did not reply for a moment, as if he were choosing and weighing his words. 'Coming from a man of your experience, Chief Inspector,' he then said, 'this is an important point, to which full attention must be given. But, after all, as you will be the first to agree, we must go by the facts. Of course personality and character are facts also. Can you be more precise in your diagnosis?'

'It's very difficult to be so. They're both what I would call inherently good living and decent. They give you that impression when you speak to them, and they have that reputation among their associates.'

'I sympathise with what you say,' Carling answered, 'but don't you think you're forgetting the special circumstances?

Murder is not like other crimes. A man of good character who would not steal or cheat or commit arson might well commit murder, if it was for the sake of the woman he loved. You know that as well as I.'

French knew it. He knew also that a hurt to a woman's love or pride may cause her to act in a way wholly at variance with her general character.

'Murder,' went on the Chief Constable, 'may represent itself as an unselfish action. A man thinking that a certain murder would benefit the woman he loves, might commit it, even if he knows he will be hanged. Such a thing has happened again and again. Another thing. Suppose Weir, angered beyond measure by Tarrant's treachery, committed this murder. Suppose Temple found it out. It might be a fine action on his part to take the blame. But it's not for us to judge.'

French knew it was true, but it was the C.C.'s next remark which finally reconciled him to what he had known all along must come.

'Besides,' Carling added, 'we're not assessing their guilt. Before they're charged they'll have an opportunity of making a statement clearing up your doubts. It's a statement you obviously couldn't ask for unless you had decided to arrest them if they failed to satisfy you, and you couldn't decide on the arrest without this conference. I recognise therefore that you could only have acted as you have. Now is there anything further to be said as to why we shouldn't bring them in tonight?'

French had nothing. It was not indeed Carling's arguments which had convinced him, but his own knowledge of their truth. To his personal regret, but to his professional satisfaction, it was presently decided that the arrests should be made at ten o'clock that evening.

19

Anthony Frobisher Hears the Story

Mr Justice Frobisher hitched his scarlet gown more comfortably into position, peered at the set of his wig in the mirror on the wall of his room, and glanced rapidly at his watch.

'Time,' he said laconically.

His usher, bowing slightly, opened the door and passed out. The Judge followed. They paced deliberately down a short corridor blocked at the end by a door. The door was opened and a buzz of conversation poured out. There were shouts of 'Silence!' and the buzz diminished. Frobisher entered the court, took his place before the great chair beneath the Crown, bowed to the standing assembly, and sat down.

It was the second day of the Assizes at Saxham St Edmunds, and this morning the big case of the session was to begin. Frobisher was looking forward to it with distaste. He was indeed in a somewhat sombre frame of mind. His Court work he always found heavy and distressing, particularly in murder cases. Despite the years he had spent at the Bar and on the bench, now so many that he no longer liked to think of them, he had never become reconciled to seeing persons on trial for their life, and that hideous business of pronouncing sentence remained for him a ghastly nightmare. Today he feared the case would prove particularly harrowing. A young man and woman of otherwise good character and pleasing personality were charged with a terrible offence: the woman with murder, the man as being an accessory after the fact. If they were guilty it would not be one of those cases in which a hardened criminal pits himself against society in a gambler's throw for wealth or security, but rather one in which weak though well-meaning human nature is overwhelmed by the force of cruel circumstances. Unhappily, cruel circumstances could make no difference to the tragic end of such a trial, should the verdict be adverse.

His thoughts went back to the Thompson-Bywaters case of nearly twenty years earlier. The circumstances were far from identical, though there was a certain similarity. Many people remembered that case with dissatisfaction. It was his business to see to that, and he must spare no effort to keep his attention fully alert and concentrated on what was happening. Lately he had been growing tired, particularly as the afternoon progressed, and when one was tired it was fatally easy to miss a point . . .

He glanced round the court. It was a comparatively new building, well furnished and roomy as courts go. It was absolutely crammed. Not a place, Frobisher was sure, was vacant, not a seat but had more persons squeezed into it than the designer intended. Already the atmosphere was heavy, and in spite of the patent ventilation, it would soon be heavier still. There were no windows, the light coming from what was practically a glass roof. From this a shaft of sunlight crossed the upper part of the room, looking like a solid bar from the reflections from myriads of floating specks. In the shaft a large cobweb slowly waved.

Formalities began at once, and soon the two defendants appeared in the dock. Frobisher glanced at them keenly. Yes, they looked just as he expected they would: young, wholesome, decent. The girl was more, she was pretty, or she would have been had her face been less pale and drawn. That would weigh with the jury, Frobisher told himself: in her favour with the men, less so with the women. It weighed with him: he would like to see her acquitted. For the matter of that, he would like to see them both acquitted. Looking at them critically, he shrank more than ever from that final scene of the trial, in case the verdict went against them. Of course in such a matter he must not have—and he would not have—feelings. He was an automaton, placed there to see, as far as any human being could see, that justice was done.

A tall, thin, lanky barrister got up suddenly. This was Hume Nesbit, and Frobisher knew him to be an extremely able counsel, particularly for the defence. 'I am appearing for the female prisoner, m'lud,' he said, 'and before the prisoners plead to this indictment I wish to make a submission and an application; namely, that the prisoners be tried separately. In my submission a single trial would be embarrassing to the defence, in that evidence may be introduced which is evidence against one prisoner but not against the other, and that the introduction of such evidence might well be prejudicial to the defence of the other prisoner.'

Another barrister stood up. His name was Cunninghame. He was short and stout, a complete contrast in appearance to Nesbit, though equally able. 'I am appearing for the male prisoner and I desire to associate myself with the submission and application of my learned friend.'

As Frobisher expected, the prosecuting counsel took the contrary view. He himself thought there was little in the submission, while it was obvious that the two trials would double the time and cost involved. After much argument, he refused the application.

The Clerk of Assize now rose. 'Merle Ella Weir,' he declared; 'you are charged on indictment with the offence of murder, the particulars being that on the 18th of March in this year, in the County of Greenshire, you murdered James Pettigrew Tarrant. Merle Ella Weir, are you guilty or not guilty?'

'Not guilty.' The voice was low and musical but clear, and as Merle spoke she drew herself up, as if to register her defiance of the powers that were threatening her life.

The formal droning of the Clerk of Assize went on: 'Peter Alwyn Temple; you are charged upon the same indictment with being accessory to the fact to the murder of the said James Pettigrew Tarrant in that, well knowing that Merle Ella Weir on the 18th day of March in this year in the County of Greenshire had murdered the said James Pettigrew Tarrant, you did on the same day and on other days afterwards receive, comfort, harbour, assist and maintain the said Merle Ella Weir. Peter Alwyn Temple, are you guilty or not guilty?'

'Not guilty.'

Though his was the lesser charge, Temple spoke with the greater distress and doubt and fear. Frobisher noted it as a point to be remembered. It would tend to confirm a certain line, were that taken by counsel.

The proceedings continued. The two in the dock were furnished with seats. The jury were called, took their places, and were sworn. Frobisher glanced at them with his shrewd old eyes. They were an ordinary lot: just the kind that one usually got on a murder jury. There were nine men and three women. The foreman was a big fellow with a red face, perhaps a butcher. He looked stupid but honest, and Frobisher felt he would be fair as far as lay within him. But with that type much depended on first impressions. Once the foreman got an idea, he would, Frobisher imagined, stick to it no matter what qualifying facts were afterwards put before him. With this man, Frobisher also thought, the pathetic charm of the female prisoner would not count at all.

Next to him was an obvious intellectual, a writer or scientist or student. He would also try to be fair, but he might be hard, expecting people to act like machines, and having little sympathy with the frailties and weaknesses of human nature. The third face was more attractive. It belonged to an elderly man: clean-cut, thin-lipped and strong yet kindly. No fool, this man looked. He would be not only fair, but he would make allowances.

The remaining men were nondescript, good enough in their several ways, but they would inevitably be led by the others. Of the women, one was stout and motherly, with a placid expression and, Frobisher was sure, a warm smile; the second was thin and acid-looking, with a spiky and rather red nose; while the third seemed in all respects the personification of the commonplace. (On the whole Frobisher was satisfied with them. They would, he believed, give a common-sense verdict, and without too much delay.

As Frobisher had known, no less a personage than the Solicitor-General was to conduct the case for the Crown. He had now risen to his feet and was toying with his brief and shooting sharp, appraising little glances at the jury, at his fellow barristers, and at Frobisher himself. Sir Reginald Massingham was a big man, with a big face, big, strongly-marked features, and a big voice. He had an aggressive expression and a dominant personality which stood him in good stead in his profession, and opposing counsel of weaker calibre were apt to be intimidated by his very appearance before the battle began. Now putting his left hand on his hip and hitching up his gown over his shoulder with his right, a characteristic gesture as Frobisher well knew, he began to speak. No longer could Frobisher allow his attention to wander.

'May it please your lordship, members of the jury. I approach this case with anxiety, an anxiety which must always be present when two persons are being tried together, and particularly when they are charged with offences of varying gravity. My responsibility is that I must say nothing in connection with one defendant which might tell unfairly against the other. You will yourselves, however, be able to distinguish as to the relevancy of the evidence relating to these two charges.

'As you have just heard, Merle Ella Weir is charged with the murder of James Pettigrew Tarrant and Peter Alwyn Temple with being an accessory after the fact. The crime is alleged to have been committed near the village of Little Bitton on the afternoon of Saturday, the 18th of March last.

'The facts of this unhappy case are a little complicated, but I shall do my best to put them before you as briefly as possible. That I shall have your careful attention I know, because I can see that you fully realise the gravity of the duty which now lies upon you.

'James Pettigrew Tarrant was born in Cardiff just three

and thirty years ago. His parents were well-to-do and he received an excellent education, specialising in science. Then his father died, leaving his mother badly off. She died shortly after and Tarrant was unable to go to college, as he had intended, but had to get work in order to support himself. His chemistry was fair, and he became a salesman with a large firm of retail chemists. After ten years in various branches, during which he had given satisfaction and been twice promoted, he went as assistant to a small chemist in the Surrey village of Lydcott. There our interest in him may be said to begin, for it was there that he met the prisoner Weir.'

Sir Reginald went on to tell of Merle's history and of her appointment at the Wilton Grange Convalescent Home, of her meeting with Tarrant, of his idea about the proprietary medicine, and of his offering her a partnership. 'That by this time she had fallen deeply in love with him is certain,' he went on. 'She has herself admitted that she agreed to become his partner for this reason, and not because of any hope of financial gain. Just when he asked her to marry him I cannot say, but evidence will be put before you that a year later she considered herself engaged to him. This engagement is the first plank in the prosecution's case.

'The partners now set up a plant to produce their proprietary medicine,' and Sir Reginald described the Koldkure establishment and the progress of the business. 'This continued for some six months and then an event took place which was to have a profound effect on these unfortunate people. Merle Weir engaged a vanman: the male defendant, Peter Alwyn Temple. Temple was not an ordinary vanman. He had been brought up in a comfortable home and had a good education, but just as had happened to the deceased, the death of his father had meant that suddenly and unexpectedly he had to support himself.' Sir Reginald then sketched Temple's career, explaining how Merle came to hear of him.

'Now a disastrous thing took place,' he went on. 'Temple fell in love with Merle Weir. This was patent to those in the works and he has himself admitted it. I call it disastrous, not because it wasn't entirely honourable, but because the prosecution submits that it was one of the factors which has led to his presence in the dock today.'

Sir Reginald paused, turned over the pages of his brief, hitched his gown up over his shoulder, and resumed. 'It was at this time, when the business was doing so well, that a difficulty arose which brought it unexpectedly to an end,' and he briefly described the fall in the Braxamin receipts, Hampden's discoveries as to the cause, and the deal made with Tarrant. 'This deal the deceased kept secret from his partner, the female prisoner. While he himself got a thousand Braxamin shares of a value of about £2,250, £1,000 in cash, and a salary of £500 a year as director, he put her off with a gift of £50, telling her that he himself had only received £100.

'After the closing down of the Koldkure works both defendants obtained other employment, Miss Weir as a nurse and Temple as a rural postman. Then some three months later the deceased approached Miss Weir with a new proposal. He wanted to start his proprietary medicine business again: the same business, carried on against the Braxamin Company in precisely the same way as before. There were, however, to be certain differences: the works were to be in a different town, far away from Exeborough, the business was to have a fresh cloak, headache powders instead of a cure for colds, and all was to be done in Weir's name, the deceased's not appearing.

'The prisoner Weir has admitted that she questioned the ethics of the proposal, and has explained how the deceased met her objection . . .' and Sir Reginald repeated the story. 'Here again he deceived the accused, deliberately lying to her on many points.

'You will hear from witnesses that during this period of work at Lincaster the accused seemed oppressed and unhappy, and you will have to consider to what extent this was or was not due to her treatment by the deceased. You will also hear the testimony of witnesses as to Temple's devotion to her during the period, and of her failure to respond to it.'

From long practice Frobisher had cultivated the power of listening critically to what was being said, while at the same time indulging in a separate thought-life of his own. Thus while he lost nothing of Sir Reginald's address, he constantly allowed his eyes to pass over the assembly, missing little which took place. Sir Reginald's restrained but effective gestures, his little forensic tricks, all of which Frobisher had himself practised in his time, the confidential way he addressed the jury, and his elaborate presentation of himself as a plain man, building his case on simple common-sense facts and avoiding fanciful or chimerical theories, all were in the best traditions of the part. How little intrinsic weight there was in all of them, and yet how much they counted with juries!

Certainly Sir Reginald had the ear of this jury, and for the matter of that, of everyone present. Only the counsel and solicitors grouped round the table in the well of the court looked unimpressed. Hume Nesbit and Walter

Cunninghame, who were appearing for Merle and Peter respectively, seemed indeed utterly bored. This, of course, was another of the tricks of the trade. That they were anything but bored was what Nesbit in other surroundings would have called a dead cert. Like hawks they were watching for the slightest slip on Sir Reginald's part, from which they might raise capital by objection or subsequent quotation.

And what of the two central figures in this grim tragedy? Frobisher observed them discreetly but continuously, for he had to make up his own mind about them. Not to lead him to distort facts of course, but appearance and demeanour were facts which had to be reckoned with the others.

Merle was dressed, not in black, but in a dark blue coat and skirt and a small dark blue hat, very quiet and restrained, yet becoming. Instinctively Frobisher approved her choice. It coupled a proper humility and appreciation of her position, with self-respect and a determination to keep her end up to the limit of her ability. But her appealing face with its clear honest eyes was looking pale and frightened. Rather excited too. Temple was also looking eager and excited. Frobisher knew those expressions. He knew that as the ghastly business dragged on they would change from eagerness and excitement to dullness, even to stupor. Then perhaps to a dreadful terror and despair. Necessary as it was, this business of trial for murder remained wholly hateful. It was, of course, up to him and those like him to carry it out in the most considerate way possible, and this he could say with a clear conscience he had always tried to do.

Sir Reginald Massingham's big voice droned on, rising and falling in well calculated modulations. 'Now,' he was saying, 'I come to the day of the crime. The week preceding that Saturday had been an eventful one for the deceased, James Tarrant. On the Wednesday afternoon he called on a Miss Jean Woolcombe . . .' and he told of the engagement, of the visit to London due to Jean's wish to keep this secret, and of Tarrant's return to Little Bitton on the Saturday. 'The deceased,' he added, 'was anxious that there should be no hitch about the engagement. He therefore prevailed on Miss Woolcombe to allow it to be announced, and he himself conveyed the news to the editor of the *Saxham St Edmunds Weekly Gazette.*'

Sir Reginald then went on to tell of the fishing expedition, the preparation of the tea-basket, Tarrant's failure to return to dinner, Miss Lestrange's tragic discovery, and the resultant activities of the police. Though many of the details were known from the reports of the inquest and the hearing before the magistrates, others had been kept secret and the story held its audience spellbound. Even the two unfortunates in the dock seemed to be carried away by it from their own plight.

'I have now to refer,' resumed Sir Reginald, 'to an incident which took place on the Friday evening, the day before the crime. On that evening the accused returned to her rooms at her usual hour and Mrs Benson, her landlady, will tell you that her manner and appearance were quite normal. She had her supper and then the evening post came. Shortly after that Temple called and stayed for a couple of hours.

'Now there is nothing in all that to invite comment, but it happened that during his call Miss Grace Benson, Mrs Benson's daughter, had occasion to go to her bedroom, which is next door to Weir's sitting-room. While there she heard Weir's raised voice. She will tell you what there was a murmur of Temple's voice, the words of which she didn't hear, and that Weir then cried: "Everything he said was false! I wish he was dead! I could kill him myself! I will kill him!" This was followed by the sound of hysterical crying. Miss Benson crept downstairs and later told her mother what she had heard.'

Frobisher glanced at the jury. It was beginning to tell. The foreman was now staring at Merle with an expression of pained surprise. The placid woman seemed distressed and the spiky one rather pleased, as if it was just what she had expected all along. The others showed less definite emotions, but they were all obviously impressed. They did not know, as did Frobisher, how much of their feelings was due to Sir Reginald's art rather than to his statements. They believed that facts were what gave a case its weight: all outsiders did. Frobisher, who had spent years studying the subject, knew that with the average uncritical mind, facts were of minor importance. It was their presentation that really mattered. Sir Reginald's voice flowed on.

'Now I do not want to make more out of what may have been a hasty exclamation than is warranted. You will have an opportunity of deciding the precise import of the female prisoner's words when you have heard Miss Benson's evidence. But here undoubtedly was a definite threat to murder, and it cannot be dismissed as if it had not taken place. There is no direct evidence as to the person to whom the accused was referring, but two facts have become known, and it will be for you to say how far they are relevant. The first is that by that post, which came after the accused's supper, was delivered that week's issue of the *Saxham St Edmunds Weekly Gazette*, to which the accused subscribed, and the second is that the paper was found in the accused's room open at a certain page, and on that page was the notice of the deceased's engagement.

'One other unusual incident occurred that night. Mrs Benson will tell you that between half-past eleven and twelve, when she was in bed but before she had gone to sleep, she heard the accused go stealthily downstairs and let herself out of the house. Such a thing had never happened before and Mrs Benson supposed that her lodger had remembered some urgent letter which had to be posted. She determined to listen until the accused returned, but though she did stay awake for a considerable time, sleep at last overcame her and she heard nothing more. I ask your particular attention to this point, to which I will refer again shortly.

'Next morning, Saturday, Mrs Benson will tell you that the accused looked worried and that she ate little or no breakfast. When she went to the works her perturbation continued. Evidence will be put before you that she could not attend to business, that she refused to deal with the day's letters, and that when appealed to on points of management she gave obviously absurd answers. About eleven o'clock she suddenly left the Works and went to the General Post Office. From there she telephoned to The Gables asking for the deceased. The housekeeper, Miss Lestrange, will tell you that in reply she explained that the deceased was from home, but that he was coming back to lunch and would spend the afternoon fishing. The accused then returned to the Works, remaining there till they closed at one-fifteen, but alone in her office, where she would see no one. She went back to her rooms, once again seeming distraught. She ate practically no lunch, and hurried out again shortly after two. She then took the two-thirty bus to Little Bitton, going on arrival, not to

The Gables, but the bank of the river, which she reached about quarter past four.

'Now can we form an opinion as to the cause of this mental upset, this threat to murder, and this visit to Little Bitton? The Crown submits that it lay in that newspaper notice of the engagement between the deceased and the heiress, Miss Jean Woolcombe. Think what that notice told Merle Weir. It told her that the man who had flouted her love, taken her money and spoiled her career, had deceived her once more. Careless of whether or not he broke her heart, he had finally thrown her over, and of this he had not even had the common decency to tell her himself, but he let her find it out from the newspapers. It will be for you to consider, when you have heard the evidence, whether this news was or was not the cause of her distress and sudden visit to where he was to be found. And in coming to a conclusion on this vital matter, you will bear in mind the significant fact that when the accused was asked had she gone to Little Bitton, she denied it *in toto*. You will naturally ask yourselves, members of the jury, in this connection, if the visit were an innocent one, why did she deny it?'

Sir Reginald made an effective pause, then his voice boomed out again: 'Members of the jury, the submission of the Crown is that Merle Weir, hurt beyond measure by the deceased's treatment of her, carried away by her sense of burning injustice and injury, went to Little Bitton for the express purpose of murdering her former lover, and did murder him by putting aconitine in his tea. As you, members of the jury, know as well as I do, love and hate are very close to one another in this strange mixture which we call human nature, and actions such as the deceased was guilty of were well calculated to change the one to the other.'

A little movement passed over the court like a zephyr over a field of ripe corn. This, it was recognised, was the climax of Sir Reginald's speech, and he himself once again paused before proceeding to his next point. The general sentiment in the audience seemed to be distress. Merle's face was ghastly and Temple looked startled and taken aback. But Merle's counsel remained imperturbably bored, while Temple's leaned over to his junior and whispered something at which both actually laughed.

'Evidence will further be put before you,' went on Sir Reginald, 'that the female defendant had all the knowledge necessary to carry out the murder. She has admitted that she was no stranger to Little Bitton. Miss Lestrange, the deceased's housekeeper, will tell you that a little time prior to the murder she happened to be walking on this very bank of the Webble along which were the deceased's fishing rights, and she there met Merle Weir. It chanced that on that day also the deceased was fishing, and the accused passed beside and must have seen his basket. Her association with him and consequent knowledge of his habits would have told her what was in that basket. When therefore she learnt on the day of his death that he was going fishing, she must have realised that a thermos would be on the bank and where to find it.

'The question which naturally suggests itself to you at this stage, members of the jury, is whether any aconitine was found in the accused's possession, or whether she was known to have obtained any? Now I admit in the fullest way that the answer to both these questions is, No. But evidence will be put before you to show that she could have obtained it, and that without the slightest difficulty. She was a nurse and head of a proprietary medicine works, and it will be proved to you that not only had she a good knowledge of chemistry, but that she was continually carrying out chemical experiments. She also had reference books, and one of these will be put before you which describes the method of extracting the poison from the plant *aconitum napellus* or monkshood. This plant, as you know, members of the jury, is common enough, and it will be proved to you that a quantity of it was growing in the front gardens of houses where she could easily have obtained it.

'It will further naturally occur to you to consider for what purpose the accused left her rooms between eleven-thirty and twelve on the Friday night before the crime, *after* she had learnt about the deceased's engagement and *after* she had threatened to murder him. The Crown submits that it was to prepare the aconitine, which she could easily have extracted in the laboratory at the works. It will be for you to say, when you have heard all the evidence, whether or not she took this step.'

Once again Sir Reginald paused. Frobisher saw that the jury were getting tired, and Sir Reginald saw it too and went on quickly.

'Up to the present I have practically confined my remarks to the female prisoner. But what of the male defendant? The charge against him is of much less gravity and I shall have correspondingly less to say about him. A very few moments and I shall have done.

'As you have already heard, Peter Alwyn Temple is charged with being an accessory after the fact to the murder of James Tarrant. For a conviction on the indictment the Crown has only to prove that Temple knew that the prisoner Weir had committed the murder, and had aided her to evade discovery.

'Now the movements of Temple have also been traced during the critical period . . .' and Sir Reginald referred again to his call on Merle on the Friday evening. 'It was during this call that the female prisoner used the words: "I wish he was dead! I could kill him myself! I will kill him." The Crown submits that not only did these words apply to the deceased, but that Temple was well aware of the fact.'

Sir Reginald then recounted Peter's absence from the works on the following morning, his further call at Merle's rooms, his false story about burnt papers, and his enquiries from Joyce Caldwell, continuing:

'I would ask you now to note a singular fact. Though neither Mrs Benson nor Miss Caldwell knew where the prisoner Weir had gone, and therefore could not have told Temple, he himself knew. He took the next bus to Little Bitton, that leaving at three-thirty.

'What Temple did at Little Bitton we do not know, though we believe he could not have himself put the poison in the thermos, as he did not arrive in time. Nor do we know where he met Weir. But that he did meet her, and that before six o'clock, is proved by the fact that at that hour they both boarded a bus at Saxham, and in it drove back to Lincaster. The conductor of that bus will tell you that his attention was drawn to the two defendants by their dreadful look of anxiety and fear. If they didn't know the truth about the murder, what caused that look? Furthermore, when asked had he been to Little Bitton that afternoon, Temple, like Weir, point blank denied it. Once again, if the visit were an innocent one, why did he do so?

'The Crown submits that when on that Saturday Temple heard of Miss Weir's strange conduct, he was filled with fear lest she really had set out to do the deceased an injury.

274

He decided to go himself to Little Bitton, possibly in the hope of saving her from the crime. Unhappily he was too late, arriving to find that the deed had been done. The Crown submits that it is impossible that on that journey home with Merle Weir he should not have known what had taken place. Further, that he lied as to his movements on that afternoon with the object of preventing this knowledge from coming out and so incriminating the woman he loved, thus giving her definite aid. If he did so act, he is guilty as an accessory after the fact. It will be your duty, members of the jury, to say whether these submissions are or are not the truth.'

The speech was over. Sir Reginald sat down, and his junior, Derek Lindsay, rose to call the first witness. But Frobisher's all-embracing eye had noted that it was nearly one o'clock.

'I think, Mr Lindsay, that this is a suitable moment to adjourn,' he said in his low but incisive voice. 'Two o'clock, please.'

Everyone rose, bows were again exchanged, and preceded by his usher, Frobisher left the court

20

Anthony Frobisher
Learns the Other Side

The afternoon was taken up by the examination of the witnesses for the prosecution. This proceeded adequately, but without a great deal of interest, due to there being no real dispute as to the facts. Sir Reginald obtained formal proof of the statements he had made, and Hume Nesbit and Walter Cunninghame, for Merle and Peter respectively, avoiding any attempt to break down the witnesses, directed their efforts towards minimization. Merle had been fond of Tarrant, but surely not so deeply in love with him as had been suggested? Temple had obviously liked and admired Merle, but was it not an exaggeration to say that he had loved her to distraction? On hearing of the engagement Merle had been undoubtedly depressed and disappointed, but could she be described as desperate? Their efforts resulted in a general lowering of the colourful tone Sir Reginald had given the story, as when the sun is withdrawn from a landscape. The highlights and the black shadows disappeared and the greys and the browns came into their own. As a result, the defendants' motives for their alleged crimes grew less compelling and their actions more normal and commonplace. It was a clever piece of work, unobtrusive, but by no means negligible. Only in the cross examination of Dr Hands was a real effort made to reverse a statement.

The doctor had declared that while the immediate cause of death was drowning, the ultimate cause was in his opinion aconitine poisoning. It was upon this statement that Nesbit seized.

'You say that you are quite positive, Dr Hands, that the immediate cause of death was drowning?'

'Quite.'

'But you are not quite positive that the aconitine was the ultimate cause?'

'Assuming that the quantity of aconitine which was in the body was that which the analyst told me he had discovered, I have no doubt of it.'

'I will grant you the assumption for the present: I understand the analyst is here and will give evidence later. With that assumption please explain to the jury how you know that it was the aconitine which caused the deceased to fall into the water?'

The point was one of some difficulty. Frobisher had foreseen it and he was interested to hear how Nesbit would handle it. If it were proved that death resulted from drowning, and that the drowning resulted from the poison, that would unquestionably be murder. But if it could not be shown that the deceased was drowned as a result of the poison, it was not quite so straightforward. At first sight Frobisher believed that in such a case he should direct the jury to acquit, but he felt he should like to give the matter further consideration. His thoughts began delving into the intricacies of constructive murder and of felonies involving acts dangerous to human life.

Dr Hands moved uneasily. 'Obviously,' he answered, 'I don't know it in the same way that I know about the drowning. That was proved by the physical characteristics, water in the lungs and so on. A similar type of proof about the other is not available. But my opinion is based on two points: first, the taking of the aconitine would satisfactorily explain the drowning, and, second, I have been unable to find anything else which would.'

'I ask you a straightforward question, Dr Hands. Do you know it, or do you only suspect it?'

'I can't say I know it exactly, but my opinion is a great deal stronger than mere suspicion.'

'You either know a thing or you do not know it. Your evidence is that you do not know that the death was due to the aconitine?'

The doctor hesitated.

'Is that your evidence or is it not?' Nesbit asked sharply.

'Yes,' Hands said at last. 'I suppose I can't say I know it.'

'You can't say you know it. Quite so.' Nesbit sat down.

Sir Reginald was on his feet at once. 'You can't say you know it, in the sense that you know that I am speaking to you,' he said gently. 'But a small proportion only of our knowledge comes to us from direct observation. If you see drops of water on the window you, know that it has rained, even though you may not have seen the rain itself. Can you—?'

Nesbit was up again. 'My lord,' he said, 'I object. My learned friend is not entitled to deliver a lecture on the laws of probability.'

'I was going to ask the witness if—'

Frobisher would not have this, even though Sir Reginald was Solicitor-General. 'Allow me, Sir Reginald,' he put in swiftly, and was gratified at the tense silence which immediately ensued. 'I think you must come to your question without further preamble.'

Sir Reginald, having said all he wanted, bowed. 'Thank you, m'lud, I was just about to do so.' He turned back to Hands. 'Can you say that, using your ordinary intelligence as well as your professional knowledge, it is your strong opinion and belief that the taking of the aconitine was the cause of the drowning?'

'Yes, that's what I've been saying all along,' the doctor retorted in an aggrieved tone.

'Now you have told us, Dr Hands,' Sir Reginald went on, 'that you examined the remains of the deceased. In your opinion was he in good health in the period immediately prior to his death?'

'Yes; I saw no signs of disease.'

'And no signs of physical injury?'

'None.'

'Would you or would you not describe his as a strong, healthy man of good physique with a sound heart?'

'Yes, I certainly should.'

'You have told us that in your opinion the taking of the aconitine would satisfactorily account for the drowning. Can you suggest anything which would account for it other than the aconitine?'

'No, I cannot.'

'You cannot suggest anything else.' Sir Reginald sat down with the satisfied air of a man who has successfully accomplished a piece of good work.

Dr Morrison, the police doctor in Saxham who had carried out the post-mortem, profited by his colleague's misfortunes. He was not going to be caught out by any hypothetical questions relative to the part of the aconitine had played in the death. He said that in his opinion the fall into the river and the subsequent drowning might have been caused by the drug, but he was not prepared to say that it had been. The remaining examinations passed off without incident.

When the Court assembled next morning Hume Nesbit rose to open the case for the defence on behalf of Merle Weir. His speech was at least a model of brevity.

'May it please your lordship; members of the jury: after the able presentation of the case against my client to which you listened yesterday, you might well think that it was so strong as to be invincible. Fortunately for my client, this is very far indeed from the truth. She has one weapon in her armoury so powerful that it must necessarily overcome any attack that even my learned friend can bring against her. That weapon is a very simple one: it is the truth. My defence for Merle Weir will be to let you hear from her own lips a statement of her movements and actions on the afternoon of Saturday, the eighteenth of last March. I am satisfied that when you have heard the story you will recognise from your own inner consciousness that it is the truth, and without further words of mine, will return the verdict which I am asking at your hands: that of Not Guilty. I now call Merle Ella Weir.'

Every eye was on Merle as she left the dock, and followed by a wardress, walked to the witness box. She looked pale and frightened, but determined, as if bracing herself up to the best fight for her life of which she was capable. Once again Frobisher approved both her appearance and manner. She was showing pluck, and pluck was what she would now need.

'Your name is Merle Ella Weir?' began Nesbit, a little unnecessarily, as it seemed.

She agreed that her name was Merle Ella Weir, and also that she had been a nurse at the Wilton Grange Convalescent Home. While there she had met the deceased. Yes, she admitted that she had fallen in love with him. It was for this reason that she had consented to join him in the medicine business. Yes, before she consented he had asked her to marry him. He had promised to marry her then, as well as on several subsequent occasions, but on various grounds he had always postponed the date of the wedding.

Some three months after the closing down of the Koldkure establishment the deceased had approached her about starting the business over again. He had told her that owing to the loss on the Koldkure venture he was again a poor man, but that he could just scrape together enough to restart. This time the business was not, he said, to run indefinitely, but only long enough to give him a lever to secure better terms from the Braxamin people. On this occasion he had renewed his promise to marry her, though by now she could not overcome her doubt of his sincerity.

'You then learnt that he had bought The Gables?' went on Nesbit. 'How was that?'

'Peter Temple saw a notice in the *Saxham St Edmunds Weekly Gazette* and showed it to me.'

'What did you think about that?'

'I was hurt by it.'

'Did you speak to the deceased about it?'

'No.'

'Why was that?'

'I just felt I couldn't.'

'You just felt you couldn't,' Nesbit repeated slowly, while he bent over his brief again. 'Did you go to Little Bitton at any time after learning that he had bought The Gables?'

'Yes, a few times.'

'Why?'

Merle for the first time hesitated. 'Curiosity, I suppose. Perhaps it was morbid, but I wanted to see the house that might have been mine.'

Nesbit then turned to the Friday before the tragedy. 'On that evening after your supper, did you receive a copy of the *Saxham St Edmunds Weekly Gazette* containing the notice of the deceased's engagement to Miss Woolcombe?'

'Yes; I had been subscribing to it for some time.'

'What did you feel about this news?'

Merle grew paler. 'I felt he had treated me badly,' she answered in a lower tone. 'I thought he might at least have told me. And I suppose it made it final. I don't know that I can explain.'

'Can I help you? Had you still in your mind a hope that he would marry you, which was now finally dashed?'

Merle shook her head. 'No,' she declared, 'I didn't really believe he cared for me. But I felt hurt. And I felt angry, too. I thought he had treated me badly and that he shouldn't get off with it.'

Frobisher wondered whether Nesbit had desired that reply. If so, it showed courage. Unless he was very sure of what was to follow, it was dangerous. His object in following this line was, of course, plain. To create the impression of truth in the jury's mind involved the volunteering of damaging as well as helpful facts.

282

'You wished to punish him?'

Braver still, thought Frobisher, though with a growing doubt as to Nesbit's wisdom.

'Not exactly.' Merle seemed to be finding her position more difficult than ever. 'I felt hurt, and I thought he should suffer for it. But I didn't think there was anything I could do.'

'Did you say the words: "Everything he said was false! I wish he was dead! I could kill him myself?"'

Merle was ghastly. 'I don't remember. I may have. I did say something like it. I didn't mean it, of course.'

'You didn't mean it?'

'No, of course not. It was just that I was upset.'

'The prosecution say you did mean it!' Nesbit's voice was caressing.

Frobisher appreciated the question. Stealing Sir Reginald's fire! Nesbit was doing well.

Merle shook her head. 'Oh, I didn't! I couldn't!' she cried. 'I might have for the moment, but not really.'

'Very well.' Nesbit went on as if making the best of a bad job. 'Now tell me, did you leave your rooms between eleven and twelve that night?'

'Yes.'

'Where did you go and what did you do?'

'I just went for a walk. I was very much worried and I couldn't sleep, and I felt I must try to walk it off.'

'And when did you return?'

'I walked, I suppose, for a couple of hours. I was tired when I got back and I fell asleep.'

Nesbit leant forward and his voice became more emphatic. 'When you were out did you pick any of the plant named *aconitum napellus*, otherwise called monkshood or wolfs-bane or blue rocket?'

'Oh, no! No, I did not.'

'Did you go to your laboratory during that period?'

'No! Oh, no!'

'Did you at any time extract aconitine from any plant?'

'No! Never!'

'Did you obtain aconitine in any other way?'

'No. I assure you I never did.'

Nesbit straightened himself up again and his manner grew more normal. 'Very well. Now let us go a step further. You came back from your walk and slept. Were you still feeling upset in the morning?'

Merle grew calmer with the change of subject.

'Yes. Yes—er—I was.'

'You went to your work as usual, but about eleven you went out and telephoned to the deceased?'

'I telephoned to his house. He was out.'

'Why? What did you want with him?'

Merle hesitated for a very long time. 'I had decided,' she said slowly, 'that it wasn't fair that he should treat me like that and get off with it. I—I—had decided to prevent it.'

'To prevent it? Do you mean that you were going to kill him?'

She winced. 'Oh, no! No! How can you say that? I meant to tell him that if he didn't break off the engagement I should tell Miss Woolcombe his whole history.'

'I see. Now tell me, did you know he was going fishing?'

'Yes.'

'And what did you do?'

'I went to Little Bitton as the witnesses said. Everything they said about the journey was true.'

'Quite. Well, you got to the bank of the river. Did you see the deceased?'

284

'Yes, I saw him further down-stream.'

'Yes? And then?'

'I went along and spoke to him.'

'You went along and spoke to him. Will you tell the jury what passed between you?'

She hesitated as if to think out her answer. Frobisher could see her hands gripping one another till the knuckles showed white. 'We . . . greeted each other and then he . . . spoke of his engagement. He seemed ashamed . . . the first time I had ever seen him like that. He spoke . . . nicely and kindly. He said that—'

'Yes?'

'That . . . that a marriage between us could never have been happy and that I'—her voice trembled—'was well rid of him. He . . . thanked me for . . . my forbearance towards him.'

Nesbit waited for a moment. 'And then?' he said gently.

'Then . . . then . . . I don't understand it, but seeing him sorry and ashamed, I suddenly wasn't angry with him any more.' A vivid flush dyed her almost marble cheeks. 'I don't know how it happened, but I saw that my only chance of happiness was to forget what he had done.'

'Did you tell him so?'

'No, I couldn't bring myself to do that. I simply said I wasn't going to reproach him, and then I felt'—again her face flushed—'an extraordinary sense of freedom.'

'A sense of freedom?'

'Yes.' Her clenched hands twisted. 'I saw that for a long time I hadn't really loved him at all and that . . . it had only been an idea and . . . I was cured and . . . free.'

'And what happened then?'

'We talked . . . for a little. Then he spoke of the business.

He said he was going to make it over to me with sufficient capital to run it, and I could either carry it on or close it down, as I liked.'

'Yes? And then?'

'That was all. I said I had to go, and he said he would see about the title deeds of the business, and we . . . parted without any . . . feeling.'

Frobisher had missed nothing of Merle's bearing and actions on the box. Every change of expression, every indication of emotion was recorded in that shrewd brain. He wondered if her story were true. If it were false, she had told it extremely well. But was it false? That was the question which was presently going to give him and the jury so much anxiety.

The jury were obviously impressed by the tale: exactly in the several ways he might have expected. The foreman's reaction seemed to be doubt: he looked as if he didn't know what to make of it. The scientist seemed sceptical, the thin-lipped man kindly but non-committal, the stout woman as if she would have liked then and there to take Merle in her arms and bear her away from the whole hideous ordeal, while her thin neighbour's expression suggested that she didn't believe a word she had heard. Of the others, those whose brows had been darkest when Sir Reginald had finished his speech seemed now most sympathetic to Merle.

'And what,' went on Nesbit, 'did you do then?'

'I intended to go straight back to Lincaster. Then I felt that a good walk would be a relief. So instead of taking the bus, I walked back to Saxham.'

'Where did you meet Temple?'

'In Saxham at the Lincaster bus. He was waiting for it, too.'

'Now tell me, Miss Weir,' and Nesbit's voice once again grew graver, 'did you expect to meet Temple there?'

She shook her head. 'No; it was a complete surprise to me.'

Nesbit paused to let this answer sink in, then resumed. 'Did you notice anything strange in his manner during the journey back to Lincaster?'

Once again Merle seemed to find it hard to reply. 'Yes, he seemed horrified about something and would scarcely speak. I didn't know what was wrong, but it frightened me.'

'Did you ask him what was wrong?'

'He wouldn't tell me then. He said it could wait till we got home.'

'He told you then?'

'Yes, he told me that James . . . was dead.'

'You mean the deceased? Then what happened?'

'I just couldn't believe it. It seemed so dreadful. Peter said he had found him . . . drowned in the river.'

'Please call him Temple. And then?'

'We talked it over and I told him where I had been.'

'Did you come to any decision as to reporting your visits to the police?'

'We decided not to do so. No one knew that either of us had been there and it would have meant difficult explanations.'

'Did you suspect murder?'

'Oh, no, it never entered our heads. We thought it was an accident.'

'You mustn't speak for yourself, please. When did you realise it was murder?'

'Temple heard it in the town: it was generally rumoured.'

'Did you not then realise you ought to report your visit to the police?'

Again she seemed deeply moved. 'I suppose so. Then I thought that as my visit had had nothing to do with . . . his death . . . I need not do so.'

'That's speaking generally: yes. But had you a special reason for keeping the visit secret?'

Merle looked this way and that, as if for a way of escape. Then with a gesture of despair she answered in a low voice: 'I thought—Temple would be blamed for not trying to help—the deceased: perhaps sent to prison.'

'That's why you kept silence about his visit. But I'm asking you about your own?'

She was almost whispering. 'I thought I might be suspected.'

'Oh. So that was the reason you lied to the police and committed perjury in a lower court? You were, in fact, determined to hush up the truth in case it might injure either Temple or yourself?'

Merle was ghastly. 'It was not keeping back anything about the murder. Our visits had nothing to do with that.'

Nesbit closed his brief. 'One last question, Miss Weir, and you must remember that you are on your oath. Did you put poison into the deceased's food or tea, or place poison anywhere that he might swallow it?'

'Oh, no, no, I didn't!'

'Or did you do anything of any kind whatsoever to bring about or to assist in bringing about his death?'

'No, no! I didn't! God knows I didn't!'

Nesbit sat down and the usual wave of movement passed over the assembly. It had, thought Frobisher, been a good defence. Nesbit had handled it skilfully, and Merle had made an excellent witness. Frobisher had little doubt that had the trial ended at that moment there would have been an acquittal. But for such a defence, the cross-examination was the touchstone.

Sir Reginald now got up to cross-examine. There was, Frobisher thought, something sinister and predatory in the prosecuting counsel's appearance as he stood, a big figure of a man, with his head thrust forward, and his large, strongly marked features set in an aggressive and pugnacious mould. One would have expected from him a harsh and raucous voice, but when he began to speak, his tones were soft as velvet. Here again Frobisher recognised his professional cunning. The man knew the jury would resent any bullying of the witness.

'Now, Miss Weir, this proprietary medicine business which you entered into with the deceased: did you consider it honest?'

'I was a little doubtful at first, but Mr Tarrant explained that it was quite all right and just—business.'

'And you were satisfied with that, I suppose?'

'Fairly satisfied, yes.'

Sir Reginald grew slightly more aggressive. 'A person is either satisfied about a thing or he is not satisfied. Now, Miss Weir, were you satisfied or were you not satisfied?'

'I wasn't altogether satisfied.'

'You weren't altogether satisfied. And yet you persisted in the business during all those months at Exeborough and agreed to start it again at Lincaster?'

'After what he said, I thought it wasn't so bad.'

'I put it to you that you knew the business was dishonest, but you went into it because of your love for the deceased?'

Merle gazed at him helplessly.

'Well, Miss Weir?'

'Yes.' Her voice was low and distressed.

'Quite. Now did you put any money into the business?'

'One hundred pounds and other small sums.'

'What was your total capital at the time?'

Again Merle seemed to find it difficult to reply. 'I had five hundred pounds in the bank.'

'Now I'm sorry to ask this question, but I'm afraid I must. Had you lived with the deceased?'

Again the warm flush covered Merle's cheeks. 'Yes,' she said in a low voice.

'I see. Has there been a child?'

'No. Oh no.'

'When you went into the business first did you think the deceased would marry you?'

'Yes, I thought so.'

'Would you have gone into it if you hadn't thought he would marry you?'

'No. I had made up my mind about that.'

Sir Reginald leant forward. 'And when you went into the Lincaster business, the honesty of which you doubted, you did so because of your hope that he would marry you, and for no other reason? Is that so or is it not?'

Very hesitatingly she answered, 'Yes, I suppose that's true.'

Sir Reginald nodded, bent forward, and once again moved the papers before him. Then again he stood up, hitching his gown over his right shoulder with his characteristic gesture.

'On the Saturday morning you telephoned to The Gables. From where did you make the call?'

'From the General Post Office.'

'Had you a telephone in your own office?'

290

'Yes, I had, but—' She stopped abruptly.

'Perhaps I can help you with a question. Why did you not use your own instrument?'

'I didn't want—I was afraid if I got through to James; the deceased, I mean; of some of the staff overhearing me. It would have been a private conversation.'

'It would have been a private conversation,' repeated Sir Reginald with a meaning look at the jury. 'Very well; now another point. Was there among the flowers at the Witton Grange Convalescent Home a large cluster of monkshood?'

'Yes.' Merle's face registered surprise at this new attack.

'Then you know the appearance of the plant?'

'Yes.' Her voice faltered as she saw its direction.

Sir Reginald stooped, picked up a book and passed it across. 'Look at this book, please. Have you seen it before?'

'Yes,' she answered, 'it's mine.'

'It's your book. Kept in your office at the Works?'

'Yes.'

'I hand it in, m'lud, in respect of Page 438. It is a standard work on organic chemistry, and on Page 438 the extraction of aconitine from the plant *aconitum napellus* or monkshood is described in detail.'

The book with ceremony was passed to Frobisher, who, having looked at the page in question, laid it aside on his desk. Sir Reginald, waiting punctiliously, resumed his cross-examination.

'Now having known the deceased so long and so intimately, you were doubtless aware of his habits and preferences? Is it a fact that he liked afternoon tea and would not voluntarily miss it?'

'Yes, that is true.'

'You heard Miss Lestrange give evidence that she saw

you on the Webble river bank about a fortnight before the tragedy. Was that evidence true?'

'I was there on the Saturday afternoon a fortnight before the tragedy.'

'On that afternoon did you see the deceased?'

'Yes, he was fishing.'

'Did you speak to him?'

'No, he didn't see me.'

'Then why did you go down to the river bank?'

This question seemed to give Merle more difficulty. 'I can hardly describe it,' she said. 'I wanted just to see the house he had chosen.'

'You felt that you should have been mistress of it perhaps?'

Merle paused. 'Perhaps a little,' she admitted, 'but really because I was just interested.'

'Very well. Now on that afternoon did you see a basket where some rocks outcrop on the bank?'

'Yes.'

'Did it occur to you what that basket might be?'

'I thought it was James—the deceased's tea-basket.'

'You thought it was his tea-basket: quite.'

Sir Reginald sat down, but Merle's immediate ordeal was not yet over. Nesbit rose to re-examine.

'With regard to my learned friend's suggestion that you thought your business dishonest. Did you think it was fraudulent, an offence for which you could be prosecuted, or were you merely afraid it was approaching sharp practice?'

'That was it: it seemed to me rather sharp practice.'

'I have only a couple more questions to ask you. Will you explain exactly for what purpose you used the book on chemistry produced in court?'

'To help with my chemical experiments. I was trying to find a better medicine than Braxamin, so as to be able to outsell it on merit.'

'I follow. One last point. You put over a hundred pounds into the business?'

'Yes.'

'Did you go into it as a partner or as a paid official?'

'As a partner.'

'Did you receive a proportion of the profits?'

'I got what I needed to live on. The rest I put back into the business for improvements.'

'By your own free will?'

'Oh yes.'

'Did the deceased put money in also?'

'Yes, as far I know, all he had.'

Nesbit sat down, and it being past one o'clock, Frobisher adjourned the proceedings for lunch.

21

Anthony Frobisher
Listens to Arguments

The examination of Peter Temple after lunch followed much the same lines as had that of Merle. Under Cunninghame's adroit guidance he spoke first of his history; of his upbringing, his education, the change in his circumstances due to the death of his father, and his appointment as vanman at the Koldkure works. Then on the closing down of the works, of his temporary incursion into the postal world, his appointment as works manager of the Lincaster business, and his success in that position. Finally, of his love for Merle, which he did not attempt to minimise, admitting without hesitation that it was the ruling passion of his life.

Cunninghame then led him to the period of the tragedy. On the Saturday Temple was to be away from the works, and on the Friday evening he called on Merle to ask her to look after some matters for him next day, of which he had forgotten to tell her. Yes, he found her very much excited and distressed over the news of Tarrant's engagement. Yes, she had used the words, 'I wish he was dead! I could kill him myself! I will kill him!' but she had then broken down, sobbed, and said she hadn't meant them. When he left her he thought she had entirely regained her composure.

On the Saturday he did not get back to Lincaster until after the works had closed. He went round to Merle's rooms, intending to ask her to go out with him. Mrs Benson's statement as to her apparent distress worried him. Admittedly he told Mrs Benson a false tale of some valued papers of Merle's having been burned. He did it to prevent gossip about Merle. Anxious to learn more as to her state of mind, he went on to see the works' forewoman, Joyce Caldwell. There he learned about Merle's preoccupation in the office. He assumed that she was still distressed about the engagement, and he wondered whether she might not have gone to Little Bitton to have the matter out with Tarrant. This opinion was largely based on the fact of the time at which she left her rooms: she could just have caught the Saxham bus. He decided to make the journey himself, in the hope of finding her and being able to comfort her. Accordingly he went to Saxham on the next bus, and happening to meet Rose Jordan, the office typist, in Saxham, learned that he was on the right track.

'And what did you do then?' asked Cunninghame.

'I went on to Little Bitten and walked down the Webble Road, and so to the bank of the river opposite The Gables. I—'

'How did you know the layout of the place? Had you been there before?'

'Yes, Miss Weir had told me on a previous occasion that she had been there, and I was curious and went to see it.'

'Why did you go to the Webble Road side of the valley? Did you know that the deceased was fishing?'

'No, I didn't know. I thought there was just a chance of seeing Miss Weir, if she had been on the terrace or in the garden. From the road behind The Gables you can't see anything.'

'And did you see her?'

'No. I therefore began to walk towards the house, but when I was getting near the footbridge leading to the garden I saw the deceased's body in the river.'

'What did you do then?'

Temple hesitated, and for the first time showed confusion. 'I didn't know what to do. My first idea was to run for help to the house, then I thought I shouldn't be in too great a hurry. So I examined the body in case he might still be alive. But he was dead.'

'How did you know?'

'There could be no doubt about it. It was cold.'

'Very well. Did you then report the occurrence?'

'No.' He spoke with obvious distress.

'Why not?'

Temple looked all round the building as if for help. 'I was afraid,' he said at last, 'in case it mightn't have been an accident.'

'Afraid? Afraid of what?'

'Afraid of being suspected.'

'Then you thought it was murder?'

'No, I believed it was an accident. But, of course, I couldn't be absolutely sure.'

'Then what did you do?'

'I took the bus back to Saxham at once.'

'Did you meet the female prisoner at Saxham?'

'Yes. When I heard her story I was frightened, for I saw that she also was liable to suspicion. But I thought she was safe, for I thought Tarrant must have been put into the river by physical violence, and of course she couldn't have done that.'

'You decided to say nothing about your visits?'

'Yes. I couldn't, in any case; it was too late. And then when we heard about the poison that was another reason.'

Cunninghame went on with his questions, but he elicited little more of interest. Then Derek Lindsay rose to cross-examine.

His first few questions were innocuous enough, and concerned Temple's early life and his love for Merle. Then he grew more searching.

'You have just stated that on the Saturday of the crime you went to Little Bitton in the hope of finding the female prisoner?'

'That is so.'

'When you were originally asked by the police where you went that afternoon, did you tell them it was to Little Bitton?'

Temple stared at him unhappily.

'Well, Temple?'

'No,' he answered in a low voice, 'I didn't mention Little Bitton.'

'Where did you tell the police you had been?'

'To Dunsfield.'

'Had you been to Dunsfield?'

'No.'

'That is to say your original statement to the police was a complete falsehood?'

Again there was no reply. Lindsay repeated the question

and this time Temple reluctantly agreed. Lindsay glanced confidentially at the jury as if to say: 'See? That's the sort of man you're dealing with,' then started off again.

'When during your visit to Merle Weir on the Friday night you saw her distress and heard her outburst in which she threatened to kill the deceased, were you at first afraid she might really do it?'

'Oh, no, I thought it was merely hysteria. She became normal before I left.'

'Next day when you heard of her strange manner and that she had left in time to catch the Saxham bus, were you afraid then she might do something rash?'

'Oh no, I—I just thought she shouldn't be alone.'

'Quite so.' Lindsay's voice was grim. 'I put it to you, Temple, that you were afraid that she might murder the deceased.'

'No.' Temple's uneasiness was growing.

'I put it to you that it was this fear which made you lie to Mrs Benson about the burnt papers?'

'Nothing of the kind.'

'You thought she was in an abnormal condition?'

'Worried and upset, yes; abnormal, no.'

'Not abnormal? Do you really ask the jury to believe that a lady of Merle Weir's temperament was not in an abnormal condition when she threatened to murder the deceased?'

'But she had got over that.'

'Do you say that it was not abnormal for a lady of Miss Weir's business ability to refuse to dictate letters and to give absurd decisions on points of management?'

Temple hesitated. 'She was upset, yes,' he said in a fainter voice.

'Upset or abnormal, I won't quarrel over the word. Now

298

you are on your oath, Temple. I put it to you again that on Saturday you feared Merle Weir might commit murder, and that you were hurrying to Little Bitton in the hope of preventing her from doing so.'

Frobisher could see the sweat glistening on the young man's forehead. He did not reply.

'Is that true?' There was a snap in Lindsay's voice like the crack of a whip.

'I suppose so.' Temple almost whispered.

'You suppose so. Now—'

Temple, seemingly at the end of his tether, exclaimed: 'Of course I was quite wrong.'

Lindsay's manner changed. 'Ah, possibly, but I have not asked you about that. Now another point. When you saw the deceased in the river, I put it to you that you thought Miss Weir had killed him?'

'Oh no. No. How could she have done so?'

'You left him lying in the river, not knowing whether he was alive or dead?'

'He was dead.'

'Have you ever learned first aid? How to give artificial respiration?'

'Yes.'

'You have? Then you must be aware that you cannot tell from observation whether an apparently drowned person is alive or dead. You left the deceased lying in the river, although you knew there was a chance that he might be alive?'

Temple was ghastly. 'I thought he was dead.'

'Perhaps, but you did not know. What you did know was that you should have taken the body from the water and carried out artificial respiration or called for help. Did you not know that?'

'I suppose so.' Again the voice was scarcely audible.

'I put it to you that the reason you left him there to die, for all you knew to the contrary, was that you thought the female prisoner was somehow responsible.'

'No,' very faintly.

'Then can you explain your action in any other way?'

'What I said,' Temple faltered. 'I was afraid of being suspected myself.'

Lindsay had apparently got what he wanted. 'Very well,' he said, 'the jury will form their own conclusion about that. Now tell me,' and he turned to the question of extracting aconitine from monkshood.

In the re-examination Nesbit tried to show that Temple's inaction when he found the body was due, firstly, to an unreasoning panic for himself, and secondly, to his conviction that Tarrant was already dead and that therefore it never occurred to him to do anything. His efforts were not particularly successful. Nor were Cunninghame's when he attempted to prove that Tarrant must have been dead when Temple found him.

A number of witnesses were then called to bear testimony to the excellence of Merle's private life, these arguing that she was not at all the type to have recourse to murder, even under severe mental strain. Most of them were not cross-examined, and when the last stepped out of the witness box Nesbit rose to address the court on behalf of Merle.

Frobisher glanced at the clock. The afternoon was wearing on. He could really adjourn now if he chose. But Nesbit was not likely to be long—in his own interests, for the jury were growing tired—and it would be better if possible to complete the defence at one sitting.

'May it please your lordship; members of the jury,' began

Nesbit in the time honoured phrase; 'the time has now come for me to put before you the defence to this charge of wilful murder against Merle Weir. I will be very brief and I hope you will bear with me patiently for a few moments.

'I will begin by directing your attention to the case made by the Crown. My client has been accused of murdering James Tarrant by poisoning him with aconitine. Now it is obvious that to substantiate such a charge, the very first thing that the Crown must do is to prove that death occurred through aconitine poisoning. But in this, as you heard, they have utterly failed. Death was due to drowning, and neither of the experts called was able to say that the drowning was due to the aconitine. I grant you that one of the doctors said he thought that the drowning was due to the aconitine, but he immediately qualified this statement by admitting that he did not know it for a fact. The other doctor declared in so many words that he was not prepared to say that the aconitine was the cause of the drowning death. No other evidence on the point was submitted.

'Now just consider the position. Two medical witnesses are called to give expert evidence on a medical point. Both agree that they cannot be certain of the point at issue, though one gives an opinion on it. The other is so doubtful that he refuses even to give an opinion.

'I submit, members of the jury, that you cannot accept this evidence as conclusive. The doctors themselves, knowing all the details, did not consider the facts conclusive. I submit that it has not been proved that the drowning was due to aconitine.

'But if it has not been proved that the drowning was due to aconitine, then it has not been proved that the death was due to aconitine. I submit further that if, considering the medical evidence, you are not satisfied that the deceased died from aconitine poisoning, then you must bring the accused in Not Guilty of this charge. That, members of the jury, is my first point.'

Nesbit paused a moment to let his remarks sink home, then resumed: 'But this, it might perhaps be argued, is a technical point. I want to do more than show you that my client is technically innocent; I want to prove her complete and entire innocence from every point of view.

'In this connection there is an admirable rule for the guidance of juries: that if apparently damaging facts admit of an innocent interpretation, that innocent interpretation should be accepted rather than another. This is simply the old rule of "Give the accused the benefit of the doubt".

'Now here you have heard from the lips of Merle Weir herself an explanation of the facts and of her conduct which, I submit to you, is absolutely satisfactory. At no point was there a contradiction. At no point were the details other than natural and reasonable. I feel sure you will agree that the statement adequately covered the facts. If this is so, I submit that on the rule of giving the accused the benefit of the doubt, you must necessarily bring in a verdict of Not Guilty.

'But still, though I feel that I can claim a verdict on this point alone, I would rather you gave it, not because you were doubtful of my client's guilt, but because you were convinced of her innocence. And as you listened to her evidence, I am sure you were convinced. You, members of the jury, are men and women of the world. You have seen life, and you are accustomed to judge character. You have seen Merle Weir in the box. Was that a liar and a perjurer that you watched and listened to? You know it was not!

Was not truth evident in her whole manner and appearance? Had she not the very stamp of truth on her features? For myself, and I am sure you will agree with me, I felt that here was no liar, no spiteful and cowardly murderess, but a woman, subject like the rest of us to the faults and frailties of our common human nature, but of upright character and honourable intention. I need say no more on this point: I am content to leave the decision in your hands.

'But if my client's statement was natural and probable, can the same be said of the case the Crown has attempted to make? I am sure you will agree with me there also, that it cannot. Would a woman of the character which so many witnesses have told you that my client possesses, commit, not a hasty and passionate crime, but a murder premeditated and sordid, as this was? I ask you, is not the idea absurd? Would a woman of kindly instincts really administer a painful poison to the man she had once loved? I cannot believe it, and I am sure you cannot either.

'Lastly, not only is the Crown case unlikely, but on one point, and that a vital point, it is absolutely impossible and self-contradictory. They tell us that my client in the middle of Friday night collected monkshood from her neighbours' gardens and extracted the aconitine, thus preparing herself for her journey on the following afternoon. But they also tell us that she only learned that the deceased was going fishing when she rang up The Gables at eleven next morning. If she only learned on Saturday that she could use the poison, how did she know to prepare it on Friday night? Was she a magician, able to read the future? I ask you to give this point your very earnest consideration, for I put it to you that it alone renders the whole of the Crown case abortive.

'It is with the utmost confidence then that I ask you for a verdict of Not Guilty. First, I ask you for that verdict because the Crown has not proved that the action of which they accuse my client really caused the death of James Tarrant. Secondly, I ask you for it because of the obvious truthfulness of my client and of the inherent probability of her story; and thirdly, I ask for it because the case of the prosecution is unconvincing and fails to meet all the facts.

'I do not call your attention to the awful results which will follow a verdict of Guilty: you are, I know, fully alive to the heavy responsibility which now rests upon you. If this young woman has taken life, then let her life be forfeit. But it is your responsibility to make sure that her life is not taken in error. I cannot of course see what is in your minds, but I do most earnestly and sincerely beg you to consider fully and impartially the views I have tried to put before you.'

The speech, Frobisher saw, had impressed the jury. Once again he believed that could the verdict be taken at once, it would be for acquittal. But Sir Reginald was a formidable antagonist. Not until he had made his reply could a reasonable forecast be made.

Directly Nesbit sat down, Cunninghame rose to address the court on behalf of Temple. Frobisher, again glancing at the clock, knew that he also would be brief, and he therefore once again refrained from adjourning the proceedings.

Cunninghame divided what he had to say into two parts. His first point was the obvious one that the charge against his client depended upon that against Merle. If Merle were found Not Guilty, the entire case against Temple fell to the ground. This was so obvious that it was unnecessary for him to labour it.

His second point was that even if Merle had been guilty of putting the poison in the tea, Temple was unaware of it, and therefore could not possibly have done anything to assist her in the affair. 'He found the deceased drowned, and he tells you that he never for a moment imagined that the prisoner Weir could be responsible. It is true that as a result of some very, may I say, *strenuous* cross-examination, he admitted that the thought of her possible guilt had occurred to him. Very natural: why not? But a thought occurring to a person is one thing, and his believing it or acting upon it is quite another. In this instance, I ask you how could Temple possibly have believed Miss Weir guilty? The deceased was a powerful man, tall and strong and wiry. You have seen Merle Weir. I ask you: had she the physical strength to drown a man like Tarrant, otherwise than by first rendering him insensible? And of such there was no sign. I suggest to you that Temple could not possibly have entertained the idea that she was guilty.

'On reaching Lincaster that evening, he talked the matter over with Weir, and do you suppose that if she were guilty, she would have said so? Is it not quite obvious that under such circumstances she would have told him the story she told here in court? And is it not obvious that he would have believed it? It would have sounded so much more likely than that of her guilt. It would have fitted in with his own preconceptions, the deductions he had made on finding the body. No, it is practically impossible that on that evening he could have suspected Merle Weir.

'But what of later, when he learned about the poison? I admit that *then* suspicion might have been possible. But this could only have been a suspicion. In no way, unless he were told by Weir, could he have *known* that she was guilty.

Under these circumstances nothing that he could have done could have made him an accessory after the fact.

'My learned friend for the prosecution suggested that Temple's failure to report the finding of the body was a proof that he suspected the prisoner Weir of murder. But why search for laboured and far-fetched theories to account for this dereliction of duty when you have Temple's own perfectly simple, straightforward and convincing explanation of his conduct? Temple did not report his discovery because he was afraid of being himself suspected. He tells you so himself, and what could be simpler and what could be more likely? Again, please put yourself, each one of you, in his place. You find this body in the river. You realise that it would be possible to prove that you had a powerful motive for desiring his death: that of freeing the woman you loved from the chains which bound her to him, and would you not think twice before admitting that you were alone with his body? Why have to explain your presence there at all? And a decision once taken—taken in the stress of the moment—could not be gone back on. I am sure you will agree that motives of self-defence would be entirely adequate to account for all Temple's actions.

'I am far from excusing his action. It was of course entirely wrong. The moment he found the body he should have pulled it out of the water and attempted artificial respiration, or at the very least hurried for help. I think it was morally an unpardonable action, and I am sure you will agree. But, members of the jury, he is not being tried for this. You are not dealing with it. He is being tried for aiding the female prisoner to evade the penalty of her crime: a totally different proposition. It is this he is charged with, and no matter how we may condemn him otherwise, it is upon this you have to give your verdict. Members of the jury, I feel absolutely convinced that when you have fully considered all these matters, you will come to the conclusion that Temple is innocent of the charge brought against him!'

It was over. That closed the defence. Nothing more for those two in the dock could now be said, except in so far as he, Frobisher, should direct attention to points in their favour. Well, he need not think of that now. It was late and he was tired and tomorrow was a new day. Without delay he adjourned the proceedings until the following morning.

22

Anthony Frobisher Weighs the Issue

The court was if anything even fuller when the third day of the trial opened. Today should see its end, for there was only Sir Reginald's closing speech and the summing up before the jury retired. A good many of those present thought the result a foregone conclusion. The defence seemed to them overwhelming: as they put it to one another, 'That nice-looking young woman would never have done it.' Others, perhaps with more experience of trials, reserved judgment. 'Wait till we've heard Sir Reginald,' they said; 'he's generally got a trump up his sleeve.'

But all were at one in the intense interest with which they awaited the closing stages of the pitiful drama.

Sir Reginald, standing up as soon as the proceedings reopened and hitching his gown up over his shoulder with his characteristic gesture, began in a low voice with his head bent over his brief. Then, having by this means secured silence and the attention of all, he raised himself to his full height, threw back his head and continued in his usual tones, forceful or caressing as the exigencies of the moment required.

He touched first on the able speeches to which they had just listened, insisting that everything which could be said on behalf of the accused had been put forward in the strongest way possible. While wishing to be absolutely fair to the defendants, his duty, he went on, was to present a more sober and dispassionate view of the circumstances, so that the jury might found their opinions on the facts and on the facts alone, without allowing themselves to be influenced by feelings and sentiments. A brief reference to their duty to the Crown, which was neither more nor less important than their duty to the accused, and Sir Reginald was in his stride.

'Before coming to the details of the case,' he went on, 'I must say a word on the first point raised by the defence, that as it has not been proved that the deceased died from taking aconitine, the defendant Weir must be found Not Guilty of the charge brought against her, and of course if this is correct in her case, it will apply in Temple's also.

'Now I submit to you that the defence is wrong upon this point, because I submit that it *has* been proved, proved beyond any reasonable doubt whatever, that the deceased did die as a result of taking aconitine. Consider the circumstances. It is known that the deceased did take a large dose of aconitine that afternoon. The effect of such a dose would be, first, to make him feel ill, and second, to produce loss of power in his limbs. What more likely than that his feeling of illness should make him start for his home, and what more likely than that the loss of power would cause him to slip off the footbridge into the water? When you add to these facts that, in all other respects, the deceased was a powerful man in admirable health and could easily have got out of the river if, he had fallen in, and that there is no other way of accounting for. his not having done so, I cannot doubt that as hard-headed men and women of the world you will conclude that the aconitine was the cause of his death. You must remember that the doctors were not asked to decide this question on common-sense lines. They were asked to give a scientific demonstration, which they naturally could not do. You must not therefore let their hesitation influence your judgment.

'Now I will first take the case of Merle Weir, and will begin it with a word as to her character. 'Admittedly she looks and speaks like a very charming and estimable young woman, and you have heard, and must give proper weight to, the excellent testimonials of character given by various witnesses. But in considering the relation of her character to the present case, I must call your attention to three points.

'The first is that she is not quite so innocent as she appears. In the past she has consistently allowed her affections to override her sense of right and wrong. She became partner in a business which was in point of fact dishonest, knowing it to be dishonest, because of her love for the deceased. That she has admitted. It does not of course follow that the converse is true: that because of her sudden hate for the deceased she murdered him, but the tendency in her character is there, and you must take it into consideration in dealing with the present charge.

'My second point is even more important. She may appear to be truthful, but she is not. All through this case she has lied. She not only lied to the police, but she committed perjury in the lower court. She has admitted it herself, and you can read her evidence. She swore she did not go to Little Bitton on the Saturday. Today her statement is quite different, and one or other version must be false.

'My third point is more general. It is, and my lord will back me up in this, that murder is less dependent on character than almost any other crime. A man of good character will not normally commit burglary or arson or blackmail, but under the stress of circumstances he may commit murder. I do not wish to elaborate this argument now: I will refer to it later. All I ask you to bear in mind is that the possession of a good character is no proof of innocence of murder.

'Now with regard to this particular crime, it is clear that your conclusion as to the accused's innocence or guilt will depend on whether or not you believe her story. Her story therefore becomes of immense importance, as also do the tests which you may apply to it on this point.

'My learned friend gave you two of these tests: first, is the story intrinsically probable and does it adequately cover the facts? and second, was the demeanour and bearing of the accused while telling it such as to convince you of its truth? I accept these two tests. Let us briefly consider their application.

'I think I may admit at once, and I imagine you will agree with me, that the story is intrinsically probable and that it does adequately cover the facts. I do not want in the slightest to minimise any advantage this may give to the accused, but it is my duty to remind you that this alone by no means constitutes a proof of innocence. For just consider, supposing she were guilty, how easily she could have evolved that story. The whole of her movements to and from Little Bitton, and for the matter of that, of Temple's also, she would tell exactly as they occurred. No invention would be needed so far. Indeed only two episodes would have to be altered. The first is that of her activities during Friday night; the second, her actions on the bank of the Webble on Saturday afternoon. If on the former occasion she had gathered monkshood and extracted the aconitine, she had only to omit these details and say she could not sleep and so took a walk. In the latter, if she put the aconitine in the flask, she had only to say she had not done so, but had passed the basket without stopping. So that here too very little invention would have been required.

'Now please let us be clear about this. What I have to impress on you is that the fact that this is a good story and fits the circumstances is not evidence of its truth, and you cannot acquit on these grounds.

'And yet is the story so very adequate and reasonable? On Friday evening the accused contemplated murdering the deceased. I do not want to make more of this than the circumstances warrant, but that is the fact. She said so in the presence of witnesses and she does not deny it. The defence says she afterwards changed her mind. Now I ask you: If she changed her mind, why did she go to Little Bitton? She first said she did not go to Little Bitton, then when she found she could not sustain this, she said it was to tell the deceased that unless he broke the engagement she would give him away to Miss Woolcombe for the forsworn lover and adventurer he actually was. Incidentally, on her own admission here was the bitterness still remaining in her heart. The Crown submits that all this lying and substitution of stories can only be accounted for in one way: that she never changed her mind, and that she went to Little Bitton to carry out her intention of poisoning the deceased, the story being modified later to account for her action.

'Her statement then takes an unusual turn. She tells you that she suddenly experienced a change of heart and saw that her only chance of happiness lay in forgiving the deceased.

'Far be it from me to deny that such things happen, but the question is: Did it happen then? Was their conversation as pleasant and amiable as she makes out? Or did she speak to him and get a cutting retort which further fanned her bitterness? Or did she not see him at all, but merely put the poison in the thermos? These questions are for you. All I have to do at the moment is to point out that her story by itself does not acquit her.

'There is another point about the story to which I must call your attention. There was, as I have said, an awkward period to be accounted for in the middle of Friday night. The accused was heard to leave the house and she remained out for a long time, its exact length being unknown. What was she doing? She says she went for a walk. Now, I ask you, is it likely that she should go for a walk in the middle of the night? Members of the jury, did she go for a walk? The Crown submits that this walk never took place; that it was an invention designed to cover the preparation of the poison.

'On my learned friend's first test, then, I submit that the adequacy and reasonableness of the story does not prove innocence. What of the second, her bearing in court, and particularly in the witness box?

'Now I am sure you were conscious, as I was conscious, of the accused's charm, and you will of course give due weight to any indications of natural feeling, honesty or truthfulness which she exhibited. But I ask you to consider what her bearing in the lower court must have been when she was swearing a lie. Was it different from her bearing yesterday? Here again, on my learned friend's second test,

I submit that Miss Weir's bearing was no proof whatever that she was speaking the truth.

'But perhaps, in spite of these considerations, you formed the opinion from her bearing that she was telling the truth? If so, I ask your particular attention to another point.

'You have seen the accused in the dock and heard her in the witness box, for her extremely distressing situations. You have not seen or spoken to her under normal conditions. Now Temple knew her very much better than you. He had in fact been extremely intimate with her over a period of many months. Moreover he loved her, thereby presumably idealising her character. But *he* thought her guilty. When he found the deceased, there was nothing to show that death was not accidental, and yet he immediately jumped to the conclusion that the accused had murdered him. That from the man who knew her so intimately and loved her so dearly! If you consider her innocent, you have to explain this belief of Temple's.

'But, you may say, how do we know that he thought her guilty? I will tell you. There is first the episode of the false story of the burnt papers. If Temple did not foresee the possibility of her guilt, why should he go out of his way to tell this lie? He says he wished to stop gossip about the accused, but, I ask you, what gossip could possibly have arisen? I suggest that he was trying to destroy what might prove to be damaging evidence. If she should have set out intending to commit murder, her excitement just before the crime would be very damaging evidence indeed. Is it not obvious that Temple foresaw the possibility and was trying to meet it? That, I suggest, is one reason why we know he thought Merle Weir guilty.

'The next is that Temple explained, or rather my learned

314

friend who is appearing for him explained, that he omitted to try to save the deceased's life or to report his discovery because he was afraid of being himself suspected. Let us examine that statement.

'I grant my learned friend that Temple's motive must have been overwhelmingly strong. This is proved by his action, which, morally at least, was indefensible. My learned friend admits as much. I think you will agree that it must have been due to fear of suspicion, either on his own behalf, as the defence say, or on that of the female defendant, as the Crown submits. In other words, if it was not due to fear for himself, it must have been to fear for Merle Weir.

'Now I must here point out to you that it could not have been fear for himself. The hour at which he left Lincaster was known; the hour at which he left Saxham was known; and from these the earliest hour at which he could have reached the body could have been calculated. But if the body was cold, as he tells us it was, death must have occurred a considerable time earlier. So there was no possible chance of his being suspected. Therefore I submit that it was not fear on his own behalf, but on Merle Weir's, which was in his heart.

'You will see from all this that the defence is not so convincing as it appears at first sight.

'And now, what of the alternative, which we say took place?' Briefly Sir Reginald went through the Crown case again. Merle, sad and disappointed from her treatment by Tarrant, but still loving him and hoping against hope that he would yet marry her and make her an honest woman, as the old phrase ran. Then the discovery of his engagement, not from himself, but through the columns of the local paper, thus not only wiping out her remaining hopes, but

315

filling her with the bitterest resentment. Her determination not to allow him to get away with it. Her providing herself with the poison, with the intention of using it on the first possible opportunity. 'To prepare for that opportunity,' went on Sir Reginald, 'it was not of course necessary that she should have known exactly when it would arise, as the defence suggests. The next day was Saturday, and on Saturday she was free from her business in the afternoon, therefore she made her preparations in case that afternoon would prove suitable.

'And here I must remind you of how she found out that it would be suitable. Merle Weir had a telephone in her own office. From there she could have rung up The Gables. But did she? No. She preferred to speak from the General Post Office, nearly a mile away. She tells you this was to prevent any of her staff from overhearing the conversation, which would have been private. No doubt it would have been private. 'Sir Reginald was finely ironical. 'I submit that it was so private that she took this extra trouble to prevent the call, not from being overheard, but from being traced. And why should she wish to prevent the call from being traced? For the same reason, surely, that she afterwards denied that she had gone to Little Bitton: for the sake of her neck.'

Sir Reginald continued outlining the case for the Crown: Merle's decision, on learning of the fishing expedition, to use the poison that afternoon. Her going to Little Bitton and putting the poison into the flask, either after seeing Tarrant, or more probably, without having met him at all. Her walk back to Saxham to enable her to put up the Dunsfield alibi. Her subsequent agreement with Temple as to their story, should inquiries be made. 'If this is not true,' he went on, 'what happened? The deceased was murdered. If he was not murdered by the accused, who murdered him? No suggestion on this point has been made.'

Sir Reginald then turned to Temple. Temple, in the view of the prosecution, had been seriously afraid for Merle on the Friday evening, but when after her outburst she had quieted down, he had thought she had grown normal. Her conduct on Saturday morning had revived all his fears, and believing she had gone to Little Bitton to murder Tarrant, he followed to try to prevent her doing so. He failed, but later decided to back up her story, as the best way of helping her.

Sir Reginald put his case with consummate skill, as Frobisher, who disliked him, had to admit. Listening to his mellow voice with its flowing periods was like seeing a film of the action, so inevitable did he make it all seem. It was having its effect on the jury. Except for the thin-lipped man and the stout woman, it looked as if Sir Reginald was leading them by the nose. It was having its effect on the accused also. Merle had looked hopeful on the previous evening when Nesbit and Cunninghame had finished their speeches. Now her face had once again grown ashen and she was staring at Sir Reginald with a growing horror in her eyes. Even Temple, who up till now had held himself erect and kept a stiff upper lip, seemed to be losing hope.

Having reached the end of his statement, Sir Reginald was too much of an artist to spoil his effort with a long peroration. In a few brief words he said that such was what the Crown submitted had happened, and that if the jury believed it, they would bring in a verdict of Guilty, no matter at what cost to themselves.

317

There was again movement through the court, inseparable from the close of an important speech. It was like the passing of yet another milestone on the long road of the trial, and signified the end of one tension and the beginning of another. Frobisher took up his notes. So far as he could tell from his observation of the jury, opinion was now fairly evenly divided, and it was clear to him that by his summing-up he could obtain whichever verdict he might desire. A reason, he told himself, to be more than ever careful to allow no inkling of his own opinion to appear on those points upon which the jury had to make a decision.

He began in a quiet, conversational voice, speaking without effort, but so clearly that every word was easily audible in all the room.

'Members of the jury: you have heard the cases for the Crown and for the defence put before you in a particularly able manner, and if I may say so, with great fairness on both sides. It is now your duty, weighing all that you have heard, and using the ordinary common sense and judgment which you normally apply to your everyday concerns, to decide on the guilt or innocence of these two persons of the crimes with which they have been charged.

'Your responsibility is heavy. Your two complementary duties—to acquit the innocent and convict the guilty—are equally and vitally important. You are here to see that these two persons, unless proved beyond reasonable doubt to be guilty, leave this court a free man and woman. That is your duty to them. But if this woman has committed murder and this man was an accessory to it, they must suffer for it. This, as you know, is not because of any such desire on your part or on mine, but because in a case like this our whole social structure is at stake. You are here in a position

318

of trust towards the community in which you live. That is your duty to your neighbour.

'You must therefore put from your minds the defendants' youth, their mental suffering, the woman's good looks and suchlike considerations, and decide for or against them on the facts and the facts alone. Learned counsel tried to intimidate you by directing your thoughts to what might follow an adverse verdict. You have nothing to do with that. That is the responsibility of others. You must, and I know you will, do your duty regardless of consequences.'

Frobisher went on to define the crimes of murder and of being an accessory to murder after the fact, then turning to the question of whether the aconitine had or had not killed the deceased.

'Here the facts are not in dispute. The deceased did actually take a lethal dose of aconitine on that Saturday afternoon. This made him feel ill: it must have done, and it is suggested that he thereupon tried to reach his home. The fact is that he did go part of the way home. He then somehow got into the river, and being unable to get out again was drowned. The effect of the poison is to produce a loss of power in the limbs, and it is suggested that this loss of power was the cause of his slipping off the footbridge. It is for you to say whether or not these suggestions are justifiable. That is your responsibility and I am not concerned with it, but I am concerned with telling you the law on the matter. If the female prisoner gave the deceased poison and he was drowned as a result of that poison, then she is guilty of murder to precisely the same extent as if he had died directly from the poison without falling into the river at all.'

The thin, clear tones went steadily on. Merle's character.

The jury had heard her praises sounded by several witnesses and they would give that testimony the weight that they considered it deserved. On the other hand she had, if they believed the evidence, gone into a doubtful proprietary medicine business with the deceased, and her two stories of how she spent the Saturday afternoon undoubtedly contradicted each other. The jury had had the advantage of seeing and hearing her, and they must make up their minds as to her truthfulness.

He turned to Merle's story, agreeing that in its truth or falsehood lay the crux of the case, and summarising at considerable length the arguments which had been put forward for its acceptance and rejection respectively. 'I do not think,' he went on, 'I can help you here. You will have to decide for yourselves how much credence you give it. If you believe it, you need go no further, and you will return a verdict of Not Guilty in the cases of both defendants. If you do not believe it, or believe it only partially, you must consider other aspects of the case in reaching your decision.'

With regard to the question of whether or not Temple believed the story, he must tell them that Temple's beliefs were quite irrelevant, and must not be taken into account. It was their opinion about the story that mattered, not that of others.

In his turn Frobisher then went through, item by item, the case for the prosecution. That Merle had been badly treated by the deceased was unquestionable, and it was for the jury to consider whether this treatment could have produced in her the urge to murder. In this they must neither overlook her outburst on learning of the deceased's engagement, nor give it greater weight than it deserved. With regard to the suggestion that Merle had gathered monkshood during

Friday night, the prosecution had shown that she could have done this, but not that she did it. He was bound to point out that this was all that was incumbent on the prosecution in order to obtain a verdict, but here again the jury could use their own discretion. They might consider, taking all the circumstances into account, whether Merle Weir was likely to risk being seen gathering monkshood from a private garden by the light, perhaps, of a street lamp, or whether she felt that if she were seen she could make her escape before being identified. He must here point out that the prosecution had brought no evidence of gardens being robbed.

The prosecution had asked the question: If this woman did not murder the deceased, who did? and had pointed out that no alternative explanation of the deceased's death had been put forward. It was his duty to inform the jury that the defence were not bound to suggest any alternative theory, and the fact that they had not done so must not be used against the accused. It was the duty of the prosecution to prove their case, and though proof of an alternative case might be a good defence, it was by no means the only one.

On and on continued the quiet but incisive voice, examining, analysing, weighing probabilities, but giving no lead towards a decision. It was very still in the court. The audience sat as if hypnotised, listening to the words upon which might depend a human life. Merle remained the colour of parchment. She seemed sunk in a stupor of despair, as if expecting the worst. On Temple's face was stamped an expression of indignant amazement as well as horror, as if he could not believe that such things could be said.

Frobisher presently turned to the case against Temple. 'Learned counsel has correctly stated that if you find the

321

female defendant Not Guilty, the case against the man breaks down, as the crime with which he is charged depends for its existence on her guilt. But the converse is not necessarily true. If she murdered the deceased, he may or may not have known of it, and if he knew it, he may or may not have "received, harboured or maintained" her, which you may take to mean to have helped her, either by the destruction of evidence or in some other way. These are the questions you will have to decide about him. Here again you will use your common sense and judgment, just as you do in settling the ordinary affairs of your daily life. You will recall in this connection his action in not reporting his discovery of the body, and you will consider whether his motive could or could not have been the fear that he himself might have been suspected of murder. If you do not think this could have been his reason, you will ask yourselves what it was. As to the story of the burnt paper, if you believe his own explanation of it, you will probably disregard it altogether. If you do not believe his explanation, you will consider how far, if at all, the incident supports the Crown case.

'All this leads up to the question: Supposing Temple did suspect Merle Weir, did this occur to him only as a mere vague possibility, or had he sufficient information to be reasonably convinced of her guilt? If the latter, you will then consider whether he gave her any definite aid towards evading the penalty of her crime. Evidence was put before you that he lied to the police as to his movements on the afternoon of the crime, and it was argued that as this suppressed material evidence, it constituted definite aid. Even if this had been fully proved, it is very doubtful whether it would substantiate a charge of being an accessory after the fact, but I am bound to point out, as counsel for the defence correctly stated, that it was not fully proved. No evidence was given that Temple was not acting in his own interests rather than in that of the prisoner Weir. It may be, members of the jury, that you will be of the opinion, after considering the evidence against the prisoner Temple, that the Crown has not discharged the onus which lies upon it in all criminal cases of proving the charge against the prisoner beyond all reasonable doubt. That however is entirely a matter for you.' A momentary pause and the final words: 'Now if there is no further information that you require from me, will you please retire and consider your verdict?'

In the charge of their bailiffs the jury filed out, Merle and Temple disappeared from the dock, and Frobisher with his little bow left his seat and retired to his room.

He was tired after the effort of summing-up, and even now when it was over his mind remained full of what he had said. Was there any material point about which he had omitted to speak? He did not think so. Had his directions to the jury been sufficiently clear and sharp cut? Yes, he believed they had. Above all, had he managed to avoid showing a bias for or against those two in the dock? Again he felt satisfied. The summing-up had been a piece of good work, and so far as he was aware, not a word could be questioned should there be an appeal. Well, he had done his best, and he had no reason to be otherwise than content with the result. And now, though it was rather early, a little lunch seemed indicated.

As he took the coffee, omelette and piece of toast he had found most conducive to clear thought in the afternoon, his mind returned to the two subjects of all this endeavour. He hoped they were having some lunch. The woman looked hysterical, and he feared she might make a scene if the verdict should be adverse. Food would help her. Well, it would be there for her if she could take it. He felt an unusual urge to sympathise with the pair, but this was a luxury he could not allow himself. So far as he was concerned, they were lay figures . . .

His mind passed on to the next case: one of murderous assault on a policeman by smash and grab raiders. This was a matter in which he would have no mercy. Bandits and gangsters should be hanged, and if by the accident of the policeman not dying these had cheated the rope, he would see to it that they had a good many years of penal servitude in which to think their conduct over.

He finished his lunch and fell to writing. In one way or another there was a good deal to be done, and the more he got through now, the less would be left for the evening. An hour passed: two. The jury were taking an unconscionable time. What were they talking about? Surely it didn't mean a disagreement? A faint misgiving that he had been too impartial seized him. Perhaps he should have given them a stronger lead. A few words would have swayed them one way or the other . . .

A knock at the door. Ah, there they were at last. Once again he entered the court, the defendants reappeared, and then the jury filed in. One glance at their faces was sufficient. They were dark and unhappy and their eyes avoided the direction of the dock.

Temple they found Not Guilty and he was quickly released. Then came the case of Merle. With all its ghastly ceremonial the trial reached its hideous end.

23

All Concerned are Satisfied

Three days later Chief Inspector French sat in his room at New Scotland Yard.

In the papers before him there lay plenty of work, but he was not working. The verdict at Saxham St Edmunds had left a very unpleasant impression on his mind and he could not keep it out of his thoughts. The doubts which had oppressed him as to the guilt of Merle had not been removed by the trial, and he felt uneasy lest a miscarriage of justice should be about to take place. Of course the fault, if there were a fault, was not his, except in so far as he had been unable to procure absolutely positive proof of guilt. For the hundredth time he reviewed his actions, and he was convinced that they had been impeccable throughout.

The beginning of this unsatisfactory end had been when he had asked for the conference to discuss his results. There certainly his conscience was clear. In the light of the evidence he had collected, it was his obvious duty to report. He had to deal with the facts as he knew them, and it was no part of his business to arrogate to himself the office of judge. He had, moreover, stated his opinion to the Chief Constable, perhaps even more forcibly than his position warranted. This was the utmost that was open to him, the final decision not being in his hands.

When the evidence had been submitted to the Public Prosecutor's department, as it was inevitable that it should be, the die was cast. The Chief Constable's decision to proceed against Merle and Temple was there confirmed. In fact French, at one of his interviews there, had been complimented on his successful efforts. Yet French could not get the doubt out of his mind, and it left him unhappy.

But though he did not know it, he was not yet done with the case. As with a final shrug he took up his papers, his telephone rang.

'I want to speak to Chief Inspector French, please,' came a familiar voice. There was an excited urgency in the tones.

'Chief Inspector French speaking.'

'This is Peter Temple. I've got some news. There's just a chance that it might help Merle. You're the only person I know who could find out, if you would. I ask you to help me for Merle's sake.'

'Why not ask her solicitor?'

'Because this would require investigation. In itself it's nothing.'

'Then why not Superintendent Hawkins?'

'He wouldn't want to upset his case. No, you're our only hope. Mr French, you were kind to us and you were fair, and Merle likes you. You can't refuse: Merle's life may be at stake.'

Refuse! Not if French knew it! Here, amazingly, was the very chance for which he had just been longing. Temple should have gone to Hawkins, but he was hanged if he was going to consider that.

'What's the point, Mr Temple?'

'I would like Miss Oates to tell you herself: she would be more convincing. She was a nurse with Merle at that place in Surrey, and now lives at Little Bitton. She and Merle have met there on different occasions. At the trial I kept on wondering why she hadn't been called to prove Merle's visits. So directly I was released, I went to look her up. I found her here.'

'Where are you speaking from?'

'The Saxham Cottage Hospital. She was knocked down by a car on the day after the murder, and has been very ill. She hadn't heard the details of the trial till I told her. She was terribly upset, because she knows that Merle wouldn't have done a thing like that. Then she said she had seen something that afternoon and it might throw a new light on the affair. Question is, Mr French, will you come down and see Miss Oates? A moment: here's matron to speak to you.'

A woman's voice sounded. 'I'm the matron,' it explained. 'I should like to add to what Mr Temple has said that Miss Oates has become very much excited and wants to see you urgently. She's scarcely fit for an interview, but the doctor thinks that if she were frustrated it would have serious results.'

'Tell her,' said French, 'that I'll be with her in the course of a couple of hours.'

'Thank you. It may save her life.'

French felt as if a load had been lifted off his mind as he rang up Carter and told him to get out a car. If he were given an opportunity to re-open the case, he really would be thankful. He somehow took it for granted that he was about to obtain some new and important information, entirely forgetting the fanciful tendency of an invalid's evidence.

In due course he reached the Cottage Hospital and saw the matron.

'It was good of you to come so promptly,' she said. 'It's clear that any hope of Miss Oates's progress is out of the question until she has seen you. But I shall have to ask you to be tactful with her. As I told you, she's not really fit for the interview, and I'm afraid if you questioned her at any length, it might prove serious.'

'I shall be very careful,' French promised. 'What about Temple?'

The matron grimaced. 'I've sent him on a message. He was excited and getting everyone on edge, and I couldn't stand him any more.'

French smiled. 'He's been through rather a lot, you know.'

'Of course, and I've every sympathy with him. But that's no reason why the place should be turned upside down.'

French's manner when he was shown up to the ward was so soothing as to earn the matron's approving glance.

'Matron tells me you have something to say to me,' he said with his pleasant smile as he sat down by the bed. 'Well, I shall be very glad to hear it. But remember that there's plenty of time and take things easily. There's no hurry at all.'

'I'll come back presently,' put in the matron, 'and if,' she smiled broadly at Elsie, 'you let him tire you, there'll be terrible trouble all round.'

'Thank you for coming,' Elsie began feebly when they were alone. 'I only hope it's not on a wild goose chase. It's about Merle Weir. She was a good friend to me.'

'Yes?' said French. 'Mr Temple rang me up to say that you had something to tell me.'

'Yes. You may wonder why I didn't report it earlier, but I didn't know what had happened.'

'I quite understand,' French assured her.

'When Mr Temple told me today about the trial it nearly finished me off, I was so upset. I simply couldn't believe it at first.'

'You don't think Miss Weir's guilty?'

'I know she's not. It's just absurd. She's one of the best.'

'Well,' said French, 'the opinion of anyone who knows her intimately is useful. But I'm afraid that alone wouldn't be enough. Now, if you know some fact which might help her, I'd go into it at once.'

She looked at him gratefully. 'Thank you,' she said, continuing with many pauses and hesitations: 'I hoped you'd say that. It seems a terribly small thing, but I do hope it may be a help. I'm afraid it's only that I saw a car on that Saturday afternoon. It was parked at the entrance to Blackhill Copse.'

'Tell me the whole story.'

'On Saturday afternoon I wanted to take a letter to the post and I left my home—you know where it is?'

'On Webble Road nearly opposite The Gables, but a little farther away from the village?'

'Yes, that's right. I started about quarter to four. I passed the lane to Blackhill Copse three or four minutes later. You know where that is, I suppose?'

French felt as if he was undergoing a *viva voce*. 'It leads off Webble Road,' he replied, 'from the opposite side from the river, and a little nearer the village than The Gables?'

'Right. As I passed, I happened to look up the lane and

I saw a car parked partially behind some trees, as if to hide it from the road.'

'It wasn't properly hidden then?'

'No. I could see it was an Austin Seven. I noticed it particularly because I had been thinking of getting one: wondering if I could afford it, you know. Then I posted my letter, and when I was going back it turned out of the lane just before I reached it, and drove off. It doesn't sound much when I tell you, but I've never seen a car there before, and from what Mr Temple said today, it was just at the time.'

'The time?'

'I mean when the poison could have been put into the flask.'

'I follow. Could you see who was in the car?'

'No. It was empty when I passed it the first time and the second I could just see a figure in the driving seat.'

'You couldn't see when it passed you?'

'It didn't pass me. It turned away from me.'

'Of course you didn't notice the number?'

'Oh yes, I did. That was a lucky chance, too. It was CVW 283. CVW I knew was Essex, because a friend of mine who lives in Colchester has a car and I've often been in it, and as it happens, 283 was our telephone number at the Wilton Grange. Strange, wasn't it?'

'Very,' French agreed absently. Little thrills of excitement were creeping up his spine. It *couldn't* be! One of the discoveries he had hoped for was that a small car of a popular make would be parked somewhere close to the Webble, about four o'clock that afternoon. He had been unable to find any trace of it, but there was a time when he would have staked a good deal on its being there. John Hampden! Could he, after all . . . ?

His brain was whirling as he drove back to Town. If Elsie Oates' recollection of the number were correct, it would be child's play to find the car. Even if the number had been changed, it should be possible to trace it. He pondered over ways and means.

He did not like to think of the blow to his own prestige if Hampden should prove to be guilty. He had often made mistakes in the past, and some of them pretty bad ones. But none had been as bad as this would be. However, such considerations could not affect his present actions.

His general call for information about the car was answered more quickly than he could have hoped. The very next day constables rang up from two garages. By a curious chance, both were from York Road, but one was the York Road which runs north from King's Cross Station, the other that which runs south from Waterloo. It appeared that the car had been sold by the King's Cross firm during the week before the murder, delivery being taken about 2 p.m. on the Saturday. It had been left at the other garage about five-thirty that same evening, with instructions for it to be sold for what it would bring. The sale had since been carried out.

French heard the news with exasperation. It was now clear why his first search had failed. Hampden had been too clever. French had visualised the hire of a car, but Hampden had evidently foreseen that a hire would in itself be traceable and had adopted a plan which had no such defect. The sale and purchase of the car, had both been known, would have been equally remarkable, but both were not known. A single purchase or a single sale could arouse no suspicion. Well, French thought ruefully, he had known that Hampden was an able man and he should have foreseen some such move.

It was not long before French, armed with his collection of photographs, was at the Waterloo garage, which, being the nearer, he decided to take first.

'It was a strange thing about that sale,' observed the manager, who seemed slightly uneasy as to the visit. 'We never paid over the money. We sent it to the address the lady gave, and it was returned "Not known". We never heard from her again.'

'The lady?' French asked sharply. 'What lady?'

'Why, the lady who sold the car, of course. Who else?'

French stared at him. 'Is she among those?' he asked, handing over his photographs.

The manager shook his head, and French asked if he might use his telephone. He put through a call to the other garage. There he learned that it was a lady who bought the car, and a description showed that it was the same lady in each case.

French was completely taken aback. Then Hampden had been even more clever than he had supposed, having been able to get an agent to do his work. French rubbed his chin as he realised how much more difficult this made his job.

One thing at least seemed clear. The passenger in that car, presumably Hampden, was the murderer. If he were not, he would have come forward on reading of the trial. And if that murderer proposed to allow Merle Weir to hang for a crime she had not committed, nothing that the law could do would be bad enough for him.

All that day French pondered over the problem of how he could identify Hampden's lady emissary, but it was not until the evening that he made any advance. Then he took the file and began a last and more careful reading than ever. Considering one by one the women whose names appeared, he stopped suddenly at one. For a moment he thought intently, then a ray of light shone across the case, which in a moment became a blinding illuminant. At once he saw— everything! Instantly it became clear not only who was guilty, but the motive and the method as well.

He drew in a deep breath. Here was the end of the case, success to himself, new life to Merle, joy to Peter Temple and death to another! Success to himself! But was it? How, he wondered, had he failed to realise the truth and to allow so false a step to be taken? Was that success or was it failure? Then he forgot about himself and was conscious only of profound thankfulness that he had made his discovery before it was too late.

Early next morning he had an interview with Sir Mortimer Ellison at the Yard, and as a result the A.C. put through a call to Major Carling at Saxham St Edmunds. The call was followed by French himself, and a long conference at police headquarters convinced the Chief Constable that he had made a terrible mistake. For a moment French recognised a tendency to put the blame on to him, but Major Carling was a fair man at heart, and presently he generously complimented French on his scruples at the time of the arrest.

That evening French and Superintendent Hawkins, with attendant constables and another warrant, drove to Little Bitton. They went straight to St Aidan's.

'We want to see Miss Maudsley,' Hawkins told the maid.

The girl looked at them with surprise. 'She's up in her room,' she said. 'I'll tell her.'

'We'll go up with you,' Hawkins declared in a tone which permitted of no contradiction.

The now frightened girl led the way up the stairs, the three heavy-footed men following as softly as they could.

Except for their muffled footsteps the house was very still. Alert and with his nerves on the stretch as French was, he could not but admire the elegance and luxury of everything he saw. Compared to these broad and easy steps, his own staircase was like a ladder. They reached an entresol at which the flight divided, going up both to right and left.

Suddenly there was a step above and a woman's voice rang out, sharp with anxiety. 'Who is it, Alice? Who's coming up?'

'Superintendent Hawkins, miss, to see you,' the girl returned.

From above there came a choking cry, then rapidly retreating steps. As if galvanised, and with a lightness surprising in one of his great bulk, the superintendent leaped up the remaining steps. A door slammed just ahead.

'Quick!' cried Hawkins. 'That's the room!'

Before they reached the door there came another sound, a short, sharp sound, the sound of a shot. Hawkins uttered a single blistering phrase and raced on. French was not a yard behind him as he threw open the door and passed into the room.

Hilda Maudsley was lying on the floor, blood oozing from her mouth, and a small elegantly chased duelling pistol in her hand. Above the body a tiny cloud of smoke hung in the air.

Later they found a letter addressed to the coroner.

When this is in your hands (it read), I shall be dead. I am leaving it in order to make confession that I murdered James Tarrant by putting aconitine in his thermos flask. When those two, Miss Weir and Temple, were arrested, I was afraid it would come to this, but

I hoped against hope for their acquittal. Now that she has been convicted, there is no longer hope for me. I will wait until her appeal is heard, and if it goes against her, one of my father's duelling pistols will do what is necessary. Lucky for me now that I kept them.

I am not sorry for killing Tarrant. I had made inquiries about him, and the world will be cleaner for his death. I could not bear to think of his ruining the life of the only person who had been kind to me since my parents died. But I did not kill him for this: I can't claim so good a motive. It was for myself—to keep my job. He would have got rid of me. I realised that he knew I saw through him and that he hated me. I had tasted happiness and security and I couldn't face losing them, because I knew what life without them can be. I am not trying to excuse myself: I know there is no excuse for me. But at least I am not going to let anyone else suffer for my sin.

Perhaps I had better say just how I did it, so that there may be no doubt that this confession is the truth.

I foresaw the engagement and determined that if it came off I should murder Tarrant. I bought books on chemistry and medical jurisprudence and learnt about poisons, deciding on aconitine and extracting it from the plant.

When the engagement took place and we went to Town it was intended that Miss Woolcombe and I should spend the weekend with some of her friends at Huntingdon. Tarrant was not invited, and he said he would go home on the Saturday and fish in the afternoon. I saw my opportunity, because, of course, I knew all about his tea arrangements, and that day I arranged to buy a second-hand Austin Seven at Burchett's Garage in York Road, near King's Cross, promising to take delivery about midday on Saturday. I told Miss Woolcombe that a friend of mine was staying at Bournemouth, and that I should like to spend the weekend with her. I was not really wanted at Huntingdon and she agreed at once.

On Saturday, after seeing Miss Woolcombe off at King's Cross, I got the car and drove to the Webble valley, approaching from the west, so as not to go through the village, and parking the car up a lane. I crept along the bank behind the shrubs, and saw that Tarrant was out of sight of his basket. I put the aconitine into the flask and returned to London in the same way as I came. I believe I was not seen. At Straker's Garage in York Road, near Waterloo, I left the car to be sold for what it would bring, giving a fictitious name and address to which the money could be sent. I then caught the six-thirty train to Bournemouth, staying at the Ridley. If I were asked what I did during the afternoon, I would have said I had been to the films. I thought I was safe, and I would have been only for this disastrous trial. Now the verdict has destroyed hope for me.

Hilda Maudsley.

For once the machinery of the law acted rapidly, and Merle heard the news as soon as it could be sent. French saw her at the time of her release, together with Peter, who had hurried to meet her.

'You know,' he said as he congratulated them, 'what happened to you was really your own fault. Why didn't you trust the police and tell the truth?'

They both recognised the kindness in his tone and told him. 'You see,' Peter said, 'Sir Reginald was right about me. I *was* afraid that if Merle got another attack of hysteria she might attempt to injure Tarrant or even commit suicide, and I *did* follow her in the hope of preventing this. Then when I found the body I was so upset that I couldn't think clearly. I feared Merle might somehow be responsible or might be suspected. Therefore I said nothing about it, but hurried away as quickly as I could.'

French shook his head. 'Very unwise, Mr Temple,' he declared.

'I see that now,' Peter admitted. 'But it all happened so quickly. Then when I talked to Merle and she told me the truth, I saw she was in real danger of suspicion. I couldn't then report my discovery: it was too late. I should have been severely blamed myself, and besides it would have brought Merle into it. Then again, my hesitation might have been interpreted to mean that I suspected her, which might have told badly against her—as it actually did.'

'So you decided to deny that you had been there?' French commented, again shaking his head.

'I know we were wrong,' Merle put in. 'But you can understand, can't you? Then, because I might have been suspected, we decided to say I hadn't been there either. Once we said that, we had to stick to it.'

French did understand. He saw neither would have lied for himself alone, but each lied without hesitation for the other.

Little more remains to be told. Two months later Peter and Merle were married, an event which brought them all the more happiness because of its ghastly prelude.

On her release Merle insisted on informing the Braxamin

directors of their Lincaster activities, and in a striking manner this act of honesty redounded to her own advantage. Tarrant was found to have helped himself to some of the firm's money, and being thus in debt to the firm, they took over the Lincaster works against it. They closed them down, but retained the services of the newly married couple at their own headquarters.

Merle's good fortune did not, however, stop here. Experiment proved that her new Digestion Remedy was better both than the original and than Braxamin itself. The Braxamin firm thereupon adopted it, giving Merle a seat on the Board and appointing Peter assistant works manager.

As for French, the case had been anything but a triumph, but he could remind himself that in the long run he had succeeded. However, it was a case of which he never cared to be reminded, and Sir Mortimer Ellison showed his kindly tact by avoiding his usual jokes.

'Hard luck not getting it first time,' was all he said, 'but all's well that ends well.'

By the same author

Inspector French's Greatest Case

At the offices of the Hatton Garden diamond merchant *Duke & Peabody*, the body of old Mr Gething is discovered beside a now-empty safe. With multiple suspects, the robbery and murder is clearly the work of a master criminal, and requires a master detective to solve it. Meticulous as ever, Inspector Joseph French of Scotland Yard embarks on an investigation that takes him from the streets of London to Holland, France and Spain, and finally to a ship bound for South America . . .

'Because he is so austerely realistic, Freeman Wills Croft is deservedly a first favourite with all who want a real puzzle.'
TIMES LITERARY SUPPLEMENT

Inspector French and the Cheyne Mystery

When young Maxwell Cheyne discovers that a series of mishaps are the result of unwelcome attention from a dangerous gang of criminals, he teams up with a young woman who is determined to help him outwit them. But when she disappears, he finally decides to go to Scotland Yard for help. Concerned by the developing situation, Inspector Joseph French takes charge of the investigation and applies his trademark methods to track down the kidnappers and thwart their intentions . . .

'Freeman Wills Crofts is among the few muscular writers of detective fiction. He has never let me down.'
                                                                    DAILY EXPRESS

By the same author

Inspector French and the Starvel Hollow Tragedy

A chance invitation from friends saves Ruth Averill's life on the night her uncle's old house in Starvel Hollow is consumed by fire, killing him and incinerating the fortune he kept in cash. Dismissed at the inquest as a tragic accident, the case is closed—until Scotland Yard is alerted to the circulation of bank-notes supposedly destroyed in the inferno. Inspector Joseph French suspects that dark deeds were done in the Hollow that night and begins to uncover a brutal crime involving arson, murder and body snatching . . .

'Freeman Wills Crofts is the only author who gives us intricate crime in fiction as it might really be, and not as the irreflective would like it to be.' OBSERVER

By the same author

Inspector French and the Sea Mystery

Off the coast of Burry Port in south Wales, two fishermen discover a shipping crate and manage to haul it ashore. Inside is the decomposing body of a brutally murdered man. With nothing to indicate who he is or where it came from, the local police decide to call in Scotland Yard. Fortunately Inspector Joseph French does not believe in insoluble cases— there are always clues to be found if you know what to look for. Testing his theories with his accustomed thoroughness, French's ingenuity sets him off on another investigation . . .

'Inspector French is as near the real thing as any sleuth in fiction.'   SUNDAY TIMES

By the same author

Inspector French: Found Floating

The Carrington family, victims of a strange poisoning, take an Olympic cruise from Glasgow to help them recover. At Creuta one member goes ashore and does not return. Their body is next day found floating in the Straits of Gibraltar. Joining the ship at Marseilles, can Inspector French solve the mystery before they reach Athens?

Introduced by Tony Medawar, this classic Inspector French novel includes unique interludes by Superintendent Walter Hambrook of Scotland Yard, who provides a real-life detective commentary on the case as the mystery unfolds.

'I doubt whether Inspector French has had a more difficult problem to solve than that of the body 'Found Floating' in the Mediterranean.'   *SUNDAY TIMES*

By the same author

Inspector French:
The End of Andrew Harrison

Becoming the social secretary for millionaire financier Andrew Harrison sounded like the dream job: just writing a few letters and making amiable conversation, with luxurious accommodation thrown in. But Markham Crewe had not reckoned on the unpopularity of his employer, especially within his own household, where animosity bordered on sheer hatred. When Harrison is found dead on his Henley houseboat, Crewe is not the only one to doubt the verdict of suicide. Inspector French is another...

'A really satisfying puzzle ... With every fresh detective story Crofts displays new fields of specialised knowledge.'
DAILY MAIL